Praise for *Oscar Wilde and a Death of No Importance*

"One of the most intelligent, amusing and entertaining books of the year. If Oscar Wilde himself had been asked to write this book he could not have done it any better."

—Alexander McCall Smith

"Wilde has sprung back to life in this thrilling and richly atmospheric new novel . . . The perfect topography for crime and mystery . . . magnificent . . . an unforgettable shocker about sex and vice, love and death."

—*Sunday Express*

"Gyles Brandreth and Oscar Wilde seem made for one another . . . There is much here to enjoy . . . the complex and nicely structured plot zips along."

—*Daily Telegraph*

"Brandreth has poured his considerable familiarity with London into a witty fin-de-siècle entertainment, and the rattlingly elegant dialogue is peppered with witticisms uttered by Wilde well before he ever thought of putting them into his plays."

—*Sunday Times*

"Fabulous . . . The plot races along like a carriage pulled by thoroughbreds . . . So enjoyably plausible."

—*Scotsman*

"Both a romp through fin-de-siècle London . . . and a carefully researched portrait of Oscar Wilde . . . Very entertaining."

—*Literary Review*

"Brandreth has the Wildean lingo down pat and the narrative is dusted with piquant social observations. A sparkling treat for fans of Wilde and Sherlock Holmes alike."

—*Easy Living*

"A lively, amusing, and clever murder mystery starring Oscar Wilde—larger than life, brilliant, generous, luxurious—with a new trait: he is now a master sleuth not unlike Sherlock Holmes . . . Brandreth is steeped in the lore of Wilde, but this doesn't oppress the story which is a cleverly plotted thriller through London's demi-monde . . . Highly entertaining."

—*The Dubliner*

"This is not only a good piece of detective fiction in its own right, it is highly entertaining, spiced as it is with Wildean sayings, both real and invented and the imagined conversations and intellectual sparring between Wilde and Conan Doyle. Future tales in the series are something to look forward to."

—*Leicester Mercury*

"Excellent . . . I'd be staggered if you'd read many better whodunnits. Brandreth demonstrates supremely measured skill as a story-teller."

—*Nottingham Evening Post*

"Wilde as detective is thoroughly convincing . . . The period, and the two or three worlds in which Wilde himself moved, are richly evoked . . . [*Oscar Wilde and a Death of No Importance*] is an excellent detective story. I'm keenly looking forward to the rest of the series."

—*The District Messenger*, newsletter of
the Sherlock Holmes Society of London

"Brandreth knows his Wilde . . . He knows his Holmes too . . . The plot is devilishly clever, the characters are fully fleshed, the mystery is engrossing, and the solution is perfectly fair. I love it."

—*The Sherlock Holmes Journal*

"A skilful and erudite piece of writing and one well worth reading, not only for the plot but for much information about Wilde and his friends at that period."

—Tangled Web

"It works quite brilliantly. This is the first of a series. You'll want to start the next the day after finishing this one."

—*Diplomat*

"A witty and gripping portrait of corruption in late-Victorian London and one of which Oscar Wilde and Arthur Conan Doyle would be proud."

—*Livewire*

"A wow of a history mystery . . . a first-class stunner."

—*Booklist*

Praise for *Oscar Wilde and a Game Called Murder*

"The second in this wickedly imagined and highly entertaining series . . . an intelligent, jaunty and hilarious mystery."

—*The Good Book Guide*

"Hugely enjoyable."

—*Daily Mail*

"A cast of historical characters to die for."

—*Sunday Times*

"A carnival of cliff-hangers and fiendish twists and turns . . . The joy of the book, as with its predecessor, is the rounded and compelling presentation of the character of Wilde. The imaginary and the factual are woven together with devilish ingenuity. Brandreth also gives his hero speeches of great beauty and wisdom and humanity."

—*Sunday Express*

"Wilde really has to prove himself against Bram Stoker and Arthur Conan Doyle when a murder ruins their Sunday Supper Club. But Brandreth's invention—that of Wilde as detective—is more than up to the challenge. With plenty of wit, too."

—*Daily Mirror*

"Gyles Brandreth's entertainment is an amusing and satisfactorily unlikely story featuring Bram Stoker, Arthur Conan Doyle, a locked room, and Oscar Wilde in the role of the series detective."

—*Literary Review*

"The plot speeds to an exciting climax . . . Richly atmospheric. Very entertaining."

"Sparkling dialogue, mystery piled deliciously on mystery, a plot with pace and panache, and a London backdrop that would grace any Victorian theatre."

"The acid test for any writer who has enjoyed first-time success is that all-important second novel. Gyles Brandreth, I am happy to report, has sailed through the ordeal with flying colours . . . Irresistible . . . Elegant . . . Rich . . . Enjoyable . . . A classic Agatha Christie–style whodunnit involving some particularly inventive murders with a few well-placed red herrings."

"As much imaginative biography as murder mystery . . . Terrifically well researched, it whizzes along."

"[*Oscar Wilde and a Game Called Murder*] is the eagerly awaited second volume in Gyles Brandreth's series of detective stories and it doesn't disappoint."

"I can't wait until the next one."

Also by Gyles Brandreth

OSCAR WILDE

and the

Dead Man's Smile

A Mystery

Gyles Brandreth

A Touchstone Book
Published by Simon & Schuster
New York   London   Toronto   Sydney

Touchstone
A Division of Simon & Schuster, Inc.
1230 Avenue of the Americas
New York, NY 10020

First Touchstone trade paperback edition September 2009

Touchstone and colophon are registered trademarks of Simon & Schuster, Inc.

For information about special discounts for bulk purchases,
please contact Simon & Schuster Special Sales at
1-866-506-1949 or business@simonandschuster.com.

The Simon & Schuster Speakers Bureau can bring authors to your live event.
For more information or to book an event
contact the Simon & Schuster Speakers Bureau at 1-866-248-3049
or visit our website at www.simonspeakers.com.

Manufactured in the United States of America

1   3   5   7   9   10   8   6   4   2

Library of Congress Cataloging-in-Publication Data
Brandreth, Gyles Daubeney, 1948–
Oscar Wilde and the dead man's smile : a mystery / Gyles Brandreth.
p.   cm.
"A Touchstone book."
1. Wilde, Oscar, 1854–1900—Fiction. 2. Doyle, Arthur Conan, Sir,
1859–1930—Fiction. 3. Murder—Investigation—Fiction. I. Title.
PR6052.R2645O734 2009
823'.914—dc22
2008054129

ISBN 978-1-4165-3485-3
ISBN 978-1-4169-8720-8 (ebook)

To Jill
In memory of Simon

Oscar Wilde and the Dead Man's Smile

Drawn from the previously unpublished memoirs of Robert Sherard (1861–1943), Oscar Wilde's friend and his first and most prolific biographer

Principal Characters in the Narrative

London, 1890–91
Oscar Wilde, poet and playwright
Robert Sherard, journalist
Arthur Conan Doyle, doctor and novelist
John Tussaud, director, Madame Tussaud's Baker Street Bazaar

London, 1881–83
Lady Wilde, Oscar's mother
James Russell Lowell, poet and United States
minister in London
George W. Palmer, businessman and philanthropist
The Reverend Paul White, prison chaplain

New York, 1882

Colonel W. F. Morse, manager, D'Oyly Carte, New York office
Aaron Budd, clerk, D'Oyly Carte, New York office
W. M. Traquair, valet

Leadville, Colorado, 1882

H. A. W. Tabor, mayor of Leadville
Eddie Garstrang, gambler

The La Grange Theatre Company, 1883

Edmond La Grange, actor-manager
Liselotte La Grange, his mother
Bernard La Grange, his son
Agnès La Grange, his daughter
Gabrielle de la Tourbillon, his mistress
Carlos Branco, his leading character actor
Richard Marais, his business manager
Pierre Ferrand, the company doctor

Paris, 1883

Sarah Bernhardt, actress
Maurice Rollinat, poet
Jacques-Emile Blanche, artist
Emile Blanche, physician
Félix Malthus, Préfecture of Police

I want to eat of the fruit of all the trees
in the garden of the world.

Oscar Wilde (1854–1900)

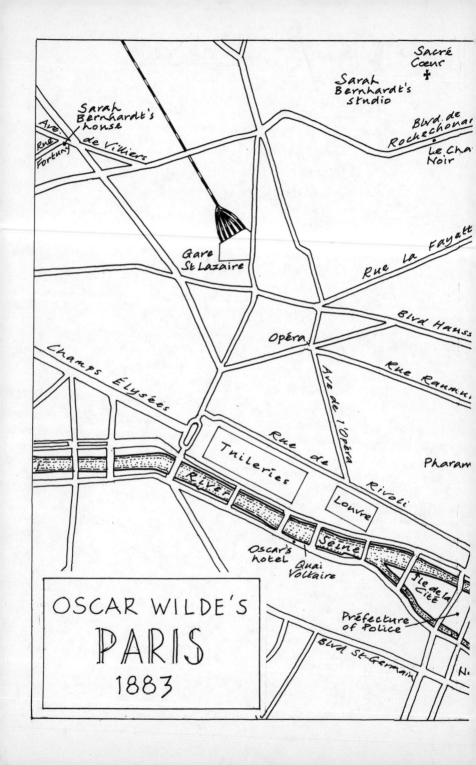

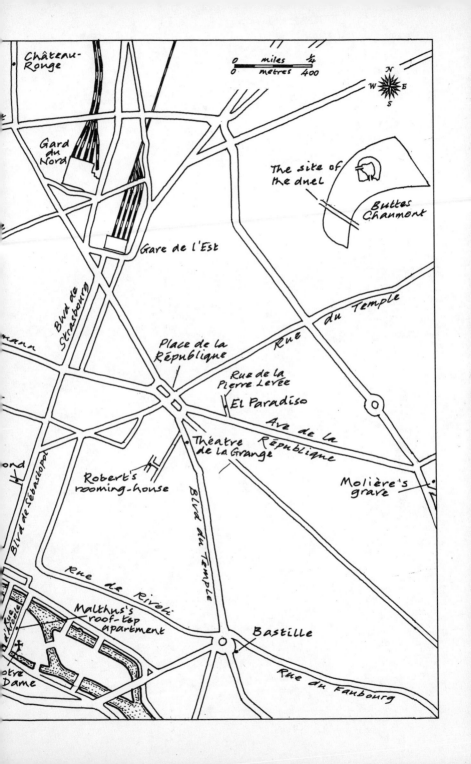

OSCAR WILDE

and the
Dead Man's Smile

London, Christmas 1890

"**D**o you recognise him?"

"I'm not sure."

"He has the look of a murderer, has he not?"

"Do you think so?"

"Yes, I do. It's his smile, Robert. Never trust a man who shows you his lower teeth when he smiles."

"But the poor wretch is dead, Oscar."

"The rule applies, nevertheless."

"And this is just a waxwork."

"But it was sculpted from life, Robert, or, at least, directly from the cadaver. It's a point of honour with the Tussaud family, you know. They will have had access to the body within hours of the execution."

It was midmorning on Christmas Eve, Wednesday, 24 December 1890, and with my friend Oscar Wilde, I was visiting the celebrated Chamber of Horrors at what was then London's—England's—the Empire's—most popular public attraction: Madame Tussaud's Baker Street Bazaar.

Oscar was at his most ebullient. As we toured the exhibits, peering through the flickering gaslight at the waxwork effigies of the more notorious murderers of recent years, my friend's moonlike face shone with delight. His eyes sparkled. His large frame—he was more than six feet tall and, now thirty-six years of age, tending to corpulence—heaved with pleasure. Nothing amused Oscar Wilde so much as the wholly improbable. " 'Tis the season to be jolly," he chuckled softly, "and we are bent on horror, Robert." He glanced at the multitude around us and beamed at me. "It is the anniversary of Our Lord's nativity and all London, it seems, is making a pilgrimage to a shrine to child murder."

Certainly, in its sixty-year history, the Baker Street Bazaar had never been busier than it was on that day. Thirty thousand people had stood in line to see Tussaud's latest sensation: an exact reproduction of the sitting room in which, only nine weeks before, Mary Eleanor Pearcey had battered her lover's wife and baby to death. Mrs. Pearcey had piled her hapless victims' corpses onto the baby's perambulator and dumped them on waste ground near her home in Kentish Town. John Tussaud spent two hundred pounds—the price of a small house—on acquiring the perambulator and other souvenirs of the murder, including the murderess's bloodstained cardigan and the boiled sweet that the innocent baby was sucking on as he was killed. John Tussaud's investment reaped a rich reward. In those days, entrance to the Baker Street Bazaar cost a shilling a head.

Oscar and I had not paid the price of admission, however. Nor had we queued to get in. We had gained access to Tussaud's via the staff entrance in Marylebone Road as special guests of the management. We were due to meet up with our friend, Arthur Conan Doyle, and Doyle was a friend of Madame Tussaud's great-grandson and heir, John Tussaud. Arthur had arranged the visit as a Christmas treat for Oscar and Oscar had arrived bearing a Christmas present for Arthur. The two men had only known each other for sixteen months, but they were firm friends. Their intimacy—their ease with one another—surprised me because, as personalities, they were so different. Oscar was Irish, an aesthete and a romantic. Oscar was flamboyant: he revelled in the outrageous. Arthur was Scottish, a provincial doctor and a pragmatist. Arthur was stolid: he respected the conventional. But both were writers of high ambition, with keen intellects and lively sensibilities, and both were fascinated by the vagaries of the human heart and the workings of the criminal mind.

Oscar was five years older than Arthur, and, in 1890, undoubtedly the better known. The pair had been introduced to one another by an American publisher, J. M. Stoddart, who, on the same evening, in August 1889, had commissioned a "mystery adventure" from each of them. For Stoddart, Doyle was persuaded to write his second Sherlock Holmes story and Oscar conjured up his novel of beauty and decay, *The Picture of Dorian Gray*. Doyle's Holmes adventure, *The Sign of Four*, was well received and helped consolidate the young author's growing reputation as a skilful spinner of satisfying yarns. In its way, *Dorian Gray* helped consolidate Oscar's reputation, too. The book was denounced as immoral. The *Athenaeum* called it "unmanly, sickening, vicious." The *Daily Chronicle* derided it as "a tale spawned from the leprous literature of the French Decadents—a gloating study of mental and physical corruption." It was banned by the booksellers W. H. Smith.

Oscar envied Arthur his creation of Sherlock Holmes. Arthur envied Oscar his way with words. Arthur had no reservations about *Dorian Gray*. He considered the work subtle, honest, and artistically good. He respected Oscar both as a writer and as a gentleman. And, amusingly, he also reckoned that Oscar had the qualities essential in a private detective: "a retentive mind, an observant eye, and the ability to mix with all manner and conditions of men." Arthur told Oscar that if ever he should write another Sherlock Holmes story he would invent an older brother for the great detective and base him on Oscar. "Do so, Arthur, please," said Oscar. "Your stories will stand the test of time and I have immortal longings."

Madame Tussaud's, that Christmas Eve morning, was packed to overflowing, but even among the crowds and in the half-light of the Chamber of Horrors, Messrs. Doyle and Tussaud had no difficulty in finding us as we hovered between the reproduction of Mrs. Pearcey's sitting room and the ghastly waxwork of the grinning murderer with the exposed teeth. Oscar was both the tallest man in the room and the most conspicuous. He was dressed for the season: his elaborate bow tie was holly red; his dandified frock coat was ivy green; and in his buttonhole he sported a substantial sprig of mistletoe.

"Merry Christmas, Oscar!" called out Conan Doyle, pushing his way through the throng towards us. "Season's greetings, Robert."

Doyle held out his right hand towards Oscar. Oscar ignored it and, passing the brown parcel containing Doyle's intended Christmas present to me to carry, embraced the good doctor in a mighty bear hug. Oscar knew that this hug embarrassed Conan Doyle, but it was the way in which he always greeted his friend: Arthur's handshake was almost unendurable. Doyle was not tall, but he was well built, sturdy, fit, and strong, and the vicelike grip of his hand was as forbidding as his fierce moustache. Conan Doyle's dark, walruslike whiskers would have done credit to a Cossack general.

"I'm sorry I'm late," said the young doctor, prising himself from Oscar's warm embrace. "The train from Southsea was delayed. A body on the line. Most unfortunate."

"Some people will do anything to avoid a family Christmas," murmured Oscar.

Arthur sniffed and furrowed his brow disapprovingly. "May I present our host, Mr. John Tussaud?" he said, taking a step back to introduce us to his companion. Mr. Tussaud rose briefly onto his toes, nodding his head briskly towards each of us as he did so. With his drooping moustache and wire-framed spectacles, he looked more like a mild-mannered schoolmaster than a purveyor of horror to the masses.

"Thank you for your hospitality, sir," said Oscar, with a gentle bow. "And congratulations on the show." He looked about us at the crowds, two or three deep—men and women, gentlefolk and workers, children and babes in arms—trooping steadily past the exhibits, mostly in silence. "It is a triumph."

John Tussaud flushed with pleasure and pushed his spectacles further up his nose.

Oscar went on: "I was particularly taken with the half-sucked sweet retrieved from the dead baby's mouth."

"Yes," said Tussaud eagerly, "the sweet does seem to have caught everybody's imagination. It's raspberry flavoured, you know."

"Good God, man," exclaimed Conan Doyle. "Did you taste it?"

"Only briefly," said Tussaud with a nervous laugh. "I felt I should. The visitors like as much detail as possible."

"I understand completely," said Oscar soothingly. "Your visitors need to know that what they're witnessing is the genuine article. The more corroborative detail you can give them the better."

Tussaud looked up at Oscar gratefully. "You understand, Mr. Wilde."

Oscar smiled at John Tussaud and touched him on the shoulder. "I was telling my friend Sherard here that all your waxwork models are drawn from life—or death, as the case may be."

"Absolutely," replied Tussaud seriously. "We insist on it—wherever possible. With the murderers, of course, we're very much in the hands of the authorities. Some prison governors let us in prior to the execution, so that we can make a model of the murderer while he's still alive. Others won't let us in at all—or only give us access to the murderer's body after the execution has taken place. That's not very satisfactory, to be candid."

"Hanging distorts the features?" suggested Oscar.

"It can do, I'm afraid," replied Tussaud, lowering his voice as a group of young ladies pressed past us. "From a waxwork modeller's point of view," he continued, sotto voce, "the ideal method of execution has to be the guillotine. My great-grandmother was so fortunate in that respect. The Revolutionary Tribunal in Paris sentenced sixteen thousand five hundred and ninety-four people to death, you know. The guillotine was invented to cope with the numbers."

"You are a 'details man,' I can tell, sir," said Oscar, smiling.

"I have the complete list," murmured Tussaud. "All the names."

"Your great-grandmother must have been spoilt for choice," said Conan Doyle grimly.

"And run off her feet," added the great-grandson. "Families wanted death masks of their loved ones. Those who were about to die wanted to be immortalised in wax. The demand was incredible—one head after another. We have the original guillotine here, you know."

"Yes," said Oscar. "Mr. Sherard and I have just been admiring it—together with the last head it claimed."

"I'm so glad," purred Mr. Tussaud. "In its way, it is a thing of beauty; almost a century old, but still in perfect working order. The craftmanship's extraordinary. It was in use until just three years ago. I acquired it from the French authorities for a tidy sum. I knew in my bones that my great-grandmother would have wanted us to have it here. She was a remarkable woman. Have you yet seen her death mask of Marie Antoinette? It's one of her best." Our host's spectacles glinted in the gaslight as he raised both hands and beckoned us to follow him.

He led us away from the throng and through an unmarked door, across a darkened corridor, and through a second door into a smaller exhibition room, entirely lit by candlelight. There were no crowds here, just half a dozen visitors standing behind a rope cordon gazing at an assortment of individual human heads lolling on scarlet cushions.

"This is my favourite room," said Tussaud, lowering his voice once more and gesturing proudly towards the exhibits. "Look. To the left, we have the revolutionaries. Robespierre is the third one along. And to the right—slightly elevated, you notice—we have Louis XVI and his queen."

"Their faces appear to be larger than those of the revolutionaries," said Conan Doyle, gazing at the waxed visages of the royal couple.

"They are larger, Arthur," said Oscar quietly. "They were better fed."

"And behind you," announced Tussaud in an excited stage whisper, "we have Citoyen Marat, murdered in his bathtub by Charlotte Corday."

"Oh, my," murmured Oscar, turning round, "that is most lifelike."

"Marie Tussaud was among the first on the scene."

"In at the kill," whispered Oscar, impressed.

"She made it her business," said Tussaud earnestly. "It *was* her business. She told the story of her time. She was an artist—a portraitist who worked in wax instead of oils. Monsieur David's famous painting of this very scene is based on her waxwork. Monsieur David was a family friend. So was Marat. And Rousseau. And Benjamin Franklin. Marie made models of them all. She knew all the great men of the age. And the women, too."

"I envy her," said Oscar quietly, turning his back on the bath and surveying once more the row of severed heads. "I should have liked to have met Queen Marie Antoinette."

"You have met Queen Victoria, haven't you?" asked Arthur playfully.

"It's not quite the same thing," murmured Oscar.

"Marie Tussaud met everybody," repeated her great-grandson proudly.

"Oscar's met everybody," I said defensively.

Oscar smiled. "Not Robespierre, alas."

"But you met the man who tried to assassinate Queen Victoria, didn't you?" I persisted.

"I did, Robert. Once. And very briefly." He turned to John Tussaud, adding by way of explanation: "The man was an unhinged versifier named Roderick Maclean. A poor poet and a worse shot."

Mr. Tussaud laughed and looked at his watch. "It's lunchtime, gentlemen. I want to hear all about Queen Victoria's failed assassin over our lobster salad and roast pheasant."

"Lobster salad?" repeated Oscar happily. "Roast pheasant?" He looked at Conan Doyle with shining eyes. "You are the best of friends, Arthur, and you have the best of friends."

"I'm taking you to our new restaurant," explained John Tussaud. "We shall dine by electric light to music provided by Miss Graves's Ladies Orchestra. They have promised to give us a selection of tunes from the Savoy operas."

"Gilbert and Sullivan," said Oscar genially. "I have met both of them."

"Oscar's met everybody," I repeated. "Poets, princes, artists, assassins . . ."

John Tussaud was leading us towards the stairway at the end of the exhibition room. We passed a familiar profile. "Yes," said Tussaud, nodding at the bust: "Voltaire. Marie Tussaud knew Voltaire."

Oscar paused. "How I envy her!" He sighed. "I met

Louisa May Alcott once," he said, "the author of *Little Women*. She *was* a little woman." He gazed fixedly at Madame Tussaud's head of Voltaire. "And I met P. T. Barnum," he added. "And, through him, of course, I met Jumbo the Elephant. It's not quite Voltaire, but it's something."

Conan Doyle burst out laughing. "You're impossible, Oscar!" he cried. "Jumbo the Elephant? I don't believe you."

"It's true," protested Oscar.

"It can't be."

"Give him the manuscript, Robert."

I handed Conan Doyle the parcel that I was carrying.

"This is my Christmas present for Arthur," Oscar explained to John Tussaud. "It's some holiday reading, something for him to puzzle over at his Southsea fireside."

The manuscript was wrapped in brown paper and tied up with string. Conan Doyle turned it over slowly in his hands.

"They're all there, Arthur," said Oscar teasingly. "Louisa May Alcott, Jumbo the Elephant, the man who tried to shoot Queen Victoria . . ."

Conan Doyle looked up at Oscar and furrowed his brow. "What is this?"

"As I say: your Christmas present, Arthur. Last year you gave me *The Sign of Four*. This year I'm giving you this. It's a manuscript—and a challenge. It's a story from my salad days, an account of a year and a half of my life—a while ago now. Before I was married. Before I was a family man. Before my responsibilities had made me fat. The story begins in 1882, when I was in my mid-twenties, footloose and fancy-free. A time when I travelled the world and came to know some remarkable men and women. Not Robespierre and Marie Antoinette, not Voltaire, to be sure, but remarkable nonetheless: Longfellow, Walt Whitman, Sarah Bernhardt, Edmond La Grange . . . Names to reckon with—and people you've never heard of."

Conan Doyle balanced the package on the palms of his hands as though assessing its weight. He brought it up to his face, as if by sniffing at it he might better estimate its value. "Is it autobiographical?" he asked.

Oscar smiled. "It's my story, Arthur, but it's Robert's handiwork. Robert is my recording angel—my Dr. Watson. He witnessed much of what occurred in France himself, as you'll discover, but I saw it all as it unfolded, from its beginnings in the New World. This is a tale that starts on one continent and travels to another. I want you to pay close attention to the beginning, Arthur. The beginning does not merely set the scene; it lays the groundwork for what is to come." Slowly, Oscar ran his forefinger along the string that held the brown paper parcel together. "This is a true story, Arthur. I suppose you'd call it a murder mystery. It can't be published—at least, not in my lifetime. Much of it is libellous. Some of it is salacious. And, as yet, the story is incomplete. The manuscript's unfinished. It lacks the final chapter. I want you to read it, Arthur. I want you to read every word, even though some of it will make you blush. If you like, you can show it to your friend, Sherlock Holmes—he's made of sterner stuff. And then, when you've read it, and pondered long and hard, I want you to tell me what you think the final chapter should reveal."

Oscar turned back to our host and widened his eyes. "Now, Mr. Tussaud, kindly lead us to your lobster salad. The sight of all these wax cadavers has given me the most tremendous appetite."

What follows is the manuscript that I gave that day to Arthur Conan Doyle.

1

America

On 24 December 1881 Oscar Wilde set sail for the United States of America. He went in search of adventure and gold. Within weeks, he had found a portion of both.

Oscar had recently turned twenty-seven and, in England, his claim to fame was that he was famous for being famous. He was a celebrity, in the tradition of Lord Byron and Beau Brummell, but more Brummell than Byron, more style than substance. "Evidently I am 'somebody,'" he noted at the time, "but what have I done? I've been 'noticed.' That is something, I suppose. And I have published one book of poems. That doesn't amount to much."

As a young man, first at Trinity College, Dublin, and then at Magdalen College, Oxford, Oscar had achieved every academic honour within his reach. He rounded off his undergraduate years by securing an Oxford double first and winning the coveted Newdigate Prize, the university's chief prize for poetry. But what was his real ambition in life?

"God knows," he said, when asked. "I won't be an Oxford don anyhow. I'll be a poet, a writer, a dramatist. Somehow or other I'll be famous, and if not famous, I'll be notorious. Or perhaps I'll lead the life of pleasure for a time and then—who knows?—rest and do nothing. What does Plato say is the highest end that man can attain here below? 'To sit down and contemplate the good.' Perhaps that will be the end of me, too."

When Oscar left Oxford, cushioned by a modest legacy from his late father, he floated down to London, the capital of the British Empire, and made his mark on the metropolis with outlandish views and an outrageous appearance. "It is only shallow people who do not judge by appearances," he declared. He had always been partial to dressing up. In his last term at Oxford he appeared at a ball disguised as Prince Rupert of the Rhine. In his first season in London he took to going out in a bottle-green velvet smoking jacket edged with braid, wearing a cream-coloured shirt with a scalloped collar and an overabundant orange tie, taffeta knee breeches, black silk stockings, and silver-buckled shoes. He became a champion of beauty and a self-styled professor of aestheticism. "Beauty is the symbol of symbols," he declared. "Beauty reveals everything, because it expresses nothing. When it shows us itself it shows us the whole fiery-coloured world."

The young Oscar Wilde was determined to be noticed.

And he was. Soon after his arrival in London, the satirical magazines of the day started to publish spoofs and squibs at his expense. He was lampooned in music-hall sketches, in stage farces, and then, most famously, in April 1881, in Richard D'Oyly Carte's hugely successful production of W. S. Gilbert and Arthur Sullivan's comic operetta *Patience*. Oscar was at the first night and gently amused. He recognised the piece for what it was: not a personal attack on him, but a pleasingly tuneful skit on the absurdities of the aesthetic movement.

The success of *Patience* changed Oscar's life. On 30 September 1881 he received a telegram from Colonel W. F. Morse, Richard D'Oyly Carte's business manager in New York, inviting him to undertake an American lecture tour to coincide with the operetta's American production. Oscar did not hesitate. On 1 October 1881 he wired his acceptance to Colonel Morse. The young poet was in want of money and exhilarated by the prospect of crossing an ocean and discovering a continent. "I already speak English, German, French, and Italian," he explained to his mother. "Now I shall have the opportunity of learning American. It will be a challenge, I know, but I must try to rise to it."

He wrote to James Russell Lowell, the United States minister in London, presuming on their nodding acquaintance to ask for some letters of introduction. The venerable Lowell, then in his early sixties, replied that "a clever and accomplished man should no more need an introduction than a fine day," but as he liked Oscar, was amused by him, and, a poet himself, admired the young man's verses, he was happy to oblige.

As well as letters of introduction, Oscar equipped himself with a new wardrobe, including a warm Polish cap and a befrogged and wonderfully befurred green overcoat; Lowell had warned him about the New York winters. And because Colonel Morse had advised him that he would be lecturing to "huge audiences in vast auditoria," in the weeks before his departure, Oscar engaged the services of an expensive expert on oratory to give him elocution lessons. "I want a natural style," he told his instructor, "with a touch of affectation." Oscar Wilde prepared carefully for his American adventure. He hoped that it might prove the "making" of him.

Oscar set sail from Liverpool on the afternoon of Christmas Eve 1881 on board the SS *Arizona*. He was apprehensive. The *Arizona* was the fastest steamship then crossing the Atlantic, the holder of the Blue Riband, and the young aesthete did not much care for speed. The *Arizona* had also recently survived—but only narrowly—a mid-Atlantic collision with an iceberg.

In the event the crossing was calm and hazard free. It was the arrival that proved more of an adventure. The *Arizona* docked in New York harbour on the evening of 2 January 1882. It was too late to clear quarantine, so Oscar and his fellow passengers were obliged to spend a further night on board ship. The gentlemen of the New York press, however, were impatient for a first sighting of the much-vaunted Mr. Wilde. They would not wait till morning. They chartered a launch, came out to sea, and, in Oscar's phrase, "their pens still wet with brine, demanded that I strut before them, like a prize bantam at a country fair."

The journalists were a little taken aback by what they found. Oscar was not the delicate exotic that they had been expecting. According to the man from the *New York Tribune*:

The most striking thing about the poet's appearance is his height, which is several inches over six feet, and the next thing to attract attention is his hair, which is of a dark brown colour, and falls down upon his shoulders. When he laughs his lips part widely and show a shining row of upper teeth, which are superlatively white. The complexion, instead of being of the rosy hue so common in Englishmen, is so utterly devoid of colour that it can only be said to resemble putty. His eyes are blue, or a light grey, and instead of being "dreamy," as some of his admirers have imagined them to be, they are bright and quick—not at all like those of one given to perpetual musing on the ineffably beautiful and true. Instead of having a small delicate hand, only fit to caress a lily, his fingers are long and when doubled up would form a fist that would hit a hard knock, should an occasion arise for the owner to descend to that kind of argument.

Oscar did not engage his interlocutors in fisticuffs, but nor, in the main, did he endear himself to them. "I tried to be amusing," he later confessed, "and engendered snarls where I had hoped for smiles. My efforts at drollery were taken for disdain." He was asked how he had enjoyed his ocean crossing. He replied, "The sea seems tame to me. The roaring ocean does not roar. It is not so majestic as I expected." His remarks appeared beneath the headline: "Mr. Wilde Disappointed with the Atlantic." He gave the impression of arrogance.

And he compounded that impression on the morning after his shipboard press conference. Disembarking from the SS *Arizona* and passing through customs, he responded to the customs officer's predictable enquiry, "Have you anything to declare, Mr. Wilde?" with a well-prepared reply: "I have nothing to declare except my genius."

Some thought this vastly amusing. Others thought that

young Mr. Wilde was riding for a fall. And, to an extent, he was. His first few lectures were not a success. He said too much, too quickly, and in too soft a voice. He failed to hold the attention of the crowd. His audiences were disappointed; the critics were unkind.

In public, Oscar was undaunted. In private, he acknowledged that he had work to do. He simplified his lecture; he improved his presentation; he moderated his language; he added some jokes that everybody could understand. He turned a potential disaster into an unquestioned triumph. Ultimately, during the course of 1882, Oscar delivered a total of more than two hundred lectures in one hundred and sixty towns and cities across North America, from New Orleans to Nova Scotia, from northern Massachusetts to southern California. "Oh, yes," he would say in later years, "I was adored once, too. In America I was obliged to engage two secretaries to cope with the correspondence— one being responsible for the demand for autographs, the other for the locks of my hair. Within six months, the first had died of writer's cramp; the other was entirely bald."

In fact, Oscar did have two companions on his travels, but neither was a secretary. Colonel Morse supplied him with a "man of business," a clerk from D'Oyly Carte's New York office, named Aaron Budd, and a personal valet, a young Negro called W. M. Traquair. "I did not care for Mr. Budd," said Oscar. "He looked after our railroad tickets and counted the takings. He was efficient, but not interesting. He rarely spoke, he never smiled, and the pallor of his skin was disconcerting. I believe he was an abstainer and a vegetarian. By contrast, I cared a great deal for Washington Traquair. His father had been a slave. He was my servant, but he was also my friend. He was not a great talker and he could neither read nor write, but he had a wonderful smile and he laughed at my jokes. You have to love a man who laughs at your jokes."

In the course of his tour, Oscar made a great deal of money and, as he put it, "a rich assortment of new acquaintances." In New York, he met the celebrated novelist Louisa May Alcott, then in her forties and at the height of her fame. "She was a small but profoundly passionate woman," he recalled. "She told me the plot of a story that she was revising at the time. It was entitled *A Long Fatal Love Chase*. As she recounted the tale, she held my hand in hers and tears filled her eyes. I asked her why she had never married. 'Oh, Mr. Wilde,' she said, 'if I tell you, will you keep my secret? It is because I have fallen in love with so many pretty girls and never once the least bit with any man.'"

It was in New York, too, that Oscar met the great showman Phineas Taylor Barnum. Oscar was lecturing at the Wallack's Theater on Broadway and Barnum came with a party of friends "to see what all the fuss was about." What Barnum made of Oscar's disquisition on "Art and the English Renaissance" history does not record, but Oscar reckoned the encounter a success. "When I spoke to Mr. Barnum of Giorgione, Mazzini, and Fra Angelico, he assumed they were a trio of Italian acrobats. Mr. Barnum lacked education, but he had style. He came to my lecture and I visited his circus. After the spectacle, at my insistence, he introduced me to his prize attraction, Jumbo, the African elephant. 'I must meet him,' I told Mr. Barnum. 'His name will be remembered long after ours have been forgotten.' 'I should hope so, Mr. Wilde,' answered Barnum. 'He cost me ten thousand dollars.'"

Oscar brought back many good stories from his year on the American lecture circuit. Probably his favourite anecdotal set piece concerned his time in Leadville, Colorado, high up in the Rocky Mountains. There he addressed audiences consisting of ordinary working-men—labourers and mine workers in the main. Because the miners were mining for silver, Oscar chose to read to them extracts from the autobiography of the great Renaissance sculptor in silver Benvenuto Cellini. "I was reproved by my auditors for not having brought Cellini with me. I explained that he had been dead for some little time, which information elicited the enquiry: 'Who shot him?'"

When, later, Oscar was asked if he had not found the miners "somewhat rough and ready," he replied: "Ready, but not rough. There is no chance for roughness in the Rockies. The revolver is their book of etiquette. This teaches lessons that are not forgotten."

The mayor of Leadville, one H. A. W. Tabor, known as the Silver King, invited Oscar to visit the Matchless Mine and open a new shaft named the "Oscar" in his honour. Oscar was delighted to oblige and, dressed in his aesthete's finery, was ceremoniously lowered into the mine inside a huge bucket. Once he had inaugurated the new shaft, employing a special silver drill for the purpose, the miners invited him to dine with them at the bottom of the mine. "They laid on quite a spread," he recalled. "The first course was whisky; the second course was whisky; the third course was whisky; I have little recollection of the dessert."

That evening, Mayor Tabor offered Oscar further

entertainment at the Leadville casino. According to Oscar, "Drinking rather than gambling appeared to be the business of the place. It was crowded with miners and the female friends of miners. The men were all dressed in red shirts, corduroy trousers, and high boots. The women wore brightly coloured evening dresses cut so low that their breasts were almost entirely exposed. The floor was covered with sawdust and the walls hung with huge, gilt-framed mirrors. In a corner of the main saloon was a pianist, sitting at an upright piano over which was a notice that read: 'Don't shoot the pianist; he is doing his best.'"

On his second (and final) night in Leadville, Oscar returned to the casino. This time, he went alone. Mayor Tabor had business to attend to in Denver; Aaron Budd, Oscar's business manager, was not a drinking man; and Traquair, the valet, was barred from entry because of his colour. Oscar began the evening by the piano, surrounded by young men in red shirts and young women with full bosoms. He made them laugh and they made him smile. Four and a half hours later, having eaten nothing and drunk too much, he found himself in a different, darker corner of the saloon, seated alone with two men in check shirts and a young woman who leant towards him across the table, dusting her breasts playfully with a little lace handkerchief. As one of the men plied Oscar with drink and the other removed his wallet from his coat pocket, two pistol shots rang out across the room. One shot blew the whisky glass from Oscar's hand; the other sent his wallet spinning into the air.

Instantly, as the shots were fired, Oscar's trio of drinking companions fled the scene, and Oscar, bewildered but unharmed, slumped slowly to the floor. The man who had fired the shots crossed the room, helped Oscar to his feet, and accompanied him out of the casino, down the deserted street, and back to his hotel. The man's name was Eddie Garstrang.

2

Eddie Garstrang and Edmond La Grange

Eddie Garstrang was thirty-seven, ten years older than Oscar. He was several inches shorter than Oscar, and slimmer, more wiry, with a small head, pale yellow hair, milky blue eyes, and a disarming, open smile. A professional gambler, he was also a professional marksman, a sharpshooter of exceptional skill and daring. At least, that's what he claimed, and Oscar saw no reason to doubt him. Garstrang boasted that the great P. T. Barnum had once seen him in action and offered him a starring role in his circus. Eddie Garstrang had decided against working for Mr. Barnum. He was determined, he said, to be his "own man." He had declined Mr. Barnum's offer politely, to be sure. He was softly spoken and a firm believer in what he termed "old-world courtesy." Garstrang was not as others were in Colorado. He did not chew tobacco or drink whisky. He did not wear a red shirt and corduroy trousers. He dressed in a tailor-made woollen suit of sober check and sported a white and lavender columbine in his buttonhole. Oscar found him fascinating.

On the morning after the incident in the casino, the pair met up for breakfast. It was not a prearranged encounter. At around ten o'clock, Oscar, unshaven and still groggy from the night before, made his way into the hotel dining room in search of coffee and found Garstrang already seated at his table.

"Good morning, Mr. Wilde," said Garstrang, getting lightly to his feet and extending a hand to Oscar.

"Good day, sir," replied Oscar croakily. "I must thank you. I recognise you. You are my rescuer from last night, are you not?"

"I have that honour," said Garstrang. He bowed towards Oscar with a smile.

Oscar seated himself at the table. "Is there coffee?" he asked, rubbing his eyes fiercely with clenched fists.

"There is," said Garstrang, pouring Oscar a cup. "And it's hot."

"And strong, I hope." Oscar lifted the cup and sipped at the coffee. He looked up at Garstrang, who was still standing, and smiled at the stranger. "I'm in your debt, sir. I know it. What do I owe you?"

"Nothing, Mr. Wilde."

"You must want something. How much?" Oscar slipped his hand into his coat pocket and produced a green snakeskin wallet. It was one of his favourite possessions, a twenty-first birthday present from his mother. He examined the scorch mark at the wallet's edge. Garstrang's bullet had done no more than lightly nick the snakeskin.

"The pleasure of your company for breakfast is all I ask," said Garstrang.

"Whisky was all my supper," said Oscar, returning the wallet to his pocket, "coffee will be all my breakfast, but you're welcome to share it." He smiled and nodded to the older man. "Be seated. Please. And remind me of your name? I'm afraid that my recollection of last night's adventure is somewhat hazy."

"Garstrang—Edward Garstrang. I don't have a card."

"But you do have a gun," said Oscar, smiling. "That I recall." He took another sip of coffee and looked about the deserted dining room. He leant across the table towards Garstrang and added, conspiratorially, "Was anyone hurt last night?"

"No, I'm a good shot—and it was very close range."

"Why did you come to my rescue? Do you mind if I ask?"

"You're a visitor, and a distinguished one at that. We don't get many poets in velvet knickerbockers passing through Leadville. You were being taken advantage of at the casino last night, Mr. Wilde, and that's not nice." Garstrang paused and smiled his disarming smile: he had tiny white teeth pressed tight together. He poured more coffee into Oscar's cup. He added softly, "Of course, in my way, I was taking advantage of you myself."

Oscar's brow furrowed. "Were you, Mr. Garstrang? How?"

"With my little gun I came to the rescue of the great Oscar Wilde. It'll make a useful paragraph in the newspaper. I could use the publicity. I need to be noticed. I like to be talked about."

"For reasons of business or self-esteem?" Oscar asked, leaning back and opening his silver cigarette case. The hot coffee was reviving him.

"Both," replied Garstrang, striking a match and leaning forward to light Oscar's cigarette. "Do you understand that? I think if anyone does, it should be you."

"I understand completely, Mr. Garstrang. A man who is much talked about is always attractive, whatever the truth. One feels there must be something in him, after all." Oscar drew slowly on his cigarette and gazed steadily into Garstrang's blue eyes. Oscar was the younger man but they sat face to face as equals. "What brings you to Leadville, Mr. Garstrang?" asked Oscar.

Garstrang laughed. "I was born in Leadville."

"You do not look like a man who was born in Leadville."

"I'm pleased to hear it. I have travelled quite widely."

"To Europe?"

"To New Orleans. I work on the riverboats that travel up and down the Mississippi and Ohio rivers. The bigger boats all have casinos now and that's where I earn my living. I'm a professional gambler, Mr. Wilde. I play cards."

"Is that exciting?" asked Oscar. "I imagine it must be."

"I don't play for excitement. I play for money. I am a gambler because, as a child, I realised that I hadn't the physique to be a cowboy or a miner and I did not wish to be a sales clerk as my father had been. My father was as most men are—nothing much. He lived, he died, he left no mark upon the world: he might as well never have been born. I was fifteen when he passed away. What did I inherit from him? A facility for mental arithmetic and an old Colt percussion revolver, that's all. I don't know why he kept the gun: he never used it. When he died I had nothing but the Colt, a few sticks of furniture, a rented room, and a change of clothes. That's when I determined to make my fortune. That's when I decided I was going to be rich. And famous. Or, if not famous, notorious." He refilled Oscar's coffee cup and sat back, folding his arms across his chest. "Do you understand what I'm saying, Mr. Wilde?"

"I could not have put it better myself," replied Oscar. "Every man of ambition has to fight his century with its own weapons. Fame and fortune are what our century worships. To succeed in our time one must achieve celebrity and gold. Nothing else will do."

A silence fell between them. Garstrang broke it, changing the subject and saying how much he had enjoyed Oscar's lecture. He had heard him in Denver at the beginning of the week. They talked of this and that: of Oscar's poetry, of Cellini's autobiography, of Garstrang's prowess at poker and his facility with a gun. Eventually, another silence fell. Oscar extinguished his second cigarette and looked carefully at his companion. It was the milkiness in Garstrang's blue eyes that made him appear so weak, he decided. And the fact that his narrow face was smooth and pale and hairless. Oscar reflected that he and Edward Garstrang were probably the only two white men in the entire state of Colorado that day not to be wearing either side-whiskers, a moustache, or a beard.

"Is your mother still alive?" Oscar asked.

"No," said Garstrang. "I never knew my mother. Rather, I knew her, but I don't remember her. She passed away when I was small."

"Do you have brothers? Sisters? Uncles? Aunts?"

"I have no family, Mr. Wilde. I travel alone. I like it that way. I'm a loner, unbeholden."

"We have much in common, I think," said Oscar pleasantly, pushing his chair away from the table and rising from his seat. "We are both outsiders, Mr. Garstrang, observing our lives even as we live them." He held out his hand towards his new friend. "To become a spectator of one's own life is to escape the suffering of life, I find."

Oscar had got to his feet because, over Garstrang's shoulder, through the open dining-room doorway, he could see the silhouette of Washington Traquair, the valet, hovering anxiously behind the glass door that connected the outer entrance lobby to the hotel itself. As a Negro, Traquair was not permitted beyond the outer lobby. "My man is waiting for me," explained Oscar. "Kansas is calling."

"Thank you for your company," said Eddie Garstrang, getting to his feet as well and shaking Oscar warmly by the hand.

"Thank you for yours," said Oscar, "both this morning and last night. This morning you entertained me. Last night you saved my life."

"I saved your wallet, that's all," said Garstrang, laughing, "and your dignity, perhaps."

"My wallet and my dignity—that's a great deal. I'm grateful. I won't forget you, Mr. Garstrang."

Oscar continued on his tour. He travelled from Colorado to Kansas to Iowa and Ohio, then up the East Coast to Canada, then down to Memphis and New Orleans, across to Texas and up to New England and Canada once again. There were more memorable encounters along the way. In Salt Lake City, Utah, Oscar was presented to the president of the Mormon Church of Jesus Christ of Latter-day Saints and met five of that fine gentleman's seven wives and one of his thirty-four children. Oscar noted that the opera house in Salt Lake City was the size of Covent Garden and "so holds with ease at least fourteen Mormon families." In Atlanta, Georgia, Oscar came close to blows with the Pullman car attendant who told him that although his valet, Traquair, was indeed in possession of a valid sleeping-car ticket, nevertheless, as a black man, he could not take advantage of it. It was against the railroad company's rules.

In Lincoln, Nebraska, Oscar got his first taste of prison. He was taken on a tour of the Lincoln penitentiary and introduced to a number of the inmates. "They were all meanlooking, which consoled me," he said, "for I should hate to see a criminal with a noble face." He was shown into the cell of a convict who was due to be hanged in a few weeks' time. "Do you read, my man?" asked Oscar. "Yes, sir," replied the convict, showing Oscar a copy of Charlotte M. Yonge's sentimental novel, *The Heir of Redclyffe*. As he left the cell, Oscar murmured to the prison governor, "My heart was turned by the eyes of the doomed man, but if he reads *The Heir of Redclyffe* it's perhaps as well to let the law take its course."

The tour ended in New York City in mid-October 1882. All in all, it had been a success. Oscar had earned himself a substantial sum (in excess of five thousand dollars, after expenses) and considerably raised his profile on both sides of the Atlantic. His mother wrote to him from London: "You are the talk of the town here. The cabmen ask me if I am somehow connected with you. The milkman has bought your picture! In fact nothing seems celebrated in London but you. I think you will be mobbed when you come back by eager crowds and will be obliged to shelter in cabs."

Oscar decided not to hurry home. He was enjoying being fêted in New York. "If my presence is advertised in advance," he reported to Lady Wilde with satisfaction, "the road is blocked by admiring crowds and policemen wait for me to clear a way. I now understand why the Prince of Wales is in such good humour always: it is delightful to be a *petit roi.*"

But Oscar stayed on in America for another reason. He was revelling in his present celebrity, certainly, but he was also making plans for the future. He had ideas for two plays that he wanted to write—period dramas that he hoped to see presented in New York the following year— and he was the recipient of an unusual literary commission from an unexpected source. The French actor-manager Edmond La Grange was preparing a new production of *Hamlet* and suggested to Oscar that he might like to assist him with the translation.

Edmond La Grange was one of Oscar's boyhood heroes. Oscar had seen him on stage in London and Dublin in several of his greatest roles. He had seen him in Paris, too, at the Théâtre La Grange on the boulevard du Temple, in *Le Roi Lear.* He had even met him once, briefly, on the seafront in Dieppe in August 1879. Oscar had felt emboldened to introduce himself because Oscar knew the actress Sarah Bernhardt—Oscar worshipped Sarah Bernhardt!— and Bernhardt and La Grange had recently appeared together in Molière's *Amphitryon.* Now, in New York, in the autumn of 1882, Oscar got to know the great man. Oscar Wilde, aged twenty-eight, and Edmond La Grange, aged sixty, became friends.

La Grange was in America doing what Sarah Bernhardt

had done before him: taking the continent by storm. There were differences between the two great players, of course: Sarah's storm was more spectacular than La Grange's. La Grange was remarkable, but Sarah was divine. And Sarah was a woman. When Madame Bernhardt toured America in 1880, her personal luggage comprised forty costume crates and seventy trunks for her offstage dresses, coats, hats, furs, and fragrances, and her two hundred and fifty pairs of shoes. Monsieur La Grange travelled with three suitcases and a makeup box. Madame Bernhardt's entourage included two maids, two cooks, a waiter, her *maître d'hôtel,* and a *bonne p'tite dame* to act as companion and secretary. La Grange came with an elderly dresser and "Maman," his eighty-two-year-old mother.

Edmond La Grange's repertoire was less extensive than Sarah Bernhardt's—he brought five productions to America: she had brought eight—and his celebrity, his "star status" as we call it now, could not rival hers. However, as actors, as masters of their craft, they were in the same league, and, according to the critics, his supporting company, though smaller, was superior to hers, and in New York, at Wallack's Theater, playing in Molière, Racine, and Corneille, in French, his takings equalled hers. And like Madame Bernhardt, Monsieur La Grange was paid in cash.

It was perhaps surprising that Oscar's and La Grange's pathways had not crossed before. La Grange's four-week Broadway season was the culmination of a four-month cross-continental tour and the great French actor and the young Irish aesthete were both appearing under the auspices of Richard D'Oyly Carte. Indeed, it was Carte's man,

Colonel Morse, who eventually effected the introduction. "Edmond La Grange speaks damned good English, but he damn well refuses to do so," Morse complained to Oscar, chewing on the small cigar that appeared permanently fixed to the corner of his mouth. "La Grange maintains that French is the official language of diplomacy and therefore the only language to be used in international relations. Whenever I dine with him after the show, he jabbers away at me nineteen to the dozen and I can't follow a word he's saying. You speak French, Wilde. You can have dinner with him. You can talk to him. He'll understand you. You might even understand him, God knows."

Edmond La Grange and Oscar Wilde understood one another well. They got on famously from the start. Oscar spoke fluent, flawless French, and was soaked in the culture and heritage of *la belle France*. He was honoured to have dinner with his hero and more than happy to talk with him. He was happier still to sit back, wide-eyed with admiration, listening to whatever the great man had to say. Oscar loved the rich, deep timbre of La Grange's voice. Oscar revelled in the orotund, slightly archaic turns of phrase the actor employed. Oscar adored La Grange's myriad theatrical stories: "They are full of base lies, of course, but they contain a higher truth." La Grange, at the time, was rising sixty-one, but he crackled with energy. He was not especially tall, but his posture was impeccable and his "presence" undeniable. He was not especially slim, but he was loose-limbed and moved with a dancer's grace. He had thick white hair swept back over a high, lined forehead. His face was weather-beaten, but he had a fine profile: strong cheekbones, a Roman nose, and huge, humorous brown eyes. La Grange was an actor to his fingertips, as dramatic in his manner offstage as on, a gambler, a risk taker, in love with the theatre, in love with life.

La Grange and his company were set to return to Europe on the SS *Bothnia* on 27 December 1882. La Grange proposed to Oscar that he return to Europe on the same ship. It was steaming to Le Havre, via Liverpool: on the journey they could work together on their translation of *Hamlet*. And Oscar, learning that, while in America, La Grange's old dresser—a faithful retainer who had been with the company for more than thirty-five years—had unfortunately died, proposed to La Grange that the Frenchman take on the young black valet, Traquair, as his new dresser. "I can vouch for him in every particular. He has laid out my shirts from Peoria to Pawtucket. He knows his business and you may trust him with your life. He has a face of jet and a heart of gold."

"Does he speak French?" asked La Grange.

"He speaks the language of devotion," answered Oscar.

On the day of departure, Wednesday, 27 December 1882, Oscar was among the last passengers to board the ship. "Saying good-bye to a continent is not something that can be rushed," he explained. Besides, at the dockside there were admirers—and the press—to contend with. When, at last, as dusk was falling, he arrived on board, he found La Grange and his entourage already comfortably installed in the *Bothnia*'s grand saloon, drinking champagne. To Oscar's surprise, there was an addition to the party. Standing immediately behind La Grange, leaning over his shoulder, whispering into his ear, was Oscar's blue-eyed friend from

Leadville, Colorado: Eddie Garstrang, the professional gambler.

Garstrang straightened himself and bowed towards Oscar, quite formally.

"What the devil are you doing here?" asked Oscar in amazement.

Edmond La Grange looked up at Oscar and smiled. "Monsieur Garstrang is my new personal secretary, Oscar. I won him at cards."

3

Crossing the Atlantic

It was true. Edmond La Grange had indeed "won" Eddie Garstrang at cards. Oscar heard the whole story in less time than it took to drink a glass of champagne. As distant cheers went up on the main deck of the *Bothnia* and the ship's siren sounded, and, in the background, stewards and porters bustled to and fro, La Grange sat in state, centre stage, surrounded by half a dozen members of his company (attendant lords and ladies), and told the tale. He told it with Gallic gusto, and extravagant hand gestures, while Garstrang stood sentinel, in silence, at his side.

"You recall the Tabor Grand Opera House in Leadville, Colorado, Oscar?" La Grange began. "A gem of a theatre with a perfect acoustic. We triumphed there, too, you know. Several months after your visit, towards the end of our tour, we played a week in Leadville—and to remarkably good business. The miners of the Midwest have a feeling for Molière as well as the English Renaissance, it seems." The sixty-year-old actor leant back in his chair and suddenly crossed and uncrossed his legs as if executing a little dance of delight. The attendant courtiers smiled. "After our first night—it was *L'Avare* and they loved it—I was taken down the street to the casino for a little celebration; and there it was that I met the redoubtable Monsieur Garstrang."

La Grange paused and looked up at his new secretary and raised his glass towards him. "We had a drink and we played cards. At Monsieur Garstrang's suggestion we played a game that he called bucking the tiger. It was called faro when I played it as a child. It's a French game, invented to amuse Louis XIV. I played it with Monsieur Garstrang in Leadville, and I won. He seemed surprised. I was not. I had just secured thirteen curtain calls—I was on a winning streak that night." He beckoned a steward to refill his glass and he drank from it greedily.

"The next night," La Grange continued, "I went back to the casino, and there was Monsieur Garstrang, waiting for me. We played again. I won again. We agreed to meet for a third night of cards, only this time Monsieur Garstrang proposed that we play poker. He said that it was a game born on the Mississippi River. We played—and he played well. But I played better. I won. And I won against the odds. That night I had given Leadville *Le Cid* and in the Rockies they don't have quite the same appetite for Corneille as they do for Molière."

La Grange chuckled and drained his glass. "We met again, on each of the next three nights. We played poker again and each time we played we raised the stakes. Monsieur Garstrang played poker much as Sarah Bernhardt plays Phèdre—with terrifying intensity. He gave it his all. He was determined to recoup his losses. But even the divine Sarah sometimes loses a game. For six nights in succession Monsieur Garstrang lost and lost heavily. And on the Sunday morning, on the day of our departure from Leadville, he came to see me at my hotel. We took breakfast together and he told me that he could not pay me what he owed me.

He told me that, in truth, he could not pay me one-tenth of what he owed me. He said that he owned a gun and could use it to shoot himself. I explained to him that my specialities are tragedy and comedy: melodrama is something I despise. And that's when we came to our agreement."

"Your agreement?" repeated Oscar, glancing between the great French actor and the pale-faced American who stood at his side.

"As you know, I lost my dresser on this tour, Oscar. He died in Chicago. He was very old. Even when he was young, he was very old. But old Poquelin was more than a dresser to me. He was a friend. We played cards together— and he played well. When I act, I want to act with good actors. When I play cards, I want to play with the best. You have kindly found a new dresser for me, Oscar, and I'm grateful. I am hopeful that Traquair will give good service, but I doubt that he plays cards. Monsieur Garstrang plays cards. He is joining the Compagnie La Grange to be my secretary by day and to play cards with me by night."

Edmond La Grange held his empty glass out towards Eddie Garstrang. Garstrang took it and held it in front of him, like a cupped chalice. La Grange banged his fists on the arms of his chair and rose to his feet. As he got up, the lords and ladies all got up, too. "It's a wonderful story, is it not, Oscar?" he asked.

"Certainly," said Oscar, "in its way. I wonder that you did not tell it to me before now."

"Oh," said La Grange, stepping towards Oscar and putting his hand on Oscar's sleeve, "I could not. A gambling debt is a debt of honour: it cannot be enforced by law. Monsieur Garstrang and I came to our arrangement in Leadville two months ago. We shook hands on it. We agreed that he would settle his affairs in Colorado and then join us here, today, in New York. To be honest, I was not entirely sure that he would turn up. But he has. And for that I salute him. He is a gentleman; though, sadly, I cannot afford to let him travel as one."

La Grange laughed and widened his eyes and looked about him: at Garstrang, who was still cradling the empty champagne glass, and the attendant lords and ladies who were moving gradually towards the saloon door. "We have done well in America, but we need to husband our resources nonetheless. The Théâtre La Grange is being refurbished in our absence. The sets for *Hamlet* will not come cheap. I like to think that I keep a first-class company, but most of them must travel steerage, alas."

He clapped his hands. It was the sign for dismissal. "The ship is moving. Shall we go and wave New York farewell? And then change for dinner. You will join me for dinner, won't you, Oscar? Eight o'clock, in my stateroom? Come looking wonderful—and with something amusing to say."

Two hours later, Oscar arrived for dinner in Edmond La Grange's stateroom dressed in a dark purple evening coat lined with lavender satin. He wore velvet knee breeches, black silk stockings, and low shoes with shiny, silver buckles. At his neck and wrists were frills of ivory lace and in his buttonhole a spray of winter-flowering cyclamen. (The florist at 61 Irving Place, at the corner of Seventeenth Street, had equipped him with a different buttonhole for each night of the crossing, each one wrapped in damp cloth to keep it fresh.) He was wearing a version of the costume that he had worn when giving his lectures.

La Grange was delighted with his young friend's appearance. "You do look wonderful," he said, beckoning him into the stateroom with one hand and handing him a crystal saucer of Perrier-Jouët '78 with the other. "And have you come in an amusing frame of mind?" he asked.

"I have come in a receptive frame of mind," answered Oscar, smiling. "The spectator is to be receptive. He is the violin on which the master is to play."

La Grange laughed. "You're a very clever fellow, Oscar. I can see that I must watch you carefully. I fear that our little circle is going to be a bit dull for you, but we'll wine you well and feed you properly, that I promise."

Dinner on board the SS *Bothnia* was a substantial affair—at least, it was for the half dozen first-class passengers dining in the La Grange stateroom. In the journal that he kept intermittently (and which he used as much to try out new lines as to record the happenings of the day), Oscar made a note of it. I reproduce it here in its entirety:

27.xii.82. Dined with ELG *en famille*. Service *à la française*. Menu *à la* Weybridge until we got our just desserts. ELG talked of Rabelais and ate like Gargantua: mulligatawny soup, fried whiting, brill with shrimps, pork cutlets, *tomates farcies,* boiled turkey in celery sauce, curried hare, roast pheasant with all the trimmings. I played Pantagruel (as required) and ate quite daintily until the jellies and meringues and *boudin à la reine* appeared, when I succumbed. I can resist everything except temptation. The wines were exceptional, notably a Chambertin 1870, a Château d'Yquem 1880, and a curious Russian liqueur that arrived with the ices. Give me the luxuries: anyone can have the necessaries.

Oscar made a note, too, of his dinner companions:

A motley crew. I had met them all before and was consequently doubly grateful to my host for seating me as he did, between himself and Mademoiselle de la Tourbillon. This was the seating plan:

ELG

Liselotte La Grange ("Maman")   **OW**

Richard Marais   **Gabrielle de la Tourbillon**

Carlos Branco

ELG placed his mother on his right hand. Liselotte La Grange (universally known as "Maman") is an insufferable old booby: spoilt, selfish, self-referential, childish, obstinate, opinionated. Her excuse is that she is as old as the century, born, it seems, on 5 January 1800. She is one of those shrill women who preach the importance of virtues she is never called upon to exercise. Wanting for nothing, she harps on the value of thrift. Being idle, she grows eloquent over the dignity of labour. Her son defers to her in everything. He even indulges her repellent bitch poodle, a cumbersome creature known, absurdly, as Marie Antoinette because she is said to be descended from one of the original poodles bred by Louis XVI. (Maman is obsessed with lineage, her own and everybody else's.) In truth, the dog lacks all breeding and spent the whole of dinner breaking wind, scratching herself, and scrabbling beneath the table, tripping up the waiters and begging scraps from the plates of Maman and her neighbour, Richard Marais.

Marais, I cannot fathom. He is the La Grange company's *homme d'affaires* and has been with La Grange for more than twenty years. He is bald and plain and appears to lack all personality. The poor man is deaf as well, a disability La Grange regards as essential in a business manager. "When the tax man comes to call, Monsieur Marais can honestly say he never heard him knocking." Marais is deaf, but not mute. He can speak, but does so rarely. And when he speaks, what he says is not interesting. We shall not be friends, I think. I cannot listen to anyone unless he attracts me by a charming style or by beauty of theme.

Carlos Branco does both. He is witty, too. Tonight he said, "I love acting. It is so much more real than life." Branco is La Grange's oldest and closest friend, the scion of a distinguished Portuguese theatrical family. ("Heritage" is everything with these people!) He is sixty, handsome, intelligent, as sophisticated as Maman is vulgar. He has been playing leading character roles in the La Grange company productions all his life. "Polonius is my destiny," he said this evening. He has humour and humanity, and warm, walnut-coloured eyes. I like him very much.

Gabrielle de la Tourbillon I adore. She is tall as a poplar, slender as a reed, and her beauty, though real, is not obvious. She has the figure and face of a boy, but the energy and guile of an ambitious woman. When first I met her, a few weeks ago, she said at once: "I am Edmond La Grange's leading lady and his mistress. He has had several of both. He is sixty now and I am thirty. I am the one who is here to stay." Tonight, at dinner, while La Grange fussed over Maman and the wretched Marie Antoinette, Gabrielle talked to me of his other mistresses—and of his wife, the mother of his twins, Alys Lenoir, who took her own life, twenty years ago, after the children were born. Gabrielle told me, too, of her own lovers—all but one of them older than her—and, as she spoke of them, saying, "An actress needs friends," beneath the table she took my hand in hers and squeezed it tight. "I like a young man who has a future," she whispered. "I like a young woman who has a past," I replied.

That evening, towards the end of the dinner, over the ices and the Russian liqueurs, the talk of the table turned to the La Grange company's return to Paris and the plans for the forthcoming production of *Hamlet*. Forty years earlier, when they were both twenty, Edmond La Grange and Alys Lenoir had played Hamlet and Ophelia together. It was how they had met. Now, their twin children were twenty years of age and their son, Bernard, was to play Hamlet, and their daughter, Agnès, Ophelia. "It is in the great La Grange tradition," declared Maman, tapping the side of her dessert dish with her spoon. "Bernard will be a fine Prince Hamlet. He has the voice and the profile. And Agnès, poor fragile thing, was born to play the doomed

Ophelia. All Paris will come." When she spoke, Liselotte La Grange addressed no one in particular. Her every utterance was a general declamation. "When Edmond played Hamlet," she continued, "his father played Claudius and I played Queen Gertrude. All Paris came. Edmond will play Claudius now. Carlos will play the old fool, Polonius, of course. Who will play Gertrude?"

"Gabrielle is to play Gertrude, Maman," said La Grange amiably, resting his hand on his mother's tightly clenched fist, "as well you know."

"She is too young," hissed Madame La Grange, pulling her fist away from her son's grasp and banging it fiercely on the table.

"She *is* too young," echoed La Grange soothingly, "but she is an actress. She can appear older than her years."

"She is too thin," insisted Madame La Grange. "Far too thin. It's disgusting."

In the corner of the stateroom, Marie Antoinette began to yap and chase her own tail. Gabrielle de la Tourbillon said nothing. Nor did she look dismayed. She appeared accustomed to Maman's tirades.

Edmond La Grange looked at his mistress and smiled. He turned back to his mother. "Gabrielle is slender, certainly."

"She has no breasts," snarled the old woman.

Oscar stirred. "Are breasts essential to the playing of the role of Queen Gertrude?" he asked.

"Yes," barked Madame La Grange. "They are, monsieur. Gertrude is a mother. A mother has breasts."

"Breasts will be provided," said Edmond La Grange. "I shall speak to the wardrobe mistress."

• • •

After that first night at sea, when the ocean was placid and the night sky quite clear, the weather changed. The remainder of the Atlantic crossing was of a piece with Maman's manner: at best unsettling, at worst tempestuous. Storms came and went quite suddenly, but the bitter wind was constant and the heavy rain relentless. Even at noon the sky was dark. Only the foolhardy—and Richard Marais taking the wretched Marie Antoinette for her twice-daily constitutional—braved the decks of the SS *Bothnia*. Oscar, finding, to his relief, that he was a better sailor than he had expected, spent most of the journey closeted with La Grange in the actor's stateroom, listening to the great man's stories of the glory days of French theatre and working with him, line by line, on the translation of *Hamlet*. It was absorbing work. All his life, Oscar would be fascinated by Hamlet's melancholy.

Now and again Oscar exchanged a word or two with his erstwhile valet, Traquair, when the young man struggled up from his third-class berth in the bowels of the ship to attend to Monsieur La Grange's laundry and to lay out his new master's evening clothes. Traquair seemed happy enough, though he said little. Eddie Garstrang said still less.

Oscar saw Garstrang each evening, briefly, after dinner. Each evening, in La Grange's stateroom, Oscar ate a similar meal with the same five people: La Grange, his mother, his mistress, his business manager, and his oldest friend. Each evening, when dinner was done, La Grange escorted Maman to her cabin and helped her fuss over her nighttime pills and potions. Each evening, he then returned to his stateroom and invited Oscar to join him and Richard Marais and Carlos Branco for cards. "We play euchre, Oscar. It is an easy game. It is your kind of game. It is the game for which the joker was invented." Each evening, Oscar hesitated (he was not averse to cards) and then declined (recognising that this was what was expected of him), at which point a steward was despatched to summon Garstrang from the second-class lounge to make up the foursome. Garstrang arrived, smiled, bowed, and took his place at the card table. Each evening, on his arrival, when Oscar tried to engage him in conversation, he demurred, explaining quietly, "My obligation is to Monsieur La Grange now—I cannot talk—I must play cards."

The transatlantic crossing took ten days, during which the La Grange evening ritual was varied only twice. On the night of 31 December the captain of the SS *Bothnia* hosted a series of New Year's Eve parties for passengers of every class. Edmond La Grange remained all evening in the first-class saloon with his mother and Marie Antoinette, while Oscar, with La Grange's encouragement, escorted Gabrielle de la Tourbillon to the principal festivities that had been arranged inside a huge marquee lashed to the ship's main deck. There the young couple—Oscar was twenty-eight; La Grange's mistress was thirty—defied the elements and danced the night away to music provided, alternately, by a palm court orchestra and a Negro band.

To Mademoiselle de la Tourbillon's delight, Oscar was eager to dance. To her surprise, he was quite nimble on his feet. To her amazement, when the Negro band started to play "Oh, Dem Golden Slippers," he declared: "This is my favourite tune in all the world!"

"And why is that, Oscar?" she asked, laughing.

"Because it is written by a friend of mine, a man named Jimmy Bland," Oscar answered, sweeping the actress around him as they glided across the crowded dance floor. "I met him in New York and I liked him at once. We were born in the same week in the same year. I felt we were brothers beneath the skin. He is black, of course, and I am white."

"And you are Wilde," she said, still laughing, "and he is Bland."

"Exactly," replied Oscar. "Names fascinate me terribly." As the music propelled them around the windswept tent, he held her closely in his arms and said, "I am filled with delight at the beauty of your Christian name, Gabrielle. It has an exquisite forest simplicity about it, and sounds most sweetly out of tune with this rough-and-ready world of ours—rather like a daisy on a railway bank!"

"You are absurd, Oscar!"

"I hope so," he answered, kissing her forehead as the band played on.

Oscar enjoyed New Year's Eve on board the SS *Bothnia*. He noted in his journal:

> I flirted with ELG's mistress all night, amused her (I believe), and pleased myself (I know). A chase after a beautiful woman is always exciting. I do not love her, of course. Does she love La Grange? She says that she does, but I wonder. Does he love her? He pays her scant attention.

His recollection of his final night on board the SS *Bothnia* was less happy:

It was Maman's birthday—her eighty-third—and in the first-class grand saloon La Grange hosted a reception in her honour. The party was not a success. The sea was calm (the Irish coast was within sight), the buffet was generous, wine flowed freely, and ELG made a gracious tribute to his mother. But it was a cold affair: Liselotte La Grange is not loved by those who know her well. I watched as the middle-aged members of the company went up to her to pay their respects. They did their duty and retreated as quickly as they could. When they leant forward to kiss her hand or cheek, they made sure their lips did not touch her withered skin. The younger actors kept their distance altogether. The old woman is to be pitied. She is arrogant, irritating, tediously obsessed with her wretched dog and the glory of the La Grange lineage, but it is her age that makes her peculiarly unlovely. Old age has no consolations to offer us. The pulse of joy that beats in us at twenty has become sluggish. Limbs fail, senses rot. We degenerate into hideous puppets, haunted by the memories of the passions of which we were too much afraid, and the exquisite temptations that we had not the courage to yield to. Liselotte La Grange is angry with the world and she has cause. Once upon a time she was young.

On the morning after the party in Maman's honour, at the break of day, the SS *Bothnia,* bound ultimately for Le Havre, docked at Liverpool to allow the British passengers to disembark. Wrapped in heavy greatcoats and wreathed in scarves, Edmond La Grange, Gabrielle de la Tourbillon, and Carlos Branco gathered on the grey and misty deck to bid Oscar farewell. La Grange embraced him in a bear hug, as a father might a son. Gabrielle kissed him tenderly, as a sister might a brother. Carlos Branco shook him heartily with both hands and then, playfully, boxed his ears. *"Au revoir, mon brave,"* he said, "come and see us in Paris very soon."

"He is coming in three weeks' time," declared La Grange. "We're only releasing him now so that he can see his mother again and sort out his affairs in London. We shall have him on the boulevard du Temple at the end of the month, in time for our first rehearsal. He is to meet my children. He is to assist us with our production." The great actor looked up at Oscar and smiled. "Now that we have found you, we're not going to lose you, are we, Oscar?"

"No," said Oscar simply. "You're not going to lose me."

Carlos Branco put a hand on Oscar's shoulder; Gabrielle slipped off her glove and ran her fingers down his cheek; Oscar and La Grange hugged one another once more. There were tears in all their eyes.

The sentimental moment was interrupted by the arrival of an English customs officer.

"Is this your trunk, sir?" asked the man, indicating a large brown leather case, bound with heavy black straps. It was being held by a pair of boy porters who appeared to be struggling with the burden of it.

Oscar gave it a cursory glance. "It is," he said.

"Are you Mr. Wilde? Mr. Oscar Wilde?" asked the customs officer, seemingly winking as he spoke.

"I am."

"Have you anything to declare this morning, sir?" asked the customs man, with a smirk. "Anything in the way of genius, I mean?"

Oscar smiled.

The customs officer chuckled. "You see, we know who you are, sir."

"I'm gratified."

"The trunk appears to be unusually heavy, sir."

"It is full of books," replied Oscar.

"You're not one for light reading, then?" said the customs officer, grinning. He seemed especially pleased with this sally. He clapped his hands together, and the cold morning air was filled with a burst of his warm breath. "Do you mind if we take a look inside, sir?"

The porters laid the case flat on the deck.

"By all means," said Oscar.

"Do you have a key, sir?" asked the customs officer.

"It's not locked. You just need to unbuckle the straps and open the lock with your hand."

One of the young porters knelt down and, without difficulty, unfastened the case and pulled back the lid.

"My, my," said the customs officer, gazing down at the opened case. "This isn't what we expected . . ."

There were no books. The trunk was filled to the brim with loose, black earth—garden soil.

The customs officer bent forward and, sitting on his haunches, dug about in the black earth with a gloved hand. "My, my," he repeated as, slowly, he displaced the soil to reveal a dog's snout and then, one by one, four upturned paws.

It was the body of Marie Antoinette, Maman's bitch poodle.

4

Liverpool, London, Paris

An extraordinary scene followed on the deck of the SS *Bothnia*.

At the very moment that the customs officer got to his feet, Liselotte La Grange appeared, a tiny figure in a fur coat, supported on either side by Richard Marais and Eddie Garstrang.

"I have come to say good-bye to Monsieur Wilde," she began imperiously, letting go of her escorts and pushing her way into the group that was standing around Oscar's opened case. "I want to tell him something important," she continued, and then, as her eyes fell abruptly on the shallow trunk overflowing with earth and she saw her wretched poodle half buried in the soil, without pause her words were transmuted into a long and piercing scream. As she cried out, she closed her eyes and turned her head, not down towards the dog, but up towards the sky. Eventually, after what seemed to Oscar to be an eternity of wailing, she paused for breath and opened her eyes and looked about her in desperation. "Is it my Marie Antoinette?" she gasped. "Can it be?"

"It is, Maman," said La Grange, gently putting out his hand towards hers.

The old actor stepped forward and took his ancient

mother in his arms. "Come, Maman," he whispered, "I will look after you." He turned and led her, sobbing, along the deck, back towards the cabins. Richard Marais and Eddie Garstrang fell into step behind them, like mutes attendant on a funeral.

"She is hysterical," remarked the customs officer.

"She is an actress," said Carlos Branco quietly. "Once, she was one of the best."

Gabrielle de la Tourbillon was staring down at the stiff body of the hapless poodle lying grotesquely in its box-like grave. "I feel cold," she said.

"Come," said Branco. "I'll get you a brandy." He put his arm around her.

"Who can have done this?" she asked, shivering as she spoke.

"And why?" added Oscar, looking down at the dead dog and reaching inside his coat pocket for his cigarette case.

"Those are certainly the questions," said the customs officer briskly. "If you don't mind coming with me, Mr. Wilde, we'll let this gentleman look after the young lady while we investigate matters further. This way, sir. The lads can bring your trunk—and its unfortunate cargo."

On that cold January morning at the memorable outset of 1883, Oscar Wilde spent a little over five hours closeted in the first officer's cabin on board the SS *Bothnia* with a dead dog for company. For much of the time, he was left alone and unattended, gazing at the unflinching animal, drinking the ship's bitter coffee, and smoking his Turkish cigarettes. Intermittently, he was cross-examined—first by the customs officer, then by two none-too-cheery (and, in

Oscar's estimation, none-too-bright) representatives of the Liverpool Docks police, and, finally, and more informally, by the ship's captain.

To each interrogator Oscar expressed his sincere regret: he would have liked to be more helpful, but he could not be. He was appalled by what had occurred, naturally, but he protested that he had no idea—none whatsoever—who might be responsible for the atrocity, nor what their motive could have been. Yes, the case that now contained the dog's cadaver was indeed his case. It was one he treasured, a twenty-fifth birthday present from his mother. He had used it to store the modest library that had been his companion throughout his American tour. On his travels, he had opened the case most days, but he had never emptied it entirely. He recalled that on the preceding evening, prior to attending the birthday party in Madame La Grange's honour, he had personally supervised the packing of all his bags and baggage. He had kept a small overnight valise in his cabin, but the rest of his luggage—including the travelling bookcase—had been stored overnight in the ship's luggage room in anticipation of his disembarkation at Liverpool the following morning. He assumed that anyone could have had access to it during the night.

"Is Madame La Grange a much-loved old lady?" asked the ship's captain during his cross-examination of Oscar. The way in which the captain asked the question—with an arched eyebrow and a knowing glint in his eye—suggested he judged that probably she was not.

"She is much respected," replied Oscar tactfully.

"Was the dog much loved?" asked the captain.

"By her owner," answered Oscar, "and by Monsieur Marais, the company's business manager—"

"But generally?" interrupted the captain.

"Perhaps not 'generally,'" said Oscar. "The poor bitch was handicapped by the absurdity of her name and by being so spoilt by her owner." He glanced briefly in the direction of the dead poodle.

"Could the animal have been killed by someone with a grudge against Madame La Grange?" suggested the captain. "Or a dislike of dogs?"

"Either is a possibility, I suppose," replied Oscar, lighting another of his Turkish cigarettes and looking again at the upturned corpse of the unfortunate Marie Antoinette.

"Did you not say that you would willingly strangle her yourself, Mr. Wilde?"

Startled, Oscar turned sharply to the captain. "I don't believe so."

"I think that you did, Mr. Wilde."

"I do not recollect saying any such thing."

"But I heard you, Mr. Wilde—last night. At the party. The dog was scurrying about your feet, making a nuisance of herself as usual. I heard you say that you would willingly strangle her. You said it to Mademoiselle de la Tourbillon. I heard you. A captain has ears."

"Did I say such a thing?" asked Oscar, perturbed. "If I did, I did not mean it. It was an expression—an expression of irritation, not an expression of intent." He extinguished his cigarette. "In any event, the dog was not strangled," he added.

"Oh?"

A silence fell between them. Oscar opened his cigarette case. It was empty. He lifted the coffee cup to his lips. It was cold.

The captain looked at him steadily. "This is my ship, Mr. Wilde. What happens on board the *Bothnia* is my responsibility. I need to clear up this business as quickly as possible so that we can move on to Le Havre. For my sake, as well as for your own, tell me everything that you know."

"I know nothing!" exclaimed Oscar.

"But you say that the dog was not strangled, Mr. Wilde. How do you know that?"

"A poet has eyes, Captain. Look at the poor beast. Look at the contusion on her forehead, above her eyes. It's obvious to any half-observant man that she was struck on the head, felled by a single blow, and then buried alive, asphyxiated in this trunk of earth. It's obvious—is it not?"

The captain stepped towards the earth-filled trunk and stared down at it. He scratched his shaggy beard. "I see the contusion," he said.

He reached inside his pocket and produced his own cigarette case. He opened it and offered Oscar a cigarette. "It's a Lucky Strike. You'll like it. It's new. And strong. The tobacco is roasted, not sun dried."

Oscar took the proffered cigarette. "Thank you, Captain," he said.

"Tell me, Mr. Wilde," the captain continued, lighting Oscar's cigarette as he spoke. "Why do you think this unfortunate animal's body was hidden in your trunk?"

"I have no idea," said Oscar, lifting his head and drawing gratefully on the cigarette. "Truly."

"There are people who don't like you, Mr. Wilde."

"I have my critics," said Oscar, looking the captain in the eye.

"You have your enemies."

Oscar laughed. "Pay no attention to the newspapers, Captain. They are written by the prurient for the Philistine."

"Do you know what Mr. Henry James said of you—at my table, on board this ship, only a month ago?"

"I trust he said he was my friend. He is an author I much admire."

"He called you 'a fatuous fool,' Mr. Wilde, 'a tenth-rate cad,' 'an unclean beast.'"

Oscar's pale face flushed. "You surprise me," he said. He turned to look once more at the dead dog, drawing deeply on his cigarette. "Even so, I doubt very much that it was an agent of Mr. Henry James who, bent on my humiliation, bludgeoned Madame La Grange's pet poodle and buried the poor creature's body in my travelling bookcase. It is possible, Captain, certainly—but unlikely, don't you think?"

While Oscar was being questioned by the ship's captain, the customs officer and the two Liverpool policemen moved steadily around the SS *Bothnia* interviewing individual members of the La Grange company and assorted members of the ship's crew. At two o'clock in the afternoon—two hours after the steamship was due to have departed Liverpool for Le Havre—they returned to the first officer's cabin.

"We've found your books, Mr. Wilde," announced the customs man.

"I'm relieved," said Oscar, now smoking the last of the captain's Lucky Strike cigarettes. "Where, might I ask?"

"Behind some potted palms on the quarterdeck, adjacent to the luggage room. It seems your trunk was not locked away for the night. According to the steward who collected it from your cabin, it was left lined up on the quarterdeck with other trunks and baggage. Anyone could have taken the trunk, emptied it, and filled it up with earth. The earth came from the bedding for the potted palms."

"Have you found the culprit?" Oscar asked.

"No," said the customs officer.

"No," echoed the docks policemen. "No."

"The dog was last seen in the early hours, lying docilely outside her owner's cabin. Mr. Richard Marais is the witness. He says the dog was asleep and snoring. He's ready to swear to it. Other than that, no one saw anything, no one heard anything."

"No one knows nothing," said one of the policemen.

"Nothing," repeated the other.

"And now?" asked Oscar. "What happens now?"

"We steam on to Le Havre?" suggested the ship's captain, looking enquiringly at the representatives of Her Majesty's Customs and the Liverpool Docks constabulary.

"You do," replied one of the policemen. "Killing a dog on the high seas is not a criminal offence."

"Importing dead dog meat without a licence is, however," said the customs officer, winking at Oscar. He turned to the ship's captain. "May I suggest that the dog is buried at sea, Captain? That's what the old lady—Mrs. La Grange—has requested." He looked at Oscar and nodded towards the dead poodle that was still lying upturned in Oscar's trunk. "You can have your trunk back, Mr. Wilde."

Oscar glanced a final time at the case and its dreadful contents. "You're very kind, but I think that my case should serve as Marie Antoinette's bier, don't you?"

"If you say so, sir," said the customs officer, smiling. "Your books have been bagged up in a sack. There were forty of them in all. They're quite safe. They've been taken ashore with the rest of your luggage. You're free to go, Mr. Wilde. My apologies for detaining you."

"Not at all," said Oscar, getting to his feet. "You have your work to do. I quite understand." He shook the customs officer by the hand, nodded briefly to the two policemen, and followed the captain out of the first officer's cabin onto the main deck. The air was cold, but a winter sun was shining.

"Good-bye, Mr. Wilde," said the captain. "I am sorry about this incident with the dog. An unpleasant business. It was someone's practical joke, I suppose."

"No doubt," said Oscar.

"And I apologise if I spoke out of turn. It's been a privilege to have had you on board. I am sure that you have many more friends than enemies."

"I am blessed with an excess of everything," said Oscar pleasantly. He shook the captain's hand. "Thank you for the cigarettes," he added. "I'll look out for them. Roasted, not sun dried, you say?"

Oscar left the ship, pulling his fur coat about him. At the foot of the gangplank, a porter was waiting with a barrow piled high with his luggage. Oscar handed the boy a shilling and turned back to look up at the *Bothnia* one last time. The captain was gone, but a few yards to the left of where he had been standing, further along the main deck, half hidden by one of the lifeboats, he recognised a familiar figure. It was the young black man Traquair. He was leaning against the ship's rail, waiting to wave him farewell.

Oscar travelled from Liverpool to London by train and spent the next three weeks in a frantic flurry of activity. By day he met up with family and friends: his mother, his brother, his tailor ("a gentleman's truest friend is his tailor"), the actor Henry Irving (to talk about *Hamlet*), the artist James Whistler (to talk about art), his old Oxford friend George W. Palmer, the Huntley & Palmers biscuit heir (to talk about life and money). By night, dressed in a new evening livery, Oscar visited his old haunts: his favourite clubs and bars and restaurants, theatres, concert houses, and music halls. He had been away a year: it was good to be back. His mother greeted him as a prodigal son returned; some of his friends pretended not to have noticed that he had been away at all.

London, he felt, had not changed. It was reassuring to find the old sights and smells as he had left them, but, also, a touch disappointing. "Has *anything* novel occurred since I've been away?" he asked George Palmer.

"A disappointed poet tried to assassinate the sovereign," said Palmer.

"Oh, yes," said Oscar. "Roderick Maclean. I read about him. I should like to meet him. I thank God that Her Majesty survived, of course, but I have a fellow feeling for any poet who fails to hit his mark."

It was good to be back, but it was something of an anticlimax, too. Oscar called on James Russell Lowell, the American ambassador, to thank him for the introductions that he had given him and to report on his American adventure. Lowell saw at once that Oscar was hungry for more. "Fate loves the fearless, Mr. Wilde," he said. Oscar was struck by the ambassador's aphorism. He made a note of it in his journal and adopted it as one of his own.

Stimulated by Lowell, Oscar determined to seek out new excitements. "The Oscar of the first period is dead," he declared to anyone who cared to listen. "I am ready to move on. I find that London is not." The familiar streets of the great metropolis were covered with a sheet of snow; gas lamps glowed; dogs ran between the wheels of carts and carriages and hansom cabs; the air was thick with yellow fog. "It's picturesque in its way," he told his mother, "but it's a scene depicted by Charles Dickens, and Mr. Dickens died in 1870."

Oscar was content to be back in London briefly, but grateful that the success of his American tour meant that he could afford to go to Paris for the spring. He had work that he wanted to do and Paris was the place to do it. "Fate loves the fearless," he repeated. "In London I am treading water; in Paris I can swim against the tide." As well as working with the Compagnie La Grange on their new production of *Hamlet,* he had a play of his own that he was determined to write. "It is to be called *The Duchess of Padua,*" he told George Palmer. "Its theme will be the pervasiveness of sinful passion—and its pardonableness. As a Quaker, George, it should be right up your street."

In London, at the beginning of the third week of January

1883, care of his mother's address in Oakley Street, by the same post Oscar received two letters from Paris. The first was a note, in English, from Eddie Garstrang:

Théâtre La Grange
Boulevard du Temple
Paris

13 January '83

Dear Mr. Wilde,

It really was not possible to talk on the ship. My commitment to M. La Grange was new. I felt constrained. Please accept my apologies for what must have appeared as discourtesy on my part. I trust that when you come to Paris later this month we can resume the comfortable relationship that we enjoyed over breakfast in Leadville, Colorado. I shall look forward to that.

Yours truly,
E. Garstrang

The second was a much longer letter, in French, penned in turquoise-coloured ink on lavender-scented paper:

Oscar, mon cher—

This is from your friend, Gabrielle de la Tourbillon. That is not my real name, of course! But you know that—you guessed that, didn't you, when you paid my name those extravagant compliments? I am an actress, so I must have a name suitable for an actress. What my real name is, you will never know. A lady must be allowed some secrets . . . What are your secrets, Oscar? Shall I ever know them? Will you ever let me see into your secret heart?

And how are you, Oscar, cher ami? Where are you? What are you doing? And with whom? Have I cause to be jealous? (Or do you not believe in jealousy? You have some very peculiar beliefs, Oscar—that much I know.)

What is your news? All the news from the boulevard du Temple is good. The Théâtre La Grange has reopened, refurbished, and looks wonderful. We are playing to good business, too—it seems that Paris has missed us! We are running all the old favourites until Hamlet joins the repertoire. I believe Bernard and Agnès will be extraordinary as Hamlet and Ophelia; perhaps that is not so surprising given their heritage. Offstage, they are wild things—impossible at times!—but on stage their discipline and magnetism will take your breath away. You will like them when you meet them. You like wild things, don't you, Oscar? And they are both very beautiful. Their mother was Indian—or half Indian. (Have I told you this already?) Her family came from Pondicherry, the French settlement in India. Try to find it on the map! It is the one part of India that your Queen Victoria does not own! Alys Lenoir was a descendant of the first French governor of Pondicherry. Her mother was a famous Indian dancer, Asha Aditi. No, I had not heard of her, either, but Maman says that she was "India's greatest dancer" and so quite worthy of the La Grange family line!

Maman, you will be relieved to know, has recovered

completely from the tragic loss of poor Marie Antoinette.
We buried her at sea (Marie Antoinette, not Maman!)
in your trunk. The ship's captain conducted a brief
ceremony on the main deck when we were halfway across
the Channel and then, together, he and Edmond and
Richard Marais heaved your trunk overboard. Maman
sobbed and wailed while the rest of us did our best not to
giggle. Fortunately the wind was very sharp so that we all
appeared to have tears in our eyes.

The day after our return to Paris Edmond found a new
poodle for Maman. She has named this one the Princesse
de Lamballe, after Queen Marie Antoinette's closest friend
and confidante. It seems a curious choice of name to me,
given the fate of the original Princesse de Lamballe. As I
recall, at the height of the revolution the unfortunate lady
was handed over to the mob, raped, beaten, and butchered
to death. Her head, her arms, her legs—even, I believe, her
breasts—were chopped off and displayed on spikes. It was
worse than a first night in Marseilles.

Anyway, Maman is now contente and because she is
contente he is content. People say that Alys Lenoir was
the love of Edmond's life. Perhaps she was. I do not know.
He never speaks of her. As far as I can tell, it is Maman he
lives for—Maman and the great La Grange heritage!

He loves me, too, of course—after his fashion. I know
that you do not believe me, Oscar, but I love him, also,
and I am grateful to him. He is my protector. I do not
know how it is in England, but in France every leading
actress must have a protector, a kind gentleman who
will feed her, clothe her, pay her rent. In France, every
actress must pay for her own costumes! It can't be done

*without a protector. Until Edmond took me under his
wing I was doing what the other girls do: going out onto
the stage each night to scan the boxes. When I caught a
particular gentleman's eye he'd give the signal—folding his
programme over the edge of his box and raising his fingers
to indicate the number of five-franc pieces he was ready to
offer for the night. Edmond has spared me all that. He is a
good man—and a great actor.*

*And he loves you. And misses you. All he wants in life
is applause—and cards—and conversation. He wants
your conversation, Oscar! He wants your company. We
all do. Traquair, in particular, asks to be remembered to
you. He works hard as Edmond's dresser, but he is lonely.
I am trying to teach him French. I have to go! The bell has
just gone. I must cover my inadequate breasts and put on
my dress for Chimène! It's Corneille tonight—not many
laughs. We want to laugh, Oscar, that's why we need you.
Come to Paris, cher Oscar, come as soon as you can.*

Oscar did as he was bidden. He travelled from London
to Paris by the boat train on Monday, 29 January 1883.

5

"What is your name?"

It was in Paris, early in 1883, that I first met Oscar Wilde. I was a callow youth of twenty-one—fair-haired, pale-faced, full of dreams and diffidence. He was twenty-eight and, so it seemed to me, the master of all he surveyed.

We met, by chance, in the refurbished foyer of the Théâtre La Grange at the fashionable end of the boulevard du Temple, at around eleven o'clock on a Friday morning at the beginning of February. I was standing by the theatre box office. I had just bought myself a single ticket for that evening's performance of *Le Cid*. Oscar stepped into the foyer from the back of the stalls. He had been attending a rehearsal of *Hamlet*. He wore a red suit and a white carnation in his buttonhole. He paused for a moment to light a cigarette. I caught his eye. I smiled awkwardly as my cheeks burnt. I recognised him at once. I had seen his photograph often. I owned a copy of his *Poems*.

"You have the advantage of me, monsieur," he said, stepping towards me with an outstretched hand. "Where have we met before?" He spoke in French. "Was it in Parnassus in other times? Or, last week, outside the *boulangerie* in the rue de Turbigo? Remind me."

"We've not met before," I mumbled in English as he shook my hand.

"What is your name?" he asked.

I hesitated. I looked up at him. He was much taller than I. "Sherard, sir," I said, "Robert Harborough Sherard."

He let go of my hand and tilted his large head gently to one side. He surveyed my appearance. He glanced at the battered attaché case that I was holding close to my chest. He narrowed his eyes and chewed a moment on his lower lip. "I don't believe you, sir," he said, smiling at me. "That's not your name. How intriguing to begin our friendship upon a lie. I think we will be friends, don't you? What is your name?"

"Robert Harborough Sherard," I repeated, now scarlet with embarrassment.

"That's not your name—or, if it is, it's only part of it. What is your real name, Robert?"

"Robert Sherard is my real name now," I said. "My name was Robert Kennedy until a month ago."

"Ah," said Oscar, blowing a long blue-grey plume of smoke into the air and following its progress with his eyes.

"I had a dispute with my father," I stammered, "a row over money, and, as a consequence, I confess it, I have changed my name."

Oscar looked down at me and disarmed me with his smile. "A lie and a confession within moments of our meeting . . . We are going to be close friends, Robert, I'm sure of that. Have you half an hour to spare? Shall we take coffee—or absinthe? Absinthe makes the heart beat faster."

Without waiting for my answer, he swept ahead of me, out of the theatre foyer, and into the boulevard du Temple. As we passed a poster for the Compagnie La Grange, he paused and ran his finger across the name of Gabrielle de la Tourbillon. "That isn't her real name, either. Everyone's pretending to be somebody else nowadays." He strode ahead, taking it for granted that I would follow. He crossed the road, weaving his way between the trundling carriages, throwing his cigarette end into the gutter, and clapping his hands together as if in anticipation of a special treat. He led me down a narrow side street and into a cobbled alley.

"Here we are," he said, pushing open the door of a small and dingy estaminet. "They'll look after us here." We sat, face-to-face, across a tiny table by the bar. "It's good to meet you, Robert. The café is Walloon, the absinthe is Swiss, I am Irish, and you are—what? English, I assume."

"English, yes, though I was brought up in Italy and Germany—and Guernsey. My father is an Anglican chaplain."

"Guernsey," said Oscar, smiling broadly. The idea seemed to amuse him vastly. "Where the cows come from."

"My parents shared a house in Guernsey with Victor Hugo," I said.

"By all that's wonderful!" exclaimed Oscar. "Tell me your story, Robert—and I shall try to spot the lies."

"It's true about Victor Hugo," I insisted. "I shall only tell you the truth."

"I'm sorry to hear that," he said, as the barman placed two empty glasses, a carafe of water, and a bottle of absinthe on the table. "A lie is often so much more amusing than the truth."

"It is because of Victor Hugo that I am a writer," I said seriously. "And because of my great-grandfather, I suppose."

"Your great-grandfather?" he repeated, pouring an inch of the green liquid into my glass.

I hesitated. "William Wordsworth," I said.

He smiled. "William Wordsworth, the poet laureate? Is this true?" From a bowl on the table he picked up a small lump of sugar and held it lightly between his thumb and forefinger.

"It is. My mother is Wordsworth's granddaughter."

"Is she?" He lifted the carafe of water and slowly, carefully, poured a trickle of water over the sugar lump into my glass.

"She is."

"I wish she wasn't, Robert." He put down the carafe and the sugar and leant forward across the table. "I wish you had continued as you began—with a pack of lies." He looked earnestly into my eyes.

"Do you?" I asked anxiously. I was confused.

"I do, Robert. You see, many a young man starts in life with a natural gift for exaggeration which, if nurtured in congenial and sympathetic surroundings, or by imitation of the best models, might grow into something really great and wonderful. But, as a rule, he comes to nothing. He either falls into careless habits of accuracy, as you seem to have done, or takes to frequenting the society of the aged and well informed. Both things are equally fatal to his imagination, as indeed they would be to the imagination of anybody, and in a short time he develops a morbid and unhealthy appetite for truth-telling, begins to verify all statements made in his presence, has no hesitation in contradicting people who are much younger than himself, and often ends by writing novels that are so lifelike that no one can possibly believe in their probability. You are not writing a novel, are you?"

"I am."

"Oh, God." He sighed. "A three-volume novel?"

"Yes."

He reached for the absinthe and poured himself a generous dose. "This is dreadful news, Robert. Is it far advanced?"

"It is nearly finished," I said.

He shook his head mournfully and peered bleakly into his glass.

"I also write poetry," I added.

He brightened a little. "In the Wordsworth vein?"

"I hope it is original," I said, somewhat stiffly.

"No daffodils?" he asked.

"I am not a plagiarist," I replied.

"Do not disdain plagiarism, Robert," he said. "You have read my poems—I plagiarise. I do so without shame. Plagiarism is the privilege of the appreciative man." He smiled at me once more and clinked the side of his glass against mine. "In a poet, plagiarism is excusable and lying quite essential. Lying—the telling of beautiful untrue things—is the proper aim of art."

That Friday morning in February 1883, in a drab café off the boulevard du Temple, as the green fairy within the absinthe bottle began to weave her spell, Oscar Wilde dazzled me with paradoxes and made me his friend for life. He charmed me in the way that all true charmers do: he made me feel that I was the only person that mattered to him. I was unaccustomed to such attention. He asked me to tell him my story and I did. It did not take long.

I was in Paris, alone, existing in a rooming house in the rue de Beauce, earning my crust with bits and pieces of translation work. I was a linguist, but my university career had come to nothing. I had left Oxford because my father had curtailed my allowance. I had left the University of Bonn because he had cut it off altogether. My father disapproved of my republican views and my bohemian ways. He despised my ambition. I had hopes of becoming a full-time writer. I had enjoyed some small success as a part-time journalist. I had secured interviews with three of the great literary figures of the day—Emile Zola, Guy de Maupassant, and Alphonse Daudet—and published accounts of my encounters. In Paris I cultivated the company of men of achievement and, when I managed to meet them, I found that they accepted me; not (I realise now) because I was remarkable or beautiful (no one has ever thought me that!), but simply because I was young. As Oscar liked to say: "Youth is a calling card that will gain you admittance anywhere—use it while you may."

As we were preparing to leave the estaminet, when we had finished our bottle of absinthe (the lunch hour had been and gone), I said to my new friend, "Oscar"—he insisted that I call him "Oscar"—"when we first met this morning, how did you know that Sherard was not my name?"

"Because when I asked you, "What is your name?" you hesitated, Robert. No man hesitates over his own name. And then, when you gave me your answer, you looked me in the eye; it was a look of defiance that said, 'Here is my name—take it or leave it.' And, of course, I noticed the battered attaché case that you were clutching to your breast, with the initials 'RHSK' neatly imprinted beneath the lock. You called yourself 'Robert Harborough Sherard.' I knew the 'K' must stand for something."

I laughed. I was quite drunk by now. "So it's Oscar Wilde, poet and detective, is it?"

"It is," he said, draining his glass and joining in my laughter. "And why not? I have come to Paris. I admire the writings of the late Mr. Edgar Allan Poe. Let his gentleman detective, le Monsieur Dupin, be my role model!" He rose to his feet, a little unsteadily, and gazed down upon me seated at the table.

I reached to the side of my chair to retrieve my tell-tale attaché case. I looked up at him and smiled. "Actually, Oscar, tell me, *why* have you come to Paris? What are you doing here?"

"I have come to write a play—a play of my own. And I have come to assist the great Edmond La Grange with his production of another man's play: Master Shakespeare's *Hamlet*." He paused and touched me lightly on the shoulder. "And I have come, also, because fate favours the fearless and I am investigating a murder."

"A murder?" I repeated, gazing up at him, amazed.

"Yes," he said, nodding at me with half-closed eyes, "the murder of a dog—an unfortunate creature called Marie Antoinette."

From that morning onwards, Oscar and I were friends. When we next met—the following evening, for a supper of oysters and champagne at his hotel on the quai Voltaire—he told me of his adventures in America and of the drama that had unfolded when the SS *Bothnia* docked at

Liverpool. "The dog was dead," he said, "but nobody really cared. Curious that."

He told me, too, that our encounter coincided with a sea change in his life. He was entering a new era in a new country and, consequently, he required a new wardrobe. "We are now concerned with the Oscar Wilde of the second period, Robert," he explained. "Let me assure you that he has nothing in common with the gentleman who wore long hair and carried a sunflower down Piccadilly." We went shopping for clothes together. I helped him to dress in the manner of a sophisticated Frenchman of the day, with a silk top hat and a well-cut double-breasted redingote (dove grey, with blue black buttons). I accompanied him and his hairdresser to the Musée du Louvre where Oscar showed us a bust of the Emperor Nero and declared that *this* was the look that he now required for his locks: "Roman and imperial."

Night after night we dined together. We always ate well (Oscar was the most generous of hosts) and, usually, we drank too much. I amused him by suggesting that white wine was misnamed and should, in truth, be called yellow. He took the idea for his own and rewarded me by telling me that my pale yellow hair was also misnamed: it was, in truth, honey-coloured.

As we wined and dined, as we walked together along the banks of the River Seine smoking our postprandial cigarettes, we talked of life and love—and women. Oscar told me of the women in his life: of Florrie and Lillie and Violet and Charlotte, girls whom he had loved and lost. He told me, too, of Constance, the girl from Dublin whom he thought he might one day marry. "She has beauty and spirit and a name that suits a wife. And, Robert, she reads Dante in Italian—and understands him!" I told him that I had never been in love.

Oscar took me to the Théâtre La Grange and introduced me to the company. With the permission of Richard Marais, the company's ever-present *homme d'affaires*, I was allowed to sit in on the *Hamlet* rehearsals as a silent observer. Oscar presented me quite formally to Edmond La Grange and to his children, the twins, the young stars of the production: Bernard and Agnès La Grange. They were a striking couple, dark and so beautiful, with skin like burnished olives. Oscar said that they were "strange creatures, wild and difficult to know." He considered the boy, Bernard, "spoilt and probably unreachable," but he believed that Agnès "could be tamed." "She has a delicate beauty and a fierce intelligence, but she is troubled and fragile. She wants the love of a good man. Why don't you fall in love with Agnès, Robert? You are twenty-one, a writer with prospects and honey-coloured hair. She is twenty, an Indian princess, gifted and unattached. She is devoted to her father and he to her, but, so far as I can tell, she has no serious suitors. Fall in love with Agnès La Grange, Robert. Live dangerously. Go on."

I did not do as Oscar counselled. Instead, I did something very foolish and much more dangerous. I fell in love not with Agnès La Grange, but with her father's mistress. I fell in love with Gabrielle de la Tourbillon.

6

Decadence

That February Oscar and I spent many days and nights within the orbit of the Compagnie La Grange. Oscar was dazzled by the great leading man and I was bewitched by the old actor's young mistress. During the *Hamlet* rehearsals Oscar and La Grange would sit together on the stage, side by side, at a small table set in front of the footlights. When La Grange (who was playing Claudius) was not required in a scene, he would direct proceedings from the table, referring to Oscar constantly. "It is our translation, but he is your poet, Oscar; you must tell us where we are going wrong."

Oscar was flattered by La Grange's attention, but embarrassed by it, too. He was anxious not to irritate the other actors. They were skilful players: they knew what they were doing. Bernard La Grange, though only twenty, was clearly going to give a performance of extraordinary grace and intelligence. Even at the first reading, Oscar realised that Bernard's Hamlet was likely to be one of the great performances of the age. Oscar decided, therefore, that except in matters that directly concerned the text and the translation, he would say as little as possible. He was grateful to be allowed a ringside seat as the production evolved and determined not to overplay his hand.

After rehearsals—they usually ran from eleven in the morning to six at night—La Grange and Oscar would retreat together to La Grange's dressing room. It was a large *cabine,* the size of a substantial caravan, built for the purpose in the downstage wing immediately adjacent to the stage. According to Oscar, inside it had the feel of an expensive tart's boudoir: "all mirrors and velvet swags, guttering candles, and overworn chaises longues." When La Grange had an evening performance, Oscar would keep him company while he changed. Oscar was fascinated to watch the transformation as the old actor applied his makeup and donned his costume for his night's work. Oscar noticed that La Grange always appeared to be a younger man when in character than when himself. On the rare evenings when he was not playing—on the nights when Gabrielle de la Tourbillon was giving her Phèdre, for example—La Grange and Oscar would still go to the dressing room and there they would share a bottle (or two) of yellow wine and smoke some of La Grange's favourite Cabañas Havana cigars.

When La Grange was dressing for a part, Traquair, the valet, was in dutiful attendance. Oscar was pleased to note that Traquair, though subdued, appeared at ease with his new master. When La Grange and Oscar were simply drinking and smoking together, Traquair withdrew to his own quarters, a tiny self-contained annexe to the dressing room: "the dresser's bedroom," a windowless cubicle not much larger than the narrow divan and washbasin it contained.

Oscar revelled in his conversations with La Grange. For the most part Oscar listened while La Grange talked. La

Grange spoke of the great acting dynasties of France—of the Baptistes, the Deburaus, the Thénards. He told stories of the travails and triumphs of his own family, going back to the time when the founder of the dynasty, Charles Varlet de La Grange, was Molière's pupil, friend, and first biographer. For Oscar's benefit, La Grange reenacted his forebear's touching description of the death of Molière. It brought tears to Oscar's eyes. "You are a very foolish, fond young man," said La Grange, raising his glass to Oscar. "When I was a boy, my father took me to see Macready's Othello." Macready gave his final performance here in Paris. There you would have wept—and with some cause. The pity of it, Oscar, the pity!"

They talked of the theatre mostly. As Oscar explained to me, "That's what most theatre people mostly do." But they talked also of literature and philosophy and were excited to discover a mutual love for the lost world of Ancient Greece. Over Sancerre and cigars, with tears of joy in both their eyes, they spoke of Socrates and virtue, of Plato and love, of Aristotle and the soul, and of Epicurus and the elements. Edmond La Grange claimed to live his life according to the teachings of Epicurus. "I believe that he does," said Oscar. "Epicurus sought the tranquil life, characterised by *aponia*—the absence of pain and fear. He did not fear death because death is merely nothingness. He did not fear the gods because they neither reward nor punish us. He believed in being self-sufficient and surrounded by friends. That's why La Grange—one of the great men of our age—lives his life entirely within a theatre and plays cards every night with his cronies."

When Oscar was closeted with La Grange, I did what I

could to spend time alone with Gabrielle de la Tourbillon. I was smitten with her from the moment of our introduction. We met where Oscar and I had first met: in the foyer of the Théâtre La Grange. Oscar presented me to her saying, "This is my friend Robert Sherard. You have something in common. He, too, is living under an alias."

She laughed. "He is very young to be living under an alias." She put out her hand to shake mine.

"He is not as young as he looks," said Oscar slyly. "He has nearly completed a three-volume novel!"

She took my hand. "He is very cold," she said. She lifted my hand to her warm cheek. "He is terribly cold," she said. "We will have to warm him up." She pulled my hands together and covered them with hers.

During rehearsals, while Oscar and La Grange sat side by side at the front of the stage, I would sit with Gabrielle in the auditorium, at the end of the fifth or sixth row of the orchestra stalls. Whenever she was required for a scene, she would slip out of her seat and move quickly and quietly through the "pass door" onto the stage. She accepted me at once as her constant and devoted companion, as though it were the most natural thing in the world. I fell into the habit of undertaking errands on her behalf: fetching her a glass of water, collecting her copy of the script that she had left up in her dressing room, running out to the patisserie in the rue Béranger to buy her a paper twist of her favourite bonbons. I did as she asked me and asked no more in return but to look at her. She was to me like a goddess: tall and slim with a long, slender neck and a perfect profile. Her hair was black and silken; her eyes were cobalt blue; and between her eyes and her high cheekbones were the gentlest traces of crow's-feet—lifelines that I wanted above all else to kiss.

Whenever, in the half darkness of the auditorium, she turned towards me and saw me gazing up at her, she took my hand in hers and whispered, "Robert, I am not a museum exhibit. I am your friend." She held my right hand gently in both of hers and, slowly, softly, ran her fingers along each of mine. Sometimes, holding my hand in her lap, she took my fingers and held them together and pressed them against her womanhood.

When I told Oscar this, he roared.

"Is this a lie?" he spluttered through his laughter. "A beautiful lie—at last!"

"No, it is the truth," I protested, blushing furiously and running my hands through my hair in my embarrassment. "It is the truth. Do you not believe me?"

He saw that my distress was genuine. "I believe you, Robert," he said at once. He smiled at me. "Indeed, I congratulate you. Gabrielle de la Tourbillon is a very attractive woman."

"But what does it mean?" I asked. "What does it signify?"

"It means that she is an actress. This is what actresses do. I fear that you will find that it signifies very little."

"'What actresses do'?" I repeated, uncomprehending.

"By custom long established, during the course of a theatrical production the leading lady has an affair with her leading man. It's almost inevitable. It's virtually compulsory. But in this instance there is a difficulty. Mademoiselle de la Tourbillon is *already* the mistress of the senior leading man—and the junior leading man is her lover's son."

He gave me a kindly grin and proffered me a cigarette. "She is having to turn her attention elsewhere."

"Does she not love me, then—even a little?"

"She is flirting with you, Robert."

"I love her," I said. I said it passionately and I meant it.

Oscar struck a match and held it to my cigarette. "Be careful, Robert. You are twenty-one. She is thirty. Take great care. You are an innocent moth and her flame burns very bright."

I heard Oscar's warning, but I did not heed it. My moments with Gabrielle de la Tourbillon, sitting in the darkened orchestra stalls of the Théâtre La Grange, were simply too intoxicating. They were frustrating, too. There were so many things that I wanted to say to her, so many questions that I wanted to ask, but there was never an opportunity. When we were in the stalls, her focus was on the stage and the rehearsals. When we were elsewhere in the theatre—or in the street outside or in one of the cafés nearby—other people were always there. We were never alone. She had no private space. She shared her dressing room with another actress, a young girl called Lisette who also served as her understudy and helped to dress her. She shared her bed with Edmond La Grange. They lived together in an apartment immediately above the theatre. It was a huge apartment, by all accounts, built into the roof of the theatre, containing a series of independent suites of assorted sizes—Liselotte La Grange (Maman), and Bernard and Agnès La Grange, and Richard Marais, the business manager, and Eddie Garstrang, as La Grange's secretary, all had rooms up there—and from its high, wide windows, apparently, you could see right across Paris, as far as the Butte de Montmartre in the north and the banks of the Seine to the south. The apartment was La Grange's territory: I was never invited there.

Oscar was rarely invited, either. "After Racine," explained La Grange, "one doesn't want brilliant conversation; one wants a bottle of Perrier-Jouët and a silent hand of euchre." When he played cards, La Grange required Eddie Garstrang to make up the foursome, and Gabrielle de la Tourbillon to pour the wine and clear the ashtrays.

Garstrang was now, evidently, La Grange's man. From what Oscar could see, he appeared to have settled immediately into the ways of the great French actor and his unusual entourage. It helped considerably that Maman accepted Garstrang. It would be an exaggeration to say that she warmed to him, but, certainly, she did not object to him. When Richard Marais was otherwise engaged, Liselotte La Grange even allowed Eddie Garstrang to take her new pet poodle for one of her several daily walks.

Garstrang's integration within the La Grange company was also eased by the fact that he spoke French. It was not classical French—it was rough, Louisiana French, learnt in the casinos of New Orleans and at the gaming tables on board the riverboats of the Mississippi—but it served. Washington Traquair had no such advantage. When Traquair was busy—dealing with La Grange's laundry, darning the great man's socks, pressing his shirts, laying out his wardrobe for the evening's performance, assisting the actor into and out of his elaborate costumes—he was relatively content. But when he was idle, he was lonely. He spoke no French. He had no friends in Paris. He was a black man in a white man's city. He spent his time—almost all his time—hidden in his tiny quarters, the window-less room (it was no more than a vestibule, really) that adjoined La Grange's dressing room at the Théâtre La Grange. When he ventured out into the streets around the theatre, he was regarded, at best, as a curiosity, a figure of fun; at worst, as an alien, an object of derision.

One day, not long after his arrival in Paris, Oscar found Traquair in his little bedroom, lying on his bed, weeping. The young man was homesick. It was as simple as that. Oscar talked to him. Oscar made him laugh. (Oscar's conversation could cure the toothache.) Oscar succeeded—at least, for the moment—in talking Traquair out of his misery. Cajoled by Oscar (who promised to teach him French), the black valet agreed to "give it six months." If, by the end of the summer, he still felt that he had not settled in, Oscar undertook to find the money to pay for Traquair's return passage to America.

That February, when we weren't with Edmond La Grange and his close-knit circle, our social life revolved around the home of Paris's other great theatrical luminary, Sarah Bernhardt. She was extraordinary. "The eighth wonder of the world," Oscar called her, "the greatest personality France has had since Joan of Arc." She was thirty-eight in 1883, at the height of her fame and fortune. Her appearance was nothing: she was skeletally thin, with pale sunken cheeks and an unruly mop of fuzzy ginger-coloured hair. Her presence was everything. "She is a force of nature," said Oscar, "as irresistible as the incoming tide, as fascinating as a rainbow, as mysterious as the moon." Oscar was intrigued by Edmond La Grange, charmed by him, and flattered to be working with him on his production of *Hamlet*. He was a great actor and an engaging companion. "But, ultimately," said Oscar, "what is he? Simply a man. While Sarah is something else: Sarah is divine!"

Sarah also had a vast range of interests beyond the stage and the card table. She was quite as passionate about her sculpture and her painting, her pistol shooting, her ballooning, her fishing, and her alligator hunting, as she was about her acting. Everything she did she did on a magnificent scale. Liselotte La Grange kept a pet poodle called the Princesse de Lamballe. Sarah Bernhardt kept a toy griffon called Hamlet—and an ocelot and a puma and, for a time, in her house on the corner of the rue Fortuny and the avenue de Villiers, a fully grown lion. She adored wild animals. She told Oscar that she had consulted a surgeon to find out if it would be possible for him to graft a living tiger's tail to the base of her spine so that she could lash it from side to side when she was angry.

The aspect of Bernhardt's character that Oscar was most drawn to was her capacity for telling "beautiful lies." She spoke always with such sincerity that, somehow, whatever she told you, you wanted to believe. When I first met her—taken to her house for lunch as Oscar's guest towards the end of the second week of the *Hamlet* rehearsals—she told me that the shah of Persia had just left Paris and, so impressed was His Majesty with the ballerinas at the Paris Opéra, that with Sarah's help he had bought beautiful tutus for every member of his harem to wear. Was it possible? Could it have been true? When Sarah told me that she slept every night in her own satin-lined coffin, I told her that I did not believe her. At once she took me by the hand

and, running in bare feet, led me through the house to her bedroom. "There!" she cried triumphantly, showing me the open rosewood coffin with her nightdress lying at its side. "That is where I sleep each night—at ease and all alone."

In truth, Sarah rarely slept alone. She had many lovers. She was reputed to have seduced all the crowned heads of Europe—including His Holiness the Pope. "I am the most lied-about woman in the world!" she wailed, casting her eyes towards heaven. When I first knew her she was married to a handsome Greek ne'er-do-well eleven years her junior: a womaniser, spendthrift, and dope fiend by the name of Jacques Damala. His party piece was to produce his hypodermic syringe at the dining table and inject himself with his narcotic through his trouser leg in full view of his wife and her guests. This was Paris in 1883, at the height of *"la décadence."* I smoked an occasional pipe of opium myself.

Edmond La Grange's circle was a small one. He spent his time in his theatre, with his family and a handful of cronies. Sarah Bernhardt, by contrast, entertained the world. She kept eight servants and an open house. Whenever Oscar and I called to see her, there were always other guests. At that first lunch party, in February 1883, I was seated between Jacques-Emile Blanche, a young artist yet to make his name, and Maurice Rollinat, a notorious poet and musician, one of Sarah's celebrated "discoveries." I took immediately to Jacques-Emile Blanche: we were exact contemporaries, and there was an openness about him—a freshness and a freedom of spirit—that I found wonderfully appealing. Oscar was equally taken with Maurice Rollinat. They found at once that they shared a passion for the works of the poet Charles Baudelaire. Rollinat's own poetry took as its themes death, murder, suicide, live burial, diabolism, disease, and putrefaction. "You don't get many laughs with Maurice Rollinat," said Oscar, "but if you're in the mood to ponder human misery, degradation, and despair, grey-faced Maurice is your man."

On the evening of that first luncheon chez Madame Bernhardt, Oscar persuaded Rollinat to take us on a guided tour of what he termed "the darkest corners of the City of Light"—the haunts of the lowest criminals and poorest outcasts of the city. "Lift the veil, Maurice," said Oscar. "Show us the showplaces of the Paris inferno."

It was a grim but unforgettable evening, made bearable by the glasses of absinthe that we consumed at each filthy bar we visited along the way. The expedition culminated at the infamous tavern of the Château Rouge in Montmartre. "Our tour is nearly done," said Rollinat, standing in the darkened doorway of the inn. "I have brought you here to show you the Salle des Morts."

"The Room of the Dead? I have heard of it," said Oscar.

With a curious smile playing on his thin, grey lips, Rollinat explained: "In London you have Madame Tussaud's famous exhibition. In Paris we now have the waxworks of the Musée Grévin. But here at the Château Rouge is a tourist attraction of a different order. La Salle des Morts is a chamber of living horrors where the desperate and the destitute—the homeless, the lame and the halt, prostitutes and drug addicts, beggars and vagabonds—crouch and huddle and lie together in near darkness to be viewed for half a sou by visitors in search of the macabre."

"Must we see this?" I asked.

"I think so," said Oscar, looking at me. "At least, I must.

I want to eat of the fruit of all the trees in the garden of the world. I must taste the bitter as well as the sweet."

"There is no hurry," said Rollinat, holding open the door to the tavern. "We have time for a drink first. Those that we have come to see will not run away."

We spent some time in the crowded, smoke-filled bar on the ground floor of the Château Rouge, sipping absinthe, talking to thieves and the saddest daughters of joy, listening to the obscene songs of a frightful old, noseless hag, and watching a group of professional beggars display the tricks by which they feigned infirmities. As midnight struck, the landlord nodded to Rollinat and beckoned to us to follow him. We made our way to a narrow wooden staircase at the rear of the bar and followed the landlord, a large, lumbering man, as slowly, breathing heavily, he climbed the stairs. "This is our pièce de résistance," the landlord wheezed. "It's a good business, too. You pay to see it and the poor bastards who live here, they pay, too—half a sou a night. It's just a room in the rafters, but it's safe, and shelter and company of a kind."

The room was as wide and deep as the bar below, but totally bereft of furniture, low ceilinged, and windowless. To reach it we had to climb a second, narrower, steeper stairway that came up through the floor into the centre of the room itself. The landlord went first, followed by Rollinat. I came next, leaving Oscar to bring up the rear.

"*Et voilà!*" declared Rollinat, under his breath. The landlord held his candlestick high in the air and slowly swung it round in a circle to illuminate each corner of the room.

It took a moment to adjust to the gloom. It took more than a moment to adjust to the stench and to absorb the horror of what we were witnessing. It was a sight to appal the eye and pierce the soul. Stretched out in every posture of pain and discomfort, many in the stupor of drink, many displaying foul sores, maimed limbs, or the stigmata of disease, all in filthy and malodorous rags, the sleepers of the Room of the Dead, with their white faces, immobile and sightless, looked indeed like corpses. Oscar read my mind. "But the dead and buried rest in peace," he murmured, "for they are in heaven. These wretches are the living dead. This is a hell on earth."

As I write this, seven years later, I can still picture Oscar Wilde's face as it was that night. I can still see his large, Neronian head just rising above the floor: his feet had refused to carry him to the top of the staircase and into the pestilential room. Seen in the flicker of the landlord's candle, there was upon its features the horror of one who looks on the Medusa: a twinge of pity about the lips, perhaps, but in the main, horror—sheer horror.

Oscar said nothing until we had regained the street. There, in the cold midnight air, for a moment he stood quite still, his eyes shut. He breathed deeply and turned towards me in the darkness. "Did you not see him?" he whispered, opening his eyes. "Did you not recognise him?"

"Who?" I asked, bewildered.

"Up there," he said, "in the Room of the Dead. Did you not see him?"

"Who?" I repeated.

"Bernard La Grange," he said. "I am certain it was him. Why was he there, Robert? Why?"

7

Curiosity

It was Saturday morning—the morning after our visit to the Salle des Morts—and Oscar had decided that we should call on Sarah Bernhardt for breakfast. It was a little after eleven o'clock and we found the great actress, swathed in a green and gold oriental peignoir, her tousled hair pinned up on her head, her face covered in a mass of white powder (as though she had dipped it into a bag of flour), seated at a little bamboo table in the ornamental orangery at the back of her house.

When the servant admitted us to her presence, Madame Bernhardt was leaning across the table feeding a sliver of grape to a large tortoise that sat on a silver salver before her. "I'm giving Methuselah his *petit déjeuner*. Don't mind us, gentlemen. Help yourselves to coffee."

Hamlet, her Belgian griffon, whimpered at her feet. Osric, the cockatiel, squawked overhead. The caged canaries (Rosencrantz and Guildenstern) twittered excitedly. Apart from the animals, she was alone. Her husband was elsewhere: befuddled and in the arms of his mistress. Her lover was elsewhere: extricating himself from the arms of another woman. Maurice, her eighteen-year-old son (*"un petit accident d'amour"*), was upstairs and fast asleep. Sarah got to her feet, picked up the tortoise with both

hands, and carrying it aloft as though it were the head of
John the Baptist, nodded to me to open the door to the
garden for her. She hadn't yet learnt my name. (I am not
sure that she ever did.) Holding it high, she carried the
reptile into the garden and laid it carefully on the earth
beneath the shrubbery. She came back into the orangery,
stroking my cheek as she passed me, and went straight
to Oscar and kissed him lightly on the mouth. "I am so
pleased you have come back so soon," she said. "There was
something I meant to ask you yesterday and quite forgot.
My new Japanese screens, Oscar—how should I arrange
them? How? How? *How?*" Dramatically she stretched out
both her arms in the direction of a pair of painted screens
that stood forlornly in the corner of the room.

Oscar looked towards the screens and pondered a moment and smiled, then lit his cigarette and, looking back at
Sarah, said, "Why arrange them at all? Why not let them
occur?"

"Oh, Oscar!" she exclaimed, bursting into a peal of
happy laughter. She clapped her hands with delight and
sat down once more. "Did you hear that, Hamlet? 'Why
not let them occur?' You are so brilliant, Oscar. You have
been up half the night and still you are so brilliant! Come,
take your coffee, bring your friend, sit by me, tell me everything. How was Montmartre? Did you see the dark side of
the City of Light? Did Rollinat show you everything? Did
you visit la Salle des Morts?"

We collected coffee from the sideboard—and black
German bread and hard Dutch cheese and slices of Italian
salami—and sat on either side of Sarah Bernhardt at her
bamboo breakfast table. She put her fingers together as if

in prayer and pressed them gently against the point of her chin. "Tell me everything," she said, widening her eyes. "Tell me all that you saw. Shock and surprise me."

"What shocked and surprised me," said Oscar, peeling a banana for his friend and handing her the fruit, "was the sight of Bernard La Grange, in rags and on his knees, pale and contorted, surrounded by a sea of vagrants and vagabonds in the Room of the Dead."

"Bernard La Grange? The wunderkind? Are you sure that it was him?" she asked, taking the fruit and breaking it to hand me a piece.

"I am certain. I think that he recognised me, too. I saw fear in his sunken eyes. He was trembling. His hands were shaking. They clawed the empty air. It was pitiful, Sarah. Why was he there? Why?"

"Curiosity," she said simply.

Oscar shook his head and lit his cigarette.

"Curiosity," she repeated, biting into the banana, "that's why he was there." She swallowed the fruit and ran her fingers soothingly across Oscar's forehead. "Don't look so anxious, my friend."

"I'm puzzled," said Oscar. "That's all. By day, he's rehearsing *Hamlet*. By night, he's sleeping in the Room of the Dead. Why?"

"Why were you there?" asked Sarah, taking Oscar's cigarette from between his fingers and puffing on it lightly. "Curiosity!"

"I went to observe the horror," Oscar protested.

"And he went to *experience* it," countered Bernhardt. She got to her feet. "He is an actor, Oscar. You are a writer. Writers describe. Actors *inhabit*. You talk airily about tasting all the fruits in all the gardens of the world—the bitter and the sweet. Well, Bernard La Grange isn't talking about it—he's *doing* it."

"He was trembling, Sarah."

"He's a fine young actor; everybody says so. He was *living* the part, inhabiting it to the full. He's his father's son."

"His hands were shaking uncontrollably."

"Perhaps he had been taking cocaine," she said lightly. "So many of the young ones do." She returned Oscar's cigarette to him and ran her fingers playfully through his close-cropped curls. "And how is his Hamlet progressing?"

"I think he will be remarkable," said Oscar.

"Exactly," purred the diva, kissing my friend on the forehead.

"I think it will be a remarkable production, all in all," Oscar continued earnestly. "Edmond La Grange will be a definitive Claudius."

"Of course. He is a great actor."

"Should I tell La Grange about Bernard? Should I tell him what I've seen?"

"Don't be absurd, Oscar." With a long, thin index finger Madame Bernhardt tapped Oscar on the nose reprovingly. "What the son does in his own time is not the business of the father. Besides, if it isn't affecting the boy's performance, Edmond La Grange won't give a damn."

"Won't he?" asked Oscar. "La Salle des Morts is a pestilential hellhole, Sarah. It can't be good for the boy's health."

"But it may be enriching his performance, deepening his understanding of the moody Dane, may it not? That's all that matters to Edmond La Grange. As long as his son gives an account of Hamlet that is worthy of the great La Grange name, nothing else counts. Believe me, I know the man. I've known him for twenty years. He's a cold fish."

"I find him agreeable enough," said Oscar.

"Of course, you do. You're not his son or his lover—you're part of his audience. He performs: you applaud. I don't believe that Edmond La Grange has any true feeling for anyone but himself—and his audience. He adores his daughter, I know, poor, fragile thing. He feels for her, you can see that in his eyes. But the love of his life, without question, is his audience." She paused and pondered for a moment. "That may be why he's such a great actor. He gives his all to his art."

Oscar chuckled. "He's kind to his poor old mother."

"He respects his heritage, certainly," said Sarah seriously.

"Madame La Grange is not an easy lady," I volunteered. I had been looking for an opportunity to make a contribution.

"She is impossible!" shrieked Sarah, throwing up her hands in a theatrical gesture of despair. "My darling Hamlet and her wretched Marie Antoinette have never got on."

"Her 'wretched Marie Antoinette' is dead," said Oscar.

"No!" cried Sarah, suddenly moved. Her eyes were pricked with tears. (The Bernhardt temperament was nothing if not mercurial.) "I should not have spoken of the poor little dog like that. When did she die? She was not that old."

Sarah picked up her own little dog and cradled the griffon in her arms as Oscar told the sorry tale of what had occurred on the SS *Bothnia*. The actress was visibly moved by the story. "Who did this terrible thing?" she asked when Oscar had finished his narrative. "Who can have been so cruel?"

"I do not know," said Oscar. "I have no idea. I've asked questions. I've made enquiries of each and every one of the members of the La Grange company who was on board at the time and none of them seems either interested or concerned. Not one of them cares."

"Are you surprised? They're all actors, after all."

"But you're an actress," I said, "and you love animals."

"There is a difference," she replied, kissing her griffon on the nose and lowering him gently to the ground. "They are French and I am not. I am Jewish."

Suddenly, her mood apparently once more transformed, Madame Bernhardt turned to me and, smiling, asked, "Would you like to meet Victor Hugo, young man? He is very old and quite harmless." Without waiting for my reply, she grasped me by the hand and pulled me from my chair.

"I've met him, in fact," I said, a little confused. "In Guernsey, when I was a boy."

"Did he try to bite you?" she asked, laughing. "He probably did. But he's quite toothless now and he means no harm. He's chained up in the cellar. We'll take him some salami. Come."

I stood, bemused, as France's greatest actress tried to entice me across her orangery with a large salami in her tiny hand.

Oscar barked with laughter and banged the bamboo table with such force that the teaspoons rattled in their saucers. "Victor Hugo is Sarah's African lion, Robert. He's a mangy old creature and stinks to high heaven. You don't want to meet him, believe me, especially when you've met the real thing." Oscar got to his feet and rescued me from the divine Sarah's grasp. He prised the salami from her and laid it back on the sideboard. He took the tiny actress in his arms and embraced her. "We must go, my friend. We will see you soon."

"I look forward to the La Grange *Hamlet*," she said. "I shall come to the first night. I imagine all Paris will be there. Will I recognise a Wilde touch or two in the production? I hope so. I collect *Hamlets,* you know. I have seen all the greats. I shall play the part myself one day."

Oscar laughed. "And when you do, will all Paris come?" he asked.

"All the *world* will come, Oscar," she answered, pulling her peignoir about her. "And do you know why?"

"No, Sarah. Tell me: why?"

"Curiosity."

By fiacre, from Sarah Bernhardt's house in the XVIIth arrondissement, we reached the Théâtre La Grange, in the *troisième,* in less than half an hour. It was an imposing building with a fine neoclassical façade, the oldest of the seven theatres that had once been situated on the boulevard du Temple. The street was known as the "boulevard du Crime," not because it was frequented particularly by the criminal classes, but because murder and melodrama had been the staple fare of all the theatres along the thoroughfare. In the early 1860s, when Baron Haussmann was charged with redesigning Paris, clearing away slums and driving arterial highways through the heart of the city,

Edmond La Grange had seized the moment to acquire the freehold of the largest of the theatres in the boulevard and redevelop it. La Grange had given the theatre his name and changed its nature, transforming it from a down-at-heel playhouse specialising in cheap sensation into Paris's leading commercial theatre with a popular classical repertoire, the only serious rival to the Comédie-Française.

The Théâtre La Grange was his home—and his life. What leisure time he allowed himself was spent in his apartment. The rest of Edmond La Grange's waking existence was passed either on the stage itself, rehearsing or playing; or behind the scenes and below the stage, supervising the building of the sets and the creation of the costumes; or in his dressing room, in the wing immediately adjacent to the stage, on the right-hand side of the proscenium arch. When his dressing-room door was open, from the mirror on his dressing-room table the great actor-manager could command a clear view of the centre of the stage.

The rest of the theatre's dressing rooms were to be found, not at stage level, but on four separate floors, reached by a single narrow stone stairway at the rear of the building. La Grange's dressing room, larger than any of the others, was the heart of his empire. It was where he planned his productions; where he learnt his lines; where, day after day, six days out of seven, he applied his makeup and donned his costumes to turn himself from whoever he was into whoever he wanted to be; and it was where, on days when there were matinées, between the afternoon and the evening performance, on his chaise longue (the chaise longue on which Molière himself was said to have breathed his last), he dozed, recollecting past triumphs, dreaming of future glories.

The dressing room was also the room in which Edmond La Grange conducted his business; where (with such high hopes!) he hired new actors and (with such deep regret!) let go those who no longer met his exacting standards; it was the room in which he and Oscar sat for long hours poring over their translation of *Hamlet*; it was the room in which he and Richard Marais sat each night by gaslight, checking and counterchecking the day's box office takings. It was not a room I had yet visited. It was a room in which Oscar felt very much at home.

"It's the holy of holies," said my friend, leading the way across the darkened stage towards the dressing-room corner. "Tread softly and speak low. Sacred are its mysteries."

"Are we expected?" I asked, lowering my voice. "Isn't there a matinée?"

"There is and we are," Oscar replied gaily, and then, abruptly, even as he spoke, he hushed himself—"Sshh!"—and held out his hand to halt me in my tracks. "Quiet!" he hissed.

We had reached the dressing-room door. We froze where we were. I held my breath. Slowly, Oscar turned his eyes towards me and inclined his ear towards the door. From within the room we could hear the sound of a woman sobbing. A man spoke—his voice was raised and angry. His words were indistinguishable. Another man spoke— an older man: there was the force of anger in his voice, too. The woman's sobs became louder and louder—and faster and faster—and then burst, like a wave upon the shore, and subsided into tears. Were they tears of anguish or tears of laughter? Oscar narrowed his eyes and leant his body further towards the door. I made to speak. I felt we had no business to be there. Oscar lifted a finger to his lips to silence me. Within the room, the two men's voices were raised once more, sharper and angrier than before. Suddenly, a third voice joined the fray. It was deeper than the others, and calmer, too. I recognised it because of the slight Portuguese accent. It was the voice of Carlos Branco. *"Mais enfin!"* he cried. *"Mais enfin!"*

Quite suddenly, Oscar pulled me away from the dressing-room door and, as he did so, the door itself swung open. In the doorway, in his dressing gown, barefoot, stood Edmond La Grange. For a brief moment—no more—I saw wild confusion in the actor's eyes. His fingers trembled at his temples. He ran them rapidly through his thick white hair. Then he recognised Oscar in the half-light of the wings and laughed. "Oscar! What are you doing here?"

"We have a rendezvous," answered Oscar, smiling.

La Grange slapped his palm against his forehead. "I'd forgotten. Forgive me." He hit himself a second time and raised his eyes to heaven and shook his head in mock despair. Behind him, close together, stood Carlos Branco, Bernard La Grange, and Agnès La Grange. From within the room, each of them stared out at us. Each of them was smiling. "We've been discussing the play, Oscar," La Grange continued. "We've been experimenting." He glanced at Carlos Branco. "Old Polonius here has had some novel ideas. We've been taking them on board."

"I must dress for the matinée," said Branco genially.

"There's no rush," said La Grange, raising his hand to

prevent his friend from leaving. "Let us finish our discussion—if Oscar will excuse us."

"By all means," said Oscar, bowing and retreating, "unless I can be of service?"

La Grange waved his hand dismissively. "It's all technical stuff," he said, "who goes where, what happens next—that kind of thing. It's for the craftsmen, not the poet. Can we meet after the matinée? Shall we have English tea? I'll get Traquair to toast some muffins."

Oscar repeated himself. "By all means," he said.

I looked at my friend and saw that his gaze was fixed on Bernard La Grange. The young actor was staring at Oscar, with his head held back and tilted to one side. There was no trace of strain in his face, no apparent signs of the after-effects of his night in the Salle des Morts.

"*À tout à l'heure*," said Edmond La Grange, closing his dressing-room door.

"*À tout à l'heure*," said Oscar.

We spent the rest of that Saturday afternoon over a bottle of absinthe in the little estaminet in the cobbled alley off the boulevard du Temple.

"You have read 'The Murders in the Rue Morgue' by Edgar Allan Poe?" Oscar asked.

"I have," I said.

"You recall the great C. Auguste Dupin's great maxim?"

I laughed. "Which one in particular?"

"There is only one so far as I am concerned, Robert: 'There is such a thing as being too profound.'" He raised his glass to me by way of a toast and then lowered it carefully to the table and contemplated its yellow-green contents with a furrowed brow. "Dupin is right, is he not?" He ran his finger around the glass's rim. "And I'm a fool, trying to dig deep in shallow ground, looking for needles where there are no haystacks, seeing weasels and whales in shapeless clouds. 'There is such a thing as being too profound.'"

I laughed once more. "There is such a thing as being a little drunk," I said.

"And yet," he continued, ignoring me, "it makes no sense. We heard three men arguing. We heard a woman sobbing. But when the door was opened, all were wreathed in smiles!"

"La Grange had a look of alarm in his eyes," I said. "At least, for a moment he did."

"Did he? Was it alarm or was it surprise? Perhaps he was simply startled to find us there."

"And there were traces of tears in Agnès's eyes."

"But she was smiling—and her smile was tender, natural, unforced. She placed her hand on her father's shoulder. She did not appear to be in the least bit distressed, did she?"

"No," I acknowledged, draining my glass. "She did not. None of them seemed distressed."

"And yet, moments before, we heard their voices raised. We heard Agnès's sobs. We heard Carlos Branco cry, '*Mais enfin!*'—and then the door opened . . ."

"And there they were, smiling out at us."

"Perhaps they knew that we were there," said Oscar, sitting up suddenly and pushing his glass away from him. "Perhaps it was a charade played out for our benefit?"

"But why? Isn't it much more likely that what La Grange

told us was the truth? They were simply discussing the play, arguing a point, as actors do."

"Tearing a passion to tatters, to very rags . . . Indeed," murmured Oscar, subsiding, and reaching for his glass once more. "You are right, Robert. There is such a thing as being too profound."

Oscar's glass was empty. He considered it briefly and then, with both hands, lowered it carefully from the table to the floor. He folded his arms in front of him and laid his head gently on them, closing his eyes. "Our liquid lunch is rounded with a sleep, Robert. We are such stuff as dreams are made on and are to have muffins for tea . . . Good night, sweet prince . . . The rest is silence."

8

Something Rotten

Oscar awoke before I did and he awoke refreshed. When I opened my eyes, my vision was bleary. When I lifted my head from the table, a sharp pain ran across my skull. It took a moment for me to realise that my friend was no longer seated in front of me. I heard him before I saw him. His voice was clear and resonant: he might have been addressing a public meeting.

"The god of this century is wealth. Art, nature, beauty, intelligence—they are as nothing to us now. Wealth is what we worship. Wealth is the deity before whom we are ready to sacrifice all: all that we are, all that we might be."

I looked around the dimly lit café. The candles on the tables had been lit. At the table next to ours, two old soldiers were seated, smoking pipes and playing dominoes. Immediately behind them, standing at the bar, was Oscar—the Emperor Nero in a blue serge suit, with an amaryllis in his buttonhole. In one hand, he held a lighted cigarette; in the other, a glass of yellow wine. To his left stood Richard Marais, La Grange's man of business—bald, plain, and deaf. To his right stood Eddie Garstrang, the blue-eyed Colorado gambler with the tiny white teeth. Garstrang was smiling. Oscar was on song and the American was amused.

Oscar saw me stirring. "Robert, awake! It is five o'clock, the hour when a Frenchman meets his mistress and an Englishman takes tea. The great La Grange has been true to his word: it seems that muffins await us in his dressing room. Monsieur Marais and Mr. Garstrang have been sent to fetch us, though how they knew where to find us is beyond me."

"I am deaf, not blind, Monsieur Wilde," murmured Marais, examining his pocket watch. "I have seen you making your way towards this establishment often enough."

"And you also *see* what I am saying, do you?" asked Oscar, looking down at the ugly little man in amazement.

"I do," he answered. "You articulate well. You have full lips and a mobile mouth."

"And you have a diction and vocabulary that belie your disability," Oscar replied.

"I know," said Marais. "I have been with Edmond La Grange for more than twenty years. I have learnt to speak by watching a master."

I got to my feet and joined the group at the bar.

"We have been talking about money, Robert," Oscar explained. "The lure of lucre, the glamour of gold—the price of *Hamlet,* to be precise. My meeting with Monsieur La Grange had been to discuss the matter of my remuneration—the translator is worthy of his hire and all that—but the great La Grange prefers not to be troubled with financial considerations, apparently." He looked in turn at each of the small men standing at his side and smiled. "The question of my fee is to be settled with his *homme d'affaires.*"

"Edmond La Grange is an actor not an accountant," said Eddie Garstrang.

"An artist not a bookkeeper," echoed Richard Marais.

"But Madame Bernhardt tells me," said Oscar, with a sly smile, "that no one in the theatrical profession is more concerned with money than Monsieur La Grange—with the possible exception of herself."

Garstrang laughed. Richard Marais looked steadily at Oscar and said, "It is a reputation he cultivates. He will be paid—in full, on time, in cash. He insists upon it. But the detail of paying others is a detail he leaves to others." Marais wiped two tiny bubbles of saliva from each corner of his mouth. "Have no fear, Monsieur Wilde. You will receive the fee that is your due. We can finalise the matter in my office at your convenience." He looked again at his pocket watch. "They will be taking the curtain calls now. We had best be on our way."

We followed Marais and La Grange out of the café and along the cobbled alley towards the side street that led up to the boulevard du Temple. Marais led the way. He had short legs and a tiny stride, but he made rapid progress, with his bald head pushed forward, like a hobgoblin forcing himself up a hill against the wind. Oscar called out to him: "Marais—not so fast!" The little man pressed on.

"He does not hear you, Oscar," said Eddie Garstrang. "He is deaf."

As we turned from the alley into the side street, we passed two large, empty milk churns standing at the pavement's edge. They were the size of small boys. Oscar paused, threw his cigarette into the gutter, and, suddenly, with considerable force, knocked the churns off the pavement into the roadway. They clanged loudly as he pushed them together and clanked and clattered as they rolled across the cobblestones. Still, Richard Marais pressed on.

"He is deaf, Oscar. He cannot hear a thing."

Before the side street reached the boulevard du Temple, there was another alley, no wider than a handcart, leading off it towards the theatre's stage door. Here, at the corner, Marais paused and looked back to see us coming up the street towards him. He waited for us, looking impatiently at his pocket watch once more. As we approached, he muttered to Oscar, "I felt the rumble of the milk churns as they hit the cobbles, Monsieur Wilde, but I chose not to dignify your little game by stopping in my tracks and turning back."

"I am embarrassed," said Oscar. His face was flushed. "I apologise."

We reached the stage door just as a small gaggle of giggling actresses was emerging. There were five of them: each as pretty as a picture when viewed from beyond the footlights; all but one of them looking, to my eye, somewhat cheap and tawdry in the harsh light of day. Their faces, caked in paint and powder, lacked finesse. The exception, of course, was Gabrielle de la Tourbillon, the tallest of them, the most elegant, the most beautiful, the most refined—and, yes, probably, the oldest of them, too. Just to see her smiling eyes set my heart racing.

As the women pushed their way through the narrow doorway onto the street, they were laughing. "An Italian count is taking us for a drive in his barouche!" one of them cried. "It's a calèche not a barouche," called out another. "He's *so* rich!"

As they passed us by, Gabrielle held out her hand and touched my cheek. She touched Oscar's and Garstrang's, too. "I'm their chaperone!" she explained, laughing as the young girls pulled her away. As they began to run together along the alleyway, she turned, breathlessly, and called out to Richard Marais, "Don't worry. We'll be back in plenty of time for tonight's performance—however rich he is!"

Inside the theatre, the backstage area was a blaze of light. In the wings, the jets of the gasoliers and gas lamps were all turned high, and at the four corners of the stage stood four huge oil burners providing additional illumination. As actors and actresses, in hurriedly donned day clothes, made their way, pell-mell, towards the stage door, stagehands and carpenters—boys and men in blue overalls—busied themselves upon the stage: lifting, shifting, laying, nailing. Richard Marais led us through the throng.

"It's Vauxhall Gardens on carnival night," said Oscar.

"No," said Marais, "it's the La Grange bear pit on matinée days. We have to dismantle *Le Cid* and build *L'Avare* in under an hour."

"What time is the evening performance?" I asked.

"Eight o'clock. But Monsieur requires silence onstage between six and seven—for his siesta."

Monsieur was waiting for us at his dressing-room door. His eyes were ranging about the stage, but we saw him before he noticed us. He was standing in his dressing gown, barefoot, legs apart, a towel thrown toga-like across his shoulder, one clenched hand planted on one hip, the other hand held high and bearing a timepiece dangling from a golden chain.

He caught sight of us breaking through the mêlée. "Ah, Oscar!" he called. "Earlier I forgot you. Now I thought that you had forgotten me." He laughed as we approached. "Come. Welcome. Bring your friend."

He pocketed his timepiece and embraced Oscar warmly. He slapped my back by way of greeting. His mood and manner were very different from when we had encountered him last. Indeed, he looked more at ease, yet more magnificent, than I had ever seen him. He was not a tall man, but he had grandeur and a head that was so striking; Oscar called it "the head of Agamemnon." In the light of the blazing oil burner, his skin glistened and his eyes shone. He shimmered with vitality. He must have read my thoughts, because as he stepped aside to let us into his dressing room, he murmured to me, "*C'est mon métier.* It's what I do. It's what I am."

Marais and Garstrang joined us in the dressing room. La Grange's mother was already there, in the far corner, by the door to the dresser's bedroom, at an old-fashioned oak sideboard, fussing over a samovar and a tray laid out with bone-china cups and saucers. Her new poodle was chasing her tail at her feet. The unfortunate odour of dog permeated the room. As La Grange pointed us towards chairs and the chaise longue, the old lady turned and held out a large lump of sugar for her pet. The dog yapped wildly and jumped up to snap it from her mistress's bony fingers. I noticed Oscar's eyes widen with dismay. He pulled a yellow handkerchief from his pocket and held it to his nose.

"Maman is preparing tea," said La Grange, seating himself on the swivel stool that stood before his dressing table and beaming at us through the dressing-table looking glass. "Traquair has gone off in search of muffins. He went an age ago. I had to undress myself, God save the mark! I hope he's not got lost."

"How is Traquair?" asked Oscar, pocketing his handkerchief and reaching for his cigarettes.

"Conscientious. A good dresser, if not what you English call 'a good companion.'"

"I am Irish," murmured Oscar, striking a light.

"You get a well-pressed shirt with Master Traquair," La Grange continued without pause, "but precious few laughs. He's a touch morose for my liking. There's not a lot of 'give' in the man, if you know what I mean."

"How's his French progressing?" asked Oscar, drawing on his cigarette.

"I don't know," answered La Grange, pulling the towel from around his neck. "He barely speaks."

"I have promised to teach him," said Oscar. "I have been remiss."

"I hope he knows the French for 'muffin,'" muttered Liselotte La Grange from her position at the sideboard.

"I wrote out the order for him, Maman—in capital letters. Serve the tea, if you'd be so kind!" He swivelled round on his stool to face us. "You can have it with lemon, *à la russe,* or with milk, *à l'anglaise.*"

Eddie Garstrang got up to help Maman serve the tea. Oscar, I noticed, was sitting back on the chaise longue, holding out his cigarette in a languid hand and observing the great La Grange as though he were the latest acquisition at the Musée du Louvre.

I smiled at our host. "Tell me, sir," I said, "how was this afternoon's performance?"

La Grange beamed at me. He sat forward on his stool

and slapped the back of his fingers loudly against the palm of his hand. "Now, that's the kind of question that I'd like to hear from my dresser! Thank you for asking, my boy." He leant towards me and tapped me gently on the knee. With a crooked forefinger he beckoned me towards him. "Since you ask," he whispered conspiratorially, "I shall tell you." He paused and waited until our two heads were almost touching, then he confided: "*Mon ami,* it was nothing short of a triumph!"

From the samovar, without turning into the room, Maman remarked, "The La Grange family has always been good to Pierre Corneille."

"And Pierre Corneille," answered La Grange, sitting back, "has always been good to us. We played to a full house this afternoon! Every seat sold: for *Le Cid,* on a Saturday afternoon—in February!"

"Bravo, monsieur," said Richard Marais, nodding and stirring the sugar into his tea *à la russe.*

"And tonight, we'll be full once more. A thousand seats—all sold."

I asked: "It's *The Miser* tonight, isn't it?"

"Yes," he answered, leaning forward to tap me on the knee once more. "That's where we seem to score over the great Madame Bernhardt. We do comedy, too." The Princesse de Lamballe growled and lay down on the floor next to the sideboard. "The divine Sarah seems to come into her splendid own only when she murders or when she dies. Well, no one wants tragedy eight times a week. You need a little laughter now and again."

"Molière died on that chaise longue," said Maman, turning and looking at Oscar.

Oscar filled the air with cigarette smoke. The Princesse de Lamballe whimpered and scratched the floorboards along the edge of the dresser's bedroom door.

"You know, Oscar," La Grange continued, "in America I played to business that was as good as Sarah's. In some theatres, I did better than she did. She has the greater fame—"

"But you have the family name," interrupted his mother. "You have two hundred years of the La Grange tradition."

"Ah, yes," he sighed, "the La Grange tradition . . ."

"And you are French and she is a Jewess."

"She is a great actress, Maman."

"The greatest," said Oscar, with finality. He put his tea-cup on the floor and reached in his pocket for his cigarettes. He looked steadily into La Grange's eyes. He was more than thirty years the great actor's junior and yet he treated him as an equal. "You've worked with Sarah, haven't you? You like Sarah, don't you?"

La Grange smiled and accepted one of Oscar's cigarettes. "Ignore Maman. She despises Sarah because she's Jewish. She won't speak with Traquair because he's a blackamoor. For forty years she's been loath to share a stage with Carlos Branco because he's Portuguese." Suddenly, the great La Grange threw out his arms, tossed back his head, and began to roar with laughter. "Maman, you are utterly absurd," he cried. He looked at Oscar. "Do I like Sarah? No, she irritates me. All the nonsense with her husband and her lovers and her ludicrous menagerie—it's all too stupid. But do I *love* her? How could I not? As an artist she is incomparable. Onstage she is unique."

"Agnès La Grange will be her equal in the fullness of time," croaked Maman from beside the samovar.

La Grange ignored the old lady and continued to smile at Oscar. He swivelled gently on his stool, turning to open a small side drawer in his dressing table. "Sarah gave me this," he said. Slowly, from out of the drawer, he pulled a large handgun. I saw Oscar flinch. "It's a Colt revolver," said La Grange, looking at the weapon admiringly, "a six-shooter." He spun the gun at speed around his index finger. He laughed. With his thumb, he cocked the hammer. "And it's loaded."

"Be careful," said Eddie Garstrang softly.

La Grange held the gun in his right hand, resting the long grey barrel across his left wrist. He pointed the weapon towards Garstrang. The smoke from his cigarette filtered up and over the muzzle. "It's called the Peacemaker. Sarah was given it by her American manager, Mr. Jarrett— 'the terrible Mr. Jarrett' she calls him—and, before I set off on my American tour, she passed it on to me. She thought that it might come in handy."

"I have heard of Mr. Jarrett," said Oscar.

"And have you heard his great line?" La Grange narrowed his eyes and spoke the line in English, with a broad American accent: "'I have made my way in life by the aid of two weapons: honesty and a revolver.'" He laughed.

"He killed a man, I believe," said Oscar.

"Yes," said La Grange, lowering his hands and cradling the revolver in his lap. "In the way of business—on behalf of one his clients, the singer Jenny Lind. He was her manager, too."

"'The Swedish Nightingale,'" muttered Maman contemptuously. "She married a Jew."

"May I hold the gun?" I asked.

La Grange released the hammer carefully and passed the revolver to me. It was heavier than I expected and rough to the touch. I turned it over in my hands and then lifted it up and pointed it towards the ceiling. I put my finger on the trigger and, as I did so, from the corner of the room came a sudden piercing scream. It was Liselotte La Grange, bent forward, clinging to the sideboard with one hand, and with the other gesticulating wildly towards the floor.

"What is it?" demanded La Grange, turning to her.

The old woman did not reply. She simply screamed more loudly and pointed at the poodle at her feet. The creature lay, motionless, on her side.

"Is the dog dead?" cried Oscar, staring aghast at the animal on the floor. "Has another dog died?"

Together, La Grange, Richard Marais, and Eddie Garstrang got to their feet and moved as one towards the corner of the room. La Grange took his hysterical mother in his arms and held her tight. "Sshh, Maman. *Du calme,*" he commanded.

Marais and Garstrang bent down to attend to the dog. "She's breathing," said Marais, resting his head against the animal's flank. "There's a pulse. She's alive."

Maman was no longer shrieking or wailing. She was sobbing and struggling for breath, while, at the same time, with small, angry, clenched fists, beating her son's back. I did not warm to her, but I sensed her distress.

"The poor wretch can't move," hissed Marais. "She's very weak. It must have been a heart attack—or a stroke."

"No!"

"No!"

Oscar and Eddie Garstrang spoke at once. Oscar was

on his feet now, hovering by the dog. Garstrang was on his knees, with his head bent low to the ground. He was sniffing along the edge of the door that led to the dresser's bedroom. "It's gas," Garstrang murmured. "It's a gas leak. Pull her away." With both hands, he pulled the animal away from the door and pushed her body towards Richard Marais. The dog remained inert. She made no sound. Her eyes were open and looked up towards Richard Marais pathetically. The bald, deaf man looked down at the dog and, with an effort, he scooped her into his arms.

"There's gas escaping beneath the door," said Garstrang. He jumped to his feet and fumbled with the door handle. He turned it this way and that. The door would not yield. "It's locked," he cried. "Is there a key?"

Maman began to sob uncontrollably. "I don't know," called La Grange. "There must be."

Eddie Garstrang turned to me. "Give me the gun," he ordered. He spoke the command with an authority that brooked no argument. I handed him the revolver and, in a single movement, he swept it from my hand, turned towards the door, and fired a shot into the door lock. Instantly, the door to the dresser's cubicle swung open and, at once, we saw the horror within.

Lying on the divan, propped up on a bolster so that his head was exactly below the unlighted gas jet fixed halfway up the bedroom wall, was Washington Traquair.

"He's dead!" whispered Oscar. "I know it." As he spoke, the black valet's left arm jerked into the air and fell across his face.

9

The Smell of Death

"**H**e's been dead some while," said Dr. Ferrand. "Certainly for two hours, more probably for three."

"But I saw his hand move as we came into the room," I protested.

"It was as if he were waving farewell," said Oscar, almost to himself. "Waving farewell—or calling for help."

The doctor smiled. He had a kindly demeanour and warm, brown eyes. "I don't think so," he said gently.

"But I saw his hand move," I repeated.

"The arm may have twitched as rigor mortis was setting in," said the doctor. "It happens." He chuckled softly and scratched his chin through his thick, bushy beard. He was dressed in a physician's frock coat, with black trousers, black waistcoat, black shoes, and black bag, but his cheeks were pink and his eyebrows snow white. He had the face of Santa Claus. "That's why the Paris morgue has so many visitors," he added. "People are fascinated to see the dead move." He gazed down on the still cadaver of Washington Traquair. "The dead move quite a bit, you know. At first, as rigor mortis arrives, it's just a twitch or a tremor, but then, as much as three days later, as the rigor evaporates and the muscles relax, you can see arms and legs moving in all directions. I've seen dead men suddenly sit bolt upright on the mortician's slab. Quite disconcerting if you're not expecting it."

He turned to Edmond La Grange. He knew the old actor well. The two men were of an age. Pierre Ferrand had been playing cards with Edmond La Grange since their schooldays. They were boyhood friends. The doctor had a house—and a wife and children and grandchildren—in the elegant suburbs, at Passy, to the west of the city, but he had a pied-à-terre above the Théâtre La Grange. It was just one small room within the vast apartment, but it was his second home. Ferrand spent as much time chez La Grange as he did *chez lui*. It took less than two minutes from the instant when Eddie Garstrang's bullet burst open the door to Traquair's death cell for the good doctor to be on the scene. He came at once, at La Grange's command, summoned by the bell that connected the actor's dressing room with the doctor's bedroom. And so steady and reassuring did he seem—so like Father Christmas with the healing touch!—that, the moment he appeared among us, his simple presence brought order to chaos, calm to pandemonium. Even Maman fell silent.

"Edmond," he said to La Grange quietly, "do you have a shawl or a coverlet I could use?"

La Grange went to his dressing table and picked up a folded linen towel. He passed it to his friend. The doctor took the towel, unfurled it, and, with care, laid it over the dead man's head and shoulders. That was the last I saw of Washington Traquair.

"Come, gentlemen," said Dr. Ferrand, "let us leave this unhappy soul. He is beyond our help." We had all crowded into the dresser's tiny room and clustered around his deathbed. Now Ferrand ushered us back into La Grange's dressing room. Oscar was the last to move. "Come, Monsieur Wilde. Close the door. No further harm can come to the poor wretch now."

I watched as Oscar came out of the dresser's cubicle and pulled the door to behind him. Because the lock had been broken by Garstrang's bullet, the door would not close. It stood ajar, and over the next half hour, as we discussed the awful death of the unhappy young valet, I saw Oscar's eyes—perturbed as well as full of sorrow—turn again and again to stare at the half-opened door.

Liselotte La Grange was now seated on the chaise longue. She appeared to have recovered her composure, and her pet poodle, lying next to her on Richard Marais's lap, appeared to be recovering her strength. The dog sniffed and yawned and stretched, and when Maman gently stroked the underside of the animal's jaw, the Princesse de Lamballe's long wet tongue emerged, gratefully and energetically, to lick her mistress's spindly fingers.

La Grange resumed his place at his dressing table, turning his back to the room and speaking, when he spoke, to our reflections in his looking glass. Oscar and Eddie Garstrang stood side by side, leaning against the dressing-room door that led to the stage. I stood with Dr. Ferrand by the sideboard. He noticed the samovar and touched it lightly with his hand. "Will the tea still be hot?" he asked. "We could all do with a cup of hot sweet tea. This has been a shocking experience."

"We have no muffins," said Liselotte La Grange tartly, "but there is plenty of tea. I prepared it myself."

"Don't move, Maman," murmured Dr. Ferrand

soothingly. He glanced at me and smiled. "This young man and I will see that everyone is served."

"I thought that tea was the English response to tragedy," said Oscar. He looked at Ferrand, who was now busying himself at the samovar. "Doctor, should we not be calling the police?"

Even as Oscar spoke, simultaneously, La Grange and his mother cried out, "No!" La Grange banged his hand on his dressing table so forcefully that the row of bottles of liquid makeup and cologne and eau de toilette ranged in front of him rattled and clanked as they rocked from side to side.

"All in good time, Monsieur Wilde," said the doctor. "There may be no need for the police."

"There is no need for the police," hissed La Grange.

Oscar looked at the old actor through the looking glass. "You are not to blame, Monsieur La Grange. I am. I brought Traquair to this country. I encouraged him. I had a duty of care which I failed to exercise. I am responsible."

"Take some tea, Monsieur Wilde," said Ferrand, handing Oscar a cup. "Calm yourself. I have heard you say that thought is more important than action. Well, let us think carefully before we do anything that we may come to regret." He looked around the room to ascertain that everyone had been given a fresh cup of tea. He returned to the sideboard and opened his black leather bag. "Before I sign the death certificate, let us establish the facts." He took out a sheaf of papers and a pencil. "Will someone tell me what exactly happened?"

"It's very simple." Eddie Garstrang spoke. "We gathered here for tea just after five o'clock."

"There were to be muffins," muttered Liselotte La Grange.

"Traquair had gone for muffins," said Edmond La Grange.

"We took tea," Eddie Garstrang continued. "We made conversation. Then Madame La Grange noticed that her dog was ill. The animal had fallen into a sort of coma on the floor, over there, by the door to the dresser's room. I went over, I put my nose to the ground, I sensed the fumes. Monsieur Marais took care of the dog and I opened the door—"

"With the gun?" interjected the doctor, looking at the Colt revolver that now lay on La Grange's dressing table.

"The door was locked," explained Garstrang.

"From the inside?" asked Ferrand.

"I presume so," said Garstrang.

"It would seem so," said Oscar, holding up a small iron key. "I found this in Traquair's room, on the floor by the divan."

The doctor stepped forward and took the key from Oscar. He placed it inside his bag and turned to Eddie Garstrang. "How was the body when you found it?"

"Exactly as it is now. Nothing's been moved."

"The head was propped up against the bolster, so that his mouth and nose pointed towards the jet of gas?"

"Yes."

"And when you entered the room, the gas was still escaping?"

"Yes," said Garstrang.

"Yes," echoed Oscar. "In the room you could hear its hiss."

"Who turned off the gas?" asked the doctor.

"I did," answered Garstrang. "At once. The moment I stepped into the room."

"Was the tap stiff? Was it easy to turn off?"

"One twist—that's all it took."

Dr. Ferrand dug his fingers into his beard, scratched his chin, and sighed. "So the poor man went into his room, locked the door, lay down on the divan, turned on the gas, and waited to die . . ."

A silence fell.

"Why did we not *smell* the gas?" I asked. "Why were we not overwhelmed by it?"

"Carbon monoxide has no odour, no colour, no taste," said the doctor. He smiled. "It makes a perfect poison."

"But in England the town gas has an odour," I said, putting down my teacup and looking the doctor in the eye. "I'm sure that it does."

"In England, I believe," said the doctor, returning my gaze, "a foul-smelling substance is added to the gas—for safety's sake. We don't do that here."

"In England, I believe," said Richard Marais from his place on the chaise longue, "suicide is still illegal. In France, suicide is not a crime. It hasn't been since the revolution. The unfortunate Traquair has not offended in the eyes of the law."

"You see," said Maman, beaming beatifically, "there is no need to call the police."

"But why weren't we poisoned by the gas as well?" I persisted.

"You would have been in time," said the doctor, with a little laugh.

"But even as the door was blown open and we entered the room, I didn't feel any ill effects."

"Carbon monoxide is odourless, colourless, tasteless, *mon ami*—and its initial effect is one of exhilaration."

"The dog chased her tail before she fell to the floor," said Richard Marais. He tugged affectionately at the Princesse de Lamballe's ears. The dog yawned appreciatively and then snapped her teeth.

Oscar dropped the end of his lighted cigarette into his teacup and placed the cup carefully on top of a wooden trunk that stood alongside La Grange's dressing table. "Doctor," he asked, "you say that Traquair died two to three hours ago? Are you certain of that?"

"The poor fellow was a blackamoor. It's not so easy to read all the signs because of the colour of his skin, but the onset of rigor suggests that it cannot have been less than two hours ago and I think it more likely to have been three."

Oscar leant towards Edmond La Grange. "When did you send Traquair to find the muffins?"

The actor sighed and rested his eye sockets on his clenched fists. "Three hours ago." He looked up at Oscar through the looking glass and corrected himself. "No, four—at least. I told him to fetch the muffins at two o'clock. Once he'd dressed me for the performance, I let him go."

"And did you see him again?"

Edmond La Grange swivelled slowly round on his stool and gazed up at Oscar Wilde. "Young man, you are a fine poet and an amusing companion. You have a feeling for Shakespeare that is rare and that I value greatly. But it is clear to me—transparently clear—that you know nothing—*nothing*—of the life and responsibilities of a leading actor. I have spent this afternoon playing Pierre Corneille's masterpiece, *Le Cid,* to a full house. The comings and goings of my dresser at the time were not of paramount concern to me."

"Of course," said Oscar apologetically, bowing his head towards the actor and stepping back to his position by the door. "I understand."

"Thank you." La Grange smiled and breathed deeply and threw back his shoulders. "Tonight, thank God, we have a comedy: Molière's *L'Avare.* I must ready myself— if you'll excuse me." He swung back towards the mirror and looked down at his dressing table. He picked up the revolver, wrapped it in a handkerchief, and placed it in the top drawer to his right, alongside a pair of silver hairbrushes. He glanced up at the mirror. He caught my eye. "Young man," he said, "will you help dress me tonight? I'd be obliged." His eyes moved around the rest of the room. "Maman, gentlemen," he said, dismissing the party, "there's work to be done."

"And the body?" asked Dr. Ferrand. "What shall we do with the body?"

"Dispose of it. Once I'm onstage. Do what you like."

The doctor nodded and, shrugging his shoulders, dropped his pencil and sheaf of papers back into his bag. With a yelp, the Princesse de Lamballe scrambled onto the floor and shook herself as Richard Marais and Eddie Garstrang helped Maman to her feet.

"Once you are onstage," asked Oscar quietly, "may we call the police then?"

"No! No! No!"

In his rage, Edmond La Grange banged his fists upon his dressing table and with a sweep of his right arm propelled everything before him—cups, saucers, bottles, brushes—onto the floor. He turned to Oscar and roared: "Do you know nothing? Do you see nothing? Do you understand nothing? This is a theatre, my friend—it's a house of cards. One puff of scandal and it comes tumbling down." He placed one hand upon his heart and threw out the other towards his mother. "We are actors, Oscar, we are pariahs. We are the fallen—we are excommunicate. We are the damned. In England, it may be different. There your actors hobnob with royalty, I know. Here, the president of the republic would not be seen to break bread with the leading player of the Comédie-Française. We wretched theatricals are like Jews and blackamoors: we cannot mix with re-spectable society. In our place, in our playhouses, we are useful enough, we serve our purpose; but we are not to be trusted. Bring the police in here and what little reputation we have goes by the board."

"The police have never had any business with the Théâtre La Grange," said Maman, looking at Oscar with gimlet eyes.

Oscar blanched and stepped back towards the door. "I feel a responsibility towards Traquair," he murmured, "that is all."

"Enough," said Dr. Ferrand, snapping shut his black bag and taking command of the room. "Let us leave Monsieur in peace. He must prepare for his performance." He spread out his arms and, like a farmer's wife shooing geese across a barnyard, ushered Maman and Marais and the Princesse de Lamballe and Eddie Garstrang and Oscar out of the dressing room and into the wings. As he pulled the door to behind him, he looked back and smiled at the old actor still seated at his dressing table. "I will arrange everything, Edmond—as always. Have no fear."

I spent the next several hours alone with Edmond La Grange. It was a curious experience. I do not believe that he even knew my name, but he treated me as an intimate, as though I had been his personal dresser for years. He called me *"mon petit."* As soon as the others had left the room, he got up from his stool and stood before me with arms outstretched and legs astride. The anger of a moment before was all gone. "You may undress me, *mon petit*," he announced, speaking of the task as if it were a privilege. I did as I was told. My fumbling with his buttons appeared to amuse him. "Frédéric Lemaître had a pirate for a dresser," he told me as I unbuckled him. "The wretch only had three fingers on one hand and a hook for the other. Did you ever see Lemaître onstage? He always looked immaculate!" When he stepped out of his drawers, he stood stark naked in front of his cheval mirror and preened himself. His belly was low slung and slack. He slapped it with pride. He turned his profile to the looking glass and glanced across his shoulder towards his grey and mottled buttocks. He placed his left hand on his hip and with his right complacently caressed his private parts. He held his member out towards me. "We have done the state some service," he chuckled, winking at me. "Do you have a sweetheart, young man?" he asked.

"Your mistress, sir," I might have answered, but I did

not. I said nothing. I sensed that when Edmond La Grange asked a question, he did not necessarily expect a reply.

He smiled at me and said, "You're young. There's no hurry. You've years ahead of you." He held out his arms once more. "My dressing gown, *mon petit.*" I helped him into it and, following his instructions, at the back of the drawer with the Colt revolver and the silver hairbrushes I found his velvet eye mask. He settled himself onto the chaise longue, put on the eye mask, lay back, and folded his arms across his chest. "I look like a dead king upon a catafalque, do I not? Charles the Fair or Louis the Fat—what do you say?"

I said nothing.

"You are a quick learner, *mon petit,*" he murmured. "I think I shall hang on to you. Wake me at seven o'clock."

I sat on his stool and watched him until he fell asleep. As he slept, he snored and, while he was snoring, I moved about the room as quietly as I could, picking up the debris from the dressing table, clearing the tea things, folding his discarded garments, restoring order. More than once I stood at the door to Traquair's room, peering into the darkness within. I had not been in the presence of a dead body before. I was surprised that I did not find it more un-settling.

At seven o'clock, the little carriage clock that stood on the sideboard struck the hour and, as it did so, without any prompting from me, Edmond La Grange sat bolt upright on the chaise longue. "*Me voilà!* Risen like one of Dr. Fer-rand's dead bodies at the morgue." He got to his feet and lightly tossed his eye mask onto the dressing table. "Fer-rand's a good man," he said, smiling at me, "a poor card player, but a good man." He threw off his dressing gown and stood naked before me once again. "And now," he announced, "Harpagon—*L'Avare*. Whatever they tell you, *mon petit*, comedy is infinitely more taxing than tragedy."

On that first occasion, dressing Edmond La Grange proved surprisingly uncomplicated. Traquair had left everything that was required inside the corner wardrobe, laundered and pressed and arranged in the order of its putting on. La Grange, as I helped him into his costume, talked without ceasing. For thirty minutes, as he pulled on stockings and trews, and fiddled with cuffs and collars, he talked of Frédéric Lemaître and Edmond Got, of Mounet-Sully and Talma and Réjane. He talked of La Grange, too: he talked much of the great La Grange heritage. "Either you can do it or you can't do it, *mon petit*. It can't be taught. It's in the blood. You are too young to have seen the incomparable Rachel, of course. Your friend Wilde worships Bernhardt—and with reason. Rachel was a Jewess, like Sarah, but she was greater than Sarah, because she could play comedy as well as tragedy. She was utterly uneducated; she could neither read nor write. She did not know what she was saying, but how brilliantly she said it! It's in the blood."

At half past seven there was a sharp knock on the door. It was the stage manager come to tell Monsieur that the stage was set and the house was open. "*Viens, mon petit*," commanded La Grange. He crooked a finger and beckoned me to follow him. Together, we walked from his dressing room into the wings and onto the dimly lit stage. Like a guard inspecting the moonlit battlements, the great actor-manager marched with even step to the four corners of his castle: upstage right, upstage left, downstage left, downstage right. In each corner, he lightly kissed his fingertips and touched a piece of the scenery. As we passed, stagehands and waiting players fell still and bowed towards him.

The ritual done, we returned in silence to his dressing room. He sat once more on his stool facing his looking glass. He peered intently at his own reflection. He picked up a stick of makeup and deepened the dark blue line he had drawn around each eye. "The eyes are everything," he said. "The people must be able to see your eyes from every corner of the house. If they don't, they won't know you and they won't care."

At eight o'clock, the stage manager knocked once more on the dressing-room door. "Follow me," said La Grange. "During the performance I change in the wings—on the far side. There'll be a table and chair waiting, and a looking glass. And a candle to see by. Do you have everything?"

Traquair had prepared the basket of costume changes. I held it in my arms: a nightshirt, nightcap, and slippers, pantaloons and gaberdine, a skullcap, gloves, and overshoes—all in the order in which they would be required.

"*Eh bien,*" he said, bracing his shoulders and taking a deep breath as we stepped from his dressing room into the wings. "Enjoy the play, *mon petit*. And watch my eyes. It's my eyes that will tell them when to laugh."

I watched his eyes. They were indeed extraordinary. Wide, protuberant, and luminous, they darted here and there: they never stopped. *He* never stopped. For more than two hours, without pause, he ran and trotted, scampered, strutted, strode, and paced about the stage. Even when he stood still, he burnt with energy. *"Je brûle, n'est-ce pas?"* he chuckled when, for the first of his costume changes, he joined me in the wings.

When it was over—when the curtain had fallen for the fifteenth and final time—he spun slowly round onstage, his eyes still wide, and called to the cast and company: *"Merci, messieurs-dames!* Bravo!" By way of reply, the actors raised their hands before them and above their heads and applauded their leader. I stood in the wings, applauding, too.

He came straight towards me and put his arm around my shoulder and squeezed me hard. It was a ferocious squeeze, almost violent. "Monsieur Molière knows his business, *n'est-ce pas?"*

"And you know yours, sir," I answered, disengaging myself and passing him the towel that I had found at the bottom of the basket. I picked up the candle from the table to lead us back across the stage to his dressing room.

He pulled the candle towards his face. His skin glistened with sweat. "Now, that's how a dresser should address his master," he said softly. "Thank you, *mon petit.* Thank you very much."

He swept back into his dressing room and began to throw off his costume even as he stepped through the door. "I think a glass or two of champagne is in order," he declared. "You can join me. There's a case in there—under the divan."

"In where?" I asked, putting down the basket on the chaise longue.

"In the dresser's room," he said, "in *your* room, under the divan."

The door to the dresser's room still stood ajar.

"Go, go!" ordered the old actor, laughing. "He's dead. He won't bite you."

Slowly, I pushed open the door to Traquair's room. There was a faint trace of lily of the valley in the air. It was Oscar's favourite fragrance. I felt a sudden longing for his company.

"Well?" barked La Grange from the other room.

I held up the lighted candle and looked about Traquair's tiny domain.

"He's gone," I said. "There's no one here."

"I'm glad," said La Grange. "Bring out the champagne."

10

Pharamond

I did not see Oscar until noon the following day. I lingered with Edmond La Grange in his dressing room until gone midnight. It was an unreal experience. Between the two of us, we must have consumed three—or perhaps four—bottles of champagne. As we drank the sparkling yellow wine, the great La Grange talked—and talked! As he talked, I helped him to undress. I bathed him; I towelled him dry; I helped him to dress again. Under his instruction, I found, sorted, and, within the wardrobe and in the basket, as appropriate, hung up and laid out the costumes for his next performance: Argan in *Le Malade imaginaire*.

"Molière was playing Argan when he died," La Grange added confidentially. "Some say it was tuberculosis. Some think it was murder. It was the night of the fourth performance: 17 February 1673." The old actor spun round on his stool, holding his glass of champagne high in the air. "What is the date today? The same: 17 February! The mighty Molière died two hundred and ten years ago tonight, *mon petit,* on that chaise longue." He began to laugh. "Or one very like it!" He laughed so much that he began to cry.

At midnight, the carriage clock on the sideboard struck and the stage manager knocked once again on the dressing-room door. "To bed!" cried La Grange. "Will there be time for cards? Perhaps." He was quite drunk. "Will Agnès tuck me up tonight? Or Gabrielle?" He pulled on his overcoat. "Oh, spare me Maman!" he breathed in mock alarm. He put his arm around my shoulder and let me lead him across the darkened stage to the stage door.

Together we stepped out into the cobbled alley that ran along the back of the theatre. The cold night air hit us both hard. "I'm awake again," he rasped, "like one of Ferrand's corpses!" He rubbed his face roughly with both hands and ran his fingers through his thick silver hair. "I'm hungry," he said. "I need some supper. Do you want some supper?"

"No, thank you, monsieur, it's been a long day."

"Yes," he said, throwing back his head and shoulders and filling his lungs, "it's been a lifetime."

We had reached the stone stairway that led up the outside of the building to the private entrance to his apartment. He was rummaging in the pocket of his overcoat to find his key. He brought out a heavy handful of silver and copper coins and, without looking at them, handed them to me. "Thank you," he said. "Marais will sort out your wages. You can use the room."

"I have a room," I said. "It's nearby." I took the money in both hands, gratefully. "Thank you, monsieur."

"It's I who am indebted to you, *mon petit*," he replied, putting his fingers gently behind my neck and pulling me forward. "An actor needs a dresser he can trust." He kissed the top of my head. "Don't betray me now," he whispered. "Good night."

I walked to the end of the alley. When I turned and looked back, he was standing in the doorway with his daughter, Agnès, at his side. In her long white nightdress she looked like an angel. She held her arms around her father's neck. He waved to me and closed the door. I climbed the street to the boulevard du Temple and stood beneath the gas lamp on the corner. I opened my clenched fists and inspected the coins that the great La Grange had pressed into my hands. In loose change, he had given me more money than I had earned from my translation work in three months.

I walked along the boulevard until a cab came by. Flush with funds, I hailed it and ordered it to take me to Oscar's hotel down on the quai Voltaire. There, the night porter was genial but adamant: Monsieur Wilde's key was on its hook, Monsieur Wilde was not at home. I stood in the street outside the hotel, uncertain what to do or where to go. Where was Oscar? I had no idea. I was already in Oscar's thrall, but I knew him hardly at all. I felt that our friendship was profound, and yet, in truth, we had been companions for no more than a matter of days—it was little more than two weeks since we had first met. I gazed across the deserted quai onto the River Seine. There was no moon: the water was black and still. The night was silent. I felt peculiarly alone. I ordered the cab to take me back to my rooming house in the rue de Beauce.

I dropped onto my narrow bed, expecting to fall asleep at once. Instead, I lay awake for hours, or so it seemed. I cannot recollect much about that night, except that the only way in which I could banish from my mind's eye the haunting image of Traquair's head and shoulders covered with La Grange's towel was to conjure up for myself a vision of Gabrielle de la Tourbillon—smiling, naked, and in my arms.

The following morning I was woken by the cruel sound of the concierge relentlessly banging her broom handle on my door. I hid my aching head beneath the bolster, but the wretched woman's brutal beating did not stop. I struggled to my feet, and found that I was still wearing my boots and overcoat from the night before. I unlocked my door and discovered the overexcited crone, grinning like a jackanapes, waving a piece of paper in her withered paw. It was a note from Oscar: "Your carriage awaits. Breakfast is served."

The concierge was impressed to see me being driven away from her grimy tenement in a carriage of any kind. I was impressed to find that I was being driven to Pharamond, named in honour of the fabled first King of France, on the rue de la Grande Truanderie. It was a restaurant of which Oscar had often spoken. "If Epicurus had come to Paris, Pharamond is where most he would have wished to dine."

I found my friend, all alone, seated in state at a large, round table at the very back of the dining room. He was wearing a worsted suit the colour of café au lait, with a sage-green silk scarf thrown about his neck. (Café au lait and sage green were his favourite colours in 1883.) He was looking strikingly youthful: fresh faced and newly shaven. There was something absurd about his carefully arranged Neronian curls, but something magnificent about his bearing. He sat quite upright, gazing wistfully towards a lost horizon, with his elbows resting lightly on the table and his arms held out to left and right, like an overgrown boy king, posing for his portrait, with sceptre and orb in either hand. In fact, his left hand was holding a pocket watch and resting on what appeared to be a gaudily decorated biscuit tin. His right hand was clutching, simultaneously, a lighted cigarette and a glass of yellow wine.

"Good morning, Oscar," I said, somewhat groggily. I had not spoken since the night before. "How are you? You look well rested."

"I have not slept at all," he said amiably, turning his head towards me and drawing on his cigarette. "But, as you can see, I have shaved, and a close shave always does me good. And I have changed, and they say that a change is as good as a rest." He raised his glass towards me by way of salutation. "Welcome! I'm glad the driver found you."

I looked about the marbled dining room. A young waiter, polishing silver at the buffet, nodded to me and smiled. There were no other diners to be seen. "What are we doing here?" I asked.

Oscar put his glass on the table and extinguished his cigarette. He glanced at his pocket watch and laid it by the biscuit tin. With both hands he picked up a folded linen napkin, unfurled it with a flourish, and placed it across his lap. "I'm on my way to the Gare du Nord. This is halfway. I stopped off for a bite to eat. You've come to join me."

"The Gare du Nord?"

"I'm going to London."

"London?" My head was aching. I rubbed my eyes. "London?" I repeated. "Why, Oscar? What has happened?"

"I have to arrange an assignation with an assassin."

"What?" I said, bemused.

"Or, at least, a would-be assassin. My friend George Palmer has promised to arrange for me to meet the man who tried to shoot Queen Victoria. I had a telegram from him yesterday. He's gone to a lot of trouble to effect the introduction with the authorities and asks me to present myself in person so my moral fibre can be tested. I mustn't disoblige him."

I had no idea what my friend was talking about. He waved towards the waiter. "Take off your coat, Robert. Sit down. When did you last eat? Yesterday morning, wasn't it? You need reviving. Have some breakfast."

The waiter came and helped me to remove my overcoat. I sat down face-to-face with Oscar and, slowly, began to take in the feast that lay before us. It was extraordinary: half a dozen different dishes, ranged side by side. Oscar scanned the table and purred: "*Terrine de queue de bœuf, l'os à moelle, filets de maquereau au vin blanc, les escargots de Bourgogne, les huîtres plates de Cancale,* fried eggs *à l'anglais.*"

"Is this breakfast?" I asked, laughing.

"This is breakfast and lunch combined—there'll be a word for it one day. Help yourself. These are merely the entrées. I've taken the liberty of ordering *la poulette de Racan rôtie entière* for our main course. That should leave us room and time for a light dessert. You'll want to try the *madeleines chaudes à la confiture.* No one who tries the *madeleines* forgets them."

"Oscar," I said. "This is absurd."

"No," he said seriously. "It is not absurd. It is as it should be. Thirteen years ago, during the siege of Paris in the cruel winter of 1870, there was famine in this city. A cat sold for twenty francs, a rat for two. Those few who could afford it dined on cuts of bison, giraffe, and zebra from the zoo."

I looked at my friend and smiled.

He was not smiling: he was in deadly earnest. As he spoke, his eyes filled with tears. "Do you not recall how Castor and Pollux, the lumbering elephants from the Jardin des Plantes, who had spent their lives carrying the children of Paris on their backs, met their deaths that winter? Slaughtered to provide food for famished families." He picked up an oyster and considered it carefully. "There is nothing to be said for starvation, Robert. There is no virtue in pain. Life should be a banquet for all. Pleasure is the only thing one should live for." He swallowed the oyster and immediately took up another. "I have found that an inordinate passion for pleasure is the secret of remaining young." He mopped his mouth with his napkin and nodded to the waiter to pour me some wine. "Eat up, Robert. Drink up. We must raise our glasses to Washington Traquair. In his brief life, how much pleasure did he know?"

"Oh, yes," I said, raising my glass at once and leaning anxiously across the table. "We must drink to Traquair's memory; and you must tell me what happened last night. Where is his body now? Did you go to the police?"

Oscar glanced at the timepiece that he had laid face-up next to the biscuit tin. "We have two hours before my train departs. I will tell you everything. But, first, tell me: how was your début as dresser to the great La Grange?"

I began to help myself to an assortment of the entrées laid before us. "A success, I think. He tipped me generously. He plied me with champagne. He seems to want me to continue."

"I'm glad of that," said Oscar. "You can be my eyes and ears while I'm away."

"Your eyes and ears?" I repeated.

"Yes, Robert," he answered solemnly, dipping a forkful of mackerel into the fried egg yolk. "There's something rotten within the Compagnie La Grange. First, a dog dies and nobody cares. Then, a man dies and nobody cares. What is going on?"

"Traquair took his own life, surely?"

"Perhaps. Perhaps not." He put the piece of fish into his mouth and chewed on it, slowly.

"The room was locked from the inside, Oscar."

"It seemed to be, certainly."

"But you found the key yourself—on the floor, by the divan."

"I did."

I put aside my napkin and leant earnestly towards my friend. "I saw the scene with my own eyes, Oscar. It looked very much like suicide to me."

Oscar finished his mouthful and mopped his lips. "In a theatre, 'setting the scene' is what they do best. It looked very much like suicide to me, also. But was it? That's all I'm asking."

I took a sip of the yellow wine and contemplated my friend. "Do you honestly think that Traquair was murdered?" I asked.

He shrugged and raised his own glass. He swirled the wine beneath his nostrils. He breathed in its bouquet. "The aroma of roses and passion fruit . . . A crisp gewürztraminer is a perfect breakfast wine, don't you agree?"

"Do you *honestly* think that Traquair was murdered?" I repeated.

"The unfortunate Marie Antoinette was murdered, that's for sure."

"But who would want to murder Traquair?" I persisted. "What possible motive could anyone have for such a thing?"

Oscar laid down his glass. "Who would want to murder Traquair? You might, Robert—for a start."

"Me?" I expostulated.

Oscar smiled. "You now have his job, after all."

"Don't be absurd, Oscar." I laughed. "Me—murder Traquair? That's impossible."

"Not impossible, Robert. Improbable, I grant you. We were together when he died; in a haze of absinthe, as I recall. But perhaps, as I slept at the table in the bar behind the theatre, you slipped out and did the dreadful deed."

"I did not murder Traquair," I insisted. "I barely knew the man—"

"And how well do I know you, Robert?" Oscar interrupted, sitting back and gazing at me appraisingly. "We met only two weeks ago!"

"You cannot believe, surely—"

"What am I to believe?" he asked, raising an eyebrow. "By your own admission, you are living under an assumed name. You tell me that Wordsworth was your great-grandfather and that you shared a house with Victor Hugo as a boy. It all sounds a bit far-fetched. What am I to believe, Robert?"

"But we are friends, Oscar!" I cried. "Surely, we are friends."

"And Judas was Our Lord's favourite apostle," he answered, picking up an oyster from the dish that lay between us.

I pushed my chair away from the table and got to my feet. "I protest, Oscar. I did not murder Washington Traquair."

Oscar swallowed the oyster and waved his napkin at me, laughing. "Sit down, Robert. I'm teasing you. Sit down, boy." He leant across the table and placed an oyster on my plate. "I believe you, Robert. I trust you. That's why I want you to be my eyes and ears while I'm away."

I resumed my seat and took up the oyster. "How long will you be gone?" I asked.

"I don't know," he replied. He raised his wine-glass towards me by way of reassurance. "I'll write to you as soon as I know my plans. And you must wire me with anything suspicious that you see or hear. We'll keep in touch."

"Why must you go so suddenly? Are you really going to meet Queen Victoria's would-be assassin?"

"Apparently so. George Palmer has said that he will arrange it and I am intrigued." He smiled at me. "I collect unusual people, as you know."

I looked at him closely.

He lowered his eyes and laid his hand to rest on the biscuit tin at his side. "But you are right, Robert," he continued. "There is another, more pressing reason for my sudden departure. I have a duty to perform. I must see that my poor valet is buried in his native soil. I must return Traquair's mortal remains to the United States of America."

"America—"

He raised a hand to silence me. "Traquair was an only

child, Robert, an orphan, the son of slaves, the first free man in his family. We did not know each other well, but he trusted me—as I trust you. Because of me, he left the land of his birth and came to a foreign country to meet his death. I persuaded him. I'm to blame. The least I can do is see him safely home and ensure that he gets a decent burial."

"Couldn't he get a decent burial here?"

Oscar shook his head and laughed. "In France? Traquair died in a *theatre,* Robert. You recall La Grange's rebuke to me last night? It was justified. In France, in *respectable* France, the theatre is beyond the pale. In the eyes of the church a theatre is the anteroom to hell! Even the great Molière died without sacrament, buried in the dead of night in the dismal corner of the cemetery reserved for un-baptised infants. What hope for Traquair, a mere dresser—and a blackamoor?"

I skewered a snail from out of its shell. "Isn't Molière buried at Père Lachaise?" I said.

"Oh, *now* he is, yes, beneath a mighty monument. Now pilgrims come to kiss his tomb." My friend chuckled softly and took a sip of wine. "There is no logic to hypocrisy."

"Did you not go to the police last night?" I asked.

"Dr. Ferrand was adamant that nothing would be gained by doing so. Accidental death by gas poisoning is a common occurrence. And death by suicide is commonplace, too. In Paris, apparently, there are at least three suicides each day. In the winter months, according to Ferrand, four or more. We didn't go to the police. The good doctor insisted that Traquair's death would be of no interest to them. We went to the morgue." The waiter arrived to clear away the entrées. Oscar lit a cigarette. "It was a sobering experience."

"I know," I said. "I've been. It's open to the public."

"Did you go on a Saturday night? My dear, the crowds! And the noise! I had no idea that death could be so popular. The superintendent told me that they are thinking of introducing an admission charge."

"You met the superintendent?"

"Oh, yes. Dr. Ferrand knows all the bigwigs down at the morgue. We were given preferential treatment. As a personal favour to Ferrand, the superintendent's deputy came to the Théâtre La Grange himself to oversee the removal of the body. He brought with him two of his ablest 'corpse-men,' as they are called. They were discretion personified. While Edmond La Grange was merrily fretting and strutting his stuff upon the stage, in his dresser's cubicle the corpse-men were bundling poor Washington Traquair into a winding sheet. I watched them as they went about their business."

"I know," I said.

"You know?" he asked. "I thought you were on the other side of the stage, watching La Grange."

"I was. I went into Traquair's room later and recognised a trace of lily of the valley in the air. It's your favourite fragrance, is it not?"

Oscar drew deeply on his cigarette. "Excellent, Robert," he murmured. "You have the makings of a fine detective." He sat back and resumed his narrative. "I watched the corpse-men as they wrapped Traquair into the winding sheet and hoisted him on their shoulders. They carried him through the darkened wings and out of the stage door without attracting the least attention. You could commit any crime of your choosing in the wings of a theatre. When the performance is in progress all eyes are upon the stage.

"Ferrand and I travelled to the morgue in the back of the body cart with the two corpse-men and the bundle that was Traquair wedged between our feet. At the morgue, despite the lateness of the hour, the superintendent welcomed us in person. He ordered that Traquair be stored in a side room, away from public gaze. He was a good-humoured, handsome man and a generous host. He took us to his office—a small room with an internal window that overlooked the main hall of the morgue—and gave us brandy, while we discussed what was to be done. Rather a fine brandy, a Cœur de Lion calvados. I told him that I wanted to return Traquair to America. I told him that I felt duty-bound to do so. He said that, in principle, that would not present a problem—at least, so far as the French authorities were concerned. Provided that I was ready, willing, and able to accept custody of Traquair's remains, he would happily sign the necessary papers."

"And did he do so?"

"Yes. There and then."

"And where is Traquair's body now?" I asked.

"Here." Oscar tapped the biscuit tin that stood beside his wine-glass on the table. "Traquair's body was cremated at seven o'clock this morning. Because he was not a Catholic, there was no difficulty about him being cremated on a Sunday." With both hands Oscar lifted the biscuit tin and held it out towards me. "The ashes are still warm," he added, smiling, as the waiter arrived with the *poulette de Racan rôtie entière*.

11

A Mother's Touch

Clutching a single capacious handbag in one hand and holding the biscuit tin containing Traquair's remains under his arm with the other, Oscar left Paris for London by the two o'clock boat train on Sunday, 18 February 1883. I accompanied him to the Gare du Nord and waved him on his way. As he stood at the window of his compartment, he looked down on me gazing up at him from the platform below. He ran his tongue across his teeth—it was a trick of his when he was emotionally engaged—and smiled and mouthed the words, "Au revoir." Our friendship was only a fortnight old, yet I knew that it would last a lifetime. I had made the acquaintance of several of the great figures of our time, but already I sensed that this was the most remarkable of them. He was just seven years my senior, yet he seemed to me to be as much a father as a friend. He was playful, yet he had authority. I wanted his respect as well as his affection.

"I depend upon you, Robert," he called through the carriage window. "You're my eyes and ears, remember." I could scarcely hear him above the station's roar. "I'll write. I'll keep in touch, I promise." Gusts of black smoke swirled between us. "Take care, Robert!"

Guards shouted; whistles blew; the railway's engine

belched and rumbled; steam hissed; sparks flew; the train juddered to life; and he was gone.

He was as good as his word. On the morning after his departure I received a brief wire reporting his safe arrival in London. Within twenty-four hours I received a further, fuller telegram:

DEAR EYES AND EARS WHILE YOU SEARCH FOR
THE CITY OF GOLD WHERE THE FLUTE PLAYER
NEVER WEARIES AND THE SPRING NEVER
FADES KINDLY ALSO SEEK OUT ULTIMATE
SOURCE OF GAS LEADING TO DRESSERS ROOM.
IS THERE A TAP OUTSIDE THE ROOM WHERE
THE GAS MAY BE SWITCHED ON AND OFF AND
IF SO WHERE IS THE TAP LOCATED?

Twenty-four hours later, I received another telegram:

QUESTIONS ARE NEVER INDISCREET. ANSWERS
SOMETIMES ARE. IF I AM RIGHT IN THINKING
THAT NEITHER OF THE TWINS WAS IN THE
CAST OF LE CID ON SATURDAY AFTERNOON
GENTLY ENQUIRE AS TO THEIR WHEREABOUTS
DURING THE FATEFUL MATINEE.

And then one more:

REMEMBER THAT LOVE IS AN ILLUSION
ROBERT AND NOT HALF AS USEFUL AS LOGIC.
LOVE DOES NOT PROVE ANYTHING AND IS
ALWAYS TELLING ONE THINGS THAT ARE

NOT GOING TO HAPPEN OR MAKING ONE
BELIEVE THINGS THAT ARE NOT TRUE. HOW IS
MADEMOISELLE DE LA TOURBILLON?

Finally, on the Friday morning following Oscar's return to England, a long letter arrived for me at my room in the rue de Beauce.

Oakley Street,
London SW
20.ii.83

Dear Robert,

How are you? Where are you? Is all as you would have it be? I have thought of you often these past forty-eight hours, wandering in violet valleys with your honey-coloured hair, pursuing our enquiries and Mademoiselle Gabrielle de la Tourbillon with equal zeal—and, I trust, with equal success. Do you yet have the answers to my questions? And has the matchless mademoiselle yet yielded to your charms? Tell me, cher ami. I need to know.

I have not written until now—it is midnight on Tuesday—because I have not had a moment in which to do so. Much has happened since we parted at the Gare du Nord. The train journey from Paris to Calais was painful. In my haste to pack, I failed to bring either Shakespeare or Virgil, pencil or pen, so that I could neither read a book nor write one. Hour upon hour, I stared out of the carriage window, marvelling at the dreariness of the French countryside, pitying the pastoral poets, and reflecting on the fact that every great writer in history has been nourished and civilised by city life. Shakespeare wrote nothing but doggerel before he came to London and never penned a line after he left. When we reached Calais I attempted to buy a book, but none was to be found—not even for ready money. There were plenty of newspapers, of course, and thinking to distract myself during the Channel crossing, I bought every one that the news vendor had to offer. What a mistake! Regardless of the country of origin, every newspaper now chronicles with degrading avidity the sins of the second-rate, and with the conscientiousness of the illiterate gives us accurate and prosaic details of the doings of people of absolutely no interest whatever.

By the time I reached Dover, I was close to despair. In the customs hall at the harbour, I waited patiently until my turn came to present my bags for inspection and the customs officer enquired, " 'ave you anything to declare?" When I answered, without thinking, "Indeed I do. Journalism is unreadable and literature is not read. The age of the Philistine is upon us," the wretched man, who had been about to put his chalk mark upon my bag and wave me on my way, blinked and looked at me, uncomprehending. He turned and called to a colleague, "We've got a right one here." Within moments I was surrounded by a posse of fascinated customs officers: half a dozen red-faced men, one of whom—alas!—recognised me. "This is Mr. h'Oscar Wilde, lads," he announced, "a proper Clown Joey. You must've 'eard of 'im. Making a mockery of us poor customs men is his favourite party piece."

I protested—in vain. I apologised—to no avail. "Search his bags," ordered the officer. "Where are they?" "I only have the one," I murmured, lamely, opening it for inspection. The man, with grubby hands, pulled out my shirts and ties and bottles of cologne and held them up to the mocking gaze of his fellow officers. When it was clear that my case contained no contraband, he turned his attention to the biscuit tin. "What's that?" he asked. "Biscuits," I lied, "French biscuits." "Oh, French biscuits?" he sneered. "We like a biscuit with our tea, don't we, lads? Aren't you going to offer them around, Mr. Wilde?" "They're a present for my mother," I bleated, now holding the tin close to my chest. "I'm sure your mother would like you to share your French biscuits with your English friends," leered the man, leaning towards me and seizing the tin from out of my grasp. As I pleaded, "No, please, no!" the customs officer prised open the lid of the biscuit tin, scattering Traquair's ashes all about him as he did so.

It was more than an hour before I was released from the customs hall at Dover Harbour. My persecutor-in-chief left his colleagues to their business as he marched me, in full and humiliating view of my fellow passengers, back along the line to what he called his "station." It was like a station of the cross to me! "What are you hiding in 'ere, Mr. Wilde?" he demanded, as his filthy fingers rummaged around in Traquair's remains. "Nothing!" I muttered pathetically. "So it seems," he grunted, eventually, taking his dirty, dusty, empty hand out of the ashes and wiping it on his coat sleeve. A gleam came into his eye. "Is it snuff?" he enquired suddenly, taking a pinch of poor Traquair and applying a dash of ash to each of his nostrils. "No," I protested. He sniffed and peered suspiciously into the open tin. "Ah!" he exclaimed, as further inspiration struck. "Opium powder!" He licked his forefinger and dipped it into the grey ash as a child might into a bag of sherbet. He tasted poor Traquair's mortal remains! I laugh that I may not weep—but I should weep, Robert. That I allowed this to happen! This was no way to treat a good and faithful servant.

Unsurprisingly, Traquair's ashes were not to the customs officer's taste. He produced a red handkerchief from his pocket and dabbed his tongue and lips. He placed the open tin on his desk and looked me steadily in the eye. "What 'ave you 'ere, Mr. Wilde? Come now, sir, I need an answer."

And, Robert, the gods graciously provided me with one. I looked back at my interlocutor, opened my mouth, and heard myself saying, with impressive authority, "If you must know, I am newly returned from Naples. I have been on an expedition to Pompeii and Herculaneum. This ash is drawn from the crater of Mount Vesuvius itself. I am taking it to the British Museum. I have no doubt that Professor Plutarch in the Department of Antiquities will vouch for me."

I was released at once. It seems people will believe anything, providing it is quite incredible.

When, eventually, I reached Victoria—several hours later than I should have done: inevitably my sojourn in the customs hall caused me to miss the ongoing boat train—I

deposited Traquair (or what was left of him; about four-
fifths in fact) with my handbag in the station cloakroom. I
did not think it prudent—or seemly—to continue carting
the poor man's remains about with me in a biscuit tin
until I had fixed on some settled plan as to what their
eventual destiny should be.

From Victoria I took a cab to Oakley Street where my
darling mother did what mothers are supposed to do:
she gave me shelter, she soothed my brow, she solved my
problem! Lady Wilde is a remarkable woman, Robert.
You will meet her one day and admire and love her as
I do. She is all that Maman La Grange is not! She is
selfless, youthful, spirited, and full of high intelligence
and bold imagination. I told her all that had befallen poor
Traquair, and she asked if I had yet said a prayer for him. I
confessed to her that I had not and she rebuked me. I told
her that I wanted his ashes laid to rest on American soil,
and she answered that it must and would be done. We'd
find a way. I told her how I had left him in a biscuit tin in
a handbag in the cloakroom at Victoria Station! "Victoria
Station?" she cried. (Oh, Robert, would that you had
heard that cry! Bernhardt herself could not have swooped
on the words to such imperious effect!) "Victoria Station!
Oscar, how could you?" "It was the Brighton line," I
pleaded, by way of mitigation. "The line is immaterial,"
she thundered, and then, suddenly, the clouds parted and
a light dawned in her eyes and, getting to her feet, and
turning to me with an undisguised note of triumph in
her bearing, she concluded, "But the handbag suggests a
solution, does it not?"

I was at a loss. "Does it?" I mumbled. "It does!" she

said. And it did. At my mother's suggestion, I wired James Russell Lowell, the United States minister in London. He agreed to meet me within the hour. He is a poet and critic as well as an ambassador, but, above all else, he is a great and a good man. I told him my story and—at once, without a moment's hesitation—he promised to provide my late, lamented valet with secure custody to the United States of America. Washington Traquair is to be conveyed to his homeland in complete safety: he will be travelling inside the minister's diplomatic bag! Yes, Robert, Washington will be laid to rest in Washington; his ashes will be scattered in the cooling waters of the Potomac River. It is James Russell Lowell, I think, who wrote: "All the beautiful sentiments in the world weigh less than a single lovely action." I had forgotten the line until just now.

It was yesterday that I met with the good ambassador. Today, at twelve, he accompanied me to Victoria Station and, together, we retrieved my handbag and the biscuit tin. I handed Lowell the tin at once, without ceremony, and as he took it he said, simply, "Your friend is in safe hands, I promise you."

From Victoria we were driven in the ambassadorial coach and pair to Grosvenor Square where my friend George W. Palmer gave us lunch. George W. is the son of George Palmer of Huntley & Palmers, biscuit manufacturers of Reading, the largest biscuit manufacturers in the world. They have a workforce of five thousand men and women, and George and his father— who is also the mayor of Reading and represents the borough in parliament—claim to know every one of the *workers by sight and many by name. The Palmers are good people and George W., while a Quaker, is nonetheless a generous host. Lunch in Grosvenor Square did not rival breakfast at Pharamond, but, given the circumstances, it was exactly comme il faut: pea soup and turbot followed by Welsh lamb, with the consolation of rice pudding for dessert. Lowell, being a diplomat, expressed a desire for cheese and biscuits as well—not for the cheese, of course, but for the biscuits.*

There was a fourth gentleman making up the party—a clergyman, the Reverend Paul White, an old friend of the Palmer family, and it is he, according to George W., who holds my meeting with the assassin Maclean in his gift. George W. had thought to invite him in case, before we ate, we thought it appropriate to stand and remember Washington Traquair. We did so. I said a few words: I told Traquair's history such as I knew it and spoke of his gentle ways and of the sweetness of his nature. I said nothing about the manner of his passing. I implied that his death had been a tragic accident, no more. The Reverend White then said a prayer in Latin and recited the twenty-third psalm. Finally, James Russell Lowell spoke some lines from a poem of his own:

> *Death is delightful. Death is dawn,*
> *The waking from a weary night*
> *Of fevers unto truth and light . . .*

That these good men, who had never known Traquair, should speak so affectingly in his memory was profoundly moving. Traquair is at rest now—God be thanked—but I

*will not rest, Robert, until I know how he met his death
and who it is who is responsible.*

*Once we had stood to remember Traquair, the
Reverend White said grace and we sat down to luncheon.
It was a very jolly affair. Lowell shared with us his
favourite beatitude: "Blessed are they who have nothing
to say and who cannot be persuaded to say it." He had
much to say and said it with felicity. In a different vein
(less felicity—more fire and brimstone!), Reverend White
was equally loquacious. He and Lowell are of an age—
mid-sixties or thereabouts—but there the similarity ends.
The ambassador is tall and bearded and wears his hair
long, in the manner of an Old Testament prophet; the
cleric is of medium height and bald and cleanly shaven.
He is an Anglican convert, an abstainer, and a vegetarian,
with decided views on sin in general and the immorality
of French theatre in particular. When I told him that I was
working with the great Edmond La Grange, he promised
to pray for me. When I said that I considered La Grange
a great actor, he replied: "And a notorious debauchee."
When I asked him how he knew this, he responded: "The
man is an actor, Mr. Wilde, and living in Paris. What more
does one need to know?"*

*Perversely, the less I agreed with the reverend gentleman
the more I found that I liked the man. Of course, he is
the victim of that terrible blindness that passion brings
upon its servants, but I was moved by his zeal and had
a palpable sense of his fundamental goodness. "Where
is your ministry, Father?" I asked him. "Among the
fallen," he replied. "I am the chaplain of Reading Gaol.
I understand that you are to visit us, Mr. Wilde." "Am*

I?" I asked. "You are," he answered, "on Monday week, five March. Roderick Maclean, the man who tried to kill Queen Victoria, arrives at the gaol that day and Palmer tells me that you are anxious to make his acquaintance."

It seems that in spite of our disagreements over the morality of the theatrical profession, I have in some way passed muster with the good reverend and indeed I shall be interested to visit the prison. But first I shall return to Paris. I need to know the truth about the death of poor Traquair. And I need to see you, dear friend. I want to hear your news. How is life among the debauchees?

Ever affectionately yours,
Oscar

12

The Flavour of Absinthe

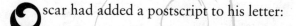

Oscar had added a postscript to his letter:

PS: I shall not return to Paris for a day or two. Tomorrow I am to take tea with Miss Constance Lloyd. She is as pretty as a picture—and the artist is Botticelli. She has the colour and bearing of his Madonna of the Magnificat in the Uffizi in Florence. She has an intelligent eye, an amiable disposition, a graceful figure, and a name that promises much. And, take note, Robert: she is three years my junior. Beware of older women—they are not to be tamed. Beware of actresses—they are not to be trusted!

And below the first postscript, he had added a second:

"In the ocean of baseness, the deeper we get, the easier the sinking." Ambassador Lowell said this at lunch. (Or was it the Reverend White who said it? Either way, I felt I should share the thought with you.)

And below the second, a third:

Please advise my hotel to expect me on Friday or Saturday, at the latest. I am hoping for an untroubled crossing; for certain, I shall have nothing to declare at customs.

In the event, Oscar returned to Paris on Saturday, 24 February 1883. He came directly to the Théâtre La Grange from the Gare du Nord. He arrived at around six o'clock, during the dead hour that comes between the matinée and the evening performance, and found me in La Grange's dressing room, alone, cleaning the great actor's shoes. My friend looked wonderfully well. There was a sparkle in his eye and a pale yellow carnation in his buttonhole. We shook hands warmly. "How are you?" I asked. I was so pleased to see him.

"Exhausted!" he cried, not sounding it in the least. "Railway stations are a nightmare. Everyone seems in such a hurry to catch a train—a state of affairs favourable to neither poetry nor romance." He glanced about the dressing room and lowered his voice. "Are we alone? Where is the master?"

"Upstairs, in the apartment."

"Asleep?"

"With his daughter. She is not well."

His brow furrowed. "Agnès is ill?"

I hesitated. "She is mad," I said.

"Mad!" he exclaimed. The sparkle in his eye turned to a glint. "Tell me more." I had expected the news to perturb him. Instead, he appeared suddenly exhilarated. He dropped his bag on the floor and clapped his hands together with relish. He produced a silver cigarette case from the pocket of his grey frock coat. He took out a Turkish cigarette and rolled it this way and that between his thumb and forefinger. He placed the cigarette lightly between his lips and, con brio, threw himself onto Molière's chaise longue. He lay back on the couch and crossed his legs. With an ostentatious flourish he lit a match and, wide-eyed, gazed at me above the flame. "Tell me everything, Robert. I want detail. What exactly has been going on while I've been away? What has brought about the madness of Mademoiselle La Grange?"

"I don't know," I said.

Oscar raised an admonishing eyebrow. "That's not very helpful, Robert. How does this 'madness' manifest itself? Are there tears and tantrums?"

"Yes."

"Wild looks and frothing at the mouth?"

"Wild looks, certainly . . ."

He drew on his cigarette. "You have witnessed this yourself?"

"We have all witnessed it. There have been rehearsals for *Hamlet* every day this week and every day, at some point during the rehearsals, Agnès has broken down."

Oscar narrowed his eyes. "When she breaks down, what happens—precisely?"

"She begins to sob, at first quietly and then the sobbing grows. It is shocking—terrible and pathetic."

"Does this happen when she is onstage, in the middle of a scene?"

"Yes. But it also happens during the breaks. Or when she's sitting on her own at the side of the stage, watching the others."

"And when she begins to weep, who comes to her aid?"

"Whoever's closest," I said.

Oscar looked at me earnestly. "Think, Robert. Please. Think carefully. When Agnès breaks down, who is it who rushes first to offer comfort and consolation? Her father? Her brother? Her grandmother? Carlos Branco?"

"All of them," I said. "And Gabrielle, naturally. Gabrielle is wonderful." Oscar smiled at me. "Carlos Branco is very caring, too," I added. "Agnès is playing his daughter in the play, of course. I think he finds her sudden outbursts particularly distressing. They often occur during their scenes together. This morning, when Agnès burst into tears, Branco followed suit."

Oscar laughed. "Actors!" he exclaimed. "Did they fall into each other's arms as they wept?"

"Branco put his arms around her and said, 'I understand, my child.' But Agnès pushed him away and shrieked, 'You don't! You don't understand—any of you!'"

Oscar held his cigarette out before him and gazed with hooded eyes upon the glowing ash. "And, from what you've observed, *mon ami*, which of poor, mad Agnès's several comforters does she find the most comforting? Who calms her most? Who restores her to herself? Think carefully."

I reflected for a moment. "Her father," I said eventually.

"Are you sure?" asked Oscar.

"Yes. Her father. And her brother."

"Thank you."

Oscar drew languidly on his cigarette. "And now, Robert," he said, turning his head towards me and smiling, "if you'd be so kind, go back to the beginning." He blew a plume of purple smoke into the air and followed its path with admiring eyes. "Go back to last Saturday, if you would; go back to the afternoon of Traquair's demise. Agnès and Bernard La Grange: where were they that afternoon? Did you ask them?"

"I did, the moment that I received your telegram."

"And?" He looked at me in anticipation.

"And . . ." I hesitated.

"Well?" His eyes widened.

"Agnès couldn't remember and Bernard wouldn't say."

Oscar swung his feet onto the floor and buried his face in his hands. "Dear God, Robert! You are supposed to be my eyes and ears!"

"I'm sorry," I mumbled with a nervous laugh. "I made the enquiries as you requested, but I drew a blank." I felt a fool. I blew my nose and straightened my back. "Oscar," I said, "you don't seriously think that Agnès or Bernard La Grange could be implicated in Traquair's death, do you?"

My friend looked up at me and shrugged his broad shoulders. "Now it is my turn to say, 'I don't know!'" he responded, with a sigh. "It is unlikely, I grant you. I have an intuition that the deaths of Madame La Grange's dog and Monsieur La Grange's dresser must be in some way connected. As yet I don't know why—or how—but if they are, I believe it puts Agnès and Bernard in the clear. The twins were not on board the SS *Bothnia* when the unfortunate Marie Antoinette was buried alive, so it is unlikely, in my estimation, that they had anything to do with the death of Traquair. It is unlikely, but not impossible. I was simply hoping to eliminate them from the field of suspects. It is a crowded field at present since it includes everyone who happened to be in the vicinity of this dressing room at the start of last Saturday's performance of *Le Cid*. If to the cast you add the stagehands and the firemen and the members of the orchestra, we're talking of upward of a hundred people. If you include the audience, we're talking of upward of a thousand!"

"But isn't suicide still the most obvious explanation?"

"I have never been interested in the obvious, Robert. Even on so brief an acquaintance you should know that of me." He sat back and pulled open his frock coat. He put his hand into his waistcoat pocket and from it produced a small maroon-coloured ball, the size of a cherry. He held it out towards me.

"What is it?" I asked.

"A sweet," he replied. "A bonbon. It tastes of aniseed. My new friend, the Reverend Paul White, gave me a little box of them. Suck on it, Robert. You'll find that it has the flavour of absinthe without any of the deleterious side effects."

I took the sweet and tasted it.

"Of course," he continued, "what the Reverend White fails to appreciate is that, for us, Robert, flavour in itself is not sufficient. The aniseed jujube is all very well in its way, but, as a substitute for absinthe, it doesn't quite come up to the mark. Do you agree?"

I sucked on the sweet. "It's pleasant enough," I said, "but I agree with you—of course." I looked at him, perplexed. "Why are we discussing this ridiculous sweet, Oscar?"

"Because I want you to understand why I do not believe that Washington Traquair could have taken his own life."

I looked at my friend, utterly bewildered. "I am lost, Oscar. I confess it."

"We are pleasure seekers, Robert, you and I. Pleasure is the only thing that one should live for. That is my philosophy. I know that the realisation of oneself is the prime aim of life, and I believe that to realise oneself through pleasure is finer than to do so through pain. I am on this point entirely on the side of the Greeks in general and Epicurus in particular. It is a pagan idea."

"What on earth has this got to do with Traquair?" I cried, suddenly exasperated.

"Nothing!" exclaimed Oscar. "That is my point. Traquair was neither a pagan nor a philosopher. He was a simple valet who knew nothing of the Greeks. He was a Christian and an American. He lived by the rules that his mother and his Church had taught him. 'Suicide is sinful.' The God-fearing Washington Traquair would not have taken his own life, however unhappy he was."

"But, Oscar," I protested, pointing to the door to the dresser's cubicle, "consider the evidence. When we found his body, Traquair's room was locked from the inside, was it not?"

"Apparently so."

"You found the key."

"I did."

"And the poor man's upturned face was lying immediately beneath the jet of gas."

"It was."

"And the gas was on but unlit. Poisonous gas was filling the air."

"I don't deny it." He got to his feet and walked over to the door to the dresser's room. The door was ajar. He pulled it open. "But I ask myself," he continued, stepping into the darkened space beyond the door, "who was it that turned on the jet of gas? Was it Traquair, alone in his room, who turned the key at the side of the gas burner and lay down to die? Or could it have been an outside agent, turning a different key in a different part of the building, hoping to poison Traquair in his sleep?" Oscar stepped back into La Grange's dressing room. He looked at me in a headmasterly fashion. "Robert," he enquired, "did you discover if there's another tap that controls the flow of gas to these rooms?"

"I did indeed, sir," I replied, unable to disguise the note of satisfaction in my voice. I turned, opened the main dressing room door, and beckoned to my friend to join me in the wings. "I followed the line of the gas pipe from Traquair's room through the partition wall into the dressing room and along the skirting board and through the outer wall—to here."

Oscar was now at my side. We stood immediately outside La Grange's dressing room, to the left of the door. I pointed to the ground. In the corner, where the wooden outside wall of the dressing room abutted the brick wall of the theatre itself, at floor level, attached to the gas pipe was a small metal tap no bigger than a florin. It was barely visible in the gloom. Holding on to my arm with his left hand, with difficulty Oscar lowered his bulky frame and squatted for a moment to inspect it.

"It's covered in dust," he said. With his right hand, he attempted to turn the tap. "It's very stiff." He struggled to his feet and examined his fingers. "And very grimy."

"And it stops and starts the flow of gas to both Monsieur La Grange's dressing room *and* the dresser's cubicle," I added. "You couldn't alter the gas flow to one room without doing it to the other."

Oscar made a low, grumbling sound and reached into his pocket for a handkerchief. As he wiped his fingers, I continued: "There is a third tap—if you'd like to see it."

He looked at me and nodded. "We must see everything, Robert. The eye is the notebook of the poet—and the detective."

"It's by the stage door, and just as grimy."

"I'll bring my bag," he said, returning to the dressing room to collect his suitcase.

I waited in the doorway, watching him. When he spoke Oscar had a precision of statement that was all his own. His way of using his hands was equally unique. He had a trick of illustrating his meaning with a gesture: a twist of his wrist or the turn of his fingers. As he stood alone in La Grange's dressing room contemplating the scene, he lifted his right hand and laid his index finger against his temple. He looked about him and murmured beneath his breath, "I am a dreamer, I admit it." He walked across the room and looked once more into the dresser's darkened cubicle. He raised his voice a little. "A dreamer, Robert, is one who can only find his way by moonlight. His punishment is that he sees the dawn before the rest of the world." He turned back into the dressing room and came to join me, pausing briefly by La Grange's dressing table. He inspected the tips of his fingers and then, very carefully, with his thumb and forefinger pulled open the dressing-table drawer. He peered inside it. "The gun," he said, "the Colt revolver—it's no longer here." He closed the drawer and looked up at me. "Where did you say we were going?" he asked.

"To the stage door."

I led the way around the edge of the dimly lit wings, pointing, as we went, to the narrow gas pipe that, just above floor level, ran along the length of the theatre wall. "The gas pipe ends up here," I explained, as we stood together in the tiny vestibule that faced the stage doorkeeper's lodge. I pointed once more towards the ground. "This is the other key that stops and starts the flow of gas that eventually reaches the gas burner in the dresser's room. As you will see, it is as stiff as the one by the dressing room."

"I do not doubt you, Robert," said Oscar, but he held on to me once more as, sighing, he crouched down to inspect the gas pipe and key. He had just, with difficulty, settled onto his knees, when the stage door swung open, admitting a gust of icy wind and the presiding genius of the Compagnie La Grange. He saw Oscar and bellowed cheerfully, "Rise, sir, from that semirecumbent posture! It is most indecorous and quite unnecessary."

Oscar looked up at Edmond La Grange and laughed. As the disciple of beauty and self-styled professor of aesthetics struggled inelegantly to his feet, France's most celebrated actor continued in his mocking vein: "A simple genuflection will suffice, Oscar. In fact, before a performance, I'm quite ready to settle for a half bow and a mere salaam." La Grange took Oscar by the hand. "Where have you been, *cher collaborateur*? We've missed you! We've needed you!" Oscar made to speak, but La Grange was in full flight: "Our production is making wonderful progress—this will be a *Hamlet* to reckon with—but, of course, we open a week on Monday so nerves are getting frayed. There's much we still need to achieve, and you've returned, I trust, to help us to achieve it."

"Yes," began Oscar, but before he could continue, La Grange had turned away from him to pull open the stage door and admit Agnès La Grange and Gabrielle de la Tourbillon. The ladies came in laughing, the fur collars of their coats turned up against the cold. From beneath their charming feathered hats, they looked out at us with wide, expectant eyes.

"Oh, Oscar!" cried Gabrielle. "You're back! I'm so glad."

"Monsieur Wilde," said Agnès, dropping a playful curtsey. "Act four, scene five—all those strange English flowers. I need your guidance." She came towards him, smiling, and offered him her hand.

He took it and kissed it and murmured to me as she stepped away, "If this be madness . . ."

"Oscar," boomed La Grange, "I have a favour to ask. Mademoiselle de la Tourbillon, Mademoiselle La Grange, and I are about to give our public more than they deserve—our all! We're offering them *Le Bourgeois gentilhomme* tonight. Uncut. When it's over, the ladies will need supper. They have had a long week—they deserve a treat. I cannot entertain them: it's Saturday night and I must see to the bookkeeping with Monsieur Marais. Would you be so kind?"

Oscar bowed towards the ladies. "Mesdemoiselles, Robert and I would be honoured to entertain you. We will be at your service the moment the curtain falls."

La Grange beamed at Oscar and then turned towards me and prodded me in the chest. "And you, *mon petit,* will be at my service in two minutes' time, if you don't mind."

"Of course, sir. Everything's laid out in your room. I was just seeing Oscar to the door."

Edmond La Grange, with a flourish of his raised right hand, led his leading ladies into the theatre. Agnès bobbed another curtsey; Gabrielle stroked my cheek as she passed by.

In the alley outside the theatre, Oscar asked me: "Are you still in love with the beautiful Mademoiselle de la Tourbillon?"

"Of course," I said. "More than ever."

"And does she love you?"

"I don't know. She might—but I think she's confused."

"She is thirty, Robert. She is too old for confusion."

"What I mean is that she might love me, but for Eddie Garstrang."

"Eddie Garstrang?" exclaimed Oscar, stopping in his tracks.

"He is pestering her," I said.

Oscar looked at me in amazement and put a hand on each of my shoulders. "Garstrang is in love with Gabrielle?" he asked.

"He is making himself a nuisance, certainly."

"Oh, Robert, let him have her. He's the right age, and he's a man who gets what he wants, as a rule."

"Not in this case," I said. "I have challenged him to a duel!"

"A duel?" Oscar began to laugh. "Don't be absurd, Robert. You can't be serious."

"I am."

"I don't believe this, Robert."

"It's true. I'll explain later. I must go now, Oscar. La Grange will be waiting. I must go."

"You are out of your mind, my friend." As I ran back into the theatre, Oscar called after me, "If anyone's mad, Robert, it's you!"

13

Le Chat Noir

I was not mad. I was in love. Gabrielle had enraptured me. I was twenty-one, gauche, naïve, impetuous, overwhelmed by desire, and wholly inexperienced in the ways of women. Now I can look back and smile at my own absurdity. At the time, I had never known a passion so disturbing or profound.

The Saturday evening performance of *Le Bourgeois gentilhomme* rattled by. I watched it from my usual station in the wings. As La Grange had promised, he and his troupe gave their all. Energy, like lightning, filled the stage, and laughter, like thunder, filled the auditorium. The moment it was done, and I had undressed and sponged and towelled the great man, and he had admired himself in his cheval mirror and donned his dressing gown, Richard Marais shuffled into the dressing room with his ink and pen and ledgers.

"Work," La Grange sighed, smiling wearily, "that is what my life has been about." He nodded to dismiss me. *"Amuse-toi bien, mon petit,"* he murmured, pinching my cheek. "Look after the ladies and take care of yourself. To-morrow is another day."

I found the ladies already ensconced with Oscar in an elegant four-wheeler at the end of the alley leading to the stage door. They were as gay and playful as they had been before the performance.

"What kept you?" asked Gabrielle, taking my hand as I climbed aboard the carriage. "We've been waiting."

"I had to undress Monsieur," I explained. As I took my place at her side, she held on to my hand and kissed my cheek. Her face was covered in theatrical makeup. It was dark in the carriage, but I could see that her cheeks were rouged and that she wore an artificial beauty spot at the side of her mouth.

"We haven't changed," giggled Agnès La Grange. "We've come in costume."

"*Tout décolleté.*" Gabrielle smiled, taking my hand and slipping it inside her cloak so that, briefly, it rested between her breasts.

"Monsieur Wilde says that where we're going we'll blend in perfectly." Agnès's golden skin was hidden behind a mask of white powder, so that her huge eyes looked larger than ever. She fluttered her eyelashes at Oscar coquettishly.

"Where are we going?" I asked.

"To Montmartre," said Oscar. He called up to the driver: "Boulevard de Rochechouart, monsieur."

As the four-wheeler lurched forward, Oscar surveyed our party with an air of proprietorial contentment. I sensed that my friend had spent the evening with a bottle of absinthe rather than a box of aniseed bonbons. "We are going to Le Chat Noir," he announced. "It is a bar and a restaurant and a cabaret room—and a way of life. Or so they say. It's notorious. It's not been open long. I've not been, but Sarah Bernhardt recommends it. Sarah claims it's the devil's idea of heaven on earth: full of mad poets and sad actors. Or is it the other way around? Anyway, she says that we will adore it and that she'll be there to make sure we're properly looked after."

"I love Madame Bernhardt," said Agnès eagerly. "I've known her all my life. I never knew my mother—she died as I was born—but I like to pretend that my mother must have been like Madame Bernhardt. Do you think that I look like her? My brother says that I do."

Oscar laughed. "You look nothing like Madame Bernhardt. Your brother is teasing you." He leant across the carriage and took Agnès's hand in his. "You have a beauty that is all your own," he said. "You look like a porcelain doll tonight."

"I am very happy tonight, Mr. Wilde," she replied. "I am in love."

"Oh?" said Oscar, sitting back and reaching for a cigarette. "Tell us more."

"I cannot," answered Agnès, turning to look out of the carriage window, "not yet. It is a secret."

A silence fell among us. We each looked out of the carriage window. It was late—gone eleven o'clock—yet the foothills of Montmartre were filled with people and traffic: drunken revellers were jostling one another, weaving their way between carriages and handcarts; dogs were rummaging in the gutters; at the street corners flower-selling gypsies, organ-grinders, and ladies of the night were plying their trade.

"Will Sarah's husband be there?" asked Gabrielle. "Or her lover?"

"Neither," answered Oscar, flicking his lighted cigarette out of the carriage window. It spun through the night air like a tiny firework and, as it landed on the cobbles, disappeared at once beneath a horse's hoof. "Le Chat Noir is for actors and artists, poets and painters, not brutes and bores. She has promised to bring Jacques-Emile Blanche."

"I know him!" cried Agnès excitedly. "He is painting my picture. He is lovely."

"I know his father," said Gabrielle. "At least, I've met him. Edmond knows him. He's a doctor, isn't he? At Passy?"

"Yes," said Agnès. "At Passy. He runs the lunatic asylum there."

Le Chat Noir was not as I had expected. To call it a bar and a restaurant and a cabaret was absurd. The whole establishment consisted of two small rooms containing, at most, a dozen tables. From the outside it looked like an unpretentious provincial café, the windows hung with red cotton curtains trimmed with lace. To gain an impression of the interior décor was difficult: the rooms were lit entirely by candle, filled with smoke, and so crowded that everybody present—whether standing or seated, whether willingly or not—was in physical contact with the person or persons next to them.

Given the extraordinary appearance of our party—with Gabrielle and Agnès in their eighteenth-century finery and Oscar looking like the Emperor Nero dressed as a Regency fop—at any other address our entrance would have caused a stir. At 84 boulevard de Rochechouart our arrival went unnoticed. With difficulty, Oscar leading the way, we pushed and squeezed ourselves through the throng. Eventually, we found Madame Bernhardt, at the far end of the second room, perched on a marble-topped table, dressed in a gold and green sarong, wearing diamonds in her russet hair, and holding a pewter tankard of red wine between her hands. *"Mes enfants!"* she cried, embracing each of us in turn. "Welcome to the Salon des Arts Incohérents. You know the boys, don't you?"

Two young men were seated on either side of the great actress. One, pale-faced and round-eyed, was the artist Jacques-Emile Blanche. He got to his feet at once and, acknowledging our arrival with a shy smile, kissed Agnès lightly on the lips. The other man—older, heavier, thicker set, with wild black hair and a walrus moustache—was the grey-lipped poet Maurice Rollinat. As we greeted him, he simply closed his eyes and let his heavy head loll back. "Maurice is exhausted," explained Madame Bernhardt, shouting to make herself heard above the hubbub. "He has been tonight's cabaret."

"Does he sing?" I asked.

"He does," she said, "but tonight he recited a poem for us. It was extraordinary—shocking. It told of . . ." She hesitated.

Rollinat opened his eyes. "Copulation," he thundered.

"Indeed," said Sarah, laughing. "The poem told of a boy and a girl who walk in the woods together and see a bull and a cow mating—"

"'La Vache au taureau,'" said Oscar. "I know the poem. It is a masterpiece. There is a true breath of nature in it. Not since Lucretius has the world read its like."

Rollinat sat forward and grinned at Oscar. His teeth were brown, but his smile was generous. "Monsieur, if you are not drunk, you deserve to be. May I buy you a drink?"

"I'm hungry," cried Agnès in a mock wail. "I need food!"

"And you shall have it," declared Jacques-Emile Blanche, "at once!" As he spoke, he caressed her cheeks with his cupped hands and then, suddenly, like a boy on a rock diving into the sea, he turned and plunged into the crowd.

Sarah Bernhardt looked at Agnès with anxious eyes. "And how are you, my child? Has the role of Ophelia driven you mad? It can, you know. I have played the part."

"I am well, Madame Bernhardt," replied Agnès. "I am happy because I am in love. And free, at last."

As she spoke, Jacques-Emile Blanche returned to the table. He held two stools above his head. Behind him came a waiter with two more. Within minutes all seven of us— three actresses, three poets, and a painter—were seated in a tight circle, like fairies in a ring, eating bread and cheese and cold sausage and sweet tomatoes, drinking rough Rhône wine and apple cider, smoking Turkish cigarettes and French cigars, and talking of life and love and death and madness. And copulation.

That night in the smoke-filled back room at Le Chat Noir I knew that I was destined to be Gabrielle's lover— and perhaps, one day, her husband. For two hours, as together we ate and drank and laughed and sighed, hidden beneath the tiny marble-topped café table her left hand rested on my right thigh. Occasionally, when Rollinat talked of carnality, of bodily appetites, and lust that runs beyond desire, her fingers strayed and pressed themselves against my line of life. I had never known a sensation so intoxicating.

Rollinat was fearless: he said things that other men dare

not even think. He spoke of murder, rape, theft, and parricide, not as crimes to be deplored, but as phenomena to be understood—and experienced. Oscar listened to him with rapt attention, now and again taking out a pencil to make a note of one of the French poet's turns of phrase. It was Rollinat and Oscar who dominated the conversation. Oscar shared Rollinat's fascination with perversity and delighted in his open contempt for conventional morality. "To be good, according to the vulgar standard of goodness, is quite easy," Oscar declared. "It merely requires a certain amount of sordid terror, a certain lack of imaginative thought, and a certain low passion for middle-class respectability."

"Can we do as we please in this world?" asked Agnès, looking up at Oscar with wide, enquiring eyes. "Does morality not matter?"

"Kindness matters," said Oscar. "Courtesy matters." He raised his glass in the girl's direction. "Beauty matters a great deal."

"But morality?" Agnès persisted. "What about morality? My grandmother says that of all our senses our 'moral sense' is the most important."

Oscar drew on his cigarette and said, slowly and deliberately: "I never came across anyone in whom the moral sense was dominant who was not heartless, cruel, vindictive, log stupid, and entirely lacking in the smallest degree of humanity. No disrespect to your grandmother, who I gather was a fine actress in her day, but I would rather have fifty unnatural vices than one unnatural virtue."

"Oscar," cried Sarah Bernhardt, waving an admonishing finger at him, "sometimes you go too far!"

"On the contrary, Sarah, I never go far enough!"

As the laughter ricocheted around our tiny table, the marble top was suddenly awash with red wine. Agnès's glass had slipped from her hand and tumbled onto the table. The glass's stem had snapped, the bowl had cracked in two. The wine was everywhere. Agnès broke into a flood of tears. "I'm so sorry," she sobbed.

Instinctively, as the glass crashed and the girl cried out, we all drew away from the table. Gabrielle took her hand from my thigh. Rollinat pushed back his stool. Sarah Bernhardt jumped to her feet and went to put her arm around Agnès's heaving shoulders. Jacques-Emile Blanche leapt up and, grabbing a cloth from a nearby waiter, began to mop up the purple liquid that was now running over the table's edge. "Who would have thought a small glass to have so much wine in it?" muttered Oscar.

"I must go home," breathed Agnès between her sobs.

"You can stay here at my studio," said Sarah Bernhardt.

"Come back to Passy," said Jacques-Emile Blanche.

The girl looked up at the young artist with anguished, red-rimmed eyes. "I am lost," she cried. "I don't know what to do."

"You're exhausted, that's all," said Sarah soothingly. "I have played the part. I know."

"Come home," said Gabrielle.

"We will take you," said Oscar. "My cab is waiting."

It was. In good times and bad, keeping his cab waiting was one of the habitual extravagances of Oscar Wilde. Gabrielle fastened Agnès's cloak around her shoulders. We murmured hurried good-byes to Madame Bernhardt, Blanche, and Rollinat, and, huddled together, leaning forward like travellers pressing across a windswept heath, we pushed our way out of the still-crowded café into the street. The cold night air was sharp and wonderfully refreshing.

"I feel much better now," said Agnès, sitting back in the four-wheeler.

"Joy comes, grief goes, we know not how," said Oscar.

Agnès smiled and wiped her eyes and put her hand into his. "I think Madame Bernhardt is right. Playing Ophelia has made me a little mad."

"We are all a little mad," said Oscar, his eyes shining. "That's what makes us interesting."

When we reached the Théâtre La Grange, the carriage waited at the end of the alley while Oscar and I walked the ladies home. We stood for a moment in the darkness at the foot of the steps leading to the door of the La Grange apartment. I touched Gabrielle's arm and tried to draw her to me; as I did so, she gently shook her head and stepped away.

"Thank you for a lovely evening, Monsieur Wilde," whispered Agnès, holding up her tear-stained face for him to kiss. "I hope I did not spoil it for you."

"On the contrary," said Oscar, smiling. "You were, you are—"

But before he could complete the compliment, he was interrupted by a rattle of bolts. A key turned in a lock. The apartment door swung open, and a man's voice barked: "Where have you been? You're late."

"Not very," answered Gabrielle, turning towards the figure in the doorway. The man stepped out onto the doorstep and swayed from side to side. He was in his shirtsleeves:

his waistcoat was unbuttoned. In one hand he held an oil lamp; in the other he held a gun. It was Eddie Garstrang.

Taking Agnès quickly by the hand, Gabrielle ran up the steps. "You're drunk!" she said to Garstrang, but not unkindly. And when he made to speak, she stopped him, pressing her lips to his. He stepped back into the darkened hallway behind him. Gabrielle and Agnès followed. As the door closed, each girl turned and looked out towards us and smiled and waved. "Good night!" "Thank you!" they called. *"A demain."* We heard the heavy key turn in the lock and the bolts slam shut.

"I will kill that man," I said to Oscar.

Oscar laughed. "It is much more likely that he will kill you."

14

Pistols at Dawn

As we climbed back aboard the waiting carriage, Oscar put his arm on mine and said, "I do hope, dear friend, that you are not serious about this notion of a duel."

"I have never been more serious, Oscar," I replied.

He shook his head and sighed. "The idea's absurd, Robert."

"It is a matter of honour."

"Don't be ridiculous."

"Many good men have fought duels over matters of the heart," I added. "The Duke of Wellington, for example."

Oscar spluttered, "The Duke of Wellington!" Suddenly, he leant forward in his seat and called up to the coachman: "Take us to Passy, driver, to l'Hôtel de Lamballe. At once."

The carriage lurched into motion. "Why are we going to Passy?" I asked.

"I'm escorting you to Dr. Blanche's lunatic asylum, Robert. There's a patient there who thinks he is the Emperor Napoléon. I suggest you have your duel with him."

I looked at Oscar: I looked directly into his eyes. "You do not understand, do you? I love Gabrielle. I will have her. Nothing can stand in my way."

My friend threw his hands in the air. "Oh, Robert,

Robert, Robert!" he cried. "She is not worth it. You have seen how she behaves."

I looked out of the carriage window. The boulevard du Temple was deserted: there was not a soul in sight, not even a scavenging dog. In the distance, a church clock struck two. I said nothing. I heard Oscar reaching for his cigarette case. He opened it and held it towards me. "You must try one of these," he said. "They're American. The tobacco is roasted, not sun dried."

I turned towards him and took one of his cigarettes, and in the light of his burning match looked upon his broad, kindly face and warm walnut eyes.

"The Duke of Wellington was a soldier, Robert," he said gently, "a man of arms, and I doubt very much that his opponent was a professional marksman."

"It's too late," I said. "I am committed. I have issued a challenge. It has been accepted." I laughed at myself. "It's pistols at dawn."

"When?" he asked.

"At dawn," I repeated, sucking on the cigarette. "Tomorrow—I mean, tonight. Sunday morning on the bridge at Buttes-Chaumont."

"Where the gallows used to stand?"

"Yes. In four hours' time."

"Good God," he murmured.

"Garstrang is bringing the pistols," I said. I drew deeply on the cigarette. "I like the flavour of this, Oscar. I know that flavour of itself isn't enough for us, but I like it all the same. What are these cigarettes called?"

"Lucky Strike," he said, and smiled. "Perhaps there is an omen there."

• • •

The early hours of Sunday, 25 February 1883, are not ones that I recall with any relish. Oscar, when he realised that I was in earnest, handed up two silver coins to our coachman and redirected our carriage towards Montmartre. "It's too late to go to bed and too far to go to Passy. If the gods are with us, we'll find Sarah in her studio. We can wait with her until dawn breaks."

Madame Bernhardt had two Paris residences. One was her town house in the XVIIth arrondissement, where she kept her menagerie and did her entertaining. The other was her studio in Montmartre, where she escaped from the world and did her sculpture and her painting. The studio was little more than a stone's throw from Le Chat Noir, along a quiet, uncobbled alley at the foot of the hill on which they are now building the mighty Basilica of the Sacred Heart. The studio itself must once have been a barn or warehouse: it was a vast, single room, with a stone floor and high, whitewashed brick walls. At one end of the room, two-thirds of the way up the wall, was a wooden balcony that served as Sarah's sleeping quarters. In the centre of the room, beneath a huge wrought-iron candelabra, was a raised dais, rectangular in shape, like a small stage, covered in sheeting and crowded with Sarah's sculptures, some in clay, some in stone, some complete, most unfinished: heads, figures, a lioness, a unicorn, an African elephant, and assorted birds of prey.

Sarah was alone. Her hair was unpinned, but she was still dressed in the gold and green sarong she had been wearing when we had left her an hour before. She greeted us, however, as if it had been months, if not years, since our last encounter. "My prodigals returned!" she cried, embracing us warmly. "Oh, Oscar, my dear! And Oscar's friend!" (She never made any attempt to master my name.) "This calls for celebration!" Barefoot, she ran over to the dais, and from behind a block of alabaster produced bottles of brandy and champagne. "You recall the famous last words of the Fatted Calf, do you not? 'I hear the young master has returned!' I am *so* pleased to see you both." She gave us each a "Bernhardt"—a thumb of brandy and a finger of champagne: "Divine, is it not?"—and, perching herself cross-legged on the edge of the dais, invited us to sit on a bed of cushions at her feet. "What news on the Rialto?" she demanded. "Is Agnès safe? I feel for her. Ophelia's such a dreadful part: first she's boring, then she's mad, then she's being carted round the stage on a bier."

"They have a waxwork for that," interjected Oscar, settling himself on the cushions with some difficulty.

"I'm glad. When I played it, the wretched pallbearers kept dropping me in the wings. They were angry because I wouldn't sleep with them. Everyone wants to sleep with Ophelia! That's what drives the poor girl mad!" She laughed wildly and refilled our glasses. "The party after the party is always the best party, don't you agree?" she said, looking between us with tears of joy and exhaustion in her eyes. "Why are you here? Why have you come to see your Aunt Sarah, do tell?"

Oscar began to explain, but did not get very far. The moment that he mentioned the word "duel," Madame Bernhardt leapt to her feet and fell upon him. Literally: she tumbled into his arms. "Oh, Oscar, I am so proud of you! Were I a man, I should be duelling every day! It is the noblest sport of all. I salute you, dear friend. What is your quarrel? Who is it with?"

"It is not my quarrel," said Oscar, attempting vainly to release himself from Sarah's tender grasp.

"You are doing this for another?" gasped the great actress. "Oscar, you are my hero!"

Oscar laughed awkwardly. "No, Sarah," he said, "you misunderstand. I am not the duellist. Robert is."

The eighth wonder of the world turned her gaze upon me. "Oh, Oscar's friend!" she cried. "I am proud to know you."

Gradually, over more brandy and champagne, with several further misunderstandings along the way, we explained the sequence of events that had brought us to her studio door. At first, Sarah assumed that it was Agnès La Grange who was the object of my desire and expressed her amazement that a mild-mannered artist of Jacques-Emile Blanche's sensibility should have taken up my challenge. Then, when she understood that it was Gabrielle de la Tourbillon whose attention I craved, she warned me that Edmond La Grange was a ruthless charmer—"by definition: he is a leading actor"—and a deadly shot: "he has Jarrett's gun: I gave it to him." Finally, when she had absorbed that my rival was neither an artist nor an actor, but an American card player of whom she had never heard, she declared: "Glory is thine, I know it. You cannot fail. But first you must have two hours' sleep to refresh you for the battle. Come!" She pulled me to my feet and took both my hands in hers. "At my house, you could sleep in my coffin. Here, you can sleep on my couch. There!" She pointed to a rope ladder that dangled from the wooden balcony at the far end of the studio. "Climb into my bed, close your eyes, and dream of victory!"

I did as I was told—except that I did not dream of victory. I dreamt of drowning, of being swept along within a never-ending tide of rolling water, spinning slowly round and round as the torrent engulfed me. And then, suddenly, I awoke and found Sarah kneeling at my pillow with a steaming cup of hot coffee in her hand. "Drink this. It's six o'clock. Oscar has a carriage at the door."

The morning was bitterly cold. As I climbed into the waiting carriage, the coachman, swathed in blankets, shrouded in mist, was pocketing yet more of Oscar's silver. He looked down at me and muttered, "I've told your friend. At the edge of the park, I leave you. I'll not be party to this. If I stay and the police are called, I lose my licence. Understood?"

I nodded and closed my eyes as I slumped next to Oscar in the back of the cab.

"Are we proceeding with this folly?" Oscar asked in a hoarse whisper.

"Yes," I said. "We must." The drive from La Butte de Montmartre to Buttes-Chaumont took less than half an hour. When we left Sarah's studio we were enveloped in darkness. By the time we reached our destination, a pale grey light had filled the sky.

The driver dropped us on the south side of the park and, accepting a final coin from Oscar, without looking back, hastened on his way.

"Where exactly are you meeting Garstrang?" Oscar asked. "Do you know?"

"On the bridge, by the Temple of the Sybil, at the top of the hill."

The hill had once been a place of public execution. For centuries it served Paris as a limestone quarry. As a centrepiece of the Universal Exhibition of 1867, Napoléon III and his bustling town planner, Baron Haussmann, had transformed it into a garden of delights. The park around the hill now included streams, a lake, a waterfall, a grotto, rocky promontories, and English and Chinese gardens. We climbed the hillside along an avenue of newly planted cedars of Lebanon.

"It is very beautiful here," said Oscar. His breath, like plumes of cigarette smoke, filled the icy morning air. "When I have finished my play, I plan to write a fairy tale. Its setting shall be this garden."

"Am I to die this morning?" I asked. My hands were trembling I was so cold.

Oscar turned to me and, putting an arm about my shoulders, whispered in my ear: "Sybil, daughter of a sea monster and an immortal nymph, is speaking through the trees, Robert. She has prophetic powers." He smiled. "You'll not die this morning."

"I am not ready to die, Oscar," I said pathetically.

My friend lifted his arm from my shoulder and laughed out loud. "Then drop the challenge, Robert! It is absurd."

We had reached the stone belvedere at the summit of the hill. Standing between the mock-Corinthian columns beneath the statue of Sybil seated upon her rock were Eddie Garstrang and Pierre Ferrand, the La Grange company doctor. Garstrang looked utterly at his ease, dapper, clean shaven, rested. The drunkenness of the night before had left no mark upon his features.

"Good morning, gentlemen," said Oscar.

"Good morning, Oscar," Garstrang replied. "I take it you've come as Sherard's second. Dr. Ferrand is acting on my behalf. In the event of injuries, he'll tend to either side—without charge or favour. He is a gentleman."

Oscar chuckled genially. "I like to think we're all gentlemen, Eddie, and relatively sane. Let's not go through with this madness."

"We must," I said, stepping forward and looking directly at Eddie Garstrang.

"You heard the lad," said Garstrang, grinning at Oscar. "He's headstrong. Don't worry, I'll not kill him. I'll just clip his wings." He nodded towards the doctor, who went over to the foot of the statue and returned bearing an ornate rosewood pistol case which he held open before him.

"You choose," said Garstrang.

"This is pure melodrama." Oscar sighed. "Tell me these are stage properties borrowed from the Théâtre La Grange and loaded with blanks."

"No," answered Garstrang. "These are .69 calibre blackpowder duelling pistols made in Paris by the celebrated brothers Le Page. The pistols are quite old, but the bullets are brand new. The guns belonged to Dr. Ferrand's grandfather. One of them has killed a man, but Ferrand says that, according to the French duelling code, we are not permitted to know which."

The bearded doctor beamed benevolently and, raising his bushy eyebrows, offered me his case of family heirlooms.

"Take your pick," said Garstrang. "Time's against us."

"The code requires the duel to take place within ten minutes of the appointed hour," Ferrand explained in French.

I chose the pistol closest to me. The gun was heavier than I had expected. The ebony handle was ice cold to the touch.

"Remove your coats and jackets, gentlemen," said Ferrand.

"He'll die of cold," exclaimed Oscar.

"It is the rule," said Ferrand. "Cowards have been known to wear body armour beneath their coats."

I handed the pistol to Oscar as I threw off my coat.

"Make your way to the centre of the bridge, gentlemen," instructed Ferrand. "Stand back to back with heels and shoulder blades touching. When I give the command, walk fifteen paces, turn, and wait. When Mr. Wilde gives the order, 'Make ready,' you may aim and say a prayer. I will then give the final command: 'Fire!' Is that understood?"

I nodded and reclaimed the gun. My hands were no longer shaking. I thought, 'I am doing this for Gabrielle de la Tourbillon and I am glad.' I smiled at Oscar and said, "Is this not what you'd call eating of all 'the fruit of all the trees in the garden of the world'?"

"It is indeed, Robert," he answered, embracing me. "Bravo, *mon brave*!"

I turned and joined Garstrang and, together, side by side, we walked down the temple steps and onto the narrow suspension bridge that ran directly from the edge of the belvedere to the facing promontory. Halfway across, we stopped and took up our positions, back to back. A hundred feet beneath ran a man-made waterfall; around us the morning mist was dissolving into dew.

"Aim for my heart," said Garstrang. "If I don't hit you first, then at least I'll not know it."

From the far end of the bridge, Ferrand called out: "May honour be satisfied! Fifteen paces, gentlemen. March!"

I walked the fifteen paces and turned. I looked on Eddie Garstrang: he was a small man, insignificant, with lank, yellow hair and weak, washed-out eyes. I was ready to kill him. "I am ready to kill you." I said the words softly but out loud and, as I spoke them, I heard Oscar's voice command: "Make ready!"

I raised my right arm. I took aim.

"Fire!"

I fired, and as I fired I heard three shots ring out.

Birds squawked and burst from the trees and bushes. I stood stock still, staring at the pistol in my hand. There was smoke coming from both the barrel and the hammer of the gun. My palm and thumb were scorched, but I felt no pain. I sensed a hand on my shoulder, warm and strong and comforting. I turned and murmured, "Oscar, my friend"—but it was not Oscar. It was Edmond La Grange.

15

Rue de la Pierre Levée

The great actor's round face was worn and lined, but full of life and wreathed in smiles. "I have lost two dressers in six months," he breathed. "I don't wish to lose a third."

I looked at him, bemused. He raised his right hand and held out before me another smoking gun. "Mr. Jarrett's Colt revolver," he said. "It's known as the Peacemaker. So let it be."

Eddie Garstrang, his pallid face now whiter than a shroud, came along the bridge towards us.

"I fired on the command, not before," said La Grange. I noticed the actor's glistening eyes: they were wide open and full of mischief. "I'm sorry, Garstrang, but it seems I am the quicker shot."

"The Colt fires a faster bullet," said Garstrang coldly.

"But I was firing from twice the distance—from the bushes." La Grange turned and indicated his hiding place at the far side of the bridge.

"I am utterly confused," said Oscar, arriving on the scene from the belvedere end of the bridge, bringing my coat and jacket with him.

"But mightily relieved, I imagine," said La Grange, laughing.

"What happened just now?" asked Oscar. "Will someone tell me?" He looked at La Grange: "Why are you here at this godforsaken hour?"

"Last night," explained the old actor, "when my Saturday-night duties with Marais were done, I played a game of cards, with Garstrang and Monsieur Branco and Dr. Ferrand, as is our custom. Garstrang lost." La Grange smiled.

"Garstrang lost and he got drunk." La Grange looked at Garstrang: the American betrayed no feeling. "Garstrang had already told me about this morning's proposed escapade," La Grange continued. "He had promised to 'wing' my dresser, nothing more: 'teach the pup a lesson,' that's what he said. But when Gabrielle returned from her supper with you, Oscar, and came to my room to bid me good night, she told me that she had just seen Garstrang in the hallway and that the poor man could barely stand." He glanced again at the silent Garstrang. "I decided therefore that, under the circumstances, all things considered, I could not trust his marksmanship." He looked down at the gun that he was holding and turned it over in his hands. "So, today, I came to do what I have done: deflect the tip of the barrel of Garstrang's pistol with a well-aimed bullet from the terrible Mr. Jarrett's Colt revolver."

La Grange turned to Dr. Ferrand, who was standing beside Garstrang nursing the damaged duelling pistol. "My apologies, Pierre. I know it is a family heirloom. I will make it up to you. I always do."

"What happened to my shot?" I asked, handing my pistol back to Dr. Ferrand.

La Grange narrowed his eyes and peered along the

bridge towards the temple belvedere. He sighed and shook his head sorrowfully. "Poor Sibyl. I imagine the bullet went straight through her heart."

I laughed. "Am I so poor a shot?"

Garstrang said quietly, "Your aim was at least a foot too high." Some colour was returning to his cheeks. He ran his thin fingers through his yellow hair and smiled at me. His smile was not unfriendly. "Have you ever fired a gun before?" he asked.

"Oh, Robert!" cried Oscar, clapping his hands in amusement. "What we do for love!"

"Gentlemen," said Edmond La Grange, turning to Garstrang and to me, "shake hands. I command you. Do it now. Go on." His eyes shone with authority, humour, and benevolence. "For my secretary and my dresser to fall out over my mistress is an absurdity. Surely we can all enjoy her? Isn't that what mistresses are for?"

"A great man speaks!" declared Oscar. "Do as you're told, Robert."

I shook Eddie Garstrang by the hand. I did so without hesitation. I felt oddly exhilarated—and curiously relieved.

"A wise man speaks," added Dr. Ferrand.

"An old man says it's time for breakfast!" La Grange slipped the Colt revolver into his coat pocket and spread his arms towards us, the palms of his hands upturned, as if about to take a curtain call. "Our carriage awaits."

Edmond La Grange had secured a four-wheeled coach and pair with a driver who had no scruples in the matter of aiding and abetting duellists. The man was waiting by his carriage with a supply of bandages and a flask of brandy.

When our party appeared, full of vigour and bonhomie, he looked positively crestfallen. "Three shots fired and no blood drawn?" he scoffed. "Have I risked arrest for this?" I displayed my scorched hand proudly: he gazed upon it with ill-concealed contempt.

We clambered aboard the vehicle and set off for town. I sat facing Eddie Garstrang: we did not speak, but we looked upon one another without rancour, no longer as enemies, nor yet as friends; simply, I suppose, as rivals reconciled.

"It is a curious thing," said Edmond La Grange, as if reading my thoughts, "but a duel does clear the air."

"It was a duel upstaged," said Eddie Garstrang.

"It was a theatrical duel," said Oscar, "a duel in the Euripidean tradition—blessed with a deus ex machina."

"My friend," said La Grange, leaning towards Oscar and touching him lightly on the knee, "do you know the inkwell story? It's my favourite story of upstaging." It was scarcely seven o'clock on a bitterly cold February morning; Edmond La Grange was sixty years of age and cannot have had more than four hours' sleep; yet he told his story with all the verve of a great vaudevillian at the height of his powers. "This is the cautionary tale of a young actor in weekly repertory who *hated* his leading man. The young actor was consumed with jealousy, and in his journal he confided the details of his obsession. 'Tonight,' he wrote, 'he ruined my finest scene.' 'Tonight, he trod on all my laughs.' 'Tonight, he killed my exit round.' Then came: 'Monday, 6:15 P.M. Dear Diary, Tonight I believe I am going to get the better of him. We open a new play and I have a speech ten minutes long. Downstage. In the light. Facing out front. And he is upstage, seated at a desk, with his back to the audience, writing a letter. I think I must win . . .' Later, a drunken hand added: '11:30 P.M. *He drank the ink!*'"

Encouraged by Oscar, as our carriage rumbled through the empty Sunday-morning streets, La Grange told story after story. He told them as if he had never told them before and delivered them, in a jolting coach to an audience of five (he made sure that the coachman was listening), with all the passion and panache that he brought to the playing of Molière to a full house at his own theatre. As I listened to his tales—all theatrical stories: he knew no other kind—I thought that Edmond La Grange was the funniest and most brilliant man alive.

Suddenly, the coach and pair drew to a halt. The driver called down to La Grange: "Is this it?"

La Grange glanced out of the carriage window. "It is. *E finita la commedia*. Breakfast is served."

We climbed out of the coach. We were not, as I had expected, back at the Théâtre La Grange. We were nearby, certainly: I had noticed us come into the place de la République while La Grange was telling his last story. I had assumed we were making for the boulevard du Temple, but this was a different street altogether.

"Where are we?" asked Oscar, looking up and down the cobbled roadway.

"Rue de la Pierre Levée," said La Grange. "It's a street of warehouses and small factories. Printing works and ceramics manufacturers in the main. The theatre is eight streets away, due west. Five minutes on foot, no more." He took us across the road towards a narrow wooden door that was let into a high, windowless brick-built wall. From his coat pocket, with a flourish, he produced a small wrought-iron key and held it up before us like a magician displaying an object that he is about to make disappear. He unlocked the door. "Follow me," he said, stepping through it.

We did as we were told, and found ourselves inside what appeared to be the warehouse to a ceramics factory. Through the gloom we discerned straw-filled wooden crates and pallets piled high with tiles, ranged in rows around the room. We followed La Grange across the darkened space and through a second door into a workshop beyond. Here the daylight, streaming down a central stairwell, almost dazzled us. "Up you go," said La Grange, indicating the steep shaft of wooden steps. One by one, we made our way up the stairs, climbing through a haze of white dust.

We reached the summit. The stairwell opened onto a huge loft, a space as wide and deep as the Room of the Dead, but filled with cold sunlight: dormer windows of assorted sizes had been cut into the roof of the building.

"Welcome to El Paradiso," said Edmond La Grange.

The room had the dimensions of the Room of the Dead, but the feel of a thriving bordello. The floor was covered with Persian rugs; the walls were hung with silks; there were cushions and divans all about and, at the far end of the room, directly opposite the stairwell, beneath a wide window that overlooked the rooftops of north Paris, a huge, unmade bed.

In the centre of the room, on a long, low, narrow table, like a diminutive altar, breakfast was laid out. There was bread and cheese, cold cuts of meat, fruit, red wine, brandy, and champagne. It was reminiscent of supper at

Le Chat Noir, except that here there was absinthe on offer, too; and, separately, carefully arranged on a wooden tray placed at one end of the table, the ingredients for lauda-num: tincture of opium and liquid ether.

"*A table, messieurs,*" said La Grange, pointing us to-wards the cushions and footstools arranged about the table. "I'll prepare the coffee—unless the combatants re-quire something stronger." He looked towards the doctor. "Pierre, make sure our guests have everything they might require."

"What is this place?" asked Oscar, his voice full of won-der. "Where are we?"

"This is my love nest," said La Grange. "The doctor knows it quite well. He has handled one or two emergen-cies here down the years. I share it with friends—with good friends, with those I truly trust."

Oscar looked about the room admiringly. I noticed his eye fall and settle on a small marble bust that stood alone on an elegant Chinese lacquered sideboard. La Grange was near the sideboard, crouching down by an oil-fired stove, attempting to light it. "I'm an Epicurean, Oscar, as you know," he called over his shoulder. "I follow my hero's philosophy."

"You pursue pleasure; you avoid pain."

"I cultivate a small circle of close friends."

"You have your public, yet—"

"I keep myself to myself." La Grange got to his feet. "Unlike other actors I could mention, I steer clear of poli-tics: public life only leads to trouble. I do as Epicurus ad-vised." He turned to the sideboard and picked up the small marble bust: it was the head of the Greek philosopher. He handed it to Oscar. "He looks like Dr. Ferrand, does he not?"

"He is handsome, certainly," said Oscar, inspecting the marble.

"He is ancient and bearded," grumbled the doctor.

"Read the inscription," said La Grange.

Oscar studied the words inscribed at the base of the head. "*Lathe biōsas.* 'Live secretly.'"

"Isn't 'Seek seclusion' a better translation?"

"Perhaps," said Oscar pleasantly, returning the bust to its place on the sideboard. "It's a year or two since I last won a prize for Greek translation."

La Grange laughed. "The point is: I think my hero would have approved of my hideaway. I hope *you* approve of my hideaway, Oscar. It's yours for the borrowing, my friend, as and when it suits you. You may bring whom you like here. No questions will be asked—at least, not by me. There is only one key. I keep it in my possession at all times. So if I lend the key to you, you can be sure that no one else has it. You can come here knowing that you will be quite undisturbed."

Oscar bowed towards La Grange, gratefully. The old actor turned to Eddie Garstrang and to me. "I'm glad, gentlemen, that we're agreed that I cannot have my secretary and my dresser fighting over my mistress. It is undignified and unnecessary. If you both want her, you must both have her—if she's willing. Bring her here by all means. She knows her way around. Bring her here—separately or together. As you please."

Over breakfast, La Grange made us take part in a playful ritual, passing the wrought-iron key around the group, making each of us kiss it in turn and swear an oath to keep the existence of the love nest a secret—especially from Liselotte La Grange!

"Mother may know best," said Dr. Ferrand, "but there is no need for her to know everything!"

"There are those who despise my mother," said La Grange. "Members of the company play a game at her expense, I know. They raise outlandish topics in her presence to see how quickly she manages to turn the subject back to herself and the glorious heritage of the Compagnie La Grange! I don't despise my mother. I love her. I am whatever I am because of her." He paused and sighed. No one spoke. He looked up and grinned at us—a little awkwardly, I thought. The way he bared his teeth turned the grin into a grimace. "Don't misunderstand me, gentlemen," he said. "I am grateful for my mother's devotion, but it is somewhat exhausting at times."

"A mother's love is very touching," said Oscar, "but it is often selfish." Oscar's eyes darted about the breakfast table as if he were taking the temperature of a public meeting. He returned La Grange's smile. "Your secret is safe with us, sir."

"Thank you," replied La Grange. "After breakfast, you may sign the book."

When we had eaten, before walking back together from the rue de la Pierre Levée to the boulevard du Temple, our host showed us the apartment's facilities—the tiny kitchen, the well-stocked linen cupboard, the bathroom with its skylight to the stars—and then, from a drawer in the Chinese laquered sideboard, produced a leather-bound visitors' book and, in turn, invited Oscar, Eddie Garstrang, and me to add our names.

"You are now official members of my little club," said La Grange, blowing dry the ink on our signatures before closing the book and replacing it carefully in its drawer.

"Is there a subscription to be paid?" asked Oscar, smiling.

"All I ask is the occasional account of your more amusing adventures here. There are no rules, no obligations."

"And only one key?" said Oscar.

"Yes, and I change both the key and the locks quite regularly. Even the maid who comes once a week—and is wonderfully thorough and completely discreet—has to claim the key from me personally."

"Did I see Sarah Bernhardt's name in the book?" asked Oscar.

"You did," said La Grange. "You are very observant, Oscar. Madame Bernhardt is our only lady member. I gave her membership by way of a wedding present. I thought that she might find it useful."

Dr. Ferrand laughed. "I'm sure she does."

La Grange stretched out a hand and placed it on his friend's shoulder. "Pierre has been a member of the club for many years. In fact, I believe he's now our longest-standing member."

"Is that since the departure of Carlos Branco?" Oscar enquired.

"It is," said La Grange, looking at Oscar and raising an eyebrow. "Did Branco tell you about the club, then?" he asked.

"No," said Oscar quickly, "not at all. There's a line through his name in the book. I noticed it. That's all."

"Ah," said La Grange, "you are *very* observant, Oscar." He began to usher us towards the stairwell. "Club membership is entirely at my discretion—at my whim, even. My old friend Carlos Branco is no longer a member of the club. His performance as Polonius is really not up to scratch."

16

The Dress Rehearsal

The next day was Monday—26 February, the feast day, as I learnt from Oscar, of St. Porphyry. My friend arrived early at the Théâtre La Grange wearing a purple tweed suit and clutching a copy of the life of the saint. He found me, alone, in La Grange's dressing room, seated on the chaise longue, polishing the great man's shoes. "You don't read Greek, do you, Robert?" he said by way of greeting, brandishing the book in the air. "I shall have to translate this for you. It's the most wonderfully lurid account of paganism in antique times. Paris in the late nineteenth century has nothing on Gaza in the early fifth!"

"You are on song this morning," I observed, looking up from my labours.

"I need to be!" he declared, dropping the book onto La Grange's dressing table and feeling in his pockets for his cigarette case. "I have a 'business appointment' with Monsieur Marais at ten o'clock. When a man offers you a meeting to discuss business, you know that whatever the outcome it will not be to your advantage." He placed a cigarette between his lips and struck a match, closing his eyes and breathing in the sulphurous fumes as he did so. "I don't want money," he went on. "It is only people who pay their bills who want money and I never pay mine."

"Very droll, Oscar," I said. "You *are* on song."

"Thank you, Robert." He offered me a modest bow and, turning to the cheval mirror that stood by the dressing table, studied his own reflection. "I don't care about money, but Monsieur Marais cares about it very much. I believe he has been swindling La Grange for years."

I looked at him, surprised. "Why? How? Marais seems devoted to La Grange."

"Why? Because he is deaf and resents the world. I don't blame him. How? By the old expedient beloved of box office managers everywhere. Have you noticed that there are thirty-four rows of seats in the stalls in this theatre?"

"Are there?"

"There are. But on the theatre plan that Marais goes through every Saturday night with Monsieur La Grange there are only thirty-three. Monsieur Marais reserves the revenue from the invisible row all to himself."

"How extraordinary."

"How simple. Marais is a swindler. At our last 'business appointment' I told him so. I told him that he might swindle his employer and get away with it, but that he wasn't going to swindle me."

I laughed. "How was he trying to swindle you, Oscar?"

"He offered me the equivalent of one hundred pounds for my work on the translation of *Hamlet*. I told him that La Grange had already promised me twice that."

"And had he?"

"No, but he might have done. Marais will pay me one fee and tell La Grange that he's paid me quite another—and pocket the difference."

"That's scandalous, Oscar."

"That's business, Robert. But I intend to stand my ground. A translator is worthy of his hire. I want twice what he offered me at our first meeting, not because I care about the money, but because I care about the principle." Oscar tugged at his waistcoat. He regarded the cut of his new suit with apparent satisfaction. He took out his pocket watch. "Why are you here so early, Robert?" he asked. "The dress rehearsal doesn't begin till twelve." Smirking, he turned back from the looking glass and gazed down at me. "Are you hoping to catch Mademoiselle de la Tourbillon before Eddie Garstrang does and commit her to a tryst in the 'club room' on the rue de la Pierre Levée?"

"Don't be absurd, Oscar. I'm here preparing La Grange's wardrobe."

"Of course, you are, dear boy; but when I arrived I noticed that you had left the dressing-room door ajar. Could it have been just in case a certain young lady chanced to float by?"

"I still love her, Oscar," I said solemnly. "I still want her, but I acknowledge that something's changed."

"Ah?" said my friend, putting away his pocket watch. "Since when?"

"Since I saw her with Garstrang on Saturday night, since I heard La Grange speak of her as he did yesterday."

Oscar smiled at me and retrieved his copy of the *Life of St. Porphyry* from the dressing table. "On one issue, at least, men and women agree," he said. "They both distrust women." I laughed. My friend put his hand on my shoulder. "That said, *mon brave,* you are young; if you get the chance, enjoy her. Every twenty-one-year-old should have the benefit of a beautiful mistress of thirty." He waved his book towards me as he made for the door. "Though whatever you get up to at Monsieur La Grange's delightful love nest, I am confident it will not rival the goings-on at the temple of Aphrodite before good St. Porphyry came along."

The little carriage clock on the sideboard began to strike the hour. Oscar departed. "I'll leave the door open," he said gaily. Through the cheval mirror I watched him go. Marais's office was an inhospitable and windowless room hidden in the bowels of the building. To reach it you had to cross the stage and make your way down a narrow flight of stone stairs in the upstage corner diagonally opposite La Grange's dressing room. In the looking glass, with some amusement, I observed Oscar's halting progress across the stage. He had left full of confidence, with a spring in his step. Now—whether because of the gloom of the darkened stage or a sense of foreboding about his meeting—his pace had faltered. I was about to shout out a wry word of encouragement when I heard a curious, distant creaking sound and then caught sight of Oscar looking upward in alarm. Suddenly, my friend cried out in distress and, as he did so, he threw himself onto the ground. As he fell, facefirst, onto the stage, a huge stage weight—a square black sack filled with iron and sand—crashed within an inch of his head.

I threw down La Grange's shoes and rushed at once to my friend's aid. As I arrived, two stagehands emerged from the darkness of the wings and ran towards him. Together, we lifted Oscar to his feet.

"How are you?" I asked.

"Alive," he said. He began to brush the dust from the

front of his tweed jacket and trousers. I noticed that his hands were trembling. The stagehands shaded the sides of their eyes and peered up into the flies of the theatre.

"Odd," said one of them.

"It's happened before," said a voice from the wings. It was Carlos Branco, standing at the side of the stage. He was dressed in a suit of armour and carrying a helmet in his hands.

"When was that?" asked Oscar.

"Last season," said Branco, coming towards us, smiling. "We did *Don Quixote,* and La Grange took the view that my Sancho Panza was not up to the mark." The old actor looked up towards the flies. "He's a hard taskmaster, is the great La Grange."

"Ah," murmured Oscar, his hands still trembling. "You are joking."

Branco put an arm around Oscar's shoulder. "It was an accident, my friend. In the theatre, these things happen all the time."

"How is the fly gallery reached?" asked Oscar, looking towards the wings.

"By the ladder at the back of the stage," said Branco. "It's the only way."

The younger of the stagehands—he was a boy of sixteen or seventeen—ran swiftly up the stage and disappeared behind a piece of scenery. "There's no one here," he called.

The other stagehand—an older, red-faced man, with a drooping black moustache—was still staring into the flies. "There's no one up there. The weight must just have slipped its moorings. It was poorly fastened."

"Are you all right, Oscar?" asked Carlos Branco, squeezing Oscar's shoulder.

"I am alive," repeated Oscar. "Thank you."

The two stagehands grunted, nodded to Carlos Branco, and picked up the weighted sack. Its weight must have been considerable: between them they struggled to carry it into the wings. Oscar took a deep breath and picked up his book off the floor. He showed the cover to Carlos Branco. "St. Porphyry teaches us not to believe in omens. He set himself against the snares of superstition." He glanced up at the empty flies and then looked at Branco and at me with troubled eyes. "I'm unnerved, my friends. I own it. A dog dies; then a blackamoor is killed; and now an Irishman is set to meet his doom."

Carlos Branco laughed. "Do you think there's a murderer in our midst, Oscar, gradually working his way through the animal kingdom?"

"It was an accident, Oscar—surely?" I said.

"Surely," said Oscar, blowing the dust from the cover of his book. "If you'll excuse me, gentlemen, I have a meeting to attend. I shall be late, and Monsieur Marais will have the advantage of me."

The dress rehearsal of *Hamlet*—the first of a weeklong series of dress rehearsals—was due to begin at twelve noon. At ten o'clock the wings of the Théâtre La Grange were deserted. By 11:30 A.M. the stage and its environs were crowded with strutting players in assorted states of dress, undress, and near-hysteria. Many were trying on their costumes for the first time, and most were volubly unhappy with the colour, the cut, the fabric, the fit, the finish, the heritage of their attire. The production of *Hamlet* was new, but the costumes and accessories were not. Bernard La Grange, prince of Denmark, protested that his wig was "grotesque"—"laughable, risible, beneath contempt"— and that he wouldn't be seen dead wearing blond curls! Maman, wardrobe and wig mistress to the Compagnie La Grange since time immemorial, explained to him that the wig had served his father and his grandfather well enough. Carlos Branco, who was to play the Ghost of Hamlet's Father as well as the role of Polonius, showed his contempt for the outsized suit of armour that he had been given to wear by marching about the ramparts of Elsinore Castle making his visor snap open and shut like the jaws of an ill-tempered alligator.

Edmond La Grange arrived with Agnès on his arm. He was at his gayest—a dress rehearsal was his happiest time—and he knew his costume well: he had worn it when he played Iago in *Othello* and Edmund Kean in the famous play by Dumas père. (Sarah Bernhardt had been his leading lady on both occasions.) Agnès made no complaint about her costume, either. She was wearing a simple white shift, trimmed and decorated with ribbons of cornflower blue: it was a dress that Maman had first worn sixty years before. Agnès looked serene and appeared much calmer than she had been when I had last seen her at the end of our evening at Le Chat Noir. She brought some flowers—white lilac blossom—to adorn her father's dressing room.

When I had finished dressing La Grange, I was despatched to offer any assistance that Maman might require. On my way to find her, in the crowded wings, I came face-to-face with Gabrielle de la Tourbillon. It was the first time

I had seen her since Edmond La Grange had said that Garstrang and I could "share" his mistress. It was the first time, too, since she had held my thigh at Le Chat Noir and I had seen her embrace Garstrang in the apartment hallway. She looked different. She looked old. She saw the confusion in my eyes. "I know," she said. "It's disconcerting. You don't recognise me, do you, Robert? It is the makeup. And the embonpoint. Gertrude is a mother. A mother has breasts."

At twelve noon, the stage manager walked through the wings and across the stage ringing a handbell. Slowly, the company began to come to order: the actors filed onto the stage and positioned themselves, according to seniority, around the ramparts; the stagehands and the wardrobe ladies hovered at the edge of the wings. No one told anyone where to stand: instinctively each seemed to know his or her place. The principals—Hamlet, Ophelia, Gertrude, Polonius—clustered centre stage. Immediately behind them stood Horatio and Laertes, with Osric, Rosencrantz, and Guildenstern just beyond. Bernardo, Marcellus, Reynaldo, and Fortinbras formed a line upstage right; the Player King and Queen and the gravediggers formed another upstage left. The English Ambassador and the Norwegian Captain stood on the battlements, with attendant lords, ladies, priests, and players ranged on either side of them.

When everyone was gathered, Edmond La Grange walked onto the stage with Oscar Wilde and Richard Marais at his side. Marais carried a wooden stool, which he placed centre stage in front of the footlights. Steadied by Oscar, La Grange stepped up onto the stool to address his troops. He smiled at them benevolently. "Good afternoon, ladies and gentlemen. We are about to perform a play with few equals in a version without equal. We can thank Monsieur Oscar Wilde for that." Oscar bowed his head as the company applauded. "This is our first dress rehearsal," La Grange continued. "You will remember our usual rules, of course—definition, clarity, energy, attack—but today our principal concerns are the costumes and the scenery. I hear that we had an accident this morning: a weight fell from the flies. Take care this afternoon, ladies and gentlemen. Watch your step. By the end of the rehearsal, I want you to feel at ease in the clothes that you are wearing and at home in the setting that surrounds you." His eyes scanned the battlements and ramparts. He glanced towards the flies. "It's painted wood and canvas, brought in and out by ropes and winches: we know that. By five o'clock, however, it must seem to you to be the very stones of Elsinore." He paused. "Any questions?"

Carlos Branco lifted his helmet's visor. "This suit of armour stinks!"

As the laughter subsided, La Grange looked down at him. "That's as it should be. You've read the play. 'Something's rotten in the state of Denmark.'"

"This wig is absurd," said Bernard La Grange, holding the mop of golden curls up in the air for all to see.

"It's a family tradition," squawked Maman from her station at the edge of the wings.

"I won't wear it!" cried Bernard.

"Don't," said La Grange. He looked down at Bernard. "It doesn't suit your colour."

"But the La Grange tradition," protested Liselotte La Grange, her arms outstretched like an aged crone in a Greek tragedy.

"The tradition is dead, Maman," snapped La Grange. "Forget it." He turned back to the company. "Live in the moment, ladies and gentlemen. We start in five minutes."

As La Grange jumped off the stool, the crowd dispersed. Eighty men and women—leading actors, supporting players, spear carriers and sailors, stagehands, flymen, carpenters and firemen, seamstresses and wardrobe assistants—moved at once, in an assortment of directions, like ants purposefully, preordinately going about their business.

Oscar and I passed one another briefly outside La Grange's dressing room. "How are you?" I asked.

"Oscar is himself again," he answered, smiling.

"And Marais? How was the meeting?"

"Not easy. Marais sat behind his typewriting machine, hammering at the keys throughout. The typewriting machine, when played with expression, is not more annoying than the piano when played by a sister or near relation, but it *is* annoying. Marais, of course, does not hear the noise it makes."

"Did you stand your ground?"

"I did. And I doubled my money. This afternoon's performance will give me twice the pleasure it might otherwise have done."

I watched the dress rehearsal from the corner of the wings closest to La Grange's dressing room. Oscar watched it from the auditorium. The performance was flawed, of course: there were technical hitches, missed lines, and botched entrances; Maman and one or other of her helpers kept appearing onstage to sort out details of costume and accessory; the stage manager and his men took an eternity to change the scenes; there was no music; the lighting was perfunctory; the whole experience lasted nearly six hours instead of three. Nevertheless, it was already clear that this production of *Hamlet* was destined to be a memorable one, with extraordinary performances, especially from the twins.

Edmond La Grange told me once that a great actor must be in possession of "energy, an athletic voice, a well-graced manner, some unusually fascinating originality of temperament; vitality, certainly, and an ability to convey an impression of beauty or ugliness as the part demands, as well as authority and a sense of style." Bernard and Agnès La Grange were blessed with all the necessary gifts.

At the end of the performance, Edmond La Grange called the entire cast and company onto the stage to give us "notes" and to rehearse the curtain call. It was then that we realised that Ophelia was missing.

17

A Night to Remember

L a Grange appeared unconcerned at his daughter's disappearance. He sent the stage manager to search for her, but when the man returned after twenty minutes with nothing to report, the great actor simply shrugged his shoulders. "She has played Ophelia to perfection. She is exhausted—to be expected. She's not required for the rest of the day; let her be."

At a little after six o'clock, the *Hamlet* company was dismissed. At eight P.M., Edmond La Grange, Carlos Branco, Gabrielle de la Tourbillon, and a dozen of the other actors were back on stage for the evening perfor-mance of *L'Avare*.

"Regretfully, the house is not full, monsieur," said Rich-ard Marais, at a little before eight o'clock, putting his bald head briefly around La Grange's dressing-room door. "I have closed the gallery."

"Very good." La Grange nodded from his dressing table. "Don't tell anyone else."

When Marais had gone, La Grange looked up at me. "And don't you tell anyone, either."

"Of course not, sir—if you say so. But may I ask why?"

"Can't you guess? If the actors know the gallery is empty they no longer play to it. They simply turn their attention to the stalls. Their performances shrink. The theatre feels a smaller, emptier place. That's not what you want, especially with a comedy. You should always play comedy as though you have a house that's fit to burst."

I looked at the reflection of the great actor's face in his dressing-table looking glass. His thick white hair was streaked with henna; his forehead was deeply lined; the tip of his nose and his cheeks were daubed with rouge; his eyes, outlined in dark magenta, glistened. He looked old and ridiculous—and yet magnificent. "Do you never get tired, sir?" I asked.

"I have been *exhausted* for forty years!" he roared. He swung round on his stool and looked directly at me. "But I go on, *mon petit,* because I must. It's what I do. And to-night, who knows, there may be one person out there who has never seen me play before and may never see me play again. For them, I must be at my best." He got to his feet and held out his arms. I slipped Harpagon's money belt about his waist and secured it tightly. "Where's Oscar?" he asked.

"I'm not sure," I said. "Taking a glass of wine, I expect. I'm meeting him later. We are going to Madame Bernhardt's."

"Of course," he murmured, "Sarah's party."

"Will you be coming, sir?"

"No, *mon petit.* I'll not be coming. I'll be playing cards. It's what I do."

That evening, Sarah Bernhardt was giving one of her celebrated soirées at her town house on the rue Fortuny. I was invited because Oscar was asked, and as La Grange was planning, as usual, to play cards in his apartment with Garstrang, Branco, and the doctor, Oscar suggested that I take advantage of the opportunity. *"Carpe diem,"* he whispered to me when I saw him in the wings of the Théâtre La Grange at the conclusion of the *Hamlet* dress rehearsal. "Bring Gabrielle to Sarah's, Robert; then take her home to bed. She's had a long day. She'll be too exhausted to refuse you! I'll have a carriage waiting when the curtain falls."

At a little before eleven o'clock, I handed Gabrielle de la Tourbillon up into Oscar's promised coach and four. In the late February moonlight, dressed in a tight corsage of satin the colour of sapphires, above a matching skirt of gauze, with a string of diamonds about her neck and more diamonds in her hair, she looked like a princess in a Russian fairy tale. She was beautiful once more.

"I love you," I murmured as I helped her into the carriage.

"I'm glad." She laughed prettily. "A lady likes to be loved."

Oscar was already inside the carriage, tucked into the corner, in full evening dress, with a sprig of lilac blossom in his buttonhole. He was not alone. Seated immediately facing him, dressed, despite the time of year, simply in black trousers, white shirt, and unbuttoned waistcoat, was Bernard La Grange. His head was thrown back against the antimacassar and his eyes were half closed.

"I have been saluting a great Hamlet," said Oscar, as Gabrielle and I climbed aboard. "And now," he added, raising Gabrielle's white-gloved hand to his lips, "I can salute the nonpareil of Gertrudes, too." He looked between the actress and the actor and smiled at each in turn. "This afternoon you were mother and son—and utterly convincing. Now you could be sister and brother, you both look so young." Gabrielle seated herself next to Oscar and leant over to kiss him on the cheek.

I seated myself next to Bernard. "How is your sister?" I asked.

"I don't know," he replied, looking out of the carriage window. The cab lurched forward, up the side street and into the boulevard du Temple.

"Where is she?" Oscar asked. "Do you know?"

"I'm not sure." The young actor turned to look at Oscar and smiled wanly. "I'm not sure where I am myself."

"You are in a good place," said Oscar, "among friends."

The coach and four passed in front of the theatre and began to gather pace. I felt a sense of extraordinary exhilaration. I looked at Gabrielle de la Tourbillon, sitting facing me, her knees touching mine, and marvelled at the intensity of my desire for her. Perhaps she read my thoughts. "Is the décolletage too much?" she whispered. "After this afternoon, I wanted to restore your faith."

"You are perfection," I said softly.

She turned towards Oscar. "Are the diamonds too much?"

"In my experience," replied Oscar, tilting his head to one side and narrowing his eyes, "when it comes to diamonds and praise and anchovy toast, one can never have too much." She laughed. "Were they a present?" Oscar asked.

"Yes—from Edmond." She caught her breath as she spoke his name and leant over and pressed her fingers to my knee. "I hope you don't mind."

I smiled, shaking my head, and said nothing. But I thought, "Why should I mind? You, too, are a present from Edmond, are you not?"

Nervously, she touched the diamonds with her hand and I could see that she was suddenly embarrassed. She looked over to Bernard anxiously. "I know it was extravagant of your father. I hope you don't mind?"

"What Edmond La Grange does with his money is nothing to me. Why should I care?"

As Bernard spoke, Gabrielle began to blush. "I'm sorry," she said, her hands fluttering awkwardly. "I—"

"No," Bernard interrupted her. "Do not apologise. I should apologise." He did not look at her: he gazed steadily out of the carriage window. "Forgive me. I am rather confused at present. It is a difficult time."

I laid a reassuring hand on Gabrielle's knee as Oscar did his best to clear the air. "You will be the belle of the ball, my dear!"

"Will there be dancing?" I asked.

"Of course," said Oscar. "And fireworks. And fire-eating. And lions and lynx and leopards wandering about the drawing room."

"I hope there will be food," said Gabrielle, rallying. "I am so hungry."

"There will be food." Oscar laughed. "And drink."

"And laudanum," said Bernard quietly. "I need laudanum. I must sleep."

In the event, there were no fireworks at Madame Bernhardt's soirée and no fire-eating. Apart from her little dog, Hamlet III, there were no four-legged creatures to be seen.

There were a dozen penguins on parade in the fountain in the garden and, on the main staircase, a trio of live mermaids. Their long, swishing tails glistened and shimmered with scales made of mother-of-pearl; the golden tresses of their hair tumbled over their naked shoulders and bare breasts. "They are real," insisted Madame Bernhardt. "And very expensive. I bought them from a pirate in the Bay of Biscay. I had to pay extra because when they sing they sing in French!"

I had not been to a party like it before. Nor have I been to one like it since. Now that we live permanently in the harsh glare of the electric light, we have forgotten the fairy-tale quality of a world illuminated by flickering flame. Sarah's house that night was lit only by candles; by tiny candles, thousands of them, candles that dazzled, then spluttered and burnt out, to be replaced by thousands more. Madame Bernhardt had thirty servants to look after her guests during her soirée: six of them were engaged entirely in the business of replacing and lighting candles.

It is worth recollecting that at the turn of the 1880s the theatres of Paris were the most crowded and celebrated in the world. Half a million Parisians went to the theatre once a week; more than a million went once a month. The leading men and women of French theatre were fêted—and employed—from New Orleans to St. Petersburg. Sarah Bernhardt and Edmond La Grange were world-famous figures, and fabulously wealthy as a consequence. La Grange was richer than Bernhardt: she earned marginally more than he did, but while he guarded his fortune, she spent hers like a profligate.

That night in rue Fortuny no expense was spared. We were fed on fresh lobster, langoustines and potted shrimps, poached salmon and grilled halibut, Cancale oysters and Persian caviar—the evening had a nautical theme—and plied with every kind of wine and spirit you can imagine. As we arrived, Madame Bernhardt pressed glasses of Vin Mariani upon us.

"Pope Leo XIII introduced me to this," she declared. "The combination of herbs, alcohol, and cocaine is irresistible. There's no tonic like it. It's the most wonderful invigorator of the reproductive organs!"

"Is that what His Holiness told you?" asked Oscar.

Sarah shrieked with laughter. "No! That's what Jules Verne told me. He's in the orangery, looking at the moon. Do find him, Oscar. You'll adore him." She kissed Oscar fondly on each cheek and then, courteously, ran the back of her hand around my jaw. "And Oscar's friend," she murmured. She glanced down and saw that the fingers of my right hand were lightly touching Gabrielle's gauze skirt. Her eyes widened: she embraced her fellow actress. "You are wearing Edmond's diamonds, Gaby," she said. "They suit you; you have the neck for them. I was with him when he bought them, you know."

"I know," said Gabrielle, smiling. "Edmond told me."

"I assume he's not coming," said Sarah. She turned to Oscar and to me and explained: "Edmond is never to be seen at private parties. You have to *pay* to see the great Edmond La Grange. It's not a bad ruse." She looked about her. "Where is Bernard? I saw Bernard with you as you came in." She turned full circle and caught sight of him through the crowd, standing in the doorway to the dining

room. She laughed. "He's found Maurice and the China-man—already! He has a homing instinct for depravity. But he is beautiful. It can't be denied. A good deal more hand-some than his father ever was."

"He is the finest Hamlet I have seen," said Oscar.

"Really?" Madame Bernhardt furrowed her brow and finished her glass of Vin Mariani. "Can an Indian half-caste play the Prince of Denmark?"

"Can a woman?" asked Oscar, smiling.

Sarah shrieked with laughter once more and, raising her arms above her head and swaying her hips from side to side, like Salome dancing for King Herod, backed away from us and disappeared into the crowd. I looked over to the dining-room doorway. Bernard La Grange and Maurice Rollinat were no longer to be seen. The Chinese manser-vant was now offering a different pair of guests a choice between jade opium pipes and what appeared to be ready-filled syringes of cocaine.

"Freedom is the only law which genius knows," said Oscar, surveying the scene. He was, as ever, the tallest man in the room. "I shall seek out Jules Verne. You two should dance. I'm sure Sarah will have a ship's orchestra secreted somewhere."

In fact, Madame Bernhardt had engaged the services of a brilliant young Polish piano player whose repertoire appeared to know no bounds. Airs by Offenbach, waltzes by Chopin, "Oh, Dem Golden Slippers" by Oscar's friend Jimmy Bland—the wild-haired Paderewski was equal to them all. As he played, we danced and, as I held Gabrielle de la Tourbillon in my arms, I knew that all I wanted from this life was to possess her, not for a night but for eternity!

At about two in the morning, Oscar found us. "I think we should go, children—before the mermaids sing!"

"Where is Bernard?" asked Gabrielle.

"You will see him in the hallway," said Oscar. "You won't miss him, I promise you."

Oscar took Gabrielle by the hand and led us both through the throng. Every room was crowded; smoke filled the air; the heat was intense; every face glistened. As we pushed past them, poets talked while muses pretended to listen; actors boasted while actresses laughed; we glimpsed a girl from the chorus of the Opéra Comique (a friend of Gabrielle's) unbuttoning the trousers of the president of the Académie française; we saw two Negroes kissing. "Life and lust, low cunning and high intelligence," Oscar called over his shoulder. "Look around you. Sarah knows them all. Touch the garb of that old gentleman as we pass him, Robert. It's Ferdinand de Lesseps. You can tell your grandchildren that you were here!"

When we reached the hallway, we left the hubbub behind. Here a hush had fallen. The mermaids were no longer on the staircase. On the stairs, around the perimeter walls, and within the four doorways that opened onto the hall itself, guests stood in silence, side by side, some hand in hand, forming a human ring. Within the improvised arena, two men, stripped to their shirtsleeves, were fighting with rapiers. They were Bernard La Grange, and the pale-faced young artist, Jacques-Emile Blanche.

"This is madness!" whispered Gabrielle, squeezing my hand tightly.

"This is youth!" breathed Oscar.

Bernard was evidently the stronger fencer of the two.

With attack after attack, relentlessly he chased his opponent round in circles. Whenever Blanche, briefly, managed a counterattack, Bernard parried it effortlessly and followed through with a theatrical riposte.

"I can't bear this!" hissed Gabrielle. "Take me away, please." As she spoke, her words were drowned by a burst of gasps and cries from the circle of spectators as Jacques-Emile Blanche lunged forward in a sudden frenzy.

"A hit!" cried Bernard La Grange, spinning round on the spot. "A palpable hit!" He fell for a moment against a group of guests standing by the dining-room door and sprang back at once into the ring, holding his arms out wide to reveal his shirt torn and crimson.

"My God!" cried Gabrielle, letting go my hand. Around the room women screamed and men cheered.

"It's *wine*!" hissed Oscar. "Red wine—the boy's an actor. Remember who his father is."

One of the guests by the dining-room door held up his empty glass to prove Oscar's point as Bernard La Grange returned to the fight. Now, beneath his breath, we heard him spitting out the moves as he made them: "Attack, attack, *croisé, coulé*, cut. Attack, attack, parry, *prise de fer*."

"Come," said Oscar, pulling us around the perimeter of the ring, "let's get you home."

"Will he be all right?" asked Gabrielle, as Oscar helped her up into our waiting carriage.

Oscar laughed. "I think the heroin will see him through."

It was gone three when we reached the side street by the boulevard du Temple once more. The night air was cold though the yellow moon was bright. Gabrielle shivered as we stood together by the coach and four at the end of the alley leading to theatre's stage door. "What now, my dears?" asked Oscar, smiling as he looked between us.

"Good night, Oscar," said Gabrielle, holding up her face to be kissed. "Thank you for a memorable evening." She put her arm through mine and held me close.

Oscar chuckled. He was quite drunk. "I think a Lucky Strike is called for, don't you, Robert? I'll take a stroll up the street while you two decide what your sleeping arrangements are going to be." He walked away from us, up the cobbled roadway. I heard a match strike and saw the burst of flame as he lit his cigarette. He turned the corner into the boulevard. I pressed my lips against Gabrielle's. She opened her mouth and her tongue met mine. It was at that moment that we heard what sounded like a desperate cry for help.

I broke at once from Gabrielle's embrace and ran up the roadway, followed by our coachman. As I rounded the corner to the front of the theatre, I saw a figure lying splayed on his back in the gutter, beside the horses' water trough. It was Oscar. His head and torso were drenched with water, his white silk shirt was besmirched and torn. Kneeling down beside him, I took him up in my arms.

"Thank you, Robert," he croaked, gazing down at his ruined apparel with half-shut eyes. "With this style, I believe the mouth is worn slightly open."

I did not take Gabrielle to my room that night. I let her return to La Grange's apartment at the theatre while I helped Oscar into the coach and four and accompanied him back to his hotel on the quai Voltaire.

He was badly bruised and severely shaken, but not seriously hurt. His account of what had occurred was lucid and to the point. As he stood in front of the theatre, enjoying his cigarette, examining the poster for the forthcoming production of *Hamlet* and trying to discover his own name by moonlight, he had heard a sudden rush of footsteps behind him. Before he had had the opportunity to turn, a man with gloved hands—he was sure that it was a man—had taken a vicelike grip on his neck and pulled him back towards the horse trough, twisting him round and forcing his head and shoulders forward into the icy water. Had he been held there he would have drowned. He struggled; he managed to pull his head free; he called out; and suddenly he was released and fell back onto the ground as the footsteps ran away. He thought that he had heard a voice cry, *"Non!"* He had a feeling that the voice was familiar, but he could not be sure. It might have been my voice. I had certainly shouted out as I had come running around the building to his aid.

As I helped my friend to undress, I did my best to calm him. But he would not be pacified. "My mind is in turmoil, Robert. I have questions, but no answers. What is going on? Who is trying to kill me? And why? And are they, in truth, trying to kill me? Or are they simply trying to frighten me? And these brutal assaults on my unhappy person—are they connected in some way with poor Traquair's mysterious death? And what about that wretched dog found dead and buried in my luggage on board the SS *Bothnia*? Is the unlamented Marie Antoinette linked in some way to what has taken place tonight?"

I had no answers to offer him. Eventually, giving him a cup of whisky and warm water, I persuaded him to climb into bed. I left him there, exhausted, sipping his drink, smoking the last of his Lucky Strikes, and reading the *Life of St. Porphyry* by candlelight. I took the carriage back to my room on the rue de Beauce and lay on my bed, fully clothed, imagining myself, naked, in the arms of Gabrielle de la Tourbillon.

At a little after ten o'clock the following morning, I collected Oscar from his hotel. We were both expected at the Théâtre La Grange for the second *Hamlet* dress rehearsal. Oscar cannot have slept for more than five hours, but he appeared quite refreshed and positively proud of his bruises. When I arrived, I found him in the hotel foyer, dressed and groomed, standing by the looking glass, appraising the purple and orange abrasions on his cheeks. He had already been out to find a matching chrysanthemum for his buttonhole.

He greeted me, not with a "good morning" or with a word of thanks for my endeavours of the night before, but with a question about "The Murders in the Rue Morgue" by Edgar Allan Poe. "You've read the story, haven't you, Robert? Does Poe have his detective ponder the mystery of the apparently motiveless crime? I don't believe that he does. It seems my hero missed a trick."

I looked at my friend in bafflement. I could not think what to say. He had his preoccupations and I—having failed to spend the night with Gabrielle—had mine. Together, in silence, we took a cab to the theatre and there, at Oscar's insistence, before the start of the dress rehearsal, sought what he called "a brief formal audience" with Edmond La Grange.

It was eleven o'clock. The actor was in his dressing room preparing himself for Claudius. He did not reprove me for my late arrival. He welcomed Oscar cordially. He did not at first notice Oscar's bruises. "Come in, sit down, *cher collaborateur*. Yesterday we concentrated on the costumes and the scenery. Today our chief concern will be the text."

"But first," said Oscar, "I have concerns of a nonliterary nature to share with you. May I?"

"Of course," said La Grange, swivelling round on his stool, turning his back on his dressing table, folding his arms comfortably across his chest, and giving Oscar his full attention. "We are friends as well as colleagues. Speak."

Oscar spoke. He spoke well, concisely, without hyperbole. He shared his concerns with La Grange just as the night before he had shared them with me. And when he had finished speaking, La Grange responded, with equal economy and ease of manner, taking each of Oscar's questions in turn and dismissing it without ceremony. The weight that fell from the fly gallery was an accident—as simple as that. The assault on Oscar in the boulevard du Temple was the work of marauding footpads—Paris was thick with them, alas. Poor Traquair had either died by chance—escaping gas fumes killed hundreds of innocent men, women, and children every year—or, yes, possibly he had taken his own life because he was lonely so far from home. And as for the business of Maman's wretched poodle discovered dead and buried in Oscar's shipboard trunk—it was obviously a joke in the poorest taste perpetrated by one or more of the sailors of the SS *Bothnia:* La Grange had warned Oscar of the dangers of fraternising with the crew.

The second dress rehearsal of *Hamlet* was due to begin at twelve noon. At 11:30 A.M. the stage manager reported that Ophelia was still missing: Agnès La Grange had not yet arrived at the theatre. Maman had looked for her in her bedroom in the apartment: she was not there. La Grange appeared exasperated rather than concerned by the news: he gave instructions that Ophelia's understudy should ready herself. At twelve noon, however, just as the dress rehearsal was set to start, Agnès slipped in through the stage door. She came into the wings, smiling, blew a kiss of apology to her father, and ran to her dressing room to change.

At the end of the dress rehearsal, after La Grange had given his notes to the cast and company, Oscar announced that he was leaving Paris that evening. He had now seen two dress rehearsals: the performances were outstanding, the production powerful, there was nothing further he could do to help. With La Grange and Shakespeare at work, there really was no need for Oscar Wilde.

He did not linger. He bade a brief private farewell to La Grange in his dressing room; and to Eddie Garstrang, Carlos Branco, and Gabrielle de la Tourbillon, whom he chanced to see in the wings; he had a final word with Richard Marais about his financial arrangements; and then asked me to come with him to the Gare du Nord.

Oscar had decided that he was not welcome in Paris. Whatever the teaching of St. Porphyry in the matter of ignoring ill omens, Oscar had seen the gathering clouds: the gods were against him remaining in France. He was going home—well, not quite home—he was not going to Dublin but to England, to London, to the home counties, to spend some time with the dull and the settled: it's what his nerves required. Besides, he had a rendezvous arranged with a lunatic would-be assassin and he was anxious to fulfil his social obligations. Would I go to his hotel on the quai Voltaire and settle up for him and send on his things? And would I be sure to keep in touch, to let him know what his Paris friends were up to?

He left on the night train to London.

The next day he spent visiting his mother and his brother in London.

The day after, he went to Reading for the weekend. He went to stay with his friend George Palmer, the biscuit king.

At eleven A.M. on the following Monday—5 March 1883, the Monday morning of the first night of the new production of *Hamlet* at the Théâtre La Grange—Oscar Wilde entered the gates of Reading Gaol.

18

Reading Gaol

Oscar visited Reading Gaol at the invitation of his friend George Palmer, and in the company of Palmer and the prison chaplain, the Reverend Paul White. The Huntley & Palmers biscuit factory was located on land immediately adjacent to the gaol, and George Palmer was a member of the prison's Visiting Committee. According to Oscar, Palmer was "an Englishman with a hearty sense of humour and a fondness for Scottish country dancing, a businessman, a keen sportsman, and a Quaker, yet the best of company despite these terrible afflictions."

Oscar knew George Palmer well, admired and trusted him. Oscar's feelings towards the Reverend White were more equivocal. In his journal at the time, Oscar noted:

White is patently a virtuous man, which always arouses suspicion. There is something about him that is too good to be true. His spoken English is so perfect it makes me think it is not his mother tongue. I have a sense that I have met him before, but he denies it absolutely. When I press him on his past, he gives little away. He declines to talk about his life before he discovered Christ, explaining that then he walked in the valley of the shadow of death and has no desire to revisit it.

What had prompted George Palmer to suggest this particular Monday morning excursion was the arrival at Reading Gaol of what he termed "a celebrity inmate": the notorious Roderick Maclean. "What you are to aestheticism, Oscar, he is to assassination."

"Really?" replied Oscar, not altogether flattered by the comparison. "The man's a lunatic, is he not?"

"So it seems. As you know, he sent one of his verses to Queen Victoria, and when Her Majesty failed to show her appreciation he sought to avenge his wounded pride. He fired a gun at her at Windsor railway station. Charged with high treason, he was found "not guilty but insane." The sovereign was not amused. The law is being changed. In future, such offenders will be deemed "*guilty* but insane." He's at Reading on his way to the Broadmoor asylum. I don't know what state he'll be in, but at least you can see him and add him to your collection of curiosities."

"I shall be intrigued to meet him, George. Thank you. I am fascinated by those who have made their mark upon the world—in whatever way. I am in awe of those determined to fulfil their destiny—whatever the cost."

Oscar was intrigued to visit Reading Gaol in any event. He wondered whether or not—and, if so, to what degree—the experience would disturb him. The year before, he had made light of his visit to the penitentiary at Lincoln, Nebraska: he had since been surprised to find how frequentl he revisited the place in his dreams, and how often th dreams turned to nightmares. More recently, he had Charlotte Brontë's account of her visit to Newgate I at the time of the Great Exhibition of 1851, and ha himself haunted by Miss Brontë's description o

the hand of a young woman who had murdered her own child and was soon to be hanged.

In his journal Oscar noted the mixed emotions that the visit to Reading Gaol provoked in him:

I was appalled, but fascinated, too. Appalled by the ugliness of all that I saw; revolted by the squalor and the cruelty; the wretched food (filthy water, grey meat, and black potatoes was all their lunch); the so-called "separate" system by which the inmates are kept apart from one another, in complete silence, hooded and masked whenever they leave their cells; the dreary, debilitating drabness of their lives—nothing happens. There is no work, recreation, or occupation, except for those sentenced to "hard labour," whose lot is either to walk the treadmill, or break stones in the prison yard, or submit to "shot drill." This last involves the prisoner lifting a twenty-five-pound cannonball up to chest height, moving it three paces to the left or right, then putting it down. The task is repeated, hour after hour, at the supervising turnkey's discretion.

I was appalled by what I witnessed and fascinated by the way in which Palmer and White—both civilised men— did not appear to question the rightness of it all. I was surprised, also, to find that this ghastly place—this hell on earth—was a prison for women as well as men, and struck by the variety of ages, types, and nationalities among the inmates: near-gentlemen and outright vagabonds, petty thieves and murderers, Arabs and Irishmen, debtors and drunkards, children and old lags close to death. "Are they treated differently, the young and the old?" I asked. "Oh, yes," said the chaplain earnestly. We were standing in the

prison's central hall. He went to a large bare-board cup-board that was fixed against a wall nearby, beckoning me to follow. From his pocket, he produced a bundle of keys, selected one, unlocked and pulled open the cupboard doors. Lined up and pinioned against the back of the cup-board, like rifles in a gun cabinet, were a dozen scourges. "These are our cat-o'-nine-tails, a necessary evil if disci-pline's to be maintained. As you can see, some are larger, some are smaller. The smaller are the ones we use on males when they are between ten and sixteen years of age. The birch rod is fifteen inches long, rather than twenty-two. The length of the flail, from the end of the handle to the tip of the spray, is forty inches instead of forty-eight. The weight is nine ounces, not twelve." I marvelled at the cruel precision of these instruments.

The tour of the prison took two hours. The promised encounter with the curiosity that was Roderick Maclean was brief. The wretched man was incarcerated on B1 land-ing, in one of the "dark cells." The room was windowless and unlit. The turnkey who unbolted the door to admit the visitors handed the chaplain an oil lamp as they entered. By the yellow light of the lamp the prisoner was clearly vis-ible. He cowered at the far end of his metal bed, encased in a straitjacket.

"Is that necessary?" asked Oscar.

"He is insane," answered the chaplain. "He is a danger to himself as well as to others."

As Oscar and the Reverend White approached the man, Maclean flinched and shut his eyes against the light. "Do not be alarmed, sir," said Oscar.

"This is Mr. Oscar Wilde," said the chaplain.

The prisoner twisted his head round and opened his eyes. He gazed intently into Oscar's face. "The poet?" he asked, in a hoarse whisper. His voice was so much more refined than Oscar had expected. "Oscar Wilde, the poet?"

Oscar bowed towards the man.

Maclean struggled in his straitjacket, straining towards the light. He leant forward and held his head up towards Oscar. There was a Scottish lilt to his accent. "You have come to see me?" he whispered.

"I have," said Oscar. "I read the poem that you dedicated to Her Majesty. It was reproduced in the newspapers. It is a fine poem, Mr. Maclean. I would be proud to have written a poem of such feeling."

Maclean stared up at Oscar and tears tumbled from his eyes.

Oscar bowed once more and backed away from the bed towards the cell door. "I must go now," he said quietly. "Good day, Mr. Maclean. I am glad to have made your acquaintance. A fellow poet salutes you."

Oscar paused on the landing outside the madman's cell as, noisily, the turnkey locked the door. He said to George Palmer, "I am sorry that I was not able to shake his hand. Is the straitjacket strictly necessary?"

"The doctor says so," answered the Reverend White.

Oscar turned and looked into the chaplain's warm brown eyes. They were not the eyes of a cruel man. "Is there nothing good in this dreadful place?" he asked.

"We are going to the chapel now," said the clergyman. "That is my domain." He smiled. "And God's, of course. The chapel is a good place."

"We can only hope that the prisoners find some measure of consolation here," said George Palmer, when they reached the chapel.

"While reflecting on the error of their ways," added the chaplain, soberly. "The chapel is designed for that purpose."

The chapel was, in fact, designed like a small Greek amphitheatre, with row upon row of individual wooden stalls rising one above the other in tiers before a simple stone altar. The stalls, to Oscar, looked like upright, open coffins, each one just large enough to accommodate a grown man. Once a prisoner had entered his allotted stall, all other prisoners were blocked from view: the only human being visible was the chaplain.

The Reverend White stood on the steps of his altar, with George Palmer and Oscar on either side of him, surveying the scene. "And with him they crucify two thieves," murmured Oscar, "the one on his right hand, and the other on his left."

"Mark, chapter fifteen, verse twenty-seven," said the chaplain. "It is a favourite text of mine, as you may imagine."

"When you look out on your congregation," asked Oscar, "when you look into their eyes, Father, what do you see?"

"I don't look into their eyes," replied the clergyman. "I do not see their eyes. The men all wear caps like hoods to mask their faces. The women all wear thick veils."

"But that woman there," said Oscar. "She wears no veil."

Oscar's head was turned towards the right. He was

looking at the front row of the wooden stalls. Seated, motionless, in the end stall but one was a woman in a black dress. Her grey hair was pulled back and tied within a netted snood. She wore the shoulders of defeat, and held in her lap hands knotted with age and pain. Her dark face (as brown as the oak stall in which she sat) was grotesquely bloated; whether by tears or drink or disease, Oscar could not tell.

The chaplain started suddenly when he saw the wretched woman. "She's not a prisoner," he said.

"Is she a ghost?" asked Oscar.

The clergyman did not laugh. "She works here," he said dryly. "She cleans the chapel, when she's minded."

The woman's head had now turned in the direction of the three men standing before the altar, but it was at the chaplain that she stared. Her gaze was unflinching. Was it insolent and full of reproach? Or devoted and heavy with despair?

The chaplain called out to the woman angrily, *"Vai-te embora! Desaparece!"**

She neither moved nor looked away.

"What is her history?" asked Oscar. "She is not English."

"Her history is unknown. She has been here for many years." He shook his head wearily. "We keep her on as an act of charity."

George Palmer was studying his half-hunter. "We'd best be on our way, gentlemen. We must pay our respects to the governor."

They departed the chapel, leaving the old woman still

---

*"Go away! Get out!"

seated in her stall, and walked briskly and in silence to the governor's office. "We'll not stay long," muttered Palmer.

"You'll stay long enough for a cup of sweet tea and a nip of brandy," said the governor, swinging open his door and taking each of his visitors' right hands in both of his. He was loud, fat, squat, red-faced, and relentlessly genial. Oscar never caught his name, but in his journal dubbed him "Colonel Pickwick." He wore a military moustache and combined a military bearing with the twinkling bonhomie, good humour, and good heart that most English readers of Dickens find irresistible but which Oscar's Irish sensibility found somewhat irksome.

"Mr. Wilde, Mr. Wilde, Mr. Wilde," he repeated enthusiastically, not releasing Oscar from his grip as he dragged my friend across the room. "I hear that friend Maclean was not at his best for you this morning. I apologise. He had a turn. He had to be tethered. I know you're fellow poets—you'd have enjoyed a chin-wag. It wasn't to be, alas. But *nil desperandum*, as you scholars say. We have a famous man for you to meet all the same!"

The governor ungrasped Oscar and threw open a glass-fronted door that led from his office to an anteroom beyond. "Ha, ha!" he cried, as the door swung back to reveal the upright figure of a tall, thin, pale-faced old man with a shock of wiry white hair and piercing blue eyes. "If Pa killed Ma, who'd kill Pa? Marwood!"

Oscar recognised the well-worn joke and recognised the features of the elderly, upright man, also. He had seen portraits of William Marwood in the popular papers often enough. Mr. Marwood smiled and revealed an ungainly row of yellow, jagged teeth. He stepped towards Oscar and pressed a visiting card into his hand. Oscar glanced down at it:

WILLIAM MARWOOD PUBLIC EXECUTIONER,

Horncastle, Lincolnshire

Oscar and the executioner shook hands.

"Marwood and I are old friends," boomed Colonel Pickwick. "He looked after my boots in the old days. He was a cobbler before he took up hanging." The governor lifted his feet one by one to show off his shiny boots. "He was a fine cobbler, but he had a higher calling. How old were you when you became public hangman, Will?"

"Fifty-four," answered the executioner pleasantly. It was a thin voice and oddly high-pitched. "I've been doing it nine years now. Thinking about it all my life, of course."

"It's the 'thinking' what does it, Mr. Wilde," said Colonel Pickwick, "you know that." The governor puffed out his chest, twitched his moustache, and winked in William Marwood's direction. "I don't know how history will mark you down, Mr. Wilde, but Marwood's place is assured. He invented the 'long drop,' you know." He looked at his old friend with pride, reaching up to rest a hand on the executioner's shoulder. "Thanks to Marwood's ingenuity, the drop between the trapdoor and the point at which the rope tightens is as much as ten feet these days. It's a cleaner, sweeter business altogether. It's stopped all that twitching and jerking during the death throes. Horrible to witness at close quarters, as the padre will tell you."

There was a knock on the outer door. "Come!" called Colonel Pickwick. A young turnkey entered the office carrying a large tray bearing cups and saucers, a pot of tea, a jug of milk, a bottle of cheap brandy, and a large dish of ham sandwiches. "Excellent," growled the governor, rubbing his hands. "Gentlemen, tuck in," he instructed. He poured a generous dose of brandy into each of the teacups. "And drink up. It's a cold day."

The five men stood in a circle around the governor's desk. "This is a most unusual tea party," said Oscar, lifting a ham sandwich to his lips. "I'll not forget it."

"Which of us is the Mad Hatter?" asked Colonel Pickwick, with a wink and a hearty laugh. "I think Marwood has a slight look of the March Hare about him, don't you, Mr. Wilde?"

The public hangman appeared to take the observation as a compliment and raised his cup of tea and brandy in the governor's direction.

"The padre can be the Dormouse," continued Colonel Pickwick, warming to the theme, "but, damn and blast, we have no Alice!"

"There's a strange old lady that we met in the chapel," suggested Oscar.

Colonel Pickwick spluttered good-humouredly: "Dear me, no. She's too far gone even for Alice in Wonderland. She's as mad as Maclean. We only tolerate her at the padre's behest." He added a dash more brandy to Oscar's cup and then raised his own. "A toast, gentlemen. To our new friend, Mr. Wilde, and our old friend, Mr. Marwood— each an artist, in his way. Your good health."

The five men raised their teacups to one another. In the glass door leading to the governor's anteroom, Oscar saw a reflection of the group and smiled at its improbability: a poet, a prison governor, a hangman, a priest, and a biscuit manufacturer, all standing in a ring. In later years, he frequently reflected that he had never drunk a toast with so motley a crew.

"There's an extra toast for Marwood," announced the governor, reaching down to the table for the brandy bottle. "He's retiring this year."

"My eye's not what it was," said Mr. Marwood, by way of explanation. "And my hand's not as steady." He held up a tremulous hand to prove the point.

Colonel Pickwick laughed. "He can afford to. He gets twenty pounds a year from the crown plus ten pounds a drop. He's a rich man."

"Rich in memories, certainly," said Marwood seriously. "I've never done it for the money."

"How many have you hanged in your time, my friend?" asked the governor.

"One hundred and sixty-four men and eight women over nine years, but I'm not retiring until the summer. I'm expecting a busy spring."

"Well, here's to it, William," said the governor, emptying the remains of the brandy bottle into the cups held out before him.

Oscar was surprised to find how much he liked these men. Colonel Pickwick was too loud for comfort, but his openness and easy hospitality were endearing. Oscar was particularly taken with Marwood and his devotion to his craft. When Oscar told him that he was newly returned from France, Marwood began an interesting discourse on the benefits of the noose over the guillotine, and a fascinating account of the "families" of executioners in both countries. "When I retire," he told Oscar, "I plan to write a history of execution and I believe that the French chapters will be the most interesting. Heritage is everything to a Frenchman." He was an especial admirer of the six generations of the Sanson family. "The French Revolution was their heyday, of course. During the five hundred and three days of the Terror, the Sansons executed a total of two thousand three hundred and eighteen men, women, and children—and not a botched head among them. Did you know that, Mr. Wilde?"

"I did not," said Oscar, "but now that I do, I'll not forget it."

19

The First Night

I n Paris, that same Monday night, the La Grange company's new production of *Hamlet* opened to great acclaim.

Le tout Paris was there. Henri-Clément Sanson and his nephew Charles, the last of the celebrated Sanson line, were seated in the stalls. The first minister of France was in the royal box. Anatole France was in a box as well, looking very young. Emile Zola was in the stalls, looking very old. I observed them from backstage via a spy hole cut for the purpose into the proscenium arch. Sarah Bernhardt was among the last to take her place in the packed auditorium: she arrived with the young artist Jacques-Emile Blanche as her escort. They sat in the centre of the stalls, in the same row as Jean Mounet-Sully, reckoned by Bernhardt to have been the best Hamlet of her time, alongside the composer Charles Gounod, and the grey-faced poet Maurice Rollinat. It was Rollinat, the laureate of mortality, who thought to bring the Sansons with him. Henri-Clément Sanson looked to be near death.

"I thought he *was* dead!" exclaimed Edmond La Grange when I reported the aged executioner's presence to the great actor a few minutes before the curtain was due to rise. "He came to see my Hamlet forty years ago and he was ancient then. He's a drunkard and a bugger, but he loves the theatre."

"I know," I said. "I have met him."

"The Sansons were to the guillotine what the La Granges have been to the drama—but it's over now."

"His nephew is with him, I believe."

"If you believe that . . . ," said La Grange, and he let the words trail away. He got to his feet and threw back his head and shoulders. He scanned his own reflection in the looking glass as though he were a connoisseur inspecting an old master. "Claudius is in command," he said. "He has the character to be a king." He turned to me and held out his arms while I fastened a leather and gold belt around his waist. "Poor, pathetic Henri-Clément lacked the cutting edge—not helpful when you're the public executioner. He couldn't cope with the blood. Brought him out in a rash. He turned to drink and boys. After eighteen performances—just eighteen executions—he abandoned his calling. Hocked the guillotine to pay off his gambling debts! It'd make a great comedy if it weren't so tragic."

The little carriage clock that stood on the dressing-room sideboard struck the hour. "Elsinore calls," announced La Grange, inspecting his reflection in the cheval mirror one final time. "I was right not to wear a beard." As he reached for the door, anticipating the stage manager's knock, he looked at me curiously. "How on earth did you come to meet Sanson?" he asked.

I hesitated. "I met him with your son—and Maurice Rollinat," I said. "At Madame Bernhardt's."

Edmond La Grange shook his head. "Sarah keeps the strangest company." He pulled open the dressing-room door. "But she is a great artist and a generous woman. She will cheer tonight."

"All Paris will cheer," I said.

"Perhaps. Unless the last of the Sansons chooses to die in the middle of the second act. That's all we need." He laughed as he made his way into the darkened wings. "Who'd be an actor?"

"I don't think anyone will die tonight."

"I wouldn't be so sure about that, *mon petit,*" he whispered. "Death is everywhere. As you'll hear Gertrude say within the hour, 'All that lives must die, passing through nature to eternity.'"

There were no deaths at the Théâtre La Grange that night. Indeed, it was a night when a legend was born: the legend of "the perfect *Hamlet.*"

The phrase was Sarah Bernhardt's. She used it in her impromptu speech, delivered from the battlements of Elsinore Castle, during the long onstage party that followed the triumphant first performance. She declared that there had been, and would yet be, interpretations of the role of Hamlet that rivalled that of young Bernard La Grange—she singled out Jean Mounet-Sully standing somewhat sulkily in the crowd—but she doubted that there had ever been, or would ever be, a production in which all the principal roles were played at such a pitch and which revealed so completely the passion, pain, poetry, heart-ache, heroism, and truth of the play. Bernhardt—who had played Ophelia herself and had a healthy respect for her own achievements—proclaimed that Agnès La Grange's interpretation of the role surpassed even her own. "I have never known madness played with such pitiful intensity. The gods will weep for this Ophelia!"

According to Madame Bernhardt, her dear friend Edmond's production was "the culmination of a great tradition, the flowering of the glory of the family La Grange. And, ladies and gentlemen, think of it: in years to come people will speak of this night—the night of the perfect *Hamlet*—and you will say, with a full heart and tears welling in your eyes, 'I was there!'" Through the cheering and applause, as Jacques-Emile Blanche and Charles Gounod stepped forward to help her from the battlements, Sarah added that she herself planned to use the new and peerless La Grange/Oscar Wilde translation of the play when, in due course, the time was right for her to essay the title role.

Bernhardt's speech eclipsed that of Edmond La Grange, who had spoken just before her, but, to my surprise, the great actor did not seem to mind. When he stood to address the company, his daughter, Agnès, sat at his feet, her arms held tight around him. He looked down at her while he spoke and gently caressed her hair. He said what was expected of him—he praised his colleagues and he thanked his friends—but he said it perfunctorily, without feeling. He spoke as if he were in another place at another time. I felt I knew the reason why. The moment that the curtain calls had come to an end—and they were orchestrated by La Grange: it was his signal to the stage manager that set each one in train—he had swept immediately off the stage. In the wings I handed him his towel and a glass of iced champagne. He drank it in a single gulp, and in the dressing room, alone, as I undressed him and sponged him down and dried and dressed him again, he demanded more champagne. He drank glass after glass, without pause.

"He is drunk," muttered Carlos Branco, chuckling, as La Grange began his speech.

"It's allowed," said Dr. Ferrand.

I was standing behind the two men. "Can I get you some champagne?" I volunteered.

Carlos Branco turned to me, smiling, and whispered, "Unlike your master, I do not need to drink tonight. I am happier than I have ever been."

It was a night for happiness. Even Maman seemed relatively content. She grumbled that Claudius had looked quite wrong without a beard and that Gertrude had been too pale to be this Hamlet's mother, but, all in all, she conceded that the Théâtre La Grange had a triumph on its hands. "We've known a few," she snapped.

When the speeches were done, the gas lamps were turned low; food and wine were served and the dancing began. The *chef d'orchestre* played the fiddle while Laertes played the accordion, and the Princesse de Lamballe, Maman's poodle, ran yelping through the throng. Bernard La Grange, the acknowledged hero of the night, took centre stage and danced like a dervish, mostly on his own, but now and then, when the music slowed, taking one of the assorted gentlewomen in his arms (it was Ophelia's understudy, a green-eyed girl with soft red hair), holding her so close to him that she looked to be in danger of suffocation. Agnès La Grange danced with Jacques-Emile Blanche; Carlos Branco danced with Sarah Bernhardt; and the ancient executioner, Henri-Clément Sanson, attempted to dance with his nephew, until both men stumbled and fell over, whereupon Maurice Rollinat, laughing and cursing, took them home.

I danced with Gabrielle de la Tourbillon. Liselotte La Grange stood with Richard Marais at the edge of the crowd, watching us in the half-light. "Do you see that?" she asked contemptuously. "Gertrude with my son's dresser. It's disgusting." She spat out the words so that we should hear her.

"Ignore Maman," whispered Gabrielle, her lips touching my ear. "She's old and jealous."

I held Gabrielle's body close to mine and told her that her performance that night had overwhelmed me utterly and that I loved her very much. She smiled and kissed my ear again and told me that she had the key to the rue de la Pierre Levée. I told her that I would prefer her to come to my room in the rue de Beauce. She whispered that she would.

It was gone one o'clock when we left the theatre. Sarah Bernhardt and her court had long since departed. Richard Marais had escorted Maman and the Princesse de Lamballe to their quarters. As, hand in hand, Gabrielle and I made to leave, we saw Agnès leading her father by the hand towards his dressing room. As they reached the edge of the wings, he stumbled and fell forward. Dr. Ferrand and Eddie Garstrang, who were nearby, ran to steady him. Garstrang caught sight of us leaving and, shrugging his shoulders, laughed in our direction—without malice.

As we slipped into the night, Hamlet was still holding Ophelia's understudy in his arms: they were no longer dancing, but standing together, intertwined, wrapped in the black velvet drapes at the back of the stage, making love. Old Polonius appeared to have carnality in mind as well: Carlos Branco was now dancing with another of the gentlewomen (Gertrude's understudy). He had pulled down her lace décolleté to reveal her breasts. No one noticed. Or, if they did, no one cared. This was the spring of 1883: this was the night of the perfect *Hamlet:* this was the Paris of *"la décadence."*

My memory of that night with Gabrielle de la Tourbillon in the rue de Beauce is unfortunately vague. I was young and I had never before shared a bed with a woman who was not a prostitute. The details of the experience should be etched on my memory, and garlanded with tangled sunbeams of gold, as Oscar might say. Alas, they are not. It transpired that, during the party, while the speeches were being made, Bernard La Grange and Maurice Rollinat, "to be amusing," had adulterated the wine with laudanum.

My recollection of the days that followed is much clearer.

On the afternoon of the day after the triumphant opening night, the company met onstage at two o'clock to be given the producer's "notes." Edmond La Grange was himself again. He began by congratulating his troops on their achievement thus far and reading out a telegram he had received from Oscar the night before:

NOT FAILURE BUT LOW AIM IS CRIME

AIM HIGHER THAN YOU THINK YOU DARE

AND GLORY WILL BE YOURS

La Grange endorsed Oscar's exhortation and then went through the play, scene by scene, raising specific issues of concern. The only member of the company who failed to appear for the meeting was Agnès La Grange. La Grange said it hardly mattered. Her performance was perfection. She was perfection.

When evening came and the second performance was due to begin and there was still no sign of Agnès, La Grange continued to take her absence in his stride. He instructed the stage manager to tell the understudy to ready herself, but predicted that, though late, which was reprehensible, Agnès would arrive at the theatre in time for her first entrance.

She did not do so. In her place, the green-eyed understudy went on.

The performance passed off well enough. I watched it from the wings: it lacked the fire of the first night and, backstage, there was an unspoken anxiety in the air, but, as yet, no sense of panic. Carlos Branco, as Polonius, Ophelia's father, was the only player whose performance was obviously thrown off balance. The girl herself rose to the occasion. Understandably, Bernard La Grange, as Hamlet, was more physically engaged with her than he was with his own sister. And when the curtain fell, the audience stood in their seats and cheered, apparently unaware that anything untoward had occurred. As Richard Marais remarked, "One mad girl with straw in her hair is much like another."

The stage manager, standing with Marais and Maman, watching in the wings, laughed. "Except that one is half Indian and the other has red hair."

Liselotte La Grange snorted, "And one is a La Grange and the other is not."

On Wednesday there was still no sign of Agnès. Edmond La Grange sent Garstrang and Marais and the doctor off in search of her. He wouldn't call in the police—not yet. Scandal would be bad for business. The audience that evening was simply told that Mademoiselle La Grange was indisposed.

On Thursday morning, I was in La Grange's dressing room, alone, preparing his costumes for the evening. I had just read two or three of the wonderful reviews from the first night that had begun to appear in the Paris papers. Sarah Bernhardt's phrase—"the perfect *Hamlet*"—was repeated in each of them. I was thinking that perhaps that morning I should send a wire to London to bring Oscar up to date with the news of Agnès's mysterious disappearance, when the door of La Grange's dressing room opened.

"Oscar, by all that's . . . What are you doing here?"

"I've come back—and for a reason."

"What reason?"

"I'm not sure that I know myself."

"You've heard the news?"

"From the stage doorman, just now, yes."

Oscar came into the room. He looked so well—like a cross between a Georgian dandy and a Roman senator. I could tell that he felt well because as he passed the cheval mirror he glanced at his reflection in the glass. "What has happened, Robert?" he asked. "Tell me everything."

But before I could answer my friend, he spun round on the spot. He had seen Edmond La Grange coming to the door behind him. He pulled off his purple glove and held out his hand. *"Cher maître!"* he said.

"Cher collaborateur!" exclaimed La Grange.

Just then, at the very moment when the two men were about to embrace, there was a sudden, dreadful noise—a woman's scream, followed by cries of anguish and a man's voice shouting. The furore was coming from somewhere on the stage.

Together we rushed out of the dressing room and into the darkened wings. Through the gloom we followed the frantic cries to the very back of the stage, beyond the battlements and the black drapes, to an area where the scenery was stored. There, behind the backcloth painted with the night sky of Elsinore, we found half a dozen people standing, frozen, in grotesque postures, their arms raised above their heads, like marionettes hanging in a toyshop window. Carlos Branco's face was contorted with grief. Richard Marais was holding up a paraffin lamp. He held it high over the bier that was used in the play to carry Ophelia's body to her grave. A stagehand was shouting hysterically. A girl from the wardrobe was alternately screaming and sobbing. Laid out on the bier was the headless body of Agnès La Grange.

20

Passy

Except, of course, that it wasn't.

La Grange saw that at once. He turned on the stagehand and the wardrobe girl, and Marais and Branco, and told them how stupid they were. "How infinitely stupid."

"Are you blind as well as deaf?" he demanded, angrily wrenching the paraffin lamp out of Marais's hands and holding it low over the body on the bier.

This was not Agnès. This was a waxwork. This was the waxwork of Ophelia's body, supplied to the Théâtre La Grange by the celebrated Musée Grévin. It was the waxwork of the drowned Ophelia used in the production every night in the graveyard scene. The head of the dead Ophelia—modelled from life on the head of Agnès La Grange—was missing for a reason. It was missing because it had been removed that morning, on La Grange's instructions, to be taken away to the workshops of the Musée Grévin so that a second head could be sculpted to look like the head of the understudy.

"Agnès has black hair and dark skin," said La Grange coldly. "Her understudy has red hair and pale skin. You may not have noticed this, gentlemen, but I rather think that the audience will." He held up one of the waxwork's arms. "You see," he added, "they have removed her hands as well."

He thrust the lamp back towards Richard Marais and turned away contemptuously. He fumbled with the black drapes as he tried to find his way back onto the stage. "Give me some light!" he roared in the darkness. "Away!"

Oscar and I followed him back to his dressing room. On his dressing table were the newspapers carrying the reviews of the production. He saw them and his mood changed. He chuckled. He lifted up the bundle of papers and tucked it under his arm. "My apologies, gentlemen. An uncalled-for outburst. I'm surrounded by incompetents and imbeciles, as you can see. Let's find a drink and talk."

We caught a cab on the boulevard du Temple and, as we crossed the busy place de la République, the old actor-manager divided up the papers between us. "Let us read our reviews, Oscar," he said.

"They are good," I said. "They are excellent. 'The perfect *Hamlet*.'"

"All critics can be bought," murmured Oscar, smoothing out the newspaper on his knee. He smiled at La Grange. "Judging by their appearance, they can't be very expensive."

When we arrived at the rue de la Pierre Levée, I was disconcerted to find that the door to the warehouse leading to La Grange's love nest was opened to us by Eddie Garstrang. He was carrying a box of bottles: dead ones, the debris of the night. He looked at me, bright eyed, and laughed. "Don't worry. I am alone."

"And he's not been with Gabrielle," said La Grange. "That I know."

The old actor took the door key from Garstrang and put it in his pocket. He laid a hand gently on my shoulder. "You will learn to be less jealous as the years go by."

Garstrang went on his way, whistling for a moment, then calling over his shoulder, "I'll be at the theatre, boss, if you need me."

"He's very dapper," said Oscar, watching him depart.

"Is that what you call it?" grunted La Grange, leading the way up the steep wooden steps out of the workshop to the floor above.

"Given that he's an American," explained Oscar, breathing more heavily as he climbed, "and a sharpshooter." We had reached the loft. It was awash with hazy morning sunlight. "Do you keep him busy?" asked Oscar.

"Not very. Marais does all the serious paperwork. Garstrang sends 'thank you' letters and corresponds with my admirers. But he plays a wonderful game of cards." La Grange held out his arms, inviting us to take our pick of the divans and ottomans on offer. "Of course, he loses all the time, but you must remember that he's playing with me. And I'm very good."

"And Garstrang's very eager to please," added Oscar, grinning and falling back onto a plum-coloured sofa. He spread his fingers and felt the texture of the velvet cushions at his side. "It is deliciously comfortable here." He sighed. He looked towards the marble head of Epicurus standing on the sideboard. "Your master would be proud of you."

La Grange found glasses and offered us absinthe,

brandy, or champagne. "Champagne, if you please," said Oscar. "We must toast 'the perfect *Hamlet*.'"

La Grange poured us our drinks. He did not take a glass himself. He never drank before a performance. "I have only three rules in my life," he said, seating himself on the divan immediately opposite Oscar, "and I've long since forgotten the other two." Oscar laughed. La Grange leant forward and offered his guest a Turkish cigarette. "What is the first rule of life for you, Oscar?" he asked.

Oscar took the cigarette and rolled it gently between his fingers before putting it lightly between his lips. "There is no good in arguing with the inevitable," he said solemnly. "The only argument available with an east wind is to put on your overcoat."

"That's wonderful, Oscar!" I exclaimed, stepping forward to light his cigarette.

"I know," he purred, cupping his palms around the flickering match flame.

"I've not heard it before."

"It's new. But, alas, not mine. It first fell from the lips of the great James Russell Lowell—poet, philosopher, ambassador, friend. I saw him in London, with George Palmer and Paul White. We dined. We drank. He talked. I scribbled." With his tongue, deftly, Oscar moved the Turkish cigarette from one side of his mouth to the other, while with both hands he felt inside his coat for his notebook. He found it—a small, slim book with a snakeskin binding—and flicked it open. "Listen. 'What men prize most is a privilege, even if it be that of chief mourner at a funeral.' Isn't that delicious?" He drew slowly on his cigarette. "And how about this? 'The greatest homage we can pay to truth is to use it.'" He looked up, beaming, and saw that Edmond La Grange was no longer seated opposite him. The old actor had got to his feet and wandered over to the vast window that overlooked the rooftops of north Paris. Oscar closed his notebook and slipped it back into his coat pocket. "Where is Agnès?" he asked. "Is she safe?"

"I do not know," answered La Grange, still gazing out of the window. "She has done this before—disappeared, I mean."

"For how long?" asked Oscar, shifting forward on the sofa.

"A day—a day and a night, at most. But she has never missed a performance before. That's unlike her. I am concerned." He turned back into the room and looked at Oscar directly. "You know that her mother, Alys Lenoir, took her own life. I fear for the children. Were they born with a self-destructive element to their natures?"

"Will you turn to the police?" asked Oscar.

"Yes," replied La Grange simply. "Maman does not want it, but I will. If she has not returned of her own accord by Sunday, I will go to the police. Meanwhile, we are looking for her. Dr. Ferrand is looking for her. Marais is looking for her."

"Marais is not to be trusted," said Oscar quickly.

La Grange laughed. "In this, he is. In other matters, not, perhaps." The old actor lifted his hands to his weathered face and pressed his heavy fingers against his eyes. He let out a long, deep breath and laughed again, more softly. "Marais is my business manager, and he has been cheating me for years. I have known it almost from the start. Please don't tell him that you know I know. It is the fear of discovery that keeps him by my side. He serves his purpose. I am content to share my money with Richard Marais; just as I am prepared to share my mistress with my young dresser here. It is my way."

We left Edmond La Grange alone in the rue de la Pierre Levée.

"A great man is made up of qualities that meet or make great occasions," said Oscar reflectively, as he pulled shut the warehouse door behind us. "Do you think La Grange is a great man, Robert?"

"He is certainly a great actor."

Oscar chuckled.

We walked together, arm in arm, up the cobbled street towards the Canal Saint-Martin. Oscar, I noticed, had an unaccustomed spring in his stride.

"You're very buoyant this morning," I remarked.

"I haven't slept," he replied. "I have the energy of the utterly exhausted! I came on the night train and the English Channel was very French last night."

I laughed. "You mean, restless, rough, and rude?"

He smiled down at me. "Something like that, Robert, but I think the joke works better if you don't explain it."

"You *are* on form," I said.

"The game's afoot," he answered. "There's a tide in the affairs of men; I'm exhilarated. I'm beginning to see through the glass less darkly."

"I'm confused. I thought that you'd gone to London because you felt there had been two attempts on your life and you were no longer welcome here. You are now of a different opinion?"

"The foolish and the dead alone never change their opinion," he declared, pulling out the snakeskin notebook from his coat pocket and brandishing it triumphantly before me. "Russell Lowell has a gem for all occasions!" He unhooked his arm from mine and put it around my shoulder. "I think perhaps that I am not in so much danger now," he said, more calmly. "I think, too, that I can fulfil my obligation to poor Washington Traquair better here than in London. He was murdered, Robert, and I will find out by whom."

We had reached the cab rank in the place de la République. We climbed aboard a two-wheeler and set off, first to my room in rue de Beauce to collect Oscar's bags, and then to the quai Voltaire, to reclaim a room for Oscar at his hotel. As we travelled, Oscar made me recount all that had occurred while he had been away. "Omit no detail, Robert. Who was with whom and when and where—and how did they appear to you. Tell me all that you saw. Tell me everything. You are a poet and the great-grandson of a laureate." He tapped his snakeskin notebook with his forefinger. "'The eye is the notebook of the poet,' we are told."

I told him all that I could recall. (I told him, too, that it was not mere coyness that prevented me from telling more of my night with Gabrielle de la Tourbillon.) He listened intently. He asked me to repeat certain details, sniffing or growling to suggest interest or surprise.

"Bravo!" he murmured, when I had concluded my narrative. "You have earned your lunch. You've painted the landscape with the eye of a Corot."

I laughed. "A little too impressionistic for your liking?"

"Far from it. Corot's eye was crystal clear. He was

classically trained. He lived here on the quai Voltaire, you know. That must be why I thought of him. Yesterday afternoon, at Victoria, I suddenly realised that what the Impressionists give to Paris, *fog* gives to London!"

"You are on form, my friend," I said.

While our two-wheeler waited outside the hotel, Oscar ordered us the simplest lunch (bread, cheese, a tomato-and-herb omelette, and a bottle of red Rhône wine) and gave me his account of his adventures in London and Reading. Customarily, Oscar was a slow eater and a leisurely conversationalist. Not on this occasion. He ate and drank and talked with almost feverish rapidity. The moment the meal was done, he threw down his napkin and got to his feet. "No time for lamentation or for coffee now," he said. "Our carriage awaits. We must be about our business. We must find Agnès La Grange."

"Do you know where she is?" I asked, amazed, hurrying after him into the street.

"I believe I do."

He ordered the cab to take us to Passy, on the western edge of the city.

Once upon a time, Passy had been a picturesque fairy-tale village, comprising a church, a small château, and a handful of stone houses set on a rocky hillside by the Seine. Now it was growing into a bustling, sophisticated Parisian suburb. I reminded Oscar that I knew it because it was where Balzac had lived and written some of his finest work. When I had first come to Paris, I had gone on a pilgrimage to see the great writer's home.

"Ah, yes," said Oscar, smiling. "Balzac, your hero. He was a most remarkable combination of the artistic temperament with the scientific spirit. He would have made a good detective. We are not visiting his house today, however, Robert. We are calling at the château next door—l'Hôtel de Lamballe, once the home of Queen Marie Antoinette's unfortunate friend the Princesse de Lamballe, after whom Maman La Grange has named her poodle. It now houses the clinic founded and run by the father and grandfather of our young friend Jacques-Emile Blanche. I believe that this is where Agnès La Grange has taken refuge."

"Among the lost and the lunatic?"

"And the illustrious," added Oscar. "The Doctors Blanche attract a very superior type of patient. This is not Reading Gaol: the patients here come voluntarily. Delacroix, Degas, Dumas, Berlioz—they've all sought sanctuary here. The Blanches understand the artistic temperament. Apparently, Gérard de Nerval was allowed to bring his pet lobster with him."

As we came up the hill towards Passy and our cab turned left through the high wrought-iron gates into the grounds of the clinic, another carriage, a closed four-wheeler, was coming out. "Did you see who that was?" asked Oscar, peering out of our cab's rear window.

"No. Who was it?"

He shook his head. "Perhaps I was mistaken."

At first encounter, the celebrated clinic of the Doctors Blanche offered a disturbing mixture of the serene and the macabre: a beautiful eighteenth-century house, flooded with sunshine, filled with freshly cut flowers, and, within it, haunted figures, mostly cowed and shuffling, wandering alone along high-ceilinged corridors. We were greeted in the marbled entrance hall by a pale young man, with sunken cheeks and bloodshot eyes, who sat at a Louis XV desk beneath an ornate Venetian chandelier, with a hypodermic syringe resting in a kidney-shaped enamel bowl at his side. He was Dr. Blanche's secretary, he assured us.

He was also a patient, he explained, as he escorted us through a series of huge and handsome reception rooms towards the doctor's study. "We're all given work to do here. It is part of the treatment." He looked Oscar up and down as we walked. "I expect the housekeeper will find something to suit you. They're always short of people in the laundry."

When we reached the last of the interconnecting reception rooms (it was a music room: Oscar was disappointed not to recognise the elderly gentleman seated at the piano), the young man directed us to the far corner and led us up a shallow flight of steps to a pair of closed double doors. He knocked on the doors briskly and, without waiting for an answer, pushed them open for us, stepping back to let us through. "I will see you at dinner," he said, retreating. "It's jugged hare tonight."

Oscar led the way into the doctor's study: it was a perfect country gentleman's library, with green-painted wood panelling between walnut bookshelves, and a broad bay window opening out onto the garden whose lawns ran down to the river's edge.

"Yes," said Dr. Blanche. "It is the library of your dreams. I know what you're thinking, Mr. Wilde. That is my business."

"And you know my name!" exclaimed Oscar.

"And Mr. Sherard's, too," said the doctor, stepping

forward from behind his desk and taking us each by the hand. "My son has told me much about you both. He values your friendship greatly. It is a pleasure to meet you."

It was a pleasure to meet him, certainly. Emile Blanche was one of the most naturally charming men I have met. I liked him the moment I set eyes on him. I trusted him. Beyond a pair of round wire-rimmed reading spectacles and a maroon-coloured velvet skullcap, he was not especially striking in appearance—he was in his mid-fifties, I suppose, conservatively dressed, clean shaven, of middling height and build—but his manner, gentle and good-humoured, courteous and inquisitive, was immediately endearing. Behind his glasses, his beady eyes sparkled. He had an upturned mouth that revealed neat, gleaming white teeth each time he smiled.

"What can I do for you?" he asked, indicating a pair of upright chairs by his desk for us to sit upon. "Apart from offer you a glass of Madeira. It's medicinal. I'm a doctor. You can't refuse."

He went to a cabinet by the window and poured us each a glass of wine. "This is the colour of old gold, is it not?" he said to me as he gave me my glass. "Jacques-Emile tells me that you call white wine yellow wine. He is a great admirer of yours."

"And we are of his," said Oscar emphatically.

"And of yours, of course," added Dr. Blanche, handing Oscar his Madeira. "He is painting a young lady's portrait at the moment and he has given her a copy of your poems to hold in her hands. He says that that way he can be sure there will be poetry in the painting, come what may."

Oscar inclined his head to acknowledge the compliment.

"Is the portrait of Agnès La Grange, by any chance?" he asked.

"No," replied the doctor, raising his glass towards us both in a silent toast, "but Jacques-Emile is indeed painting Agnès. She is a beautiful girl. Exquisite. She is staying here at the moment. Jacques-Emile brought her. With her physician's approval, of course. Dr. Ferrand lives here in Passy. He is a fine doctor and a good man. Agnès was eager to come to us: to get away from the theatre, to get away from her troubles. She is troubled, poor child. She is in love with her father."

"With Edmond La Grange?"

"Yes. He was here a moment ago. You've only just missed him. He comes to see her every day. He is very concerned for her." Dr. Blanche looked anxiously at our puzzled faces. "But you knew all this, surely?" He set down his wine-glass on the desk.

"No," said Oscar quietly, "we did not know."

Dr. Blanche looked to me. "I thought that Jacques-Emile had told you."

"No," I said.

The doctor sighed and removed his spectacles. His eyelids flickered. He took a handkerchief from his coat pocket and polished his glasses. "I have spoken out of turn," he said. "I assumed that you knew. I apologise." He replaced his spectacles.

"No harm is done," said Oscar. "We are friends of Agnès. And of her father."

"I know," said Dr. Blanche, picking up his glass of Madeira once more. "Jacques-Emile has told me."

Oscar leant forward in his chair. "You say that Edmond

La Grange was here just now . . . ," he began tentatively.

"Visiting Agnès," I added. Oscar glanced at me. I could see that I had spoken out of turn.

"Don't misunderstand me, gentlemen," said the doctor quickly. "Monsieur La Grange loves Agnès deeply, but as a father should love a daughter." He looked between us and smiled reassuringly. "Her love for him is more complicated—that is all. It's her age. It's the fact that she has had no mother. It's her life in the theatre. It's playing the role of Ophelia. It's all sorts of things. I am not unduly worried. She'll come through. Indeed, she already seems much happier than she was when she arrived. She couldn't sleep. Now she's fast asleep."

"May we see her?" asked Oscar.

"I have made you anxious," replied Dr. Blanche, putting down his glass once more. "And suspicious."

"Not suspicious," said Oscar smoothly.

"Suspicious, Mr. Wilde. I read minds. That is my business." The doctor got to his feet. "I understand your concern. You care for Agnès." He smiled at us disarmingly. "You may watch her sleeping, certainly."

Dr. Blanche walked to the walnut bookcase by the fireplace, bent forward, and turned a small handle half hidden beneath the mantelpiece. The bookcase sprang open. "This way, gentlemen."

We followed the doctor through the concealed doorway and up a narrow circular stone stairwell to the floor above. The stairs opened immediately onto a wide, deserted corridor, with cream-coloured painted walls and a polished wooden floor. The austerity of the décor contrasted markedly with the elaborate furnishings of the floor below. "We have rooms for thirty patients," explained Dr. Blanche, leading us along the corridor. He spoke barely above a whisper: even so, his voice echoed all around. We stopped outside the third room. There was a small, square pane of glass cut into the upper panel of the door and partially covered with a thin piece of cotton curtain. Dr. Blanche stood to one side to let us look through the little window. Agnès was lying on a narrow bed in the corner of the room. She was wearing a long white nightdress. Her feet were bare; her eyes were closed. She looked serene.

"Sleeping Beauty," murmured Oscar.

"We are to wake her at five," said the doctor. "She wants to go to the theatre tonight. She wants to return to her role."

"Is that wise?" I asked.

"I wouldn't necessarily advise it," replied Dr. Blanche, "but our patients are not our prisoners. And work is good. We all need to work. 'Thank God every morning, when you get up, that you have something to do that day which must be done, whether you like it or not.'"

"James Russell Lowell?" suggested Oscar quietly.

"So you, too, read minds, Mr. Wilde," said the doctor, smiling.

"No," said Oscar, "I read books."

21

"The readiness is all"

We left the clinic confused. Why had La Grange allowed the world—and us—to think that Agnès was missing when he knew all along where she was?

"And the good Dr. Ferrand knows, too," mused Oscar, climbing back up into our cab.

"At least the poor girl is alive and well," I said.

"Apparently so," said Oscar.

Oscar was due to take tea with Sarah Bernhardt that afternoon. I was due back at the theatre. Oscar dropped me off in the boulevard du Temple and told me that he would come on to find me as soon as he was able. "I'm not in the mood for the divine Sarah." He sighed. "The demands of divinity are unremitting. But I sent her a wire to tell her I'd be there. I am expected and she is a true friend, so I shall go."

He went, and, in retrospect, he was glad that he had done so. He found that Maurice Rollinat and Bernard La Grange were also of the party. Darjeeling tea and Swiss absinthe, cucumber sandwiches, and pipes of hashshashin were served. The quartet—two actors and two poets—talked much of money (as actors and poets do), but also of love and lust, of failure and success, of excess, decadence, and murder.

"I want to eat of the fruit of all the trees in the garden of the world," Bernard La Grange declared, lying back with his head nestling in Bernhardt's lap and his left hand gently caressing Rollinat's thigh. "It's your line, Mr. Oscar Wilde. It's your philosophy. You talk. I act. I want to experience *everything*. The heights. The depths." He glanced towards Oscar and widened his almond eyes. "Especially the depths. I feel that I am most alive when I visit the Room of the Dead. Is that not strange?"

"Speak to me of murder," said Oscar, sucking on his clay pipe of hashshashin. He returned Bernard's gaze. "Charles Baudelaire, I seem to recall, encouraged the idea that hashshashin tempts men to murder."

"Give me more, then!" cried Bernard, reaching out his hand towards Oscar's pipe. "I must experience everything!"

"Even murder?" asked Sarah, stroking the beautiful young actor's silk-soft head of hair.

"Would you kill or be killed?" asked Rollinat, taking the boy's hand and putting it once more against his thigh.

"Either," said Bernard seriously. "It is the experience which counts."

Sarah Bernhardt laughed and leant forward and kissed young Hamlet's forehead. "Don't die too soon," she said. "You've had such lovely notices."

Bernard La Grange sat up abruptly. "I don't read reviews, Sarah. They're meaningless. You must know that."

Oscar smiled. "Bernard is right, Sarah. You should not read reviews. You are an artist. Why should an artist be troubled by the shrill clamour of criticism? Why should those who cannot create take it upon themselves to estimate the value of creative work? What can they know about art? I despise critics!" He drew deeply on his pipe and closed his eyes.

"Do you not read the newspapers, then, Oscar?" asked Madame Bernhardt playfully. "You are always in them."

Oscar looked towards the actress from beneath hooded lids. "I will not rise to your bait, dear lady," he murmured. "I despise all newspapers, with their dreary records of politics, police courts, and personalities. I have long ago ceased to care what they write about me. My time is all given up to the gods and the Greeks!"

Bernard La Grange was leaning back against the divine Sarah once more. He turned his head towards Oscar. "Have you yet tasted Greek love, Oscar?" he asked. "Have you? Do you dare?" Oscar made no reply. "Maurice and I will take you to the Café Alexandre. It's near the theatre. There are boys there like Greek gods, with skin as smooth as alabaster and vine leaves in their hair."

"Do you not love me, then?" asked Sarah Bernhardt, leaning over the young actor once more and kissing him gently on the temples.

"I love you, Sarah. Of course, I do." He put his hand up and stroked her cheek with the back of his long, dark fingers.

Madame Bernhardt looked down and smiled on him. "I am old enough to be your mother. I know that."

Bernard La Grange gasped with delight and sat up once again. "I shall play Oedipus to your Jocasta!" he declared excitedly.

"Oh, yes!" cried Sarah. "You shall!" And then she laughed and took his head between her hands and turned his face towards hers. "But tonight you must play Hamlet to Mademoiselle de la Tourbillon's Gertrude."

"And to your sister's Ophelia," said Oscar, laying down the pipe and foraging for a cucumber sandwich. "I understand Agnès is returning."

"I prefer the understudy." Bernard La Grange laughed, getting to his feet. He stretched out his arms and yawned. He looked about and reached for a glass of absinthe.

"You allow yourself to drink before a performance," observed Oscar, tilting his head to one side and studying the handsome young man. "You do not follow the example of the great Edmond La Grange."

"What do I care for him?" asked Bernard, draining his glass.

"He is your father," said Oscar. "He is a great actor."

"He represents a great tradition," said Sarah.

"He represents the past," said Bernard. "He represents the past." He repeated the sentence as though it were an exercise in elocution. "The past. That's all over. Gone. Done with. Dead. Buried. I am interested in the present." He kissed Madame Bernhardt on the forehead. "And the future." He kissed Maurice Rollinat on the lips.

At the Théâtre La Grange, as usual, I prepared the great man's wardrobe for the evening performance. His costumes for Claudius were not elaborate, but he required me to polish the leather and the silver on his boots and belts until they gleamed. "Claudius is a usurper," he reminded me. "The trappings of kingship count with him. He has to look the part because he cannot altogether feel it."

When he arrived at his dressing room, just as the clock

was striking five, Edmond La Grange appeared at his most mellow. He was humming a tune that Traquair would sometimes whistle: "Carry Me Back to Old Virginny." It was a song by Oscar's friend Jimmy Bland.

"How are you, sir?" I asked awkwardly, avoiding his eye, uncertain what to say.

"How are you, *mon petit*?" he replied, standing in the middle of the room, waiting for me to assist him in the removal of his overcoat. He was so accustomed to being dressed and undressed by another that at such moments he simply stood with arms outstretched, awaiting the service that he took for granted. "Have you been busy?" he asked. "Have you been with Monsieur Wilde?"

"Yes," I answered, pulling off his coat.

"You have been searching for Agnès, I think?" he said, catching my eye in the cheval mirror and raising an eyebrow enquiringly.

I looked away. "Yes," I said. "We found her."

"Ah." He laughed softly. "I thought so. I thought that it was you who arrived at the clinic just as I was leaving."

As I hung up his coat and busied myself laying out and unbuttoning his shirts, Edmond La Grange sat on his swivel stool before his dressing table and, with an insouciance that seemed quite unforced, told his story. He explained that it had been Agnès's idea to get away for a few days of rest and recuperation. She had told him where she was going: he had approved. He had consulted Dr. Ferrand, who had given the plan his blessing. Dr. Ferrand was a friend and colleague of Dr. Blanche and put great store by him. La Grange had not told anyone else of Agnès's whereabouts because that was what Agnès had wanted. He

apologised for deceiving us: he hoped that I would convey his apology to Oscar. He regretted its necessity. He had felt obliged to respect Agnès's wishes: he had wanted to protect her privacy. He trusted that we would understand. He was certain that we would. And the good news was that Agnès was now feeling much better. Indeed, she was ready to return to the play. The present plan—agreed with Agnès and Dr. Blanche that very afternoon, only minutes before our carriages had passed one another beneath the entrance gates to l'Hôtel de Lamballe—was that Agnès would spend her days at Passy, resting, and then, so long as her strength permitted, drive into town each evening for her performance. La Grange asked me to call the entire company onstage forty-five minutes before the performance and he would explain the position to everybody then.

I listened to his narrative without interruption. As he finished it, he flashed a brilliant smile at me and inclined his head as though taking a modest bow. He turned back to his dressing table. "I must sleep now," he whispered. He pulled open the right-hand drawer of the dressing table and began rummaging about in it, searching for his eye mask. As he pulled open the drawer, his Colt revolver slid forward. I watched him as he touched it fondly. Over his shoulder he murmured to me, teasingly, "No more duelling, now."

He found the velvet eye mask and got to his feet. "Mo*n petit*," he said, reaching into his trouser pocket. "Here the key to rue de la Pierre Levée. Use the place tonight. yours. Enjoy. I think—I *hope*—you will find Mademois de la Tourbillon in the right frame of mind. I know free. Garstrang is joining me for cards."

He sat down on the edge of the Molière chaise longue and pushed forward his feet for me to pull off his shoes.

"May I ask you something, sir?" I said.

"Of course, *mon petit*. Anything." He lay back on the chaise longue as I adjusted a cushion behind his head.

"Is this really the couch on which Molière died in 1673?"

He laughed quietly and closed his eyes. "I doubt it very much." He pulled the velvet mask over his eyelids. "It's a story told by actors and, as you should know by now, stories told by actors are rarely to be trusted."

As Edmond La Grange slept, I went around the theatre conveying his instructions to the company. At 7:15 P.M., as required, the La Grange troops gathered onstage. Bernard La Grange was the last to arrive. He had no foreknowledge of the meeting. He came in with Oscar: they had travelled together from Sarah Bernhardt's. They stood side by side at the edge of the crowd, behind Maman, who was seated on a small chair being attended to by Eddie Garstrang. "I am dying," the old woman cried, "and nobody listens. Nobody cares."

Edmond La Grange addressed the company from the front of the stage. He was not a tall man; he stood on top of a small flight of wooden steps (part of the ramparts of Elsinore Castle) put in position by the stage manager. Richard Marais stood on the stage at his side. La Grange made a good speech: it was (as he told me it would be) a rallying cry. He saluted his company—the company that had created "the perfect *Hamlet*." He thanked them for their loyalty and for pulling together during the past few

difficult days. He had happy news, he announced. "Our Ophelia is herself again!" She had not gone missing: she had been unwell; she had been resting. However, she was returning to the theatre tonight and, if the gods willed it, would play her part as advertised for the rest of the run.

As La Grange concluded his address, Agnès, with timing worthy of her calling, appeared by the footlights at the front of the stage. We all applauded.

The speech done, the cast and company returned to their stations. Richard Marais took charge of Liselotte La Grange. "At least he can't hear her squawking," observed Eddie Garstrang. Garstrang and Oscar went into the auditorium, to the circle bar to find a drink. They then watched the performance from one of the stage boxes. Oscar was intrigued that Garstrang—an American from the Rocky Mountains, a professional gambler whose command of French was no more than adequate—appeared utterly transfixed by the play. Oscar reflected that the two men had not been so comfortable in each other's company since that breakfast in Leadville, Colorado, nearly a year ago.

I watched the performance standing in the downstage wings, as was my custom. That night it was not a perfect *Hamlet:* there were uncertain moments. Agnès appeared more fragile than ever, and in her scene with old Polonius twice lost her way; but the ovation at the end suggested that the audience was well satisfied.

Afterwards, La Grange gave me a scribbled note to take up to Agnès's dressing room. I read the note. Perhaps I should not have done so, but, momentarily, I found myself alone by a lighted gas lamp on the stairwell leading to the first-floor dressing rooms, and I did. The note said simply:

You were wonderful.

Your future is certain.

I love you. ELG.

When I reached Agnès's dressing room, I found Gabrielle de la Tourbillon standing outside the door. "She's not there," she said, leaning forward and kissing me gently on the mouth. "She's gone."

"Are you sure?"

"She takes off her makeup as soon as she's been drowned. When she comes on for the curtain call she's all ready to leave." She looked back at the dressing-room door. "I wanted to tell her how well she'd done, but she's gone. Exhausted, I imagine." Gabrielle stepped towards me and let her peignoir fall open to reveal her breasts. She laughed. "I still have to dress. Are we having supper?"

"Yes," I said. "I have the key."

"I won't be long."

I returned at once to La Grange and gave him the news. He shrugged and took back his note, folded it over, and slipped it into his dressing-table drawer.

Fifteen minutes later, I found Oscar, alone, waiting by the stage door. He was leaning against the wall, underneath the lamplight, smoking. "Look what Garstrang gave me," he said elatedly. "A Lucky Strike!"

I told my friend that I could not have a late supper with him, after all. "Will you forgive me?" I said. "I am going to have supper with Gabrielle."

He smiled. "Do you have the key?" he asked.

"Yes," I answered.

"I'm glad. Enjoy. And go easy on the laudanum. I'll go back to my hotel. I have plenty to think about."

They found her in the morning. It was one of the stage-hands who made the discovery. He was sweeping the floor: it was the first task of the day, done as soon as the theatre opened up at ten A.M. Agnès La Grange was found right at the back of the stage, behind the black velvet drapes, in the scenery dock, floating face-down in the shallow tank of water used in the play to simulate the pool in the stream in which Ophelia drowns herself.

The police doctor reckoned that she must have died at around midnight.

22

"It's in the blood"

L a Grange had summoned the police at once. By the time that Oscar and I arrived at the theatre, soon after two o'clock, the body of Agnès La Grange had already been removed from the building, and the police, under the brisk direction of one Brigadier Malthus, were concluding a series of preliminary interviews with those whom Malthus described as "essential witnesses."

"You fall into that category, gentlemen," Malthus said to us pleasantly, as we presented ourselves at Edmond La Grange's dressing-room door. "At least, I think you do."

The dressing room was crowded with people, yet quiet as the grave. Malthus, two younger policemen in uniform, and eight senior members of the La Grange company were standing, side by side, shoulders touching, ranged around the walls, like mourners at the graveside. Dr. Emile Blanche was also there. He had arrived from his clinic an hour before, not because he had heard the news, but because he was concerned that Agnès had not returned to Passy the night before as he and his staff had expected. Dr. Blanche was perched on the edge of the Molière chaise longue, next to Liselotte La Grange. He held the old woman's hand in his. (Not knowing her well, he instinctively offered her the comfort that those close to her no longer could.) Carlos Branco stood slumped against the back of the dressing-room door, his head lolling forward, his eyes open, gazing blankly at the ground. He wore a brightly coloured striped dressing gown, put on before he had heard the news.

The great La Grange sat in the midst of this throng, almost invisible, bent over his dressing table, his arms folded, his eyes closed, his head tilted at a curious angle, as if he were still in the act of flinching away from unseen horror. Brigadier Malthus stood at his side. Occasionally, the police officer placed a reassuring hand on the old actor's shoulder. The two men were friends. They were of an age. Edmond La Grange, Pierre Ferrand, and Félix Malthus had been at school together.

Brigadier Malthus was not an Englishman's idea of a French policeman. He was impressively tall, cadaverously thin, yet upright and youthful-looking for his age, clean shaven and silver-haired, with high, prominent cheekbones and a large aquiline nose. He was dressed in a well-cut, dark blue serge suit. On his lapel he wore the distinctive ribbon of a commandant of the Légion d'Honneur. He had the appearance of a lawyer or a banker, combined with the surprising, gentle, slightly teasing manner of a mildly eccentric university professor.

"You have heard the dreadful news?" he asked, once he had confirmed that we were indeed who he had taken us to be.

"A moment ago," said Oscar. "From the stage door-keeper, as we came in."

Brigadier Malthus sighed and let his tongue loll momentarily over his lower lip, like a lizard feeling for food. "It is very distressing," he said. (His voice was not the voice of a Paris policeman, either. It was cultivated, refined.)

"Most terrible," said Oscar. "Tragic." Tears pricked his eyes.

"I am just trying to establish who might have seen Mademoiselle La Grange last," Malthus continued lightly. "To assess her state of mind. You understand?" Oscar nodded. "Everyone saw her take her curtain call, of course. But nobody seems to have seen her since." The policeman looked around the assembled company and smiled. He had pale blue eyes. Slowly, he turned them in my direction. "Monsieur Sherard," he said amiably, "you are Monsieur La Grange's dresser, as I understand?"

"Yes, sir," I said.

"Monsieur La Grange tells me that he gave you a note to take to Mademoiselle La Grange at the end of last night's performance."

"Yes, sir."

"But you brought back the note because Mademoiselle La Grange was not in her dressing room."

"Yes, sir."

"Her room was empty."

"I can vouch for that," said Gabrielle de la Tourbillon. She was standing at the back of the room, in the far corner by the sideboard, half hidden behind Eddie Garstrang and Dr. Ferrand. I had not noticed her presence in the room before. I had not seen her that morning. After our night together in the rue de la Pierre Levée, I had woken at dawn to find her gone. Seeing her suddenly, hearing her speak, I blushed.

Brigadier Malthus appeared not to notice my

embarrassment. He looked round to where Gabrielle was standing. "As you have told us, mademoiselle," he said courteously. "It is noted." He pushed out his lower lip once more and turned his gaze on Oscar. "Monsieur Wilde," he began.

"I cannot help," said Oscar. "Alas. I watched the play with Mr. Garstrang. When it was over, we left the theatre with the rest of the audience and made our way in a leisurely fashion around the building to the stage door. Mr. Garstrang told me that he was going to play cards with Monsieur La Grange, as usual, and bade me good night. He went up to the private apartment above the theatre, while I waited outside the stage door, smoking a cigarette."

"Did you see Mademoiselle La Grange leave the theatre?"

"The stage door is always crowded after a performance. There is always a rush to leave. I saw several of the actors depart. I spoke with Bernard La Grange, briefly, when he came out—to congratulate him. I did not see Agnès."

"Thank you, Monsieur Wilde," said the police officer, bowing towards Oscar. He looked around the room once more. "Thank you, ladies and gentlemen. You have all been most helpful in the most trying of circumstances. I shall need to speak to one or two of you more fully in the coming days"—he nodded in the direction of Dr. Blanche and of the stagehand who had found the body—"but it seems all too clear what has happened, does it not?" He laid a kindly hand on Edmond La Grange's shoulder as he continued to address the room. "Suicide is not a crime—"

"It is a sin!" cried Liselotte La Grange.

"It is a tragedy. It is heartbreaking. I offer my sincere condolences to all those who knew and loved Agnès La Grange."

"Her mother committed suicide," said Liselotte La Grange loudly, staring directly at Brigadier Malthus. "Suicide is an inherited characteristic."

Dr. Blanche caressed the old lady's hand. Madame La Grange pulled it away from him angrily. "It's in the blood," she squawked. "It's in the blood." No one paid her any attention.

Brigadier Malthus leant over Edmond La Grange and spoke into his ear. "I should see Bernard at some stage. He's not here. Do you know where he is?"

La Grange opened his eyes and looked up at the police officer wearily. "No. I've not seen him since last night." He turned his head towards the doorway and looked at Oscar. "Monsieur Wilde found Agnès yesterday. Perhaps he can help you find Bernard today."

Brigadier Malthus turned to Oscar with eyebrows raised.

"You might try the Room of the Dead," suggested Oscar.

"Thank you," said the police officer. "I'm obliged. That is all for now. We will take our leave."

As Malthus and his men departed, slowly the dressing room began to clear. No one looked anyone directly in the eye. No one spoke, except Liselotte La Grange. She pulled herself to her feet, leaning on Dr. Blanche's arm. "The play must continue," she barked.

"Of course, Maman," said Edmond quietly.

As the room emptied, I watched La Grange closely. Gradually, his back straightened and his eyes began to gleam again.

Word of Agnès's death spread quickly. Members of the company began to arrive, drifting into the theatre hours earlier than usual. Members of the press arrived, also. Richard Marais marshalled them together on the stage and, at five o'clock, La Grange emerged from his dressing room to give a brief statement. To one of the journalists—an old friend, a card-playing crony—he granted an interview. I stood in the corner of the dressing room while the two men talked: La Grange remained calm throughout. He spoke of Agnès without tears but with heartrending affection; he described her contribution to "the perfect *Hamlet*" with unashamed pride. His self-control was extraordinary, but, early in the evening, when I left him alone in his room to take his usual preperformance siesta, as I stood in the wings, I could hear him sobbing.

The police did not find Bernard La Grange at the Room of the Dead. Oscar found him, as he had expected that he might, at Sarah Bernhardt's studio in Montmartre, with Maurice Rollinat. It was Oscar who broke the news to Bernard of his sister's death. Outwardly, the young actor took it calmly, stoically, just as his father had done. He said nothing—or, rather, as Oscar described it to me later, he began quoting a line from a poem by Baudelaire, and then, "seeming to recognise how trite the rhyme sounded in face of the reality of what had occurred, fell into silence." Oscar told Bernard what little he knew of the circumstances of Agnès's death and that the police officer investigating the tragedy appeared to be competent and conscientious: "a decent and civilised man, in fact."

"Is it Malthus?" asked Bernard.

"It is," said Oscar. "He is a friend of your father's, I think."

Bernard La Grange laughed. "But he can be trusted, nonetheless. What does he think?"

"Malthus? Of Agnès's death? He believes that it was suicide."

"Yes," said Bernard softly. "It's in the blood."

Sarah Bernhardt took the young actor in her arms and embraced him as a mother might. Maurice Rollinat embraced him, too, and as he did so (as Oscar noticed, but Sarah Bernhardt did not) slipped three small, glass phials of liquid opium into his coat pocket.

At six o'clock, Oscar brought Hamlet back to the theatre by cab. Bernard La Grange was neither shocked nor surprised that his father—and his grandmother—wanted to continue with the evening's performance. It was what he wanted, also. "It's what we do," he said.

La Grange, *père et fils,* gave magnificent performances that night, thrilling in their intensity. Agnès's understudy rose to the occasion, equally. "She is a fine young actress," Edmond La Grange murmured to me as we stood together in the wings. Other members of the company were much less assured in their playing: Gabrielle de la Tourbillon was more muted than I had ever known her to be onstage, and Carlos Branco forgot his lines on several occasions. "He's playing Polonius," Edmond La Grange muttered to me scornfully. "Polonius is an old fool. No one will notice. No one will care."

At the end of the performance, La Grange sent me to find Oscar and Bernard to invite them to join him for a drink in his dressing room. "If you see Garstrang or Marais, get them to take care of Maman," he added as I made to leave. "I don't want her here. I have had enough of Maman."

I found Bernard at the stage door, talking to a young woman. She was a pretty girl, in a blue cape and bonnet, a member of the audience, who had come to ask him for his autograph. Oscar was with them, smoking a cigarette. Bernard gave the girl his signature and kissed her hand with a Gallic show of gallantry. I told him that his father wanted to see him. "Must I?" he asked wearily.

"I think you must," said Oscar.

I brought them back to La Grange's dressing room. The old actor had undressed and dressed himself again. He had already opened a bottle of champagne. We raised our glasses to Agnès's memory—and to the Théâtre La Grange and "the perfect *Hamlet*."

La Grange announced that, for once, he was not in the mood for cards. He had ordered Marais to fetch a cab. He proposed to take us out to supper—in Agnès's honour. "I have reserved a table at Pharamond. It is Oscar's favourite. Oscar shall speak to us of Shakespeare's heroines and of mortality. Will you not, Oscar?"

"If that is what you wish," answered Oscar.

Bernard got to his feet and said that, alas, he could not join us: he was committed to going to Le Chat Noir with

Maurice Rollinat and Jacques-Emile Blanche. He was sure he had mentioned it earlier.

"Le Chat Noir?" repeated Edmond. "Tonight?"

"I have not seen Jacques-Emile since the news of Agnès . . . He loved her very much. He will be desolated. I feel that I should see him."

Edmond La Grange drained his glass and placed it on the dressing table. "You did say so, and I understand," he said. "Go. Take a cab. I'll pay for it. In fact, take the cab that's at the stage door now. I'll order another."

Bernard embraced his father, asked Oscar for a cigarette, wished us good night, and went on his way.

"Take care," said Oscar, opening his cigarette case and giving Bernard two or three of his cigarettes.

We remained in the dressing room, finishing our wine. The clock struck the half hour. "Perhaps we'll forget Pharamond," said La Grange. "This is cosy. Shall we just stay here and open another bottle?"

A minute later, as I was fetching a second bottle of Perrier-Jouët from the case that was kept in a corner of the dresser's cubicle, we heard a dreadful hubbub coming from the wings: shouting, cries of alarm, running feet. The dressing-room door burst open violently.

It was Eddie Garstrang, distraught. "It's Bernard!" he cried. "In the street . . ."

"He's dead?" gasped Edmond La Grange.

"Almost certainly."

"Consumed by fire?" asked Oscar.

"Yes. Exactly."

23

The Elements

As we ran from the dressing room, La Grange stumbled in the darkened wings. Oscar and Garstrang helped him to his feet. We ran on, desperately, out of the stage door and down the steps into the cobbled alleyway. We smelt and heard the fire before we saw it: the stench of burning leather, the spit and crackle of burning wood. There, at the far end of the black alley, like a bonfire on a hilltop, stood a horse-drawn four-wheeler with its carriage all ablaze.

The carriage was a ball of fire, a roaring furnace, and outlined against it were the silhouettes of men frantically trying to douse the flames. The cabdriver, the stage doorkeeper, Richard Marais, Carlos Branco, actors, and stagehands were darting to and from the blaze with buckets filled with sand, and water from the nearby horse trough. They did well: they contained the fire; it did not spread. The horse was saved, but not the carriage, nor the single figure within it: Bernard La Grange.

"My God, Oscar," I whispered, "we could all be dead." We stood helpless, halfway along the alley, transfixed by the horrific scene. Repeatedly, La Grange tried to run towards the flames, but Garstrang held him back. "There's nothing to be done," he said.

It must have taken half an hour for the fire to subside and the remains of the burnt-out vehicle to cool sufficiently for us to get inside the carriage and retrieve the charred body of the once beautiful young man. La Grange and Carlos Branco, both in tears, attempted to lift the body out of the carriage. The boy's limbs came apart in their hands.

"What is the meaning of this?" wailed La Grange.

At Oscar's suggestion, Richard Marais was sent to fetch the police.

"Ask for Malthus," said La Grange.

"It's midnight," said Oscar. "Bring anyone who will come."

The remains of Bernard's body were carried into the theatre and laid out in the wings. From the rail of costumes that stood at the edge of the stage Carlos Branco fetched a cloak: it was the cloak he wore as the Ghost of Hamlet's Father. He placed the cloak over the corpse. We stood around the dead boy's body in dismay.

Gabrielle de la Tourbillon, alerted by the noise, had come down from the apartment. She was wearing a hooded winter cloak over her nightdress. She brought us tumblers of brandy.

"Where is Maman?" asked La Grange.

"In bed, asleep," answered Gabrielle.

"Good," mumbled La Grange. "Leave her be."

Within the half hour, Marais had returned. The police officer he brought with him was not Brigadier Malthus. I did not catch the man's name, but I smelt the wine on his breath and the sweat on his uniform. He did not detain us long. La Grange formally identified the victim's body as that of Bernard La Grange: the young actor's silk-soft black hair was burnt to a stubble, but his face, though scorched and charred, was recognisable. The cabdriver confirmed what had happened. At half past eleven o'clock—he had heard a church bell strike—a young man came out of the stage door and walked briskly up the alleyway towards the waiting cab. The alley was quite crowded—the performance was not long over—but the cabdriver noticed the young man at once because he was walking directly towards him and walking with purpose. As he reached the carriage, he called up to the driver: "It's only one passenger, after all. Le Chat Noir in Montmartre, if you please." Then he climbed aboard.

"Was he alone when he got into your cab?" asked Oscar.

"He was on his own, yes, but there were other people nearby, if that's what you mean."

"Did he open the cab door himself?"

"Yes. No." The coachman hesitated. "I don't recall. Possibly not. He was lighting a cigarette at the time. I remember that."

"Thank you," said Oscar.

"Thank you," said the police officer, looking at Oscar with a weary eye. He licked the tip of his pencil and glanced down at his notebook before turning back to the cabdriver: "And then?"

"And then—a moment later, just as I was releasing the brakes to move off—I felt the explosion. The carriage rocked. It was like a small bomb going off, a sudden burst of noise and heat. I jumped down, uncoupled the carriage and pulled the horse to safety."

Carlos Branco looked at the cabdriver in disbelief. "You saved the horse before the boy?"

The cabman shrugged his shoulders.

"It was a ball of fire," said Eddie Garstrang. "There was nothing to be done."

"And there's nothing more that we can do tonight," said the policeman, closing his notebook and suppressing a yawn, "except leave you to your prayers."

"Will you not examine the carriage, at least?" asked Oscar.

"Not tonight," said the officer coldly. "It's late, it's dark. I'm going to bed. I advise you to do the same." The officer stared at Oscar, defying him to speak again. Oscar kept his silence. The officer turned to Edmond La Grange: "I shall leave a man in the street overnight."

A police hearse had arrived to bear Bernard La Grange's body to the morgue. Two porters—"burly men with butcher's faces" is how Oscar described them in his journal—arrived in the wings and, without speaking or acknowledging our presence, went straight about their business. Ignoring the cries of distress from La Grange and Carlos Branco, they uncovered the corpse, throwing Branco's cloak unceremoniously to one side, and rolled the dead body, like a pig's carcass, onto a canvas stretcher. Together, with a single grunt, they lifted the stretcher and, without pause, carried their grim cargo away.

"Flights of angels sing thee to thy rest," whispered La Grange, watching them depart.

The police officer looked about the group of bleak and bewildered faces. "My condolences," he said. "Good night. Brigadier Malthus will take charge tomorrow. Please be so good as to stay in the vicinity in case any of you is needed for questioning again."

"We shall all be here," said Edmond La Grange calmly. "We have a performance of *Hamlet* to give tomorrow night."

"No," protested Branco. "You cannot play *Hamlet* without the prince." Desperately, he looked at La Grange and then at the policeman. "We have lost our Ophelia. We have lost our Hamlet. They were without equal. We cannot go on."

"The understudy knows the lines," said La Grange. "The play goes on."

"No," pleaded Carlos Branco. "For pity's sake, no."

The police officer departed. The moment he had gone, Oscar touched my arm, pulling me gently from Gabrielle's side. "I think that we should be on our way as well," he said. He offered his hand to Edmond La Grange: "I know not what to say . . ."

"Say nothing," answered La Grange quietly. "We will speak tomorrow." Oscar nodded and turned to leave. Suddenly, raising his voice, the old actor called him back. "*Mon ami,* one thing before you go," he asked. "Please." Oscar turned round. "When we heard that Bernard was dead, you said at once, "Consumed by fire." How did you know?"

Oscar looked at Edmond La Grange. "Maman's dog died buried in a case of earth," he said softly. "Your dresser—my poor friend Traquair—died by breathing poisoned air. Agnès was drowned. Earth, air, and water; there was only element remaining: fire."

• • •

On the morning following the horrific death of Bernard La Grange, Oscar picked me up by cab from my room in the rue de Beauce and, together, we drove out to Passy.

"Do you honestly believe that these deaths are all connected?" I asked my friend.

It was eleven o'clock and the sky was overcast. Oscar was dressed in a most improbable (and unseasonable) suit of canary yellow. He laid a straw boater hat on the seat between us and, from a paper cornet, offered me an aniseed ball. "Breakfast?" he enquired. He was at his most shiny faced and playful. "Are the deaths connected?" he murmured. "Yes," he said emphatically.

"And by the elements of earth, air, water, and fire?"

He nodded. "I'm inclined to think so."

I looked at him and shook my head. "And I'm inclined to think that this time, Oscar, you have allowed your creative juices to flow to excess."

"Are you indeed?" He laughed. "Creativity, we're told, is not the finding of a thing, but the making something out of it after it is found."

"Precisely. And I think you've made rather more out of it than the facts of the matter justify. Death—murder or suicide—by earth, air, water, and fire? Frankly, Oscar, I'm incredulous."

"Oh, don't be that, Robert," he cried, pressing another aniseed sweet upon me. "Incredulity robs us of many pleasures, and gives us nothing in return."

"Last night's tragedy could have been an accident, Oscar. Have you considered that possibility?"

"I have, Robert, of course, I have. Like you, I heard the

coachman tell us that Bernard was lighting a cigarette as he entered the cab."

"You noticed that?"

"I did. But could a simple lighted match cause such a sudden conflagration?"

"He had a lighted match in his hand—and in his pocket three phials of laudanum!" I said, with a note of quiet triumph in my voice. (I had been waiting since last night to point this out to Oscar.) "You saw Rollinat place them there. You told me so."

"I did. And, yes, Robert, laudanum is a tincture of opium: it is prepared with ether. It is highly flammable. Somehow the lighted match could have come into contact with the laudanum; but by accident? Is not murder much more likely? Is it not much more probable that as Bernard La Grange stepped unsuspectingly into the cab, some unknown hand threw an incendiary device into the carriage after him?"

"Or perhaps it was suicide," suggested Dr. Emile Blanche gently. "I do think, gentlemen, that suicide is the most likely explanation."

We were ushered into the great man's presence the moment we reached the clinic at Passy. We appeared to be expected: in the doctor's library, coffee and Madeira were already set out on a tray by the bay window. Blanche blinked at us endearingly from behind his gig lamp spectacles. "As old Madame La Grange reminded us yesterday, suicide is an inherited characteristic. It runs in families. Agnès La Grange took her own life. She was Bernard's twin. Bernard will have felt that in losing his sister, he had lost half of himself. Bernard's mother took her own life; Bernard's sister took her own life. In doing so, they had given Bernard permission to do the same."

"It is all very sad," said Oscar, somewhat dreamily, holding up his glass of Madeira and gazing through the liquid gold towards the bay window and the grey sky beyond.

"It is heartbreaking," said Dr. Blanche. "And not only for the La Grange family. My poor Jacques-Emile is profoundly distressed by the news."

"Yes," said Oscar, coming suddenly out of his reverie. "Jacques-Emile. I feel for him. In truth, Doctor, it was to see him that we came out to Passy this morning."

"You have missed him, I am afraid. He has gone over to Montmartre to be with his friend Rollinat." He sighed briefly and offered us more wine. "These poetic nihilists like young Rollinat, they talk of death easily enough, but the reality of it bites all the same. Bites—and hurts."

"Jacques-Emile and Bernard La Grange were friends?" I asked.

"Close friends," replied the doctor, smiling at me. "The closest. They fought together, mano a mano—they wrestled and they fenced. It was through their sparring that they expressed their love. It is often the way with men."

"And Agnès?" enquired Oscar. "Did Jacques-Emile love Agnès?"

"You know that he did. Passionately. Deeply. Desperately."

"And did she love him?"

"Like a brother!" The doctor gave a hollow laugh. He removed his wire-rimmed spectacles and shook his head mournfully. "As I told you the other day—when I should not have done so: I thought that you already knew—Agnès's father was the love of Agnès's life."

"Was that love—" Oscar hesitated. "Was that love—*achieved*?" he asked.

Dr. Blanche sat forward and put on his spectacles once more. "What do you mean, Mr. Wilde?"

"Was it *consummated*?" asked Oscar.

"Good God, no." Dr. Blanche got to his feet and moved towards the window, as if to get closer to fresh air. He turned back and looked at Oscar. "What an idea!" he exclaimed, shaking his head.

"You are certain of this?" said Oscar, leaning forward, with supplicatory hands outstretched. "Forgive me for persisting, but you see the significance; under the circumstances."

"I do, of course," said the doctor, calming himself. "If Agnès and her father had been lovers, self-loathing might have driven her to suicide—or shame might have driven him to murder."

"Quite so," said Oscar dryly.

"But they were not lovers," the doctor continued, picking up the decanter and pouring us each a further glass of Madeira. "I am sure of it. Delicate as it was, I raised the matter with them both, separately and together. Edmond La Grange loved his daughter—naturally. That he should have known her carnally is inconceivable. He told me that the very notion of such a thing filled him with disgust. He told me so privately and, again, later, in Agnès's presence."

"And you believed him?" asked Oscar.

"I believed him. I have been a doctor for more than

thirty years, Mr. Wilde. I know when my patients are lying to me." He resumed his seat and sipped at his wine reflectively. "And I believed Agnès's denials, equally. Her love for her father was complicated. It contained what nowadays we call an 'erotic charge.' Are you familiar with the term?"

"It sounds expensive," said Oscar. "Eros always was the costliest of the gods."

Dr. Blanche obliged Oscar with a little laugh. "Agnès's feelings for her father troubled her," he went on. "They may indeed have been what drove her to her suicide; but, if they were, it was because of frustration, not fulfilment."

"So Agnès and Edmond La Grange did not make the beast with two backs?" mused Oscar, draining his glass slowly. He glanced towards the doctor. "Are you familiar with the term?"

Blanche smiled. "No, but I catch its drift. It sounds uncomfortable." The doctor got to his feet and turned towards Oscar, putting his hands together behind his back and raising himself on his toes as though he were addressing a classroom of students. "Mr. Wilde," he said, "La Grange and his daughter were not lovers, I'm certain of that. Agnès told me that she was ready to take an oath on the Holy Bible that she had not shared her father's bed. She knew that to do so would be a sin. She told me that she would never share the bed of a man she could not marry."

"She spoke of sin, did she? She had thoughts of matrimony even? You surprise me." Oscar placed his empty wine-glass on the side table next to him. "She was a virgin, then?" he asked, sitting forward and looking up at Blanche.

The doctor raised an amused eyebrow. "I did not say

that, Mr. Wilde. She was an actress. She had a lover, I believe. Quite recently acquired."

"Not your son?"

"No, not Jacques-Emile—though she spoke of him to Jacques-Emile."

"Did she mention his name?"

"I don't believe so. He was an older man, I think."

"Ah," sighed Oscar. "'The older man': there's a term with which we're both familiar. I don't know a more depressing turn of phrase, do you?"

24

The Face at the Door

When Dr. Blanche's decanter of Madeira was empty, we took our leave. In the cab going back into town, Oscar sat with his legs stretched out before him and his straw boater pulled over his eyes.

"You're in mellow mood, *mon ami*," I said.

"We have been in congenial company," he replied. "And though my eyes are closed, I begin to see the way ahead. I had a glimmer of it in Reading Gaol. It is becoming clearer now."

"You amaze me, Oscar. I'm totally lost. Tell me more."

He pushed back the boater and opened one eye. "I only *begin* to see the way, Robert. Don't rush me. But a beginning is a beginning. I'm content with that." He felt in his pockets for his cigarette case. "As we know, with any creative endeavour, the hardest part is to begin. A blade of grass is no easier to make than an oak."

"You are an odd fellow, Oscar," I said, contemplating my friend as, eyes closed once more, he placed a cigarette between his lips and lit it successfully with a single match. "Last night we witnessed a terrible tragedy. Yesterday morning Agnès was discovered drowned. And yet, this morning, you seem positively gay."

"I did not know them well, but I do grieve for Agnès

and Bernard La Grange," he said quietly, letting the white cigarette smoke filter slowly from his nostrils. "They were beautiful and gifted and too young to die. I grieve for Washington Traquair even more so." He half opened his eyes and turned his head towards me. "I am not heartless, Robert, you know that. But today I am happy. I cannot deny it." He sat up and doffed his hat in my direction. "I am in love."

"In love?" I repeated, surprised.

"Yes, Robert. You may congratulate me. That violet-eyed little Artemis, so grave and slight, with her flowerlike head that droops like a blossom and her wonderful ivory hands . . ."

"The young lady that you saw in London? You have spoken of her before."

"I have seen her in London, Robert, yes. And in Dublin. And in my sweetest dreams. And I have spoken of her, naturally. Have I told you that she is perfection? She has all the delicate grace of a Tanagra figurine." Suddenly, he threw his cigarette out of the cab window and from his inside coat pocket produced a small cream-coloured envelope which he kissed and then flourished before me. "If I am especially gay today it is because she has written to me; and what she has to say is most encouraging."

"Ah," I cried. "She reciprocates your feelings."

"It seems so, Robert," he said, beaming from ear to ear. "I know friend Rollinat is a doughty champion of the pleasures of perversity and the dark delights of fornication among the fallen, but I am not for love among the ruined. I am for Constance! I have seen the tender purity of girlhood look out from her dreaming eyes."

"Ah, yes, *Constance,* that's her name."

He leant towards me eagerly. "The name has an exquisite forest simplicity about it, does it not? It sounds most sweetly out of tune with this rough-and-ready world of ours—rather like a daisy on a railway bank!"

"Oscar!" I reproved him. "You've used that line before—about another lady's name."

"Have I?" He began to laugh. "Surely not."

"You have, Oscar. You used those very words to Gabrielle de la Tourbillon. When you danced with her, crossing the Atlantic. She told me all about it."

"She did?" He appeared quite unabashed. "And has Mademoiselle de la Tourbillon told you the truth about her own name?" he asked.

"I have not asked her. I did not like to."

"Oh, you should, Robert," he continued teasingly. "You most certainly should if you're to marry her."

"I'm not going to marry her, Oscar," I protested. "Don't be absurd."

My friend laughed. "I am sorry to hear it—especially since it turns out that you both have notable great-grandfathers. Gabrielle was born a Guillotin! She's a direct descendant of the professor of anatomy who gave the guillotine his name."

I looked at my friend in amazement. "Is this true? How do you know?"

"Because she told me, because I asked. Names do fascinate me so. Gabrielle and all her family changed their surname because of its macabre connotations. I think that's a great pity. I do hope my grandchildren don't decide to change their name."

"They won't," I chided him. "Wilde is a wonderful name."

"So is Guillotin," he cried. "Guillotin has the edge. You can't deny it!"

My friend, still laughing, dropped me at the corner of the place de la République and the boulevard du Temple and drove on to Montmartre in search of Jacques-Emile Blanche and Maurice Rollinat.

I, rather more soberly, walked down the cobbled side road adjacent to the Théâtre La Grange and turned into the narrow alleyway that led to the stage door. The burnt-out carriage had been taken away. A solitary policeman stood on the corner smoking a cigarette and watching, without any show of interest, as half a dozen stagehands, armed with wheelbarrows, brooms, and shovels, cleared away the remaining evidence of the conflagration. Eddie Garstrang was watching them, too.

I stopped and stood with him for a moment. Curiously, since our duel, my feelings towards the American had changed. I no longer despised him or viewed him as a rival. He was not a friend. Beyond Gabrielle, we had no interests in common, but because of Gabrielle—because we had fought over the same territory and it was territory that we now shared—we were, after a fashion, I now felt, comrades in arms. He offered me a cigarette.

"Thank you," I said. "What's happening?" I asked, nodding towards the theatre.

"Your lord and master is running the understudies through their lines. The matinée is cancelled, but the evening performance goes on. Mr. Branco says it is an insult to the dead. Marais says it is essential. The theatre needs the money. The old crone says the glory of La Grange requires it. I've no idea where Gabrielle is. She's all yours if you can find her. I'm on my way to a bar to get drunk."

I smiled. "I thought you didn't drink before playing cards."

"I don't. But I'm not playing cards tonight. And I didn't play cards last night. I don't have to play cards anymore." He drew deeply on his cigarette and, holding it tightly in the corner of his mouth, exposing two rows of tiny white teeth, returned my smile with a grotesque, lopsided grimace. "I am a free man," he purred. "I have been since the stroke of midnight. I was contracted to La Grange and I've served my time. I've cleared my debt. I've paid my dues."

"Bravo!" I said, putting my hand forward to shake his.

"Thank you, son," he said, laughing. "It feels good."

I left him and went in to the theatre. La Grange was on the stage, working with the understudies. I stood in the wings watching them until I caught his eye. "I'm here, monsieur," I mouthed.

He called to me: "I want the company onstage at six o'clock." I nodded. "Take the message round, *mon petit*. This will be a night to reckon with. You can tell your grandchildren you were here!"

His shoulders were hunched, but there was a lustre in his eyes. Hissing the word "Yes!" beneath his breath, he turned back to the actors.

I turned round to find Richard Marais at my shoulder. He was so close that our faces almost touched. His bald head was brown and blotchy. His left temple throbbed rhythmically. He was a very ugly man.

"It's done," he whispered.

"What's done?" I asked.

"The call for the meeting—at six o'clock. Everyone knows. He asked me to set it up an hour ago."

"Good," I said, excusing myself. "Thank you."

I went to La Grange's dressing room and set about my duties in the usual way: sorting the laundry, cleaning the hairbrushes, laying out La Grange's Claudius costume, polishing his belt and boots. When I had completed the tasks, I felt suddenly weary. The door to the dresser's room—the cubicle beyond the dressing room—was ajar. I pushed it open. There was no light in the room, but I could discern the outline of the divan. I lay down on it and closed my eyes and thought of Washington Traquair.

At six o'clock the great Edmond La Grange stood on top of the small flight of wooden steps that formed part of the ramparts of Elsinore Castle and addressed the company that bore his name.

He spoke affectingly about Bernard and Agnès, about their youth and beauty and great talent, about their contribution to "the perfect *Hamlet,*" and about the heritage of the family La Grange. Now, he explained, he had no heirs: the La Grange name had been at the heart of Paris theatre from the era of Molière until this moment. When he died, it would be over. "But the play must go on."

"The name must go on," croaked Liselotte La Grange. The old woman sat on a chair at the edge of the stage, with her dog scratching and snuffling at her side. Eddie Garstrang stood behind her, smiling.

Carlos Branco—"our Polonius"—had wanted to cancel

tonight's performance, La Grange continued, "out of respect for Agnès and Bernard." Polonius was wrong: "Polonius is an old fool; he has been overruled." As La Grange said these words, I watched Carlos Branco standing at the edge of the wings. He was staring at the ground. As La Grange spoke, slowly, without looking up, he shook his head. "Tonight," La Grange concluded, "Hamlet and Ophelia will be played by the understudies, young actors who are here not because they are anybody's children, but because they are fine practitioners of their art." He invited the pair forward to take a bow. We gave them our applause.

As the speech finished, I saw Oscar appear at the back of the crowd. He moved towards Gabrielle de la Tourbillon and put a hand on her shoulder. As she had listened to La Grange, I had seen her eyes fill with tears. She turned to Oscar and embraced him.

The company dispersed; the stage emptied; La Grange returned to his dressing room. I followed him, congratulating him on his speech. When we reached his dressing room, as we entered I saw his eyes scan the room. "Is everything prepared?" he asked.

"Of course," I replied. "As ever."

"Thank you," he said, turning to me and smiling. "I'm grateful." He sat down on his stool and looked at me in his dressing-table mirror. "I shall dress myself tonight," he said. "For once, I'd like to be alone."

"I understand, monsieur," I said.

"Go and find your friend Oscar," he added, waving his hand to me through the looking glass. "Watch the play from the front tonight. You may see a great *Hamlet*—so long as Polonius doesn't forget his words." He laughed and swivelled round on his stool to look at me directly. "The boy and girl are good actors, perhaps as good as Bernard and Agnès, for all we know."

He turned back towards his dressing table and raised his hand again to wave me on my way. I left the room, closing the door behind me. As I closed it, I heard La Grange moving within the room. I paused. I heard him crossing the floor. I wondered if he was about to call me back. He wasn't. To my surprise, I heard him turn the key in the lock of the door. I had never known him lock his dressing-room door before.

I began to walk up the dimly lit wings when I heard Oscar's voice across the stage. It was not loud—Oscar never spoke loudly—but it was unmistakable. Oscar's way of speaking, whether in English or in French, was unique: effortless, ever flowing, oracular. As I crossed the empty stage, I heard him say, "Women are meant to be loved, not to be understood." I followed his voice and found my friend in the wings in the top left-hand corner of the stage, hidden behind a piece of scenery, close by the spot where the drowned body of Agnès La Grange had been discovered. He was talking with Gabrielle.

When I arrived, she looked around and said, "What time is it? Everyone's gone. I must change or I will be late." She kissed Oscar lightly on the cheek. "I will see you later," she said. As she passed me, she paused and put a hand to my face. Oscar looked away. We kissed, as lovers kiss, but it was not as it had been. This was the end of the affair and, without a word being spoken, we both knew it. She hurried away to her dressing room.

"Well," said Oscar, when Gabrielle had gone, "how goes it with the great La Grange? Shouldn't you be about your duties?"

"My services are not required this evening," I said. "He's going to dress himself. He wants to be alone."

Oscar looked perturbed. When I told him how La Grange had waved me on my way and locked the door of the dressing room after my departure, he stepped out from behind the scenery and peered across the empty stage towards La Grange's dressing room. I looked over his shoulder. We could see the closed door from where we stood.

Abruptly, my friend pulled me back. Walking down the wings on the other side of the stage was Carlos Branco. He was already dressed in his costume as the Ghost of Hamlet's Father, wearing his cloak (the cloak that had covered the body of Bernard La Grange the night before) and his helmet and visor. He walked briskly towards the door of La Grange's room. He knocked on the door and waited a moment. Briefly, he glanced in our direction. He turned back to the door and took off his helmet and visor and knocked again. The door opened. La Grange appeared. The great actor gave a wintry smile and nodded, as Branco entered the room.

Oscar pulled me back behind the scenery. "Did they see us?" he whispered.

"It's very dark, but Branco might have seen us. He looked directly at us."

"Did La Grange see us?"

"I don't know. Does it matter?"

As we spoke, we heard a sudden gunshot.

We emerged from behind the scenery and ran across the

stage towards La Grange's dressing room. The door was open. La Grange was seated at his dressing table. His body was slumped over it. His head was lying in a glistening pool of purple blood. His Colt revolver was resting by his outstretched right hand. He was quite dead.

25

The Truth

"**H**e's blown his brains out," said Eddie Garstrang, surveying the scene.

"I'm not surprised," said Carlos Branco.

"Dear God," gasped Richard Marais. "It is all over."

Garstrang and Branco were the first to reach the dressing room. As Oscar and I ran across the stage, we saw them hurtling through the darkened wings. They were followed immediately by Richard Marais and two stagehands. We arrived at the door as they did.

Within the room everything was still. There was no sound apart from the gentle ticking of the little carriage clock on the sideboard. We stood, frozen, seven men in a silent semicircle, gazing down on the ruin of the great La Grange. No one spoke.

"Shouldn't we get the doctor?" I asked eventually.

"He's dead," said Oscar. "There's no doubting that."

"Look at the blood," said Garstrang. The blood was everywhere: splashed across the looking glass, spread across the dressing table, trickling onto the Turkish rug at La Grange's feet.

"Is this the promised end?" murmured Oscar.

The clock began to strike seven. "The performance

25

The Truth

"He's blown his brains out," said Eddie Garstrang, surveying the scene.

"I'm not surprised," said Carlos Branco.

"Dear God," gasped Richard Marais. "It is all over."

Garstrang and Branco were the first to reach the dressing room. As Oscar and I ran across the stage, we saw them hurtling through the darkened wings. They were followed immediately by Richard Marais and two stagehands. We arrived at the door as they did.

Within the room everything was still. There was no sound apart from the gentle ticking of the little carriage clock on the sideboard. We stood, frozen, seven men in a silent semicircle, gazing down on the ruin of the great La Grange. No one spoke.

"Shouldn't we get the doctor?" I asked eventually.

"He's dead," said Oscar. "There's no doubting that."

"Look at the blood," said Garstrang. The blood was everywhere: splashed across the looking glass, spread across the dressing table, trickling onto the Turkish rug at La Grange's feet.

"Is this the promised end?" murmured Oscar.

The clock began to strike seven. "The performance

page 296

must be cancelled," said Carlos Branco. "Now we have no choice."

"I agree," said Richard Marais.

Oscar turned abruptly on Marais. "How do you know what Monsieur Branco has just said?" he asked. "He is standing behind you. You cannot hear him and you cannot see him to read his lips."

Richard Marais looked up at Oscar contemptuously. "Young man, you are not nearly so clever as you think. I can see Monsieur Branco's face quite clearly—reflected in the cheval mirror by the door." He pointed to the full-length mirror that stood between the dressing table and the doorway. Carlos Branco smiled.

Oscar lowered his head, suddenly abashed. "I apologise," he muttered.

Outside the dressing room we could hear footsteps and voices.

"We must go and tell them what has happened," said Branco.

"Yes," said Marais, turning to the stagehands. "There's business to attend to. The performance is cancelled. I'll inform the box office and the front-of-house staff."

"Should I address the company?" asked Branco.

Oscar hesitated. "Or should Madame La Grange do that?" he asked.

"Dear God!" Marais sighed and looked once more at the bloodied body of Edmond La Grange slumped across the dressing table. The glistening blood was beginning to congeal, the purple colour turning to a brownish black. "Someone must tell Maman."

"Shall I tell Maman?" suggested Carlos Branco. "I've known her longest."

"Who will tell Gabrielle?" I asked.

"And someone must call the police," said one of the stagehands quietly. The stagehands' faces were pale with shock. In their eyes I saw fear as well as dismay.

"Quite right," said Richard Marais. "We must call the police. And Dr. Ferrand. He may be in the building anyway."

Marais broke from our semicircle and moved towards the dressing-room door. Branco made to follow him. "If we get the company together onstage, I'll speak to them."

"And what will you tell them?" asked Oscar.

"The truth," said Branco briskly. "What else is there?"

"What is the truth of this?" asked Garstrang, looking about the room and shaking his head wearily.

"Forgive me," said Oscar, moving towards the door himself, and laying a hand on Carlos Branco's sleeve, "but, for the moment, I think that you should remain here."

"What on earth are you talking about?" said Branco, pulling his arm away.

"Let Monsieur Marais speak to the company," said Oscar, "while Mr. Garstrang fetches the police." He placed himself between Carlos Branco and the dressing-room door. Oscar was considerably taller than the actor and less than half his age.

"Get out of my way," growled Branco. "You've already made an idiot of yourself with Marais. Spare me your impertinence."

Oscar stood his ground. "I don't wish to be impertinent,"

he said softly, "but I think that you should stay here with us until the police arrive."

"Why?" barked Branco indignantly. "In God's name, tell me why?"

"Because," said Oscar simply, "my friend Mr. Sherard and I saw you enter this room only seconds before the fatal shot was fired."

"Don't be absurd!" roared Branco. "I was nowhere near the room when the shot was fired. I was at the back of the stage searching for my cloak and helmet."

"And before you ask," added Marais, his hand on the door, "I did not 'hear' the gunshot. I saw the stagehands running and followed them."

"Enough of this charade," said Branco, pushing past Oscar. "La Grange is dead. He shot himself. That's plain for all to see." He turned and looked Oscar in the eye. "Now there's business to be done. You can guard the body, *mon ami*. With your friend. Until the police arrive. We'll see to the rest. It's our theatre: we know how it works."

Marais pulled open the dressing-room door and, together, he and Carlos Branco joined the gathering throng outside. Eddie Garstrang and the two stagehands followed them. One of the stagehands—the one who had spoken— turned as he left and looked back at the body of Edmond La Grange. The young man's eyes were filled with tears.

The moment they were all gone, Oscar pulled the door to and turned the key in the lock.

"You let him pass," I said, amazed. "You let Branco go."

"Did I have a choice?" asked Oscar. "I don't carry handcuffs about my person. I could hardly knock him down."

"You should have done."

"There's a dead man in the room, Robert. A brawl would not be seemly."

We both turned and gazed once more on the still corpse of Edmond La Grange slumped across the dressing table.

"Branco is a murderer," I said.

"He'll not escape—nor try to," said Oscar. "After forty years, he is ready for his moment centre stage."

I stood at the far side of the dressing table looking down on the blood-soaked head of the man who had become my master. I could not claim to know him well, but I had relished my short time in his service. His was a household name and I was twenty-one and not immune to the glamour of fame. Edmond La Grange was a "great man"—a man "born to play kings," as the French say—a man who commanded applause, night after night for more than forty years. I had not grown to love him yet, but I enjoyed his company—I was honoured by it—and I recognised his particular genius. I put out my hand towards him and, for a moment, touched his shoulder.

I turned to Oscar, who was now slowly pacing the room, inspecting the walls, the floor, the ceiling. "Why should Carlos Branco want to kill Edmond La Grange?" I asked.

"All sorts of reasons," murmured Oscar distractedly. "Envy, jealousy, hurt, betrayal . . ."

I protested: "But they were friends!"

"Most men are murdered by their friends," grunted Oscar, kneeling down behind the cheval mirror near the doorway, "just as most women are murdered by their lovers." He paused. "But did Branco murder La Grange, I wonder?" he asked.

"We saw him enter the room only a moment before the shot was fired."

"We did," said Oscar, getting to his feet. "And, look, here are his cloak and helmet—discarded behind the looking glass."

"It can only have been Branco," I said, taking the pieces of costume from Oscar and laying them on the chaise longue. "There was no one else in the room when I left it. La Grange was alone in here when he locked the door behind me. I'll swear to that."

Oscar was now standing close to the dressing table, peering over it, examining the bloodstained hairbrushes and the Colt revolver that lay by La Grange's open hand. " 'Tis strange," he murmured, "passing strange."

"There is no mystery here, Oscar," I said emphatically. "Branco came to the door and knocked on it. We saw him. He knocked on the door a second time. We saw him. La Grange opened the door to him—and welcomed him, with a smile. We watched it happen, Oscar."

"We did."

"We saw him enter the room and the door close."

"We did."

"And a moment later, we heard the shot ring out."

"Quite so."

Oscar straightened himself and turned to me, feeling in his pocket for his cigarettes. "A brawl would have been unseemly, but I think a cigarette is permissible, don't you?" As he lit our cigarettes, he asked, "From the moment we heard the gun fire, how long did it take for us to come out from behind the scenery and begin to cross the stage? Long enough for Branco to throw off his cloak and run out of the dressing room?"

"Yes," I answered, "quite long enough." I spoke eagerly: I was so accustomed to being a member of Oscar's admiring audience, I felt oddly flattered whenever he sought my opinion. "Remember," I said, "he removed his helmet as he entered the room. He only had to drop the helmet and the cloak onto the floor, place the gun by the body, and run out into the wings. As we came across the stage, he turned tail and came back towards the dressing room as if he were arriving for the first time."

"And he shot La Grange with La Grange's own revolver?" mused Oscar, gazing down once more at the long grey barrel of the Colt six-shooter.

"Yes, it was in the drawer, and already loaded. We all knew that La Grange kept it there."

Oscar ran his fingertips along the barrel of the gun. "It's called the Peacemaker, you know. Sarah Bernhardt gave it to La Grange as a present. It had belonged to her American manager—the terrible Mr. Jarrett."

"I remember," I said. "Sarah will be distressed when she hears the news."

My friend smiled and drew slowly on his cigarette. "Yes and no," he murmured. "You are familiar with the Chinese proverb: 'There is no pleasure so great as watching an old friend fall off the roof.'" He wandered from the dressing table to the sideboard and peered down at the little carriage clock. It was almost half past seven. "I wonder how long the police will be?" he asked. "I liked Brigadier Malthus, didn't you? I trusted him."

The police arrived just as the clock was striking eight and Carlos Branco was about to address the company onstage. Moments before, in the wings, we had watched Branco offer his condolences to Liselotte La Grange. He leant towards the old lady and bowed and then, awkwardly, attempted to embrace her. Maman, who had lost her only son and both her grandchildren within the space of days, stared up at him blankly. Her withered face betrayed no feeling. Behind her was Richard Marais, pale as a corpse, and at her side, holding her hand, stood Gabrielle, her eyes puffed up from crying, her cheeks blotched with tears.

Brigadier Malthus, when he arrived, marched immediately onto the stage with a quiet authority that brooked no argument. He silenced Carlos Branco even as he was about to speak, and turned to face the assembly himself. He apologised for his intrusion, regretted its necessity, and offered both his sincere condolences and his complete assurance that matters would be conducted as expeditiously as the proper pursuit of justice allowed. Standing on the ramparts, where La Grange had stood before him, he explained that no one—"no one at all"—would now be able to leave the building without his permission, adding, smiling gently as he did so, that he had men stationed outside each of the theatre's several entrances. He invited the actors to return to their dressing rooms and the stage staff to resume their posts until further notice. Glancing at his pocket watch, he expressed the hope that his business would be done within two to three hours—"by midnight at the latest."

He was better than his word.

By 8:30 P.M. Malthus's men had removed the body of Edmond La Grange from the theatre that bore his name. They also removed his dressing table and all its contents, including the terrible Mr. Jarrett's Colt revolver, and the bloodstained Turkish rug and the swivel stool on which La Grange was sitting when he was shot. Between 8:30 P.M. and 10:30 P.M., Brigadier Malthus interviewed those he termed "the essential witnesses." In the space of two hours, assisted only by a young officer who took notes in shorthand, Malthus conducted a dozen interviews. His manner was courteous and urbane, enquiring, of course, but never aggressively so. Oscar said later that Malthus reminded him of a benevolent headmaster trying to bring the best out of his boys rather than a senior police officer charged with the investigation of a gruesome killing. He began his interviews with Oscar and me, followed by Carlos Branco, Richard Marais, Eddie Garstrang, and the two young stage-hands. He also questioned the theatre's stage manager, the stage doorkeeper, the company doctor (his old friend Pierre Ferrand), and, finally, the mother and the mistress of the deceased. At just after 10:30 P.M., he arrested Carlos Branco on suspicion of murder.

We did not witness Branco's arrest, but we heard him being dragged from his dressing room on the first floor, angrily protesting his innocence. His cries were those of a desperate man, and, projected by an actor's voice, they echoed around the building. As he was bundled down the stairs to the stage door—it took four policemen to restrain him, according to the stage doorman—he cursed the name of La Grange, blamed Oscar's "false witness" for his wrongful arrest, and shouted repeatedly: "Marais heard it all!"

Once Branco had been locked into the police wagon and was on his way to his first night in the police cells, Brigadier Malthus walked through the theatre gathering up what he called "my old friend La Grange's intimate circle," and invited us to join him in the actor's dressing room for a drink in the great man's memory.

La Grange's dressing room without La Grange was a different place. Brigadier Malthus stood in the centre of the room, where La Grange's dressing table had stood. We arranged ourselves around him: he was the master now. "This is Denmark under Fortinbras," murmured Oscar. My friend and I stood together, with our backs to the wall, at the edge of the gathering, by the dressing-room door, half hidden behind the cheval mirror.

As the room began to settle, Malthus caught my eye. "Will you help Dr. Ferrand serve the wine?" he asked. The pink-faced company doctor was in the dresser's cubicle opening the champagne. His hands were shaking slightly and there were traces of tears about his eyes. I assisted him as I was bidden. (Later I asked Oscar what he thought it was about Malthus that enabled him to be so effortlessly commanding. "Is it his height? His age? His integrity?" Oscar laughed. "You know that he's a policeman. We're all frightened of policemen. And he's a polite policeman. That's very disconcerting.")

When the doctor and I had ensured that everyone had a glass, Malthus looked down at Liselotte La Grange, who sat on Molière's chaise longue gazing up at him, and said, "Let us drink to the name of La Grange. In the theatre, there is none greater."

The old woman was dry-eyed and calm. She sat bolt upright, her head erect. It was not yet five hours since her son's death, but she was already dressed in full mourning. She looked more poised and self-possessed than I had ever known her. With both hands cupped around her glass, she held it up to lead the toast. "Thank you, Félix," she said, nodding to Malthus. "You were always a good boy." She looked around the room to find the doctor. "And you, too, Pierre." She turned back to the police inspector. "I never trusted Branco," she breathed. "*Never.*" She spoke the word with such sudden vehemence that the wine spilt over the edge of her glass.

Malthus took the glass from her, and Gabrielle de la Tourbillon—also already dressed in black, I noticed—knelt down by her side and mopped up the wine with a little lace handkerchief. (It was a gift of mine: I was embarrassed to see it now. When young love evaporates, our love tokens remain to mock us.)

"That man has killed my son," cried Liselotte La Grange. "He has killed my grandchildren. He killed my dog, my darling Marie Antoinette. He murdered the blackamoor, too. I know it."

"You know it?" asked Brigadier Malthus, returning Maman's wine-glass to her.

"I know it!" she repeated, holding the glass out towards Dr. Ferrand to be refilled. "A mother knows."

"We have only charged him with the murder of Edmond La Grange," said Malthus softly.

"He is guilty of them all," cried the dead man's mother.

"But one charge is sufficient," said Malthus. "One murder is enough. He can only face the guillotine once. A life for a life. That will do."

"It is certain that it was him?" asked Eddie Garstrang. "There is no doubt?"

"He must have done it," I said. "We saw him enter the room. No one else was here."

"He did it," screeched the old woman. "He was jealous of Edmond all his life. He was envious of us all." She drank greedily from her glass and held it out towards Dr. Ferrand once more. "I never trusted Branco. He's Spanish."

"Portuguese," Gabrielle de la Tourbillon corrected her.

"He killed them all," barked Liselotte La Grange. She looked around the room defiantly. She was more than eighty years of age, but her eyes blazed with rage and drink.

"Is it possible?" asked Eddie Garstrang. "Even the dog?"

"It's certainly possible," said Oscar from the corner of the room. "Carlos Branco might have killed the dog as an act of spite, for no other reason than to hurt Maman. He might have murdered Traquair because, for forty years, the great La Grange had the luxury of a personal dresser and he had never had one. Perhaps he also murdered La Grange's former dresser, the one who died in America. It's possible . . ."

"You are right, monsieur," said Liselotte La Grange, turning towards Oscar and raising her glass in his direction. "Branco hated us because without us he was nothing—just another actor who told funny stories."

"He was a fine actor," murmured Dr. Ferrand.

"There are plenty of those," snapped Maman. She looked up at the white-haired doctor and her eyes softened. "He was a good actor, Pierre. I grant you that. He was more than adequate in the right part." She accepted more of the proffered champagne and looked about the room again. She was now holding court exactly as her son was wont to do. "Let us agree that this man Branco was a good actor; perfect as Polonius. He was not a great actor. There is a difference. He was not a La Grange—and he knew it. All his life he resented us."

"He was jealous of the glory of La Grange," said Gabrielle softly.

"So he put a stop to it?" asked Eddie Garstrang. "Is that the idea? Sick and tired after a lifetime of hearing about the great and glorious family that had dominated French theatre for a century and a half, he murdered them: the father, the son, the daughter. He put an end "to the glory of La Grange" once and for all. Is that it?"

"I believe so," answered Brigadier Malthus, narrowing his eyes. "Perhaps Monsieur Marais can tell us more." The policeman looked down at the mottled, bald head of the La Grange company's man of business. "When we arrested Branco, he said that you had 'heard it all,' Monsieur Marais. What did you hear?"

"I heard nothing," answered Marais, looking up at the policeman with watery eyes. "I hear nothing."

"Forgive me," said Oscar, leaning around the cheval mirror to look Marais in the eye, "but earlier this evening, in this very room, as I recall, you heard Branco speak."

"I heard nothing," said Marais, looking at Oscar

308

contemptuously. "I read his lips—in that looking glass, as I told you."

"But in a looking glass," said Oscar quietly, "the image is reversed. Can you read moving lips when they are the wrong way round?"

Marais snorted with derision and turned to Brigadier Malthus. "So be it. I can hear a little—when voices are raised. This afternoon I heard Branco and Monsieur La Grange arguing."

"In here?" enquired Malthus.

"Yes."

"And you were with them?"

"I was outside, in the wings."

"But Branco knew that you were there?"

"He saw me when he came out of the room."

"And Branco knows that you can hear?"

"I can only hear a little, but Branco knows. Yes. He knows my secret. And I know his."

"And what is his secret?" asked Brigadier Malthus.

"For twenty years, I have reserved a small percentage of the theatre's box office takings to myself—to supplement my income. Fifteen years ago, by chance, Monsieur Branco discovered what I was doing. He threatened to tell Monsieur La Grange, unless I agreed to share the proceeds with him."

"He blackmailed you," said Brigadier Malthus quietly.

"Yes," said Marais.

"This is no secret, little man!" snapped Liselotte La Grange. She turned and looked on the small and charmless figure standing at her side. "Edmond knew about your petty larceny, knew about it almost from the start. And he knew that Branco was party to your little subterfuge—that Branco shared in the proceeds. He's known about the pair of you for years. He knew, and he did not care. What you stole from him was chicken feed. My son's murder has nothing to do with money, little man."

Marais said nothing. Brigadier Malthus put out a hand and touched him on the arm. It was a kindly gesture. "I am grateful to you for your confession, monsieur, but I believe Madame La Grange is right," he said.

"Of course, I'm right," cried the old woman. "I know what happened. It's clear what happened. This afternoon, when Carlos Branco wanted tonight's performance to be cancelled, he was overruled—and humiliated. My son called him an old fool, to his face and before the whole company. It was one humiliation too many. It drove Branco over the edge. When Edmond had finished his speech, he returned to his dressing room and, shortly afterwards, Branco, already in costume, followed him there and shot him, in cold blood. That's what happened. That's the truth of it."

"Yes," said Brigadier Malthus, looking at Liselotte La Grange in admiration, "that's the truth of it."

26

The Higher Truth

"**B**ut Carlos Branco did not murder Edmond La Grange."

"So you say, Mr. Wilde," replied Brigadier Malthus. "Thank you for your telegram. Thank you for coming to see me. You have arrived rather earlier than I expected."

"I apologise," said Oscar. "I could not sleep. Forgive me."

Malthus pulled together the lapels of his dressing gown with one hand, while beckoning us forward with the other. "There is nothing to forgive, except my appearance; and the chaos here and the fact that I have nothing to offer you for breakfast apart from coffee and cigarettes."

"I can imagine no more civilised start to a day," replied Oscar, smiling.

"Then, please, gentlemen, help yourselves," said the policeman, with an apologetic shrug, indicating a chest of drawers covered in books and papers, on top of which was perched a wooden tray bearing an assortment of cups, an earthenware coffeepot, and a tin of Algerian cigarettes. "If you'll excuse me, I'll just finish shaving."

It was not yet eight o'clock on the morning following the death of Edmond La Grange. Oscar and I had barely slept. When we had left the theatre it was gone midnight. When

we reached Oscar's hotel on the quai Voltaire, without pre-
amble or explanation, my friend declared that "a terrible
injustice" was about to be done and that we must send a
wire to Malthus at once. "And we must see him at once or
it will be too late." I looked at him uncomprehending, but
all he would say was: "A man may die, Robert—and on our
say-so. If he does, neither of us deserves to sleep again."

Oscar's telegram reached Brigadier Malthus at the Préfecture of Police on the Ile de la Cité shortly before two
A.M., just as the officer was concluding a second, brief
interview with Carlos Branco in his cell. On reading the
wire, Malthus had sent an immediate reply, inviting Oscar
to come to his apartment in the morning.

It was a beautiful rooftop apartment on the rue
d'Arcole, overlooking the cathedral of Notre Dame: a
huge, single room, long and wide, with oak-panelled walls
and a high plasterwork ceiling. It was filled with furniture
and flowers and sunlight. Malthus was evidently a man of
taste and learning. There were prints and pictures set up
on easels around the room; every surface was covered with
papers, books, and manuscripts. In one corner of the room
a Japanese screen half hid an unmade bed. In another a
wooden hatstand carved in the shape of a Russian dancing
bear and a complete human skeleton stood side by side,
both decked out in assorted items from the policeman's
wardrobe. Malthus appeared to live alone.

I poured the coffee while Oscar lit a cigarette and Malthus returned to his ablutions. His washstand was set by
the open window. Frost-white morning sunshine streamed
into the room: a cool breeze blew through billowing white
lace curtains. With a dozen quick, clean strokes of his

razor, Malthus completed his shaving and bent over the basin to rinse his face. His hair was silver, his eyebrows were grey and full, but his skin was remarkably unlined for a man of his age. He dried his smooth face on a white linen towel and slipped off his dressing gown. He had long, pale, muscular arms, and powerful thighs. His chest and belly were covered in a blanket of soft, white hair. As he pulled on his shirt and trousers, he called out to us to clear the chairs of paperwork and make ourselves at home.

"You are a scholar," said Oscar, picking up a pile of papers from an elegant Louis XV parlour chair and placing them carefully on one of the several occasional tables that were spread around the room.

"I am a policeman—with enthusiasms," answered Malthus, coming over to join us and clearing a chaise longue of assorted books and bric-a-brac. He sat down on the chaise and leant forward, his elbows on his knees, his hands clasped together under his chin. His smile was most beguiling.

"Can I get you a coffee?" I asked.

"No, thank you," he replied.

"You do not seem like a policeman," said Oscar, waving away a small cloud of cigarette smoke, the better to observe our host.

Malthus laughed. "And you do not seem like a detective, Mr. Wilde."

"I'm not one, alas," said Oscar with a mock-heroic sigh. His eyes darted about the room. "If I were, I would be able to detect your particular field of interest. I'm surrounded by clues, but I can't tell whether it's Napoleonic France or ancient Athens or the Spanish Inquisition that holds you in its thrall."

Malthus sat up, amused, and looked around at the volumes piled high on every surface. "You are keen eyed, Mr. Wilde. You have scored two bull's-eyes. I have no interest in the Spanish Inquisition, but France under Bonaparte and Greece in the third century BC are certainly the places where I spend what leisure the Préfecture allows me. Napoléon is my particular hero." He turned and nodded towards a framed silhouette of the great Corsican. "He founded the Préfecture, you know. When I was a boy I wanted to be a priest. Then I discovered Napoléon and decided to become a policeman."

"*Ne pas oser, c'est ne rien faire qui vaille,*"* said Oscar lightly.

Malthus smiled. "I am compiling an anthology of Napoléon's aphorisms, as it happens. He rivalled even you when it came to conjuring up a telling turn of phrase, Mr. Wilde."

"And Epicurus?" asked Oscar, looking towards the crowded mantelpiece that dominated the room and indicating a small marble bust that stood at one end, its head turned in profile to the room. I had not noticed it until then: it was the head of the Greek philosopher, the identical sculpture to the one that Edmond La Grange kept in his loft on rue de la Pierre Levée.

"Edmond La Grange gave me that," said Brigadier Malthus. "He gave one to Pierre Ferrand as well. Edmond used to say that Dr. Ferrand must have been a descendant

---

* "Without daring, nothing is achieved."

of Epicurus, they looked so alike. Encouraged by Edmond, I have been trying to write a life of Epicurus. It's not been done before—in French, at least. If ever I complete the book, I shall dedicate it to the memory of Edmond La Grange, my friend. He was a true Epicurean—and a great man."

"He was a great actor, certainly," said Oscar, extinguishing his cigarette in the small brass ashtray that Brigadier Malthus passed to him.

"He was a meteor who burnt bright and lit up his century."

"And it was not Carlos Branco who killed him," said Oscar emphatically.

"Ah!" cried Malthus. *"Revenons à nos moutons."** The police officer got to his feet and fetched his tin of Algerian cigarettes. He offered the tin first to Oscar, then to me. He lit a spill and held it for us while we lit our cigarettes. He resumed his seat and took up his former position, leaning forward with his elbows on his knees, his fingers intertwined beneath his chin, his attention focused entirely on my friend. "Speak, Mr. Wilde. I am listening."

"Have you charged Branco with La Grange's murder?" asked Oscar quietly.

"I have."

"And when will he appear in court?"

"The preliminary hearing will be tomorrow, at ten o'clock. That's just a formality, of course. The trial proper will follow in two or three weeks, a month at most. It's a clear-cut case, quite straightforward."

---

* "Let us return to our sheep" = "Let us return to the subject in hand."

"Have the papers yet been submitted to the court?"

Malthus laughed. "No, Mr. Wilde. We only arrested the man last night! Napoléon had the capacity to toil till dawn, his energy undiminished, his judgement unimpaired, but I am not Napoléon—alas! I'll be seeing to the paperwork this morning when I get to the office."

"Then it is not too late," murmured Oscar, puffing on his cigarette. "Thank God." He leant earnestly towards Brigadier Malthus. "Monsieur," he said, "I beg you: withdraw the charge."

Brigadier Malthus threw out his arms: "But *why*, Mr. Wilde? Carlos Branco is guilty." He glanced towards the window. "It's as clear as daylight." He looked between us both and straightened his back as he asserted his authority. "Branco had the motive, the means, the opportunity; and with your own eyes you saw him enter La Grange's dressing room moments before the fatal shot was fired. You told me so." Malthus tilted his head in my direction and smiled. "Mr. Sherard told me so. I have your statements."

"Tear them up!" cried Oscar. He sprang to his feet and began to pace the room. Oscar Wilde had both friends and close relations who were barristers: he was an instinctive advocate himself. Over the next several minutes he addressed Malthus as he might have done a judge and jury at London's Old Bailey. He spoke rapidly and, as he spoke, I noticed a trace of the Irish accent of his boyhood return. "Carlos Branco had a motive, I grant you that. Resentment. Branco was a fine actor who spent his life in the shadow of a great one. Madame La Grange had her poodle; Edmond La Grange had his Polonius. For forty years Branco played second fiddle to the great virtuoso, humbled and humiliated by him in turn. No doubt Carlos Branco's resentment of Edmond La Grange bubbled and festered within him for years; but you can resent a man, you can *hate* a man, without murdering him." Oscar stopped in his tracks and looked Brigadier Malthus in the eye. "Branco denies the murder, does he not?"

"He does," said the brigadier, looking up at Oscar with a half-raised eyebrow. He seemed both gripped and amused by Oscar's performance. "Branco denies the murder, absolutely."

"But he admits the larceny?" asked Oscar. "He was certainly complicit in Marais's fraud. We're sure of that. And he concedes as much, does he not?"

"He does," said Malthus. "He acknowledges that he has been taking money from Richard Marais, week in, week out, for fifteen years. He claims that La Grange won all the money back—and more—playing him at cards."

Oscar laughed. "I believe Carlos Branco is telling you the truth, Brigadier Malthus. Carlos Branco did not kill Edmond La Grange."

"So you keep saying, Mr. Wilde. I hear you! But if Carlos Branco did not kill Edmond La Grange, who did?"

"Edmond La Grange killed himself."

Malthus's brow furrowed. I held my breath. Oscar walked quietly to the window and stood gazing out over the flying buttresses of Notre Dame.

The policeman got to his feet and helped himself to another cigarette. "*Why*, Mr. Wilde? *Why* should Edmond La Grange kill himself?"

Oscar turned and stood framed in the window casement. The light behind him was so bright we could no longer see his face. "Because the game was up," he said simply. "The long run was over. The golden age of the Théâtre La Grange was ended—and he was the man responsible. Like Samson, he brought the temple down upon himself."

"I don't follow you," said Malthus, shaking his head and drawing slowly on his cigarette. I was bewildered equally, but I said nothing.

Oscar continued: "Edmond La Grange was a man to whom nothing mattered but the theatre—and his place in it. Do you agree?"

Malthus hesitated. "Yes," he said eventually. "Yes, I suppose that's true."

"He was a great actor and, when he chose to be, a genial enough companion."

"He was my friend," protested Malthus. "We were at school together."

"And you are loyal to his memory, as a consequence. That does you credit, sir. But how well do we know the friends of our childhood? Because they have always been there, perhaps we cease to see them as they really are. I encountered Edmond La Grange only recently. I admired his genius; I enjoyed his company; but I recognised him for what he was."

"He was unique."

"No. As an actor, he was very special—up there with Bernhardt and with Irving. And as a man he was unusual— a phenomenon of a kind, but not unique. I did not know him as you did, as a friend from boyhood whose peculiar nature you took for granted. I observed him as an outsider given privileged access to his inner circle. I found that Edmond La Grange was a man with no morals, no scruples, no code of conduct beyond that of his own devising. People meant nothing to him. He shared his mistress with all comers. He didn't have friends: he had card-playing cronies who played on his territory on his terms. Money meant little to him. He allowed Marais—and Carlos Branco—to steal from him for years. All that mattered to Edmond La Grange was the pleasure of the moment and his place in the theatre: the La Grange heritage. He kept his mother beneath his roof—he tolerated her intolerable presence—not because he loved her, but because she was his father's wife and bore his name. La Grange mocked his mother, despised her as a woman. But he'd not rid himself of her, because she was part of his heritage."

Brigadier Malthus resumed his place on the chaise longue. He was evidently intrigued by Oscar's line of argument. "Do you think it could have been La Grange, then, who killed Maman's dog—out of spite?"

"To amuse himself and distress her?" Oscar shrugged. "It's possible. Anyone could be forgiven for asphyxiating Marie Antoinette. She was a horrid creature." Oscar stood at the window gazing out over the cathedral rooftop. "Carlos Branco might have killed the wretched dog," he mused. "Branco's capable of murdering a dog, that I'll concede. Murdering a defenceless animal and sharing in the proceeds of petty theft: that's Branco's level."

"And the dresser?" asked Brigadier Malthus, leaning back over the chaise longue to study Oscar. "Who killed your friend the dresser, Monsieur Wilde?"

Oscar spun round slowly on his heels and gazed directly at the policeman. "Am I not responsible for Traquair's death?" he asked dramatically. "I encouraged La Grange to offer him the job. I persuaded Traquair to take it. It was because of me—and me alone—that the unfortunate young man—the son of a slave, God save the mark!—was induced to travel to a foreign land where he did not speak the language and had no friends."

Malthus smiled. "But you did not kill him."

"No, not directly, but if he took his own life I share a responsibility for that, just as La Grange shared a responsibility for the deaths of Agnès and Bernard."

Malthus reached for his tin of cigarettes once more. "Edmond La Grange did not kill his own children!"

Oscar came back into the centre of the room and accepted another of the policeman's cigarettes. "Not with his own hands, of course," he said softly, lighting his cigarette from Malthus's, "but he was the author of their destruction. And he knew it. And when he realised what he had done, he had no choice but to destroy himself."

Félix Malthus got to his feet and put a hand on Oscar's shoulder. "These are extraordinary allegations, Monsieur Wilde."

"I know," answered Oscar, gazing steadily into the policeman's eye.

Malthus lifted his hand from Oscar's shoulder and moved across the room to the mantelpiece. He stood by the bust of Epicurus. He looked back at Oscar enquiringly. "You say that La Grange 'destroyed' his own children before 'destroying' himself. What precisely do you mean?"

"Agnès La Grange was in love with her father."

The policeman smiled. "Many young women are in love with their fathers. Does it signify? Agnès had no mother and her father was a powerful and charismatic man."

"This was no run-of-the-mill infatuation," said Oscar. "This was obsessive love—passionate, romantic . . ."

"And unrequited, I assume?"

"I do not know," said Oscar lightly, drawing on his cigarette.

Brigadier Malthus turned towards him. "Are you suggesting, Mr. Wilde, that my old friend Edmond La Grange and his young daughter were *lovers*? If you are, I have to tell you that I simply don't believe it. I knew the man for more than half a century. He was flawed. He had his weaknesses. But Edmond La Grange would not have taken his own daughter to his bed."

I spoke up. "Dr. Blanche was adamant on this point as well," I said.

My friend glanced in my direction. "Indeed, he was, Robert," he murmured. He turned back to Malthus to explain: "We called on Dr. Blanche at his clinic in Passy yesterday morning. Dr. Blanche was emphatic. Agnès was his patient. La Grange was his friend. The doctor is certain that their relationship, while complex, was not physical."

"I'm pleased to hear it," said Malthus.

Oscar continued: "But the doctor's son tells a different story. Yesterday afternoon, when Robert returned to the theatre, I went on to Montmartre and met up with Jacques-Emile Blanche and Maurice Rollinat at Le Chat Noir. Jacques-Emile loved Agnès, but she made it plain to him that she could not love him because she loved another. In recent days, Agnès spoke to Jacques-Emile of her lover and confessed that he was an older man. Jacques-Emile believes that it might have been her father."

"Is there evidence?" asked Malthus.

"No," said Oscar.

"Then forget it, Mr. Wilde. It was not so."

Oscar laughed. "If you say so, Brigadier! You are the police officer in command of the case. Let us accept that Edmond and Agnès were not lovers." He clapped his hands. "That's that." He looked Malthus steadily in the eye once more. "But what cannot be denied is that Agnès was in love with Edmond. Her passion for her father was obsessive and it destroyed her. It drove her to madness—and to suicide."

"That I can believe," said Malthus, nodding slowly. "That I will accept."

"And her death provoked her brother's," said Oscar. "Suicide, as we keep hearing, is an inherited characteristic. Death was never far from the thoughts of Bernard La Grange. Death was his peculiar obsession. Robert and I once came across him in the Room of the Dead, but, unlike us, he was not there out of curiosity as a passing tourist. He was a dedicated student of mortality. Death, to him, was life's ultimate experience. Self-destruction fascinated him. He talked of it often with Maurice Rollinat and the other nihilists of his acquaintance. And inspired by Agnès's death, he resolved to seize his own. Bernard La Grange burnt himself to death—he sacrificed himself in the wake of his sister's demise, like a young Indian widow committing sati. He had Indian blood in his veins, after all."

Brigadier Malthus said nothing. He had taken a small notebook from the mantelpiece and was writing in it with a pencil.

Oscar went on: this was his summing-up, his peroration to the jury. "And when Bernard was gone, what had Edmond left? Nothing. So he killed himself—in his own dressing room, with his own gun, on the night he brought the La Grange heritage to a close."

Brigadier Malthus pocketed his notebook and pencil and threw his cigarette into the empty grate beneath the mantelpiece. "Mr. Wilde, you are very persuasive. I can believe that Agnès La Grange took her own life and that Bernard La Grange did likewise. I can even accept that their deaths might have led Edmond La Grange to contemplate suicide himself. But there is a difficulty."

I looked up at my friend. I anticipated the difficulty. "We saw Carlos Branco walking into the dressing room, Oscar, a moment before the shot was fired."

"No, Robert. We saw a man dressed in a cloak, wearing the helmet and visor belonging to the Ghost of Hamlet's Father, enter the room. It could have been anyone."

"Are you saying it was not Carlos Branco?" I asked, amazed.

Oscar smiled. "It was not Carlos Branco, Robert."

"Then who was it?" demanded Brigadier Malthus.

"It was Edmond La Grange," said Oscar.

"But, Oscar," I protested, "we saw Edmond La Grange open the dressing-room door. We both saw him. He was inside the room, Oscar. We *saw* him."

"We were deceived, Robert."

"But how?"

"I will show you." He moved towards the apartment door and held out his hand as if offering to lead the way. "I will show you both. Please. Come with me."

27

The End of the Story

We climbed aboard the cab that Oscar had kept waiting on the rue d'Arcole and set off for the Théâtre La Grange for what turned out to be the very last time. Given the hour and the circumstances, Oscar was remarkably effervescent. "I'm always stimulated by exhaustion," he explained.

"There's more to it than that, Mr. Wilde," said Brigadier Malthus, who was seated opposite Oscar in the cab, their knees almost touching. "I think you enjoy the thrill of the chase. You don't look like a hunting man, and yet . . ."

Oscar grinned. His smile was lopsided and his teeth beginning to show signs of decay. He completed Malthus's sentence: " . . . we all have our secrets. Isn't that it, Brigadier?" From his coat pocket he produced his favourite silver cigarette case. "Shall we move from Algiers to Istanbul?" he suggested, offering us each one of his Turkish cigarettes. He lit them for us and, savouring the aroma of the burning match, closed his eyes and murmured, "Learn to breathe deeply, gentlemen. Relish the moment—and the cigarette. Laugh when you can, cry when you must, and, when you sleep, try really to sleep. Live life to the full. You will be dead soon enough."

He opened his eyes and turned to me and touched me on the sleeve. "Forgive me, Robert, for not taking you with me every inch of the way. I know you understand. We are a team, of course, but occasionally a line of enquiry has to be pursued on a freelance basis. Sometimes a man walks faster when he walks alone."

Brigadier Malthus breathed out a cloud of blue grey smoke. "I recognise the quotation, Mr. Wilde," he said. "Napoléon Bonaparte has some great lines, does he not?"

"Oscar has plenty of great lines of his own," I said, rising to my friend's defence. "You were speaking of hunting, sir. Have you heard Oscar's definition of the English country gentleman galloping after a fox? 'The unspeakable in full pursuit of the uneatable.'"

Malthus chuckled obligingly. Oscar smiled and drew on his cigarette. "The line comes from my brother, Willie, in fact," he said, "but I don't intend to give him credit. Giving Willie credit is never advisable—as his banker can tell you."

We all laughed. I glanced out of the cab window and noticed that we were crossing the rue de Turbigo, passing Oscar's favourite *boulangerie*. I had known him for only a matter of weeks, but I realised that already I was wholly *Oscarisé*, totally in my new friend's thrall.

He leant towards Brigadier Malthus and tapped him lightly on the knee. "The thrill of the chase may be part of the story, but in this instance, please note, I don't lust for a kill. It's a reprieve I'm after. If Carlos Branco is brought to trial, he'll be found guilty."

"And it is too late to reprieve a man when the drop has fallen," said the policeman.

Oscar sat back and rested his large head against the shabby leather of the cab seat. He looked at Malthus steadily and his eyes smiled. "Is that your line or Napoléon's, I wonder?"

"It can be yours in due course, Mr. Wilde," said the policeman, drawing on his cigarette.

It was not yet ten o'clock when we reached the stage door of the Théâtre La Grange. A solitary gendarme stood in the alleyway, at the foot of the steps leading to the La Grange apartment. He threw down his cigarette and saluted as Brigadier Malthus strode past. The stage doorkeeper was at his post, drinking a foul-smelling horse-meat broth. "My breakfast," he grunted.

"Breathe deeply, gentlemen," said Malthus wryly. "Relish the moment. You'll be dead soon enough."

We passed through the stage door vestibule into the theatre's deserted wings. Malthus, leading the way, stumbled on the costume rail that stood just inside the doorway.

"There's no rush," murmured Oscar. "Let's accustom our eyes to the gloom."

We stood still for a moment, looking about us. To our right, on the stage itself, we could discern the outline of the battlements of Elsinore. Ahead of us, we could see—more clearly because by it a gasolier burnt low—the door to Edmond La Grange's dressing room.

"Was the light any brighter than this last night?" asked Oscar, his voice barely above a whisper.

"I don't believe so," I replied. "This semidarkness is how it is between performances."

"Indeed," answered Oscar. "Quite so."

"Well?" enquired Brigadier Malthus briskly. "What now?"

Oscar turned his head towards the policeman's. "A little show for your benefit, sir—a ten o'clock matinée." Oscar touched my arm. "Robert, kindly escort Brigadier Malthus to the far side of the stage. Take him, if you would, to where you and I were standing yesterday, talking with Gabrielle. Take him to the very spot from which we saw Branco apparently entering La Grange's dressing room. Wait there—behind the scenery. Do not emerge until I tell you."

I nodded and beckoned to Félix Malthus to follow me. Carefully, in the half-light, we made our way across the empty stage. As we set off, Oscar was rifling through the costumes on the rail. We glanced behind us and saw him making his way down the wings towards La Grange's dressing room. We heard him enter. A few moments later we heard the dressing-room door open and close again.

Oscar's voice called out across the stage: "Are you hidden behind the scenery, gentlemen?"

I called back, "We are!"

Malthus looked at me and raised a quizzical eyebrow.

Oscar called again: "When I tell you, and not before, come out from behind the scenery and look across the stage—exactly as we did yesterday."

"I understand," I answered.

We waited in silence. "Your friend is extraordinary," whispered Malthus.

Suddenly, Oscar shouted, "Come! Come now!"

I took Brigadier Malthus by the elbow and propelled him from behind the piece of scenery to the very position that Oscar and I had occupied some fifteen hours before. Then, across the stage in the far wing, we had seen Carlos Branco walking towards the door to Edmond La Grange's dressing room. Now, he appeared to be there again— except that this time it could not have been Branco. Branco was locked up in a police cell at the Préfecture on the Ile-de-la Cité. Oscar was re-creating the scene: a figure wearing the cloak and helmet and visor worn by Branco in the role of the Ghost of Hamlet's Father was walking steadily towards La Grange's dressing-room door.

"It could be anyone," breathed Malthus.

"It's Oscar," I said.

The figure reached the door to the dressing room. He looked briefly in our direction—precisely as the figure had done the night before—and then knocked on the dressing-room door.

"Who is his accomplice?" Malthus murmured to himself.

"There is no one else, I'm certain."

The cloaked figure knocked on the dressing-room door once more—and the door opened. And as the door opened, the figure took off his helmet and, suddenly, within the doorway, facing us, we saw Oscar's beaming visage appear . . .

"My God!" Malthus cried out. "I see!"

"Yes," answered Oscar, looking towards us. "You see. And what you see is an illusion: a reflection of my face in a looking glass." The cloaked figure standing at the door slowly turned around and, as he did so, Oscar's face disappeared from within the doorway to be replaced by a reflection of the back of his head.

Malthus strode across the stage, his hand outstretched towards my smiling friend. Oscar unclasped the cloak that was fastened around his neck. I took the cloak while the policeman shook Oscar warmly by the hand. Just inside the doorway, to the left of it, facing us at a slight angle, was Edmond La Grange's cheval mirror. Across the stage, over the back of his cloaked shoulder, we had seen Oscar's face reflected in the mirror—just as the day before, in the same mirror, we had seen the reflected face of Edmond La Grange.

"Edmond La Grange was an actor," said Oscar, "a man of the theatre. Not surprisingly, he created a little drama to introduce his own suicide. He had determined to kill himself. He had his reasons. His children were dead; the La Grange tradition was over; "the perfect *Hamlet*" was the perfect production with which to take his leave. And as he made his exit, by way of revenge, he thought it might be amusing to cast some suspicion on Carlos Branco, "the old fool, Polonius," who, with Richard Marais, had conspired to rob him over all these years."

As Oscar unfolded his story, he took centre stage. He stood where La Grange's dressing table had stood and commanded the small room with that curious mixture of authority and charm that he used to such effect on the lecture platform. As he spoke his eyes darted about the room and he used his hands constantly to emphasise a point or to illustrate his meaning.

"At just after six o'clock last night," he continued, "when Edmond La Grange had finished his speech and the La Grange company had begun to disperse, the great actor returned to this room, his dressing room, noticing, perhaps, as he did so, where I was standing, talking with his mistress, at the back of the stage. For his pantomime to succeed, La Grange needed an audience, if only a small one." Oscar turned to me and smiled. "He sent you to find me, Robert—you recall?"

"I do," I answered, "of course. He locked his door behind me."

"And, moments later, he unlocked it and opened it and looked out. He saw that the wing was empty, but I imagine that he heard us in conversation behind the scenery at the back of the stage and decided to seize his moment. The readiness was all."

As Oscar reached into his coat pocket for his cigarette case, Brigadier Malthus reached into his for his notebook and pencil. For the remainder of my friend's narrative, the police officer took notes. Oscar watched him carefully, and whenever Malthus was busy scribbling, the Irish storyteller would draw slowly on his cigarette to give the French policeman time to catch up.

"La Grange seized the moment," repeated Oscar. "He slipped out of his dressing room and up the wing to the costume rail. He found Branco's cloak and threw it about his shoulders. He put on Branco's helmet and pulled down the visor. Dressed as Branco he walked back to his own dressing-room door, turning round when he reached it to make sure that he had the audience that he had hoped for. He did." Oscar paused and turned his eyes from Malthus's to mine. "We were there, Robert, you and I. And, knowing that we were there and knowing that we were watching, he knocked on his own door—and knocked again. And then he opened the door with one hand while pulling off his helmet with the other. As the helmet came off, the door swung open and in the looking glass, that looking glass"—Oscar pointed to the cheval mirror that stood by the dressing-room door—"La Grange's face suddenly appeared. We stared at him as he gazed at us. And as the cloaked figure, over whose shoulder we could see La Grange, stepped into the room, we assumed that what we were watching was Branco entering La Grange's dressing room and that La Grange disappeared from view because he was stepping forward to welcome his old friend and colleague."

Oscar paused while Brigadier Malthus's pencil scurried across his notebook's page. Oscar smiled and contemplated the ash at the tip of his Turkish cigarette. Eventually, when Malthus's pencil came to a stop, Oscar continued: "Inside the room, La Grange closed the door behind him, threw off the cloak and tossed it and the helmet to the floor, sat down at once at his dressing table, lifted the waiting gun to his own head, and, without a moment's hesitation, shot himself."

Malthus wrote nothing. As Oscar drew slowly on the last of his cigarette, the policeman gazed at him fixedly. Oscar smiled. "Were there any marks on the gun to suggest that anyone other than La Grange had handled it?" he asked the policeman.

"None," answered Malthus, still looking at him steadily. "But the gun was not in his hand. It was lying on the dressing table."

"It fell from his grasp as the shot was fired," suggested Oscar.

Brigadier Malthus stared down at his notebook once

more. "So it was La Grange, not Branco, who fired the fatal shot."

"Exactly," said Oscar, moving over to the sideboard on which stood La Grange's little carriage clock and extinguishing his cigarette in the ashtray that he found there.

"Carlos Branco is guilty of killing a dog, perhaps; guilty of petty embezzlement, certainly. He is not guilty of murder. It would be wrong to charge him with murder. With Maman's special pleading, the court would find against him—without doubt. And it would be wrong to execute a man for a crime he did not commit."

Brigadier Malthus closed his notebook and returned it to his coat pocket. He crossed the dressing room to where my friend was now standing. "You are a remarkable young man," he said. As the carriage clock struck the half hour, the policeman, smiling and looking Oscar in the eye, shook him, quite formally, by the hand. "I hear what you say, Mr. Wilde," he said. "And I accept your argument. Indeed, I am overwhelmed by it."

Within the hour, Carlos Branco was released. He was released without charge. By his own admission, he and Marais had defrauded the Théâtre La Grange over a period of many years, but who had they really harmed? And what evidence was there? Marais, the keeper of the La Grange company books, had destroyed them all. Besides, did anyone care?

The deaths of Edmond, Bernard, and Agnès La Grange were reported in newspapers throughout France and in many countries overseas. Rumours about the mysterious nature of the deaths rumbled on in the French press for several weeks and then petered out. In due course, before the start of the autumn theatre season, Richard Marais and Carlos Branco joined forces and came to an accommodation with Liselotte La Grange. Maman had inherited all the assets of the La Grange company from her son. Marais and Branco went into partnership with her, founding the Théâtre Branco–La Grange. Marais felt "it must be done—the *scandale macabre* will be so good for business." Maman, who mourned for her son but grieved without tears, felt that she owed it to Edmond's memory and to the tradition established by her late husband's forebears. Carlos Branco, broken by his experiences, weak and humbled by tragedy, knew no other life.

The new Théâtre Branco–La Grange maintained much of the old company's repertoire, broadened somewhat to include melodrama and farce alongside the established classics. Gabrielle de la Tourbillon (née Guillotin) became the company's leading lady. I never shared her bed again. From time to time, by chance, we met in public places (in restaurants, in theatre foyers, at parties in other people's houses), but when we met it was as if we were strangers, as if the intimacy we had known had never been. I imagine that if you encountered Gabrielle today and mentioned my name to her, it would mean nothing.

I will never forget Gabrielle de la Tourbillon—how could I? She was my first *affaire,* but I will confess that I did not pine long for her. A week to the day after the death of Edmond La Grange, at the coroner's court, in the rue du Temple, I met a delightful young lady named Odile. She was just twenty, a petite girl with a trim figure, black glossy hair, a doll's pink cheeks, and the sweetest smile and softest laugh you can imagine. She was a nursing sister, on duty in the court in case any of the witnesses should become ill. I told her that I was lovesick from the moment that I set eyes on her!

I attended the coroner's court with Oscar. Brigadier Malthus, Dr. Pierre Ferrand, and Dr. Emile Blanche were called to give evidence, and the coroner's verdict on the deaths of Agnès, Bernard, and Edmond La Grange was the same in each case: death by suicide.

That evening—it was to be Oscar's last night in Paris for a while—my friend and I went up to Montmartre and took dinner at the Le Chat Noir with Sarah Bernhardt, Maurice Rollinat, and Jacques-Emile Blanche. It was a night to remember. We sat, the five of us, crowded around a small table at the back of the café, our hands touching, our heads close together, our eyes shining in the flickering candlelight. We ate *moules marinières* and drank champagne and, as Oscar put it, "told sad stories of the death of kings."

"He *was* a king!" cried Madame Bernhardt. "He was a sun king—the greatest actor of his generation. He was *glorious*."

"But he ruined his daughter," said Jacques-Emile Blanche starkly. "He seduced her."

"Did he?" asked Sarah earnestly. "Did he really? Do we know that for certain? Who is the witness? Who saw them in bed together? No one!"

"And does it matter?" asked Maurice Rollinat, rubbing his eyes with his knuckles. "Why shouldn't they be lovers?"

"It's not natural," I said.

"Oh, but it is!" cried Rollinat. "Animals do it all the time. In the farmyard and the forest incest is absolutely comme il faut." He laughed and reached for the champagne bottle and poured more wine into each of our glasses.

"Keep your depravity for your poetry, Maurice," murmured Madame Bernhardt, gently caressing Rollinat's cheek with the back of her hand. "It's quite amusing there."

Jacques-Emile Blanche stared at the burning candle in the middle of our table. "Edmond La Grange seduced his daughter and the shame of it killed her," he said. He spoke so softly we could barely hear him. "I loved her and now she is gone forever."

"Not forever," said Oscar kindly. "There is your portrait of her. That will last. In your painting she will never grow old. Thanks to you, her beauty will endure."

Madame Bernhardt dipped a piece of bread into the *marinière* sauce. (For so slight and birdlike a creature, the divine Sarah had a remarkably hearty appetite.) "We still have no *proof* that father and daughter were lovers. Their suicides suggest it, I agree, but there is no *evidence*."

"And Jacques-Emile's father is adamant that neither of them would have countenanced such a thing," Oscar added. "They were both 'good Catholics,' as we say, and incest, as we know, is a mortal sin."

"That's what makes it so attractive," chuckled Rollinat, wiping champagne bubbles from his black moustache. I had not seen the melancholy poet in such happy form before.

"God knows the truth," said Oscar. "He alone is privy to all our secrets."

"And we all have secrets, do we, Oscar?" asked Madame Bernhardt playfully.

"We do," answered Oscar seriously. He sipped at his champagne and eyed the bottle on the table. It was almost empty. He held it up in the air, high above his head, until a waiter appeared. He ordered a second bottle and, pressing a silver coin into the young man's hand, added, "Why not bring us the third at the same time?" Smiling, Oscar turned back to the table. "Yes, young or old, beautiful or plain, rich or poor, we all have secrets. Even that waiter. Even Brigadier Malthus."

"Who is Brigadier Malthus?" asked Madame Bernhardt.

"An intellectual policeman," I said. "A most civilised man. He's been in charge of the case."

"I know him," said Maurice Rollinat. "Tall, slim, handsome, sixty. Clean shaven. Silver haired."

"That's the man," I said.

"You know him?" asked Oscar, leaning forward towards Rollinat.

"I do," replied the poet, smiling broadly. "I know him quite well. He's a flagellator. He whips himself—for pleasure."

"For pleasure?" repeated Sarah, still wiping her dish with bread.

"For *pleasure!*" echoed Rollinat with relish, letting the word roll lubriciously around his mouth. "There's a disused chapel near the Room of the Dead where he gives master classes in the flagellator's art. I have been once or twice. Three or four times, in fact. He is a fine teacher."

Oscar laughed. "I'm pleased to hear it."

"Oscar!" exclaimed La Bernhardt, looking up at our friend reprovingly. "Don't encourage him."

"I mean, Sarah, that I'm pleased to have my suspicions confirmed," said Oscar, by way of explanation. He lifted Madame Bernhardt's tiny hand and kissed her fingers lightly. "I had a feeling that there was a touch of the Toms de Torquemada about Félix Malthus." Oscar turned to me and grinned. "You recall that I suggested that the Spanish Inquisition was one of his interests, Robert?"

"He denied it," I said.

"Indeed," replied Oscar. "But I saw a flail in his coat stand and I saw the weals on his back."

"When?"

"When he was shaving. When, for a moment, he stood naked before us."

"I didn't see his back."

Oscar raised an eyebrow and said slyly, "You were studying his front, no doubt, while I was studying his back."

"He didn't turn his back towards us," I insisted.

"No," said Oscar. "He did not. But he stood naked by his washbasin and, behind him, hanging on the wall above the basin, was a mirror. I saw the reflection of his back in his looking glass." Oscar raised his champagne to me teasingly. "We all have our secrets, Robert, and some of them are hidden in the looking glass."

"Where are yours hidden, Oscar?" asked Maurice Rollinat.

"In the stars!" replied my friend airily.

"And next to his heart," I said, leaning across the table towards Oscar and putting my hand inside his blue velvet jacket.

"Robert!" he remonstrated, but it was too late. In my hand I held a small cream-coloured envelope. It was my turn to tease my friend.

"May I?" I asked, beginning to open the envelope.

"If you must," he said.

I opened the envelope and took out a small, square photograph. I held the picture lightly between my thumb and forefinger and put it near the candlelight so that our companions could see it.

"Who is she?" asked Sarah Bernhardt.

"She is beautiful," said Jacques-Emile Blanche.

"Her name is Constance Lloyd," said Oscar. "She has violet eyes and a pure heart."

"And you love her?" asked Sarah.

"I believe that I do," said Oscar, smiling.

"And might you marry her?" asked Jacques-Emile, looking at Oscar excitedly.

Oscar laughed. "Dear friend, I do believe that I might."

Maurice Rollinat, topping up our glasses once more and spilling wine over his fingers as he did so, turned sharply towards Oscar. "What happened to eating 'of the fruit of all the trees in the garden of the world,' my friend?" he asked.

"Surely 'the fruit of all the trees' must include the mulberry bush of matrimony, Maurice?" replied Oscar smoothly. "Mr. Henry James may consider me to be an unclean beast and a tenth-rate cad, but I see myself as a happily married family man."

My friend took the little photograph from my hand and carefully placed it against the candlestick on the table in front of him. He looked down at the picture of Miss

Constance Lloyd and I saw love, as well as tears and laughter, in his eyes.

"Here's to love!" I said, raising my glass.

We all raised our glasses and brought them together across the table and clinked them. "Here's to love!"

"To love!"

"To love!"

Gently, Oscar put his hand on Jacques-Emile Blanche's arm. "Death is nothing. Love is all. You loved her. She had that."

London, New Year, 1891

"**W**hat happened to the American?" asked Arthur Conan Doyle. "What happened to Eddie Garstrang the gambler?"

On New Year's Day 1891, as planned, we met up once more at Madame Tussaud's Baker Street Bazaar with our friend the physician and celebrated creator of Sherlock Holmes, Dr. Arthur Conan Doyle.

He was in rumbustious form. Christmas had been a jolly affair in the Doyle household. There was much happiness—Arthur now had a plump baby daughter, Mary, to dandle on his knee—and, thanks to Sherlock Holmes, the wherewithal to do a "proper" Christmas, with all the trimmings. And though a proper, happy family Christmas, there had still been time for quiet contemplation, for sitting by the fireside cracking nuts, for counting one's blessings, and for reading.

Doyle had read our story, had read with care ("with *great* care," he said) my humble account of Oscar's remarkable year, the year that took him from Leadville, Colorado, to the Théâtre La Grange, by way of Reading Gaol. Arthur had read my narrative (and "enjoyed it, enjoyed it hugely"), but he had questions to ask—not least about my style. "It's very *bold,* Robert. There are intimate details

I'm not sure that I'd dare share with my readers. Some of your frankness is quite shocking. I know it's mostly set in France, but all the same . . . And you write about Oscar as though he were dead."

Oscar laughed. "I'll need to be before it's published!" he cried. Oscar leant eagerly towards the young Scottish doctor and, lowering his voice to a conspiratorial murmur, enquired: "But what did you make of the *story*, Arthur?"

"Ah," breathed Arthur, patting the manuscript that lay on the table beside him. "The story." He looked between us both with stern, appraising eyes. "Is it all true? Is it gospel? Is there no invention here?"

"It's all true, Arthur," Oscar replied. "Every word." My friend glanced in my direction and smiled. "But the story's not quite complete. A few loose ends remain to be tied. There are one or two questions we've left unanswered."

"There most certainly are," declared Conan Doyle emphatically. "For a start, what happened to the American? What happened to Eddie Garstrang, 'the man who never loses'?"

"I'm glad you asked, Arthur," said Oscar, looking back at the bright-eyed doctor. "And I shall tell you." Oscar widened his own eyes. "In fact, I might even show you."

Conan Doyle tugged at his thick moustache and chuckled. "And while you're about it, you can tell me who really killed the dog, the unfortunate Marie Antoinette. It wasn't Carlos Branco, was it?"

"No," said Oscar. "Carlos Branco is not the killing kind."

"And that's why you told the police that Edmond La Grange had taken his own life. You needed to convince

Brigadier Malthus that La Grange's death was suicide, otherwise Malthus would have charged Branco; and if Branco had gone to trial he would have been found guilty, and guillotined."

"Exactly," said Oscar. "I have my faults, Arthur, but I don't like to see a man condemned to death for a crime he didn't commit."

"I'm pleased to hear it," responded Doyle, nodding genially. "So who did kill Edmond La Grange?"

"He killed himself, surely?" I interrupted, confused. "Oscar established that—beyond doubt. He showed us how it happened."

Oscar turned and gazed upon me beadily. He was now thirty-six years of age, but because of his excess weight and the wateriness of his eyes, the discolouration of his teeth, and the blotchiness of his puttylike skin, he seemed older. I was now twenty-nine, but, at times like this, I felt I was a schoolboy again, receiving an admonition from the housemaster for an offence whose nature I did not fully comprehend. "Edmond La Grange might have killed himself, Robert," said Oscar deliberately, "but, in fact, he did not do so. I know that now. And, I confess, I knew that then. I encouraged others—you included, Robert—to think that La Grange had taken his own life because it was necessary at the time in order to save the life of Carlos Branco. La Grange's death was not suicide. It was murder."

"I'm lost," I said bleakly.

Oscar laughed softly. "Whereas Arthur's in his element!"

"Indeed," responded the doctor happily, "the 'elements'

are very much a feature of the case, are they not? Earth, air, water, fire: they're at the heart of it, aren't they?"

"They are. They're the thread that drew me through the labyrinth."

"Take us with you, Oscar," cried Conan Doyle, smacking his lips and eyeing the pastries now being laid out on the table before us. "May we tuck in as you guide us through your maze?"

We sat at the far end of the Grand Tea Room of Madame Tussaud's, at what was then known as the Directors' Table, drinking afternoon tea and picking at an assortment of cakes and fancies (and Huntley & Palmer biscuits), while Oscar Wilde took us through the tangled tale of the La Grange murders.

"Where shall I begin?" asked Oscar, as soon as our waitress had retreated.

Conan Doyle glanced around the room. The tables nearest ours were all unoccupied. We had our privacy. "Begin at the beginning," he suggested. "Begin with the gifted and beautiful twin children, Agnès and Bernard La Grange." He helped himself to a slice of lemon and ginger sponge and looked up slyly at our mutual friend. "They were not La Grange's children, after all?"

"Bravo, Arthur! The twins were not La Grange's children, after all." Oscar dropped two lumps of sugar into his teacup with a little flourish. "Their father was not their father and their mother was not their mother." As he stirred his tea, he glanced in my direction. "Your eyes are downcast, Robert."

"I am confused," I said.

"And a little hurt, I think. You have taken great care in

writing up your account of my adventures in America and
Paris. At my behest, you kept copious notes at the time.
Over the years, we have discussed the details in extenso.
But now, suddenly, you sense that I have not always taken
you into my full confidence and you feel betrayed."

"Not betrayed," I said quickly. "That's too strong a
word." I looked up at him. "Disappointed, perhaps."

My friend rested his hand on mine. "Forgive me, good
friend," he continued, speaking gently in that delicate,
lilting way of his. "I have been remiss, but consider what I
am, Robert, and try to understand. I am a storyteller and
a playwright. I need to keep my readers turning the page
until the last; I want my audience on the edge of their seats
until the curtain falls. I must have my dénouement. Don't
begrudge me my element of surprise."

I laughed. And I forgave him: he was irresistible. "I
begrudge you nothing, Oscar," I said, now taking some
sponge cake for myself, "but I'm confused nonetheless.
I thought that their mother had died at the time that the
twins were born."

"Alys Lenoir, the wife of Edmond La Grange, did indeed
die soon after the twins were born. She took her own life—
as you tell us in your fine narrative. But the twins were not
her children and Alys Lenoir could not live with the lie of
pretending that they were. She could not live with herself,
having failed to provide the great La Grange with any
heirs."

"The twins were not her children?" I repeated. "But she
was half Indian, from Pondicherry. The twins looked like
her."

"No," said Oscar. "The twins looked like beautiful

344

young people with Indian blood because that is what they were, but Alys Lenoir was not their mother. Their mother was a maid, a servant girl from Goa. I have met her, as it happens."

"What?" I gasped.

"From Goa?" murmured Conan Doyle. "An Indian girl from Portuguese Goa . . ." He banged the table with his teaspoon. "Carlos Branco was Portuguese, wasn't he? This girl worked for the family of Carlos Branco?"

"She did, Arthur. Well done." Oscar beamed upon the creator of Sherlock Holmes, who rewarded himself with a look of quiet satisfaction and a slice of cherry cake. Oscar continued: "Branco was enchanted by the girl. Branco seduced her. Men, being men, do these things. She was a servant, and not much more than a child, and easily seduced. And when Branco's friend and employer, Edmond La Grange, was desperate to find a woman who could give him children, Branco proposed his little, simpleminded Goan serving girl for the purpose. La Grange took her, gratefully. She was the answer to his prayers. Where else in Paris could he have found a girl of Indian blood to be the mother of his children? She fell pregnant at once, and when the twins were born, La Grange presented them to his wife as *their* children—*her* children, La Grange children, ready made. The Goan girl supplied the great La Grange with his heirs, and Carlos Branco secured his position as La Grange's "leading character man" for life. To La Grange the La Grange inheritance was everything—and he knew his secret was safe with Carlos Branco. Branco was his creature."

"What happened to the Goan girl?" asked Arthur.

"La Grange instructed Branco to dispose of her, and Branco did as he was told. Branco always did as he was told. Branco lived in awe of La Grange—and in fear of him. For all his bluff and bluster, Branco was a weak man. Strong actors often are."

From my coat pocket I produced my notebook. I turned its pages, trying to gather together the strands of Oscar's story. "You are telling us that the twins were not fathered by Edmond La Grange: they were fathered by Carlos Branco. And that the Goan girl was already pregnant by Branco when she was taken by La Grange."

"Exactly so."

"And the world knew none of this, Oscar? No one suspected?"

"Why should they? Alys Lenoir was dead and Branco said not a word. Why would he? He was ashamed of what he had done. The twins had the look of their supposed half-Indian mother because they were part Indian, too. And they appeared to have some of the talent of their famous father, Edmond La Grange, because they were the children of another fine actor—Carlos Branco."

Conan Doyle flicked some crumbs of cake off his heavy moustache. "When did La Grange discover the truth?"

"Not for twenty years: not until the start of the rehearsals of the La Grange production of *Hamlet*. It was, in Sarah Bernhardt's estimation, 'the perfect *Hamlet*,' you'll recall. Branco watched Agnès and Bernard in rehearsal: they were magnificent, and they were his children! They had genius, and it was genius that belonged to him and not La Grange! He could bear to keep silent no longer. He revealed his secret—not to the world, but to La Grange, and to the children, Agnès and Bernard. He did it not to hurt, but to undeceive. He did it because he was so proud. And he was glad that he had done it. On the first night of *Hamlet,* he told Robert: 'I am happier than I have ever been.'"

Conan Doyle's fingers were spread out on top of the manuscript that lay on the table before him. "Carlos Branco told the twins that he was their true father. Did he tell them about the Goan girl? Did he tell them who their true mother had been?"

"I cannot be sure," said Oscar, "but I think not." He glanced towards Doyle's fingers on the manuscript. "You'll recall from Robert's splendid narrative—chapter twenty-two, I think—that Bernard, on learning of Agnès's supposed suicide, said, "It's in the blood." Bernard believed that he and his sister were the children of Alys Lenoir."

Oscar leant forward, resting his elbows on the table and bringing the tips of his fingers together in front of his chin. "Carlos Branco wanted to share his pride in his children while continuing to hide his shame in the matter of the Goan girl." He glanced towards me. "Robert and I arrived on the scene at the moment of revelation—or just after it. We came towards La Grange's dressing room and heard voices raised within. We heard a woman sobbing—whether with tears of sorrow or of laughter we could not tell. We heard Carlos Branco declare, *'Mais enfin!'*—we were certain of that."

"'*Mais enfin!*'—'But at last!'" I translated.

Arthur lifted his hand from the manuscript and raised it as though he were a schoolboy anxious to make a point in class. "Branco was Portuguese," he volunteered. "How accurate was his French accent? Could he have been saying, '*Mes enfants!*'—'My children!'?"

"He could," answered Oscar, smiling. "It was one or the other, for sure." Oscar lifted his cup of sweet tea and raised it in Dr. Doyle's direction. He took a sip, before continuing: "When we arrived at his dressing-room door La Grange seemed perturbed, distraught, but he recovered himself at once. 'Old Polonius here has had some novel ideas,' he told us. 'We've been taking them on board.'" Oscar looked towards me. "Do you recall the four faces in the dressing room that afternoon, Robert? They were not easy to interpret. We sensed the presence of mixed emotions, but who was feeling what—and why—we could not tell."

"A secret should be kept a secret," murmured Conan Doyle, now picking up crumbs from his plate with his forefinger. "Once it is no longer a secret, it becomes a serpent—it goes where it will."

"So it would seem, Arthur," replied Oscar, smiling at our Scottish friend's gnomic utterance. "Branco's revelation shocked La Grange, angered and confused him. He struck his friend's name from the visitors' book at his hideaway in the rue de la Pierre Levée. What Branco had told him had turned his world upside down. But, in one respect, at least, Branco's startling revelation gave La Grange a freedom that had not been his before. Edmond and Agnès were indeed drawn to one another—but Dr. Blanche was right. They were 'good Catholics': for each of them, as for most of us, incest would have been a temptation too far. The old man had lusted after the young woman, as old men will, and the girl had loved the older man, as sometimes happens. It had been a futile attraction, they knew that. But if Edmond La Grange and Agnès were not father and daughter . . ."

Oscar lowered his eyes discreetly as Conan Doyle widened his and breathed: "They could become lovers. There was now no taboo."

"Exactly," declared Oscar, looking up and smiling. "And so it came to pass."

Conan Doyle found a napkin with which to wipe his lips. "My, my," he murmured.

"But the ecstasy did not last long," Oscar continued blithely. "That's ecstasy's way, alas. Agnès was excited to have Edmond as her lover and was ready to share her joy with the world. 'I'm free at last,' she said when we all had supper at Le Chat Noir. But La Grange was not so certain. He was wary of the girl's emotional instability, alarmed by her devotion, and conscious that his desire for her was unlikely to stand the test of time. Love might last, but lust rarely does. There was no future for them as father and daughter—nor as man and mistress. A mistress needs to be like Gabrielle de la Tourbillon—a woman of the world who knows the rules. Agnès, young and vulnerable, and passionately in love with him, could only bring brief enchantment. Ultimately, it was doomed. Her love for him made public could well bring down the mighty house of La Grange. The great actor was keenly aware of his profession's vulnerability to the wrong kind of scandal; he made that very clear to us in an unexpected outburst in his dressing room. When it came to his calling, Edmond La Grange was a passionate man. But, as a character, he was 'a cold fish.' Sarah Bernhardt, who knew him well, told us so. Edmond La Grange quickly realised that this lovesick child would prove more trouble than she was worth. She must be disposed of. She was."

Conan Doyle's brow was deeply furrowed. He was contemplating a further slice of lemon and ginger sponge.

"And Bernard?" I asked.

"What of Bernard?" answered Oscar derisively. "He was not La Grange's son. We heard him say it—more than once. 'What do I care for Edmond La Grange?' And we heard La Grange publicly repudiate his so-called son—had we but realised it. At the dress rehearsal, when La Grange told Bernard that it did not matter which wig he wore as Hamlet and Maman bleated about the 'La Grange tradition,' Edmond declared: 'The tradition is dead—forget it.'

"To La Grange, Bernard was now another man's bastard—the old fool Polonius's bastard—and too dissolute, too fond of laudanum. To have such a creature pretending to be the next La Grange: it was not to be endured. Nor to be risked. Might not Bernard reveal the truth of his paternity? La Grange decided to rid himself of Bernard, too. What did he care for either of these young people? They were not his children. They were impostors. And, as actors, were they so extraordinary? Were they really any better than the understudies? Wasn't it the name 'La Grange' that had given them their special allure?"

Conan Doyle was cutting his slice of cake into squares the size of postage stamps. "So you are telling us that Edmond La Grange killed Agnès and Bernard," he ruminated.

"Not with his own hands. He had them killed. He was a man accustomed to giving orders—and to having them obeyed."

Conan Doyle looked up sharply. "Who killed them, then?"

"The same person who killed the wretched dog and poor Traquair," said Oscar quietly. "A creature who did La Grange's bidding—and did it in his style."

"Back to the elements," murmured Conan Doyle. "Earth, air, water, fire."

"Yes," said Oscar, with a sudden burst of energy. "The use of the elements gave a pattern to the murders. It was both a poetic idea and theatrical: typical of La Grange. Commit four murders and commit each one involving a different element. Epicurus was fascinated by the four elements. To La Grange Epicurus was a hero. But La Grange could not have committed the murders himself—"

"Why do you say that?" interrupted Conan Doyle.

"Because Robert and I were in the room with La Grange at the moment that young Bernard was killed. We were La Grange's incidental alibi. He might have been the instigator of the fire that consumed the boy, but he could not have lit the match. He must have had an accomplice, but who could that accomplice be? His mother? Unlikely. She was an old woman—mad enough, certainly, but not capable. Gabrielle de la Tourbillon? Possibly. She was La Grange's mistress—his creature, in her way—but she did not strike me as a murderer."

"I'm pleased to hear it, Oscar," I muttered. My skin was burning, but I do not think that Conan Doyle noticed.

"And could La Grange have trusted her?" continued Oscar. "Would he have done so? I think not." Oscar reached into his pocket for his cigarettes. "Besides, these murders did not strike me as being woman's work. A woman could certainly have struck the dog and buried it alive; a woman could have struck the match that lit the flames that devoured Bernard. But could a woman have tipped Agnès into the tank of water and held down her head until she drowned? Could a woman have asphyxiated Washington Traquair, held the pillow across his face until he died?"

I interrupted Oscar's flow. "Traquair was killed by gas poisoning, surely?"

"So it seemed," said Oscar, lighting his cigarette. "Gas was escaping into his room, certainly, but not, I think, enough to kill a man. I believe that poor Traquair was smothered as he slept and that the gas jet was then turned on above his divan to give the impression that he had taken his own life."

"This was a man's doing . . . ," I began, and then I faltered.

"And a man who was present when we burst into Traquair's cubicle," Oscar continued. "He had locked the door to the dresser's room from the outside once he had murdered him. He returned the key to the room by dropping it on the floor by the divan when we broke our way into the room and discovered poor Traquair's body."

"Richard Marais?" I suggested.

"It might have been. It was Marais who made the cackhanded attempts on my life: attempting to drop a weight onto me from the theatre's fly gallery; attempting to drown me in the water trough in the boulevard du Temple. I think that Marais meant to scare me, not to kill me. He wanted me to go away. He was concerned that I might reveal his fraud to his master—but his master knew about it all

along. Marais was a petty villain and not quite so deaf as
he pretended, but he had a redeeming feature."

Conan Doyle, examining a small square of cake,
chuckled. "He was a dog lover. He was devoted to Maman's wretched poodles. He was unlikely to have been the
butcher of Marie Antoinette."

"Bravo, once more, dear doctor! It was not Marais."

Conan Doyle laid his knife across his plate and pushed
temptation to one side. He looked up towards Oscar and
smiled. "Eliminate all other factors, and the one that remains must be the truth," he said. "It was the American. It
must be. It was Eddie Garstrang, the gambler."

Oscar sat back and, for a moment, let his eyes stray
about the tea room. We were the only customers remaining. At the far end of the room, at the cake counter, two
waitresses stood together gossiping. Oscar drew slowly on
his cigarette and watched the thin plumes of pale purple
smoke as they rose from his nostrils and filtered into the air
above us. "Bravo again, Arthur," he said eventually. "Bravo
indeed." He continued, almost languidly: "In certain respects, Garstrang was the most fascinating man of all the
unusual men I met during that extraordinary year. We were
not destined to be friends, yet, from our first encounter, I
sensed we had much in common. Garstrang observed his
life even as he lived it. He was an outsider, as I know I am.
He was a risk taker, as I hope I am. He wanted fame and
fortune, as I know I do. He was ready to hazard everything
on a single throw of the dice—regardless of the conse-
quences. I like to think that I would have the courage to do
the same."

Oscar leant across the table and put his face close to

Doyle's. "In Colorado, Garstrang played cards with Edmond La Grange and he lost, as you recall. He went on playing—and losing—long after he had anything left to lose. He played cards with Edmond La Grange until La Grange owned him—lock, stock, and barrel." Oscar held out his cigarette and contemplated the length of it. "The barrel was not insignificant: La Grange, a fine shot himself, was entertained by the notion of having an outstanding marksman as part of his entourage."

Conan Doyle chuckled. He was holding his new pipe in his hand (it had been his Christmas present from his little girl), and poking at the unlit tobacco leaves with a matchstick. He looked up at Oscar and smiled. "So La Grange struck a deal with Eddie Garstrang—yes? He could clear his debt, he could buy back his freedom, in easy stages."

"Yes, Arthur, in four easy stages. All Garstrang had to do was kill to order—four times—and then he would be free to leave La Grange's service, his debt repaid, his fortune restored. To make the game more amusing—for both men—La Grange introduced the conceit of the 'elemental murders': death by earth, air, water, and fire."

"Why was the dog killed first, Oscar?" I asked. "What harm did the dog ever do to anyone?"

"The killing of Maman's dog was just an *amusebouche*, Robert, a preliminary entertainment designed by La Grange to put Garstrang to the test. The dog's death was neither here nor there. As La Grange knew, no one would care about the dog, except perhaps for Maman and Richard Marais—and Edmond La Grange cared little enough for them."

Conan Doyle set down his pipe. His moustache twitched.

"Was not La Grange devoted to his mother?" he asked. Arthur was touchingly devoted to his.

"I think that Edmond La Grange rather despised his mother," replied Oscar, who was devoted to his mother, also. "He owed her everything and that does not always bring out the best in a man. He accepted her place in his life, but her foibles irritated and her pretensions infuriated him. More than once I heard him say, 'Maman, you are utterly absurd.'"

"A cold fish indeed," murmured Conan Doyle, sucking on his unlit pipe. "He was entertained by the idea of having a personal assassin at his disposal, even before he had specific victims in mind."

"He was." Oscar smiled at his friend. "And in Garstrang he sensed that he had picked a man well suited to his purpose. Garstrang killed the ghastly Marie Antoinette in style: burying her in earth in my book case. I imagine that La Grange was much amused by that. La Grange had a lively sense of humour." Oscar struck a match to light another cigarette. "Garstrang proved that he could kill a dog—but could he kill a man?" He dropped the lighted match into the dregs of his tea. "It seems he could."

I looked at Conan Doyle. His eyes had taken on a mournful aspect. "Poor Traquair." He sighed.

"Yes," echoed Oscar. "Poor Traquair. On that fateful day in La Grange's dressing room on the boulevard du Temple, when Carlos Branco unleashed his secret upon the family La Grange, where was the hapless valet? Where was Washington Traquair? The poor wretch was in his *cubicle,* of course, adjacent to the dressing room—alone and lonely. Had he heard Branco's revelation? Had he heard the row that followed it? Most probably. But had he understood what he had heard? Almost certainly not; but La Grange could not be sure of that and dared not take the risk. Besides, he could rid himself of Traquair so easily. He had the man for the task to hand—and in his debt. La Grange instructed Garstrang to kill Traquair: 'He's a valet, he's a blackamoor, he hardly counts.'

"Garstrang did as he was bid and did it well. He was an artist in his way. And he served La Grange to perfection. La Grange valued him highly." Oscar looked at me. "I believe, Robert, that he came to intervene in that duel of yours, as much to ensure Garstrang's safety as your own."

I lowered my head over my notebook and shaded my eyes. Even after so many years the absurdity of that duel—and of my infatuation with Gabrielle de la Tourbillon—was still a source of embarrassment to me. From behind my hand, I glanced towards the counter where the waitresses had been standing. They were gone: we were alone in the tea room now.

"La Grange needed Garstrang," Oscar continued. "There was business to be done. The twins must be disposed of. La Grange instructed Garstrang to kill them both. It was not difficult to achieve, even within the rules of the game. Agnès was easily drowned and Bernard was very simply set alight. Garstrang took a bottle of ether from La Grange's 'love nest'—we saw him leaving the apartment with a box full of such bottles—and used it to douse the seat and floor of the cab that La Grange had ordered to send his so-called son on his way to Montmartre. He told us that the cab had been ordered to take us to Pharamond. It was not so. He had no plans to go out for supper. He knew that if he offered Bernard a carriage at his expense, the boy would take it. Garstrang saw Bernard into the cab and, as he closed the cab door on him, threw his lighted cigarette into the cab to ignite the furnace."

"Horrible," muttered Conan Doyle.

"So it was Eddie Garstrang who killed Agnès and Bernard La Grange," I said, underscoring Garstrang's name in my notebook.

"Yes, on Edmond La Grange's instructions."

"But who killed La Grange?" asked Conan Doyle. "La Grange wasn't bent on self-destruction."

"No," answered Oscar, "though death held few terrors for him. Epicurus had taught him that 'death is nothing': 'for that which has been dissolved into its elements experiences no sensations, and that which has no sensation is nothing to us.'"

I was still staring down at my notebook. "With the twins dead," I said, "Garstrang was once more free."

"Indeed," replied Oscar. "When you saw Eddie Garstrang on the afternoon of La Grange's death he told you that he had been a free man since midnight. He told you that he had been 'contracted' to La Grange for six months and that, now, his time was up. But what he said made no sense: it was more than six months since the Compagnie La Grange had visited Leadville and less than six months since Garstrang set sail for France on board the SS *Bothnia*. No, Garstrang was free because he had fulfilled his side of the bargain."

Suddenly, quite softly, Arthur Conan Doyle began to growl. It was a low rumble, the noise a terrier might make on sniffing out a rathole. He narrowed his eyes and looked towards Oscar expectantly. "But Edmond La Grange decided that he did not want to let his murderer go?"

Oscar grinned at the doctor. "You should be writing detective stories, Arthur. La Grange told Garstrang that he needed one more murder: the fifth element, what Epicurus called 'the quintessence.' Just one more murder and then La Grange would repay him all the money he had lost at cards—and give him his freedom, too."

"The American protested that he had already fulfilled his obligation."

"Naturally, but La Grange reckoned that he now had the upper hand. Since Garstrang had already committed four murders, he was deep in blood—and vulnerable. 'Just one more, that's all I ask. Kill Carlos Branco for me and then you're free. Shoot him; use my gun. Here it is. A pistol shot combines the elements of earth and air, fire and water. Shoot Branco and then we're done.'"

Oscar paused and, eagerly, Arthur took up the story: "But Eddie Garstrang knew that he'd never be 'done'! Kill Branco and then who would be next? He had fulfilled his pledge. He was an honourable gambling man and he'd paid his dues. If La Grange was not ready to keep his side of the bargain, La Grange was the man to be killed—and, then, it would indeed all be 'done.'"

"How he did it we know," said Oscar, dropping the remains of his cigarette into his teacup. "He disguised himself as the Ghost of Hamlet's Father. He put on the cloak. He put on the helmet and visor. He went to La Grange's dressing room. La Grange opened the dressing-room door; what we saw was La Grange himself, standing at the door, between the door and the mirror. Garstrang entered the room.

I imagine he explained his curious disguise with a reference to Carlos Branco, indicating that he was now ready to kill Branco if that was indeed La Grange's wish. He invited La Grange to give him his gun for the purpose. The old actor did as he was asked and the die was cast. Garstrang took the gun and, at once, without hesitation, turned it on La Grange and shot him. The moment the deed was done, he placed the gun on the dressing table, threw off the cloak, threw down the helmet, and left the room, returning almost at once, arriving with Carlos Branco."

"Why did you not tell all this to the police at the time?" I asked.

"For the same reason that Carlos Branco did not simply tell the world that the twins were his. Who would have believed me? La Grange was dead. What evidence was there? Branco looked to be the guilty man. He had motive, opportunity, and means—and you had seen him entering La Grange's dressing room moments before the murder, Robert. You had seen him with your own eyes. You were very firm about that."

Arthur Conan Doyle was looking about the tea room. "We are alone." He consulted his pocket watch. "It's nearly six o'clock."

"We must be on our way or we'll be locked in with the waxworks," said Oscar, pushing his chair away from the table and getting to his feet. "Where is our bill?"

"We're Tussaud's guests, I'm happy to say."

"Ah." Oscar smiled, pulling on his gloves. "It is Marie Antoinette who has let us eat cake."

I picked up the brown paper parcel containing our manuscript. "I've some work to do here," I remarked.

"Don't rush," said Oscar lightly. "It's to be a posthumous publication, remember."

We walked through the deserted tea room, back towards the exhibition halls. "Oscar," I asked, a thought suddenly occurring to me. "How do you know for certain that Agnès and Bernard were, in truth, Carlos Branco's children?"

"Because," replied my friend, "like the act of suicide, the fact of being a twin can be an inherited characteristic."

"But Agnès and Bernard did not commit suicide," said Conan Doyle. "Alys Lenoir committed suicide, but she was not the twins' mother."

"Exactly," said Oscar. "Alys Lenoir committed suicide, but she was not their mother. But Carlos Branco was their father—and he was a twin."

"How do you know that Carlos Branco was a twin?" I asked.

"Because I have met his brother. I have met the twin of Carlos Branco. He was another of the remarkable people I encountered in the course of that memorable year. I met him through my friend George Palmer, the biscuit king. Branco's twin was a clergyman—a convert, a zealot, an Anglican priest, of Portuguese descent. He came to England as a young man to join the Evangelical Alliance. When I first met him I sensed that his English accent was too perfect to be true. It was only when I met him for the second time that I realised who he might be. His eyes, his gestures, his way of speaking, all had seemed familiar, but whereas Carlos Branco at sixty was overweight and red-faced, Paul White was thin and pale. Branco is Portuguese for 'white,' as you know. And Paul was the name he had chosen at the time of his conversion. Paul White was thin and pale—and ashamed. You recall how La Grange told us that, in France, actors count among the damned. Paul White was ashamed of his brother and of his brother's calling—and ashamed of the favour that he had done his brother twenty years before.

"Carlos had sent him an unfortunate Goan girl, a simpleminded family servant who had become a fallen woman. Carlos Branco had hoped that she could be his brother's housekeeper. Paul White, the evangelical, would not have her in his house, but he found a place for her, working in the prison where he was chaplain. I met her on the day I went to Reading Gaol. I met her in the chapel there, a sad, brown-faced creature in an old black dress. Paul White called out to her in a language I half recognised. I thought that it was Spanish. I realised later that it was Portuguese."

We stood in silence beneath the great glass dome in the entrance hall of Madame Tussaud's. "And the American," asked Conan Doyle, sucking on his pipe. "What happened to Eddie Garstrang?"

"Oh," said Oscar lightly. "He fulfilled his ambition. He became famous in his way. Or notorious, at least. It was what he wanted."

"I've not heard of him," said Conan Doyle.

"He's not famous for the way he lived. He's famous for the way he died."

"Did he go back to Colorado?"

"No, he stayed on in France. He returned to the life of a professional gambler. I sent a note to Brigadier Malthus advising him to keep an eye on him, and he did. And three years ago, Eddie Garstrang was arrested. He had shot a man in cold blood—over an unpaid gambling debt. Eddie Garstrang was executed. It was a notable event. He was the last man to be beheaded by the original guillotine. That's why Eddie Garstrang's here, in the Chamber of Horrors." Oscar glanced up at the clock that hung on the wall above main doorway. "It's ten to six, gentlemen. Let's go and take a look at him before the exhibition closes. Robert can't see the likeness, but I can. He has the look of a murderer. It's in his smile. Never trust a man who shows you his lower teeth when he smiles."

Acknowledgements

Readers of my series of Oscar Wilde murder mysteries frequently ask me the same question: "How much of this is true?" My answer is, "All of it. Or almost all. Certainly, much more than you would think." Oscar's friendships with Robert Sherard, Arthur Conan Doyle, George W. Palmer, and Sarah Bernhardt are well known. His encounters with Louisa May Alcott and P. T. Barnum and his interest in prison visiting and social reform are also well documented, if less well known. The places I have taken Oscar to in this story—Leadville, Colorado, New York, London, Paris, Reading—are all locations in which he was to be found on the dates on which I place him there. W. M. Traquair was indeed his valet on the American tour of 1882.

In this book, as in the others in the series, I have tried to be as accurate as possible. (If you have noted any errors, I would be grateful if you would let me know.) In this endeavour I have been assisted over several years by conversations with an assortment of remarkable individuals, among them: my late father, Charles Brandreth, who knew Robert Sherard in the 1930s; John Badley (the founder of Bedales School, where I was a pupil in the 1960s), who was a friend and contemporary of Oscar Wilde; Sir Donald Sinden, who knew Lord Alfred Douglas in the 1940s; and Merlin Holland, Oscar Wilde's only grandson.

In the preparation of *Oscar Wilde and the Dead Man's Smile* I have been particularly assisted by the following: Isobel Morrow, Independent Monitoring Board, HM Prison and Young Offender Institution, Reading; Pauline Bryant, Governing Governor, HM Prison, Reading; Anthony Stokes, Senior Prison Officer at HM Prison, Reading, and author of *Pit of Shame: The Real Ballad of Reading Gaol* (2007); Pamela Pilbeam, author of *Madame Tussaud and the History of Waxworks* (2003), who introduced me to *The Theatre Industry in Nineteenth-Century France* by F. W. J. Hemmings (1993); and His Excellency Osman Korutürk, the Turkish ambassador to Paris, who kindly showed me and my wife around his residence, l'Hôtel de Lamballe in Passy, formerly the home of the Princesse de Lamballe where the Doctors Blanche ran their famous clinic.

Among the special people I would like to acknowledge for their contribution to the making of the book are: Madame Gabrielle de la Tourbillon (who, in 1965, gave me her copy of *Réflexions sur le Théâtre*, dedicated to her by its author, Jean-Louis Barrault); the artist Anthony Palliser; the author Anne Perry; the writer and lecturer Paul Ibell; the composer and lyricist Susannah Pearse; Roger Johnson and Jean Upton of the Sherlock Holmes Society of London; and my friend Jo James.

As ever I am indebted to my literary agent, the incomparable Ed Victor, and to two members of his team in particular: Linda Van and Morag O'Brien. For their sustaining enthusiasm and detailed input I am equally indebted to three remarkable publishers: Kate Parkin in London; Trish Grader in New York; and Emmanuelle Heurtebize in Paris.

The other question I am most frequently asked by readers is this: "Which biography of Oscar Wilde do you recommend?" Of course, I recommend *Oscar Wilde* by Richard Ellmann (1987), but, magisterial as it is, the book is riddled with inaccuracies and must be read in conjunction with *Additions and Corrections to Richard Ellmann's 'Oscar Wilde'* by Horst Schroeder (2002). I also recommend, and without reservation, *The Wilde Album* by Merlin Holland (1997). The two books that, for me, take the reader closest to "the real Oscar Wilde" are *The Complete Letters of Oscar Wilde* edited by Merlin Holland and Rupert Hart-Davis (2000) and *Son of Oscar Wilde* by Vyvyan Holland (1954).

For details of the other and forthcoming titles in the series, reviews, interviews, and material of particular interest to reading groups, see:

www.oscarwildemurdermysteries.com

OSCAR WILDE

and the
Dead Man's Smile

For Discussion

1. As a reader, what were your first feelings toward Eddie Garstrang? What were your first impressions of Edmond La Grange? How did your emotions toward these characters change throughout the book? What were major turning points for you?

2. *Oscar Wilde and the Dead Man's Smile* is set in America, London, and Paris. Each of these places has unique characteristics, but all share some general similarities. How are these places similar and different?

3. What was the effect of reading the story through Robert's eyes? How would it have been different if Oscar had done the narrating?

4. Oscar writes in his journal of Madame La Grange, "Old age has no consolations to offer us. The pulse of joy that beats in us at twenty has become sluggish. Limbs fail, senses rot. We degenerate into hideous puppets, haunted by the memories of the passions of which we were too much afraid, and the exquisite temptations that we had not the courage to yield to" (page 47). Do you agree with his harsh words about old age?

5. Speaking to Robert, Oscar says, "[M]any a young man starts in life with a natural gift for exaggeration which,

if nurtured in congenial and sympathetic surroundings, or by imitation of the best models, might grow into something really great and wonderful. But, as a rule, he comes to nothing. He either falls into careless habits of accuracy . . . or takes to frequenting the society of the aged and well-informed. Both things are equally fatal to his imagination" (page 67). Is Oscar right? Is this meant to describe the fate of young men or the essence of imagination?

6. Throughout the novel, rumor and innuendo play a large role in shaping people's perceptions. What is different about rumors in the 1890s versus the present day? What is the same? In which time period did rumors play a larger role?

7. Of morality Oscar says, "I never came across anyone in whom the moral sense was dominant who was not heartless, cruel, vindictive, log stupid, and entirely lacking in the smallest degree of humanity. . . . I would rather have fifty unnatural vices than one unnatural virtue" (page 168). Do you agree? What does this quote reveal about Oscar's perception of the world around him? Do you trust Oscar?

8. How does the author use language and imagery to bring the characters to life? Did the book's characters or style in any way remind you of another book?

9. "It's a story told by actors and, as you should know by now, stories told by actors are rarely to be trusted" (page 262). Which of the actors in the story did you trust the most? Trust the least? Why?

10. Whose story is this? If you had to pick one, is it Oscar's story, Robert's, or the La Granges'? Why?

A Conversation with Gyles Brandreth

Authors often remark that they put a little bit of themselves into their characters. How strongly do you identify with each of your main characters? How are you different?

As a writer, I'd like to be like Oscar Wilde. As a human being, I'd like to be like Conan Doyle. In reality, I am Robert Sherard. I admire Wilde's way with words—and his extraordinary personal style—and I envy his philosophy, but he had genius. Conan Doyle had genius, too. Sherlock Holmes is arguably the most celebrated fictional character ever created. But Conan Doyle was also a wonderful human being: courteous, courageous, compassionate. He was a great man. Robert Sherard (a real person, genuinely Wilde's first biographer) is what I am, however: a hero worshipper, an observer, a journalist, and a biographer who spends much of his life with great men but is aware of his own limitations—and vulnerability.

You have a deep knowledge of Oscar Wilde's character and personality. If you were to meet him in person, what would you want to ask him first?

"Why, in 1895, did you bring your own house down upon yourself by instigating the legal action that led to your downfall? Why, between trials that spring, when you could have escaped in safety to France, did you not do so? What is the moment in your life you most regret? And the moment in your life in which you felt yourself most 'realised'?" Actually, what I'd probably ask him first is: "Have you read my books? What do you think? Have I got it right?"

Why did you set this book in the place and time that you did? Do you have a special link to the American West or the theatre in Paris?

Oscar's first visit to America was an important experience for him—and I have a feeling for the United States in that era because my father's great-grandfather, Dr. Benjamin Brandreth, was an American and a "big man" in his way in the America of that era. He was a New York state senator, a millionaire medicine salesman, and a friend of P. T. Barnum, among others. Paris was central to Oscar's life: that is where he met Robert Sherard; that is where he died. French culture in general, and the French theatre in particular, were always important to Oscar. They have been to me. I went to a French school. I have been visiting the theatre in France since I was a boy. I have a tiny apartment in one of the Paris streets featured in this novel. I know the streets of Paris—these streets—well. I love them.

Your novel is tremendously engaging and can easily be read in one sitting. Oscar and Robert's path in this book is a whirlwind. Did you work on the book for a long time or finish it very quickly?

This is the third in a series of mysteries featuring Oscar Wilde and his circle. In a way, what I am trying to do is write a sort of serial biography of Wilde, my flawed hero, and at the same time a series of traditional mysteries. Essentially, while the rest of the world is living in the twenty-first century, I am living at the end of the nineteenth. I am completely absorbed in this period and in the lives of all the characters: I know their biographies, I walk the streets they walked. Writing each novel takes roughly a year:

three months planning the plot and doing extra research; nine months writing. I do other things (I am a television reporter and presenter, and I do radio in the UK) but on writing days I am very disciplined. I start at eight A.M. and I continue until seven P.M., and I aim to achieve one thousand words. (They always need revising! The lighter they feel, the heavier has been the workload to get them that way.)

What is your favorite book by Oscar Wilde? What is your favorite quote?

My favorite book? *The Complete Works*. Seriously. It is the range of Wilde that I find fascinating. Of course, I love the fairy tales and *The Importance of Being Earnest* is a truly wonderful play, but dip into the *Complete Works* at any page and you will find something to warm the heart and challenge the intellect. What is intriguing about Oscar Wilde is the way that he is thinking all the time. My favorite quote? Given that my hero is a detective and these are mysteries, it has to be: "There is nothing quite like an unexpected death for lifting the spirits" (except now I can't quite remember if he said it first—or I did).

How was writing this novel a different experience from writing your first two Oscar Wilde mysteries? What was harder about the process? What was easier?

You can read my Oscar Wilde mysteries in any order. I wrote *Oscar Wilde and a Death of No Importance* first and, in it, I reckon I worked harder on establishing Oscar as a personality (and as a credible sleuth) than I did on the mystery itself. Now I think my priority is to create a good story, a strong plot, a real mystery that is a satisfying puzzle. That done, I then let Wilde and his friends loose and we see what happens! It has not got easier or more difficult, and it's still fun. As well as writing about these real men and women, I am also hoping to write a mystery that is a tribute to the tradition of the great Victorian and Edwardian pioneers of detective fiction.

What was your inspiration for this story?
Oscar's visit to Leadville, Colorado. It really happened. That's where I began. I simply took it from there. I also wanted to show readers how Oscar and Robert Sherard first met, so I had to go to Paris when I did—because that's when they were there. And I have the book begin and end as it does because I needed Conan Doyle to feature. Incidentally, all that I tell you about Conan Doyle and John Tussaud is true.

As you relate in your author's note, much of the book is centered on actual history. What is your research process like? How does your research directly or indirectly affect your writing?
I try to make my research process meticulous. I want you to read this book confident that what you are learning about Wilde and his circle—and Wilde's American tour and the Paris theatre of the 1880s and life in Reading Gaol, etc.—is accurate. The research is important to me because I enjoy it and I learn from it. Yes, it inspires: it triggers ideas for the plot. For example, I had the duel taking place in the Bois de Boulogne in my plot outline, but then I visited the Buttes Chaumont in Paris just before

starting to write the novel and realized, suddenly, "Yes, this must be where the duel took place." My description of the place is based on personal observation. The same is true of the house of the Princesse de Lamballe where the Doctors Blanche had their clinic. As the guest of the current resident (the Turkish ambassador to France) I visited it. (That reminds me. I must send His Excellency a copy of the book. It is available in French. Indeed, the series is appearing in a variety of languages and countries. For news of these, check out www.oscarwildemurdermysteries.com.)

To what other writers would you compare your writing style? Who do you enjoy reading? What books influenced you to become a writer?
I don't compare my writing style to anybody's. I am the only guilty party here! Of course, I was brought up on the mysteries of Agatha Christie and Dorothy L. Sayers. I love a traditional English mystery. I am sure that shows. Who do I enjoy reading? The Victorians mostly and all the obvious ones: Austen, Gaskell, Dickens, Thackeray, Trollope. My favorite novel is either Thackeray's *Vanity Fair* or *The Old Wives' Tale* by Arnold Bennett. Influences? Well, Sherlock Holmes has been my fictional hero since I was quite a small boy and *The Trials of Oscar Wilde* was the first nonfiction book I ever read! So the true answer to the question is Oscar Fingal O'Flahertie Wills Wilde and Arthur Conan Doyle.

Do you have plans for your next Oscar Wilde book?
Yes, I already have detailed plans for nine more—and ideas for several beyond that! The joy of Wilde is that he knew

everybody and went everywhere and had a roller coaster of a life. The possibilities are infinite. Eventually, I will be writing mysteries based on his time in prison and after—when he eked out a living in France doing detective work under the name of Sebastian Melmoth. I have not quite decided which story I am going to begin writing up next. It may be a Christmas tale—I have a fondness for snow and the color of blood on snow. Or it may be *Oscar Wilde and the Vatican Murders*. You know that Oscar Wilde had a private audience with Pope Pius IX. You didn't know? Well, he did. He really did. And they talked of murder . . .

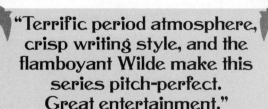